BROKEN BLOOD BONDS

M KAY NOIR

A WORD OF CAUTION

This book is intended for a mature audience only. It is set in a dark, traumatic world and often includes graphic scenes, some of which venture into dubcon.

Refer to mkaynoir.com for the full TW/CW list (on-page and off-page mentions).

If at any point this book makes you feel unsafe, please take a break and consider whether you want to continue.

Mental health matters.

PLAYLIST

1. Velvet Desires - *Bite Me Harder*
2. Ari Hicks - *Good Boy*
3. Alice Merton - *Vertigo*
4. The Kills - *Doing It to Death*
5. Ash to Eden - *Beg (On Your Knees)*
6. LEAP - *Do or Die*
7. AFI - *Snow Cats*
8. Red Hot Chili Peppers - *Dark Necessities*
9. Radiohead - *Ful Stop*
10. After Agatha - *City Light Sunrise*
11. Seabadoobee - *Don't You (Forget About Me)*
12. Phantogram - *When I'm Small*
13. Florence + The Machine - *Everybody Scream*
14. Slothrust - *Happy Together*
15. Hooverphonic - *Full Moon Duel*
16. Glass Animals - *Love Lockdown*
17. Odelly - *Mon Démon*
18. Bishop Briggs - *Baggage*
19. Lahra - *Leave Me When I Need You*

**LISTEN ON SPOTIFY

CONTENTS

For those who love with an endless appetite
and are told to starve. May you find someone
(at least one, maybe three) who hungers for
every piece of you.

CHAPTER I
THE HUNGER

(ADRIANA)

The hunger is winning.

Three days without feeding, and my body is no longer mine to control.

I reach for the wine glass, watching in horror as ice slowly spreads across the surface. Not exactly normal for someone born a fire witch.

Not good at all. I need to get some fresh blood in my system, and soon.

It may not solve my ice issue, but it should pacify my vampire nature, albeit momentarily.

It's impossible to think with this constant thrumming in my head, the all-consuming hunger tugging at every edge of my deteriorating body.

Focus, Adriana. Dinner.

Across the dimly lit burlesque club, my target—a greasy-haired creep in his fifties—inappropriately gropes another waitress. *Strike three.*

Perfect. He's absolutely perfect for what I need.

Not as a person, obviously. The man is human garbage, and his memories will taste like bile when I drain him. But that makes him perfect.

I used to be more selective about feeding.

Used to have standards.

But a lot can change in nine years.

The performer on stage, a petite blonde with a barbed-wire tattoo coiling around her thigh, sheds another layer to collective gasps from the audience.

She's cute. Cyrus would've liked her. The thought rises unbidden, but I push it down immediately. I can't think of him now.

Blood. I need blood.

Gripping my glass tighter, I return my attention to the target.

As the performer continues her show, the creep's heartbeat spikes with lust, his pudgy fingers reaching for his zipper under the table.

Nausea claws up my throat, sharp and unrelenting, but I force myself not to look away.

No shame. The fucker is touching his dick right here, thinking he's safe in the shadows, that nobody can see him being a pervert in public. But I see. *I see everything.*

The performance on stage is reaching its crescendo, but I'm no longer paying attention. The ten tables around me have been reduced to only one as my supernatural senses hone in on my prey.

But something is off.

The sound of his racing pulse should be music to my ears, should make my fangs ache with anticipation.

Instead, it's giving me a migraine.

That's new. That's wrong.

For nearly five centuries, the sound of blood pumping

through mortal veins has been the most glorious composition I've known. Now it hammers in my skull, competing with the relentless gnawing in my stomach that grows worse every hour I delay feeding.

I shouldn't have waited this long.

Three days without fresh blood shouldn't be a challenge, not for a vampire of my age. But the hunger has been returning more frequently now.

That's not the only issue.

Feeding has become...*complicated.*

Last week, it took me four attempts to successfully compel a victim. Four!

I blamed it on fatigue, on stress, on anything except the obvious truth: I'm dying. Slowly, inevitably, dying.

My stomach growls again, bringing me back to the present, to the club.

Focus, Adriana.

The asshole with the unseen target on his back drains his beer and stumbles toward the exit, his entertainment concluded, fresh cum drying on his pants.

Scum.

Leaving cash on the bar, I follow him into the night.

As the city swallows us up, I step into the shadows between two buildings, intending to materialize ahead of him on the next block. But something isn't right. My shadow-walking falters.

The familiar sensation of dissolving into darkness begins, then stutters, like a car engine trying to turn over. For a moment, I'm caught between forms, neither solid nor shadow, drowning in the nauseating vertigo of existing in two states simultaneously.

When I finally solidify, I'm only halfway to my destination, pressed against a brick wall.

Cazzo! I swear silently as I rush to catch up to the target who's stumbling down the sidewalk.

Usually, I move faster than the human eye. But today's not a good day. The hunger is exacerbating the symptoms.

My dinner almost gets away as I try to stop the world from spinning. It shouldn't be this hard.

Finally, I get close enough to grab him, yanking the man with the sticky pants into the alley with me before he can react.

"Hey!" His southern drawl is slurred with alcohol and confusion.

Not bothering to reply, I pin his arms behind his back, pressing him against the brick wall as my fangs extend.

I'm too desperate, too hungry to bother with anything but brute force.

He tries to shake me off, but even weakened, I'm still stronger than any human.

The relief should be instant.

That's how it's been for hundreds of years.

The moment my teeth pierce human flesh has always been pure euphoria, the hunger satisfied, warmth flooding my veins, strength returning to every cell in my body.

But not today.

His memories hit me with the force of a baseball bat to the gut: childhood trauma, wedding bells, the terrible things he's done to his nieces. Usually, I can filter the emotional overflow, take only what I need while leaving the rest. Now it all pours into me unchecked: his pain, his guilt, his sick desires mixing with his blood until I can't tell where he ends and I begin.

The sour taste invades my mouth. I try to pull back, but my control is gone, my usual hypnotic influence reduced to nothing.

He stares at me with pure terror as the puncture wounds heal over, half-dead but fully aware of what just happened.

"Asshole." I try my best to compel him as I shove him away. But I doubt it will hold.

I should kill him for what he's done to his nieces, for what he knows, for the simple satisfaction of ending something vile.

But I can't.

Not like this.

Not when I'm barely functional enough to feed, let alone commit a clean murder.

Instead, I leave him in the alley and saunter off into the night.

THE OCTOBER AIR bites into my skin as I make my way through the city streets. Even the cold feels wrong now, sharper than it should be, like my body can't regulate temperature like it used to.

Feeding should have restored me. Instead, I remain hollow, the hunger temporarily silenced but not satisfied.

A group of college students stumbles past, laughing, their pulses singing in harmony. My fangs ache. Still hungry. Always hungry now.

I duck into a side street, away from temptation, just as my phone buzzes.

A text from Dimitri:

> Package secured for tomorrow night.
> Client confirmed.

Half a million for a Byzantine manuscript. Money like

that used to matter. But now it's a mere means to an end, funding my search, keeping up appearances, maintaining the infrastructure of a life I'm not sure I'll be around to live for much longer. Not at this rate.

My fingers are trembling. I stare at them, willing them to be steady. They don't listen.

Another buzz. This time, an email notification from a rare book dealer in France. My heart, my stupid, non-beating heart, lurches with something dangerously close to hope.

I shouldn't open it. Not here, not in some filthy alley with the taste of a pedophile's memories still coating my tongue.

But I do.

Just as expected—another dead end.

How many does that make? Two hundred? Three?

I close my eyes. Count to ten in Latin, then Italian... then English.

The brick wall is cold against my back. I slide down until I'm sitting on the dirty street, knees pulled up, phone clutched in my hand like it might offer answers instead of disappointment.

Nine years of searching, and I'm no closer to finding that damn spellbook than I was the day it was stolen, also known as the day my undead body started falling apart.

There's a reason vampire-witch hybrids usually don't survive their turning. I used to think I was special, lucky, that I found a loophole. But loopholes only get you so far.

And nine years after the Grimoire containing the living spells holding my opposing natures in balance was stolen from me, my time is finally running out.

A rat scurries past my foot. I don't bother moving. *What's the point?* Even the rats no longer fear me.

I used to be powerful, untouchable. I walked through the world like I owned it because, in many ways, I did.

Now I can't even feed properly. Can't shadow-walk without nearly killing myself. Can't go three days without feeding before my insides threaten to tear themselves apart.

It's strange not being able to trust your own body. The constant worry that it might fail you in new ways. It's a long way removed from the feeling of invincibility I carried with me for half a millennium.

My phone screen glows in the darkness, still showing my email inbox. All the same message, variations on a theme: *Nothing yet. Still searching. Will keep you posted.*

Empty promises from people who don't understand what's at stake, who don't understand that every day I go without finding that Grimoire, I lose a little more of myself.

My fire magic is turning to ice, my vampire abilities flickering like a dying lightbulb. The two natures that should never have coexisted in the first place are finally tearing me apart as nature always intended.

I should get up, go home, maybe plan tomorrow's search…I should do *something*.

But for a moment, one heavy moment, I let myself sit in this filthy alley and endure the full weight of my failure.

I can't keep going on this way. I've been going in circles for nearly a decade; still nothing.

With a sigh, I pull up the list on my phone. The list that's consumed so much of my recent life, organized by city, cross-referenced by reputation and likelihood.

I cross off *Morning Manuscripts*.

Another dead end.

Nobody there was even remotely useful.

The shop assistant didn't even look up from his phone when I inquired about Renaissance catalogs. Just waved me away, telling me to look on the shelves if I need anything.

I had hoped to find a competent research assistant by now, someone who could look at this puzzle with fresh eyes, but they're all disinterested, too full of themselves to even bother with the test I've set up to filter out the inept candidates.

When did humans become so apathetic?

Only four shops are left in this city, according to m y list. Four more chances before I have to move on to the next place, the next disappointment.

Morrison's Rare Books is next on the list; tomorrow's mission.

They won't know anything about my book; they never do.

Why do I keep getting my hopes up?

The bookdealers have been as useless as the underground collectors.

I've searched hundreds of shops across three continents. Bribed collectors, intimidated dealers, hunted rumors through the black market with single-minded obsession, only to watch each trail go cold.

The definition of insanity is doing the same thing over and over and expecting different results. *So, what does that make me?*

A rat scurries past my foot again, bolder this time.

The audacity. His head makes a satisfying crunching sound under my foot as the squeaking dies down to silence. I kick the carcass away from me.

Shoving my phone into a pocket, I push myself to my feet, ignoring how my legs protest.

I can't stay here all night. Tempting as it is to give up, to let nature run its course until there is nothing left of my body but vulture food, I force myself to move.

The city continues bustling around me, unchanged, oblivious, as I walk the familiar streets. Life continues for everyone who isn't slowly disintegrating from the inside out.

Morrison's tomorrow.

It will be a waste of time.

I'll go anyway.

Because what else is there?

INVISIBLE

(JUDE)

I'm restocking the mythology section when a customer walks right into me. Not just a light bump, but solidly into me like I'm not even there, like I don't take up 6'3" of space in the cramped bookstore aisle.

Her shoulder bag catches my arm, sending me stumbling backward into the oak shelving that houses our folklore collection.

A leather-bound volume on Celtic mythology tumbles to the floor with a muffled thud before I can catch it, and my heart clenches at the thought of damaging such a precious item.

"Oh!" The patron looks genuinely startled, as if I've materialized from thin air. Which, in her perception, I probably have. "I'm so sorry, I didn't see you there."

Of course, she didn't.

I crouch to retrieve the fallen book, running my fingers over the worn spine to check for damage. "No problem at all." I force a smile. "Are you looking for anything specific today?"

But she's already moved on, drifting toward the rare manuscripts display like I never said a word.

The little bell above the door chimes as another customer enters. It's Mr. Davidson, one of our regulars. He nods vaguely in my direction, as though I'm a piece of furniture that happens to be in his line of sight.

But I have bigger concerns right now.

When old man Morrison emerges from his office, red-faced and huffing, I already know what's coming.

"Jude!" His voice cuts across the hushed atmosphere of the shop like a whip crack. "Where the *hell* have you been? I've been looking for you *everywhere!*"

The clumsy patron from earlier glances up from the manuscripts, her eyebrows raised. Even Mr. Davidson pauses in his browsing to look up at me.

Now I exist. Now I'm visible.

But only because my boss is making a scene.

"I've been here since nine," I say quietly, keeping my voice steady and respectful, despite the anger bubbling under the surface.

"Don't lie to me." Morrison's face grows even redder as he waves his crooked finger around. "I came out here twenty minutes ago and you were nowhere to be found."

The old man is losing it.

I was right here but he walked past the counter without seeing me.

I could point to the sales receipts I processed while he was supposedly looking for me, but that would only make him angrier. Contradicting Morrison when he's in one of his moods is asking for trouble.

"I'm sorry," I say instead, because it's easier. Because it's what he expects. "It won't happen again."

Morrison grunts, already losing interest now that he's established dominance. "See that it doesn't. And for god's sake, dust the rare books section. It looks like a mausoleum in here."

He stomps back to his office, leaving me standing there with my cheeks burning.

The clumsy patron has returned to pretending I don't exist. Mr. Davidson is suddenly fascinated by whatever book he's holding.

Keeping my eyes low, I grab the feather duster from behind the counter and make my way to the rare books section, which Morrison knows perfectly well I dusted yesterday.

Anywhere but here would be nice right about now. I'm surrounded by epic tales of heroes and villains, passionate romances, dark fantasies where ordinary people discover they're extraordinary, myths of magical beings that may or may not be real. Meanwhile, I can't even get my own boss to remember I exist.

I had somehow imagined that my life would be different by now.

Twenty-four years in, and I'm still a ghost in my own existence.

※

IT'S NEARLY CLOSING time when the bell above the door draws my attention from the leather-bound first edition in my hands.

A woman I've never seen before stands in the doorway,

13

a large black umbrella shielding her from the downpour outside.

She surveys the shop slowly and steps inside.

I nearly drop the book.

Don't stare, Jude.

But I can't help it.

Dressed in dark colors from wrist to ankle, she's beautiful in a way that seems almost otherworldly. Porcelain skin contrasts against long, black hair that falls in waves past her shoulders. Probably around mid-thirties, I'd guess.

She walks right up to me, sizing me up under an intense gaze.

And me? I remain frozen in place, book in hand, like I've been turned into a salt statue by some mischievous god.

"Good afternoon." Her voice is low, melodious, with a hint of an accent I can't place. Maybe European?

"H-hello." The word comes out all muddled. I clear my throat and try again. "Can I help you?"

"I'm looking for a book," the new customer says, her voice carrying an assertive undertone that makes my pulse quicken.

"A catalog, actually. Sixteenth-century Italian. *Inventario della Biblioteca Privata della Casa De Crevena*, published 1547." She pronounces the Italian words effortlessly, her voice changing to wrap around the foreign syllables.

The detail catches me off guard. Most customers ask for "something old" or "anything about Fae lore." This woman knows exactly what she wants, down to the year.

"That's...incredibly specific," I say, my academic brain immediately engaged. "A private library catalog from the

De Crevena family. Are you researching Renaissance collections?"

She rewards me with a smile. "You know the family."

"A bit," I admit, carefully putting down the book I've been holding.

This period was within the scope of the PhD I never finished. The De Crevena family came up in more than just footnotes during my research into the dark mysteries of the world.

"The family was quite famous," I continue, watching her intently. "Or infamous, depending on who you ask, I suppose." I'm rambling now, but her undivided attention makes me want to keep talking. It's a rare occasion for someone to take an interest in a subject I care about.

"Exactly." The word comes out as a purr, and heat rises in my cheeks. "You understand the significance."

No one has ever looked at me this way while I discuss medieval manuscripts. Like my knowledge is fascinating instead of boring. Like *I'm* fascinating.

It's doing something weird to my insides.

Usually people see the size of me before they see anything else, and stop looking after that. *Let me feel your abs* or *how fast do you row*—never *what did you read last week*.

"Let me check our catalog system," I say, moving toward the outdated but somehow, miraculously still functional computer terminal.

The woman in black follows, close enough for that intoxicating scent of jasmine to tickle my nostrils.

I type in various search terms, hyperaware of her presence behind me. Unlike most customers, she doesn't fidget or check her phone as she waits. No, she simply watches, her attention so focused, I can't escape it; it envelops me.

"Nothing in our current inventory," I murmur,

scrolling through the results. "But that doesn't mean it's impossible to find." I turn to face her, and she's standing closer than I expected. Close enough to see the gold flecks in her glassy, sea-green eyes. "It might take a while, but—"

"Time is of utmost importance," she interrupts. "And discretion." Her gaze travels over my face like she's searching for something.

"I could make some calls," I manage, despite my words threatening to fail me.

"I'd like that." Her voice has dropped to something above a whisper. "If you could locate this catalog," she continues, reaching into her purse, "I would be willing to pay well above market value. And I would prefer that you handle the transaction *personally*."

She slides a business card across the counter.

It's made of expensive paper that is heavier than normal, thicker. No company name, no title, no email. Just her name in elegant gold script and the phone number beneath it.

"Call me when you've found it," she says, and something commanding in her voice makes my stomach flip, though I don't entirely understand why.

When I find it. Not *if*.

"Day or night," she adds. "It's urgent."

She picks up the medieval poetry book I'd put down earlier, placing a crisp hundred-dollar bill on the counter. The book only costs thirty-five dollars.

"Keep the change," she says, adding, "for your troubles," when I start to protest.

"I don't even know if I can find it," I reply, but she's already moving toward the door.

"You will," the lady in black says with absolute certainty, and something about how she says it makes me believe her. She looks at my nametag briefly, then finds my eyes again. "You have the right mind for this work, *Jude*."

My name on her lips sends a shiver down my spine. Before I can stop myself, a breathless "Yes, Ma'am," leaves my lips, freezing her by the door.

Her look is sharp as she pins me with her gaze. I wish the world would swallow me whole. *What is wrong with you?* I scold myself.

"Honorifics are earned." Her voice is stern, commanding, and I damn near melt into a puddle of shame and desire.

"Fuck," I curse under my breath. "I'm so sorry. I-I… *fuck*." My cheeks are blood red as I stutter; I know they are.

Her brow relaxes, the stern look easing. "Call me when you have news," she repeats, offering a small smile. "I very much look forward to hearing from you."

The bell chimes as she leaves, and the shop becomes ordinary again, empty, all the color drained from the world.

I stare at her card, running my thumb over the raised letters of her name. My heart is still racing, my pants straining uncomfortably.

That, I did not anticipate.

I've never responded to someone so immediately, so intensely. Most of the time, my sex drive is pretty low on my list of priorities.

Who is she?

The puzzle pieces slowly click as I reread the shiny embossed letters on the business card.

Adriana De Crevena.

I take a step backward, nearly knocking over the display of bookmarks behind me.

How did I not see that?

De Crevena. The same family name as the catalog she was seeking. The same family I'd just spent five minutes discussing with her like a complete mansplaining twat.

My mind starts racing, running through the variables like it's trying to unjumble a Rubik's Cube.

Coincidence? Highly unlikely.

A descendant? Possible, though the De Crevena bloodline is well-documented and has been destroyed in its entirety, wiped off the face of the earth by their rivals. There was an entire chapter on it; I remember it from my thesis work.

No, it can't be.

But what if it was?

I flip the card over again, looking for more information I know I won't find. The little piece of cardboard is mysterious, like her.

Her voice echoes in my head: *Call me when you've found it.*

She'd said it like a command rather than a request...

Fuck me. That tone.

I tuck the card into my shirt pocket, my mind spinning with possibilities.

I'd be lying if I said I wasn't intrigued. More than intrigued. This period in history is precisely what my PhD was about. All those hours I spent researching supernatural beings that may or may not have existed...perhaps all that work could finally be of use.

Not that the erection tenting in my pants has anything to do with academics...

Oh no, that's all for her.

Adriana De Crevena.

CHAPTER 3
POTENTIAL

(ADRIANA)

My mouth waters despite having fed yesterday.

Get a grip, I chide myself as I leave the bookstore, clutching the book of poems I didn't intend on buying.

Yet I can't shake the experience.

The memory of the shop assistant's heartbeat still thrums through my veins, a rhythm I haven't heard in my own chest for years.

Jude. It's a nice name.

He wasn't afraid.

His heartbeat was steady for the most part. When it sped up, it wasn't from fear. The scent of arousal was unmistakable on him.

Most humans sense what I am on some primal level, even when they can't consciously identify the threat. They naturally recoil, pull away from me. But Jude seemed genuinely at ease, almost curious about the stranger asking esoteric questions about Renaissance manuscripts.

Fascinating. And potentially useful. He seems to genuinely be interested in finding the catalog.

The spike in his pulse when the *'Ma'am'* slipped from his lips also didn't escape my notice. I replay the moment: the slight flush creeping up his neck, the dilation of his pupils, his breath catching for a fraction of a second as he swallowed hard...

No!

I push the memory down.

I can't go through that again. Not after how it ended the last time. Men who call you 'Ma'am' are the whole reason I'm in this predicament in the first place.

Resisting the urge to look back at the bookstore, I slide into the back of the black sedan with the tinted windows waiting outside, ordering the driver to take me back to the penthouse.

Adriana De Crevena, printed on the card. He'll have noticed by now. The question is what he'll make of it.

I'm not usually in the habit of dropping cards with my real name on them. But for the helpful young man from the Morrison's, it's a test. Just like the wild goose chase for that catalog.

I know precisely where the catalog in question is; I always do.

But I need someone with keen research skills, someone determined, interested, who can think outside the box. Someone who won't give up when the trail goes cold or dismiss anomalies as clerical errors.

Someone like Jude.

He's different. I know it before I've finished looking at him. For a human, nothing should warrant a second glance: just plain jeans, plain t-shirt, sneakers that have never seen a designer label.

But something about him refuses to be dismissed.

The contradiction, perhaps.

He's built like a man who has spent years being useful with his body, yet carries himself like he'd rather not be noticed—shoulders curved inward, head angled down, apologizing for taking up space with his whole body.

Yet, he had so much confidence when it came to books; he spoke about that time period like he was there, like he could see past the romantic veneer historians love to paint over centuries of brutality. The wonder in his eyes when he discussed illuminated manuscripts—

Foolish boy. There was nothing wonderful about that period. It was all violence and suffering and the slow, grinding weight of survival in a world that viewed knowledge as heresy and women as property.

Still, his passion is genuine. And passion, properly directed, can accomplish what mere competence cannot.

Maybe he's exactly who I've been searching for.

I catch myself smiling and immediately stop.

This is mere professional interest, I remind myself. Academic utility; nothing more.

I don't care that he has kind eyes or that his voice went soft when he spoke about preserving history. And I definitely don't care how his hands moved when he explained my family's reputation.

Stop it, Adriana.

I pull out my phone to distract myself, scrolling through messages I've already read. Three texts from dealers in Europe. Five queries about manuscripts I've sourced. Nothing about the Grimoire. Never about the Grimoire.

Forty minutes later, the driver drops me off with a polite greeting and then heads out again, and I rush inside to the safety of the building's shade.

The transition from car to building takes four seconds —I've timed it—but today those four seconds are pure fire. The late afternoon sun, filtered through cloud cover, presses against my skin, pricking my skin.

"*Merda,*" I curse under my breath as I yank the door open with shaky hands.

Usually, I avoid going out during the day, but the bookstores on my list tend to close earlier than I'd like, and time is not a luxury I can afford anymore.

Quick trips, that's my only option now.

Still, the exhaustion weighs heavily on my shoulders from the simple outing as I cross the foyer.

When I had the Grimoire, the sun did nothing to me. I could walk among mortals, unaffected by the celestial forces that make other vampires burst into flame or crumble to ash.

But like most of my powers now, I have good days and bad days. Often on the same day.

As long as I don't wait too long between feedings, I've been able to manage it.

But it's getting more unpredictable.

Nodding at the concierge as I pass, I'm barely holding my head up by the time the elevator deposits me in the hallway outside my double-story penthouse, thirty-nine floors above the bustling city. *So tired...*

My apartment is a soothing pitch-black when I enter, the expansive floor-to-ceiling windows tinted dark by the automatic blinds I had installed upon moving in.

Without bothering to turn on any lights, I head straight to my office upstairs. It's the space I spend most of my time in, the only part of the penthouse that has any personality.

A large Flemish oak desk, imported from Belgium, sits at the center, framed by large windows with automatic blinds. To the left, the entire wall is stacked with books; to the right, some sentimental art pieces I've finally hung up after staring at the bare wall for over two years. Some chairs, a small sitting area with a large couch, and a coffee table older than most humans decorate the space, every item intentional.

The red light on my security panel next to the door blinks steadily. No breaches, no unexpected visitors.

I key in the code to review the day's surveillance footage, fast-forwarding through hours of empty hallways. Paranoid, perhaps, but paranoia has kept me alive this long.

Reaching for the antique drinks cart in the corner, I pour myself a glass of wine that tastes like nothing. *Old habits*. What I wouldn't give to be a little bit tipsy right now, to be distracted from my reality. But alas, comfort is not meant for creatures like me. The sheer amount of alcohol it would take to achieve that effect is simply not worth it.

Back to work.

I check my email first, scrolling through the messages again to add each response to my tracking spreadsheet, color-coding them by likelihood of producing results. Red for dead ends, yellow for follow-ups needed, green for potential leads. The document is a sea of red with scattered yellow dots. No green in sight.

I close the spreadsheet. Open it again. The red cells multiply and spread across the columns, consuming everything like an infection. I count them: 217 dead ends,

23 pending follow-ups, zero confirmed leads. The numbers should be even. *They need to be even.*

I delete a yellow cell and reassign it to red. 218 and 22. *Better.*

My hands hover over the keyboard. This is ridiculous. The color-coding doesn't change the reality: I'm no closer to the Grimoire than I was nine years ago.

But I can't stop myself from adjusting the column widths, making sure each one is precisely the same size.

When the spreadsheet is perfectly aligned, I finally allow myself to close it.

My phone buzzes again. It's a text from a contact in Hong Kong:

> Renaissance manuscript at estate sale...

> Leather-bound, damaged binding

> Sending photos.

My hand stills on the wine glass I don't remember refilling.

This is it. This is the one. I know it.

Don't, I warn myself. *Don't hope.* Everyone knows that hope is what kills you in the end, not the actual dying.

But my treacherous heart, the one that doesn't beat but somehow still aches, dares to dream.

I scroll through the attached images, my pulse quickening despite myself.

The photos load with agonizing slowness, each line of pixels rendering like a countdown. *Come on. Come on.*

The leather looks right, the size matches, even the edge-gilding appears correct. The binding shows the right amount of wear too.

But when I zoom in on the visible pages, my heart sinks. The calligraphy is wrong. My mother's 'e's always had a distinctive tail, her 'g's a particular loop. This is machine-printed, probably from the nineteenth century at the earliest.

It's not her work. Not even close.

Cazzo! The wine glass shatters in my grip.

I stare at the blood-red liquid spreading across the glass desk, mixed with fragments of crystal that glimmer in the laptop light. The wine pools in the grooves of the wood grain, following paths of least resistance, finding its way to the edge. It drips onto the white carpet below…one drop, two drops, three. I count them because counting is better than feeling.

My hand is bleeding. I shift my gaze to the blood welling up in the fresh cuts, dark and sluggish. Even my blood doesn't work right anymore. It's too thick, too cold. It should've healed right over, like it used to.

It's all falling apart.

I should clean up the wine, the glass, my hand. Instead, I sit there, watching as the wine continues to drip on the expensive carpet, counting the drops. *Fifteen drops. Sixteen. Seventeen.*

Finally, I force myself to move, wrapping my hand in a silk scarf I pull from a desk drawer.

I need to find that damn Grimoire, I think for the umpteenth time as I grab another glass from the drinks cart and top up my wine.

The trail of breadcrumbs is there, but I keep chasing my tail, coming up empty-handed.

Research has never been my strong suit. That's why I need someone like Jude.

The young man has potential. More than potential, he

has an obsessive attention to detail that turns good researchers into great ones.

Having a human ally, someone who can move in daylight, who can access records and databases I don't even know exist, would be invaluable.

He's the most promising candidate I've had in nine years.

Or maybe just another red cell to add to my spreadsheet.

Don't get your hopes up, Adriana.

CHAPTER 4
DIGGING

(JUDE)

I don't tell old man Morrison about the visit from the mysterious patron with the hypnotic voice that affects me more than I know how to process. He doesn't need to know.

I've seen plenty of rich collectors come through the bookstore in the year I've worked here. The big-shot executives hunting for first editions to impress their golf partners. Vapid customers with little personality and lots of attitude demanding collections that would 'make me look smart.' They all carry themselves with entitlement, demanding and loud and desperate to prove their worth through acquisition.

The woman from earlier was different. She had the aura of authority that you could sense without her needing to say a single word.

The sleek business card sits snugly in my shirt pocket when I lock up for the day and head back to the commune.

I've already memorized every letter, every number on that expensive piece of cardboard.

Adriana De Crevena. I keep repeating the name in my head, as if it could unlock the mystery of her lineage.

As I pass by the restaurants with their tempting aromas, my stomach growls loudly, reminding me that I haven't eaten anything since this morning, when I ended up devouring the stale cereal straight from the box because one of my housemates finished the milk again without replacing it.

But Morrison doesn't pay me the kind of wage that allows for splurging on things like restaurants or takeout. It barely covers rent and the cheapest groceries. Well, that is if he even pays me. He's late again.

There should be a packet of instant noodles somewhere in a cupboard back home—hopefully.

Two buses and more than a mile's walk later, I'm finally outside the grim building with the chipping paint and cracking walls that some call *home*. Not me. This shit-hole will never be my home, just another temporary stopping point.

The building looks like an architectural afterthought squatting against the skyline. It's the sort of place land-lords buy cheap and rent expensive to students and desperate workers who don't have better options. Which is to say, people like me.

I head straight to the kitchen, a cramped space with overflowing shelves and cupboards that no longer fully close, their hinges sagging from years of aggressive use by tenants who treat shared spaces like they're disposable.

The smell of something cooking on the stove sends another pang of hunger to my gut.

But my stomach drops when I realize my housemate is making my last pack of noodles. That's what I'm smelling.

The evidence is right there, irrefutable: the empty shelf where my name is stuck on with a label that is curling around the edges; the ripped noodle packet on the counter, torn open with the casual violence of someone who doesn't give a shit about property rights; the bowl she's stirring with one hand while scrolling her phone with the other.

"I think that's mine." It takes all my remaining energy to speak up when every instinct tells me to retreat, to avoid conflict like I've been doing since childhood.

The curly-haired redhead looks up briefly from her bowl—barely a glance, really—and then dismisses me with a single flick of her wrist. "I don't know what you're talking about." Her attention drops back to her phone, cutting me out like I'm not even there.

"It was the last one. C'mon," I try again, in vain searching through the shelf to make sure there is nothing left on it, hoping against logic that maybe I've missed something, that maybe there's another packet hiding behind the expired spices and someone's forgotten jar of pasta sauce.

No luck.

"Fuck off, you're disturbing my meal," she replies simply, continuing the scroll.

"But, I—"

"Stop being a creep." She takes her bowl and leaves, walking right past me without even looking up again, close enough for the scent of her fruity shampoo and the steam rising from my stolen dinner to assault my senses.

No apology, no acknowledgment of guilt...nothing.

And I let her.

Again.

Like I always do.

With a sigh, I fill a glass of water from the tap—at least she can't steal that, though I'm sure she'd find a way if she tried—and sink down at the splintering wooden table with its worn patches where countless students have eaten their miserable meals and studied for exams they'd probably rather forget.

They're always eating my shit. *Bloody students.* Though that's unfair. I'm a student too, technically. Or was. Or something in between—scholarship athlete turned PhD candidate turned dropout, depending on which year you asked.

The categories don't matter when you're sharing space with people who've never had to choose between food and rent, who treat shared living like an extended sleepover rather than a desperate economic arrangement.

But I can't afford to live anywhere else. The mathematics of poverty are brutally simple: you take what you can get and you don't complain, because complaining doesn't change the zeros in your bank account.

There is no one left to bail me out, to *save* me.

My good-for-nothing father fucked off when I was three, finding his end six years later in a car accident, according to my mother. She wasn't sad.

No siblings either. They only ever made one baby.

Probably for the best.

My poor mother had a hard enough time working herself into an early grave, holding down two shitty jobs to get me through school, her hands permanently stained with industrial cleaning chemicals, her back perpetually aching from hours spent bent over other people's messes.

She wasn't a bad mother; she did what she could. But I only have a few happy memories of us together.

My grandmother raised me for the most part, keeping me in check while my mother slaved away to put food on the table.

But that mean bitch died on my 11th birthday.

And now, there is nobody.

Just me and the weight of making it work without any of the safety nets that other people take for granted. No family money, no connections, no fallback plan beyond pure stubborn refusal to give up.

Which means taking on my housemates about my food, for the umpteenth time. Despite how much I detest conflict or how confrontation makes my chest tight and my hands shake with the old childhood fear of making things worse.

Some good that did.

I rinse the glass and put it away, then head to the little space in the corner of this decrepit building that I call 'mine.'

The old key turns with force, and for a second, I fear it might break—because of course that would be my luck, to be locked out of the one space that belongs to me—but then it does its job and the creaky door swings open.

My room is as dark as it was when I left early this morning to make it to work on time, the autumn sun having shifted away from my single window hours ago.

The overhead light fixture hasn't worked in months, but the landlord is as apathetic to my requests as my house-mates. He merely ignores me, adds my emails to whatever spam folder he uses for tenant complaints about habitability.

With a sigh, I turn on the little bedside lamp, which

provides barely enough light for me to squint in. But it's something.

Exhaustion threatens to close my eyes for good when I slouch down in the chair by the desk overflowing with projects I'll never finish.

But I'm too intrigued to go straight to bed.

My laptop is slow and in desperate need of replacement. The fan whirs constantly now, a mechanical death rattle that probably means the hard drive is dying, but it boots up and connects to the internet, and that's enough. It still works, as do all my logins and passwords that should've been stripped along with my bursary when I dropped out last year to look after my dying mother.

I don't even have to dig too deep.

There is a lot of information archived about the De Crevena family. Influential in European politics and even in wars, their name appears in diplomatic correspondence and military records throughout the centuries.

My finger follows the family tree of names as they scroll by, each generation documenting births and deaths and marriages that shaped the continent, history most people never learned in school.

There is no Adriana in the lineage. None that I can find, anyway.

But there is no denying that the woman who walked into the store today has an uncanny resemblance to some of the portraits staring back at me, painted in the style of the times, haunting and gothic, beautiful in that other-worldly way that Renaissance artists reserved for saints and nobles. The bone structure is too similar to be coincidental.

She must be a descendant somehow, tracking her

family's artifacts, perhaps researching her genealogy for legal reasons or simple curiosity.

Makes sense. Rich families often hire specialists to recover lost heirlooms, to piece together histories that got scattered.

Except it doesn't; there is so much that doesn't make sense.

The questions are piling up in my mind, burning.

Academic puzzles are my weakness, the intellectual equivalent of gambling addiction.

I need to speak to her.

Even now, I keep thinking back to that interaction, replaying every word, every inflection. Such a magnetic voice. The mere memory is making my dick stiffen.

What is happening to my body?

I'm not usually the type to get aroused by mysterious strangers or commanding voices, but there was something about her that bypassed my rational mind entirely and went straight to some primal part of my brain.

My hand absentmindedly finds its way to my dick as I close my eyes to remember her scent, the way she said my name.

Good god, and those full breasts, pressing against her dress, threatening to spill over. How would it feel to have your face buried in those, to be smothered by them? What would one have to do to earn such privileges?

My imagination goes wild as I jerk myself to completion with the image of Adriana De Crevena on my mind. In the fantasy, I'm naked while she's still fully clothed. She calls me a 'good boy' and pulls down her top, offering me a breast. I latch on greedily, suckling on her tender nipple as she reaches for my cock and gives me a hand job, letting me finish all over her tits.

I come unceremoniously into my hand a few minutes later with a muffled gasp.

Instantly, shame floods my circuits, warming my ears.

'What is wrong with you, Jude?' My grandmother's voice echoes through my mind as I dig through my drawer to find a tissue to clean up my mess. *'Stop being a little creep.'*

Tossing the soiled tissue in the bin, I stare at my laptop, unmoving, trying to pull my mind out of the gutter. But it keeps returning to her, to Adriana.

It will drive me mad if I keep thinking about it, but I can't find a way to steer my mind in any other direction.

Like a song that's stuck in your head, I know the only way to get rid of it is exposure: I need to see her again.

And there is only one way I will see that gothic goddess with the soothing voice again…

So, I throw myself into my research, diving into all the legal (and illegal) threads and subreddits where one can find such things, digging until my laptop fan's whirring grows so loud, I fear it might explode. Yet I don't stop, don't go to bed.

For the first time since the crushing weight of grief and the finality of leaving my hometown for good—our small house reclaimed by the bank to pay my mother's estate fees, everything I'd ever called home reduced to a legal document and a set of keys handed over to strangers—I have a purpose.

I have to find that catalog for her.

Have to.

CHAPTER 5
WATCHERS

(ADRIANA)

I'm tending to the plants in the foyer when my phone rings.

11:47 PM. It's Dimitri.

He's late.

I set the plant down, answering without preamble, "Everything go according to plan?"

"Affirmative. Package delivered. Client satisfied," he pauses. "But—"

"What is it?"

The hesitation in his voice is as unmissable as the change in his breathing. In my experience, when Dimitri gets nervous, it's worth paying attention.

"We had *watchers* tonight." His Russian accent grows thicker, vowels stretching. "Professional types."

I don't like the sound of that.

The Byzantine manuscript deal should have been routine, in and out, no complications. Nobody else knew about the drop-off.

"Did they give you any trouble?"

I put my phone on speaker to free up my hands, pouring myself a glass of wine as Dimitri recounts what happened at the docks tonight.

"They stayed in the shadows most of the time," he continues, voice tight. "Didn't approach, didn't interfere. Just...observed."

"How many?"

"Three, maybe four. Hard to tell. They moved *wrong*."

Pacing the foyer, I grow more restless as he describes the moving shadows, the sense of being observed by eyes that reflected light like an animal's.

Dimitri's voice drops lower. "One of them smiled at me, Adriana. When he stepped into the light, he had teeth like—" He stops himself.

"Like what?" I ask despite knowing exactly what he means.

"Nothing. Forget it. I'm probably just being paranoid."

But he's not. We both know he's not.

I hang up without a goodbye.

Not good. Not good at all.

There is only one possible answer—*vampires*.

Not just any vampires, either. Not if they moved in a pack like Dimitri said.

We're predators; we like our space, our turf. We don't just *watch*.

No, there is only one group of vampires who behaves like that: *La Famiglia Eterna*.

When it comes to lurking in the shadows, none do it better than those ancient criminals and their network of unsavory characters.

Far more sinister than their name suggests, The Eternal

Family—or 'The Family of Devils,' as I like to call them—is a shadow organization that operates like the human mafia, but infinitely more powerful and better connected. If something horrible, something pure evil, is going down, they're usually behind it, in my experience.

But why would *La Famiglia* care about me? I've stayed off their radar for centuries, kept my head down, avoided their territories, never interfered with their operations.

They have no reason to be surveying me. Unless they've learned something new.

The thought sends a chill through me that has nothing to do with my failing temperature regulation.

They can't know about the Grimoire, about my hybrid nature. *Can they?*

I've been so careful.

Everyone who knows is dead now.

Except for Cyrus…

I move to the window, peering through the blinds. From thirty-nine floors up, the city spreads below like a glittering circuit board, cars reduced to streams of light, people to invisible specks. Nothing moves in the darkness of nearby buildings, but that doesn't mean nothing is there.

I count the windows on the tower across from mine. Twenty windows per floor, visible floors…I lose count. Start again.

What do they want? Why now?

Stop it. You're spiraling.

With shaky hands, I drain my glass in three swallows, then pour another. The wine still tastes like nothing, but the ritual of it steadies my hands.

As I take another sip, my breath mists in the warm

room, a visible reminder that I'm losing control. Vampire bodies don't breathe unless we choose to, don't produce the telltale signs of mortality unless trying to blend in. Yet here I am, exhaling fog, reduced to some ordinary human caught in winter air.

Merda, I curse silently.

If anyone is watching closely enough, they might notice these symptoms and start asking questions about why a vampire is showing signs of instability. They might realize I'm vulnerable, weak, easy prey.

I move away from the window, suddenly aware of how exposed I am. Thirty-nine floors up means nothing to creatures who can scale buildings or shadow-walk. The automatic blinds are closed, but are they enough?

I pull the heavy blackout curtains across as well, layering protection. The security panel shows no alarms, all clear. Just in case, I replay the last hour of footage. But there's nothing.

I'm safe. For now.

But I need to be more careful, more discreet. And I need to find that damn spellbook before *La Famiglia* decides it's time to do more than hide in the shadows and spook my business partners.

That's where Jude comes in…He could be useful.

Careful, Adriana. He's mortal.

Yet I can't purge the thought of the boy with the stormy eyes that somehow look both startled and intrigued simultaneously. What is he looking at so intensely? *What does he see?* It's always the quiet ones who hide their secrets best. He's not built like a quiet one, though; quite the opposite. *Who are you, Jude?*

Still deep in thought, I abandon my gardening

activities and move back upstairs to my office with my glass in hand.

The pile of unopened mail is stacked neatly on my desk. I know I should deal with them, but instead, I open my laptop.

It's just a routine background check for a potential employee, I tell myself as I stalk *Morrison's Rare Books'* threadbare social media presence.

The last Facebook post was dated five months ago. It was a link to a local newspaper article about the bookstore, how it's been in Morrison's family for fifty years, blah, blah, blah.

I don't care about the story; it's the photo that draws me in. Morrison is standing by one of the displays, and there, beside him, is Jude, looking out of place in his own skin. *He should straighten out those shoulders.*

Stop it, Adriana!

The most important piece of information in the entire boring article about Morrison's white privilege is the photo caption, the one that lists the two people in the photo: *Andrew Morrison (left) with his shop assistant, Jude Cole.*

Jude Cole. I like that. It suits him.

Closing the neglected Facebook page, I type Jude's name into my browser. *Just a routine check.*

The search yields more than expected, though none of it feels personal. Regatta results, a varsity rowing roster, a sports profile that lists him as stroke seat of the university eight two years running. A PhD fellowship and an academic history that trails off without explanation. And a small obituary in the online archive of an unknown newspaper, dated June of last year.

Miranda Cole, age 44. Leaving behind her only son, Jude Cole, age 23.

No immediate family. No mention of anything else. No Instagram, no Twitter, nothing beyond that neglected Morrison's Facebook page. Every trace of him online has been recorded by others, nothing offered willingly. For someone his age, the absence is striking.

A loner. *Just like Elijah was.*

No!

He's nothing like Elijah.

But the similarities between Jude and my former familiar are undeniable in a way that makes my silent heart clench.

That same devotion in his eyes, as he could worship you, like he could let you care for him, provide for him, protect him from a world that's clearly been unkind.

I close the laptop with more force than necessary and the sound echoes in the quiet room.

Careful now. Look how it ended last time…

Nearly ten years later, and the betrayal still cuts deep.

No, I won't make that mistake again.

I haven't kept to myself all these years, to be seduced by boyish charm and intimate knowledge of the 16th Century. No matter how many times I've imagined Jude falling to his knees before me since I left *Morrison's Rare Books* earlier.

He'd look so pretty on his knees.

No! Stop it.

I'm getting nostalgic, which is never a good idea when you have five-hundred-plus years of regrets you can't forget.

I should delete Jude's information and find another

researcher. Someone more neutral, less likely to trigger my protective instincts.

But I don't want to.

Instead, I return to my desk and reopen the laptop. His sporting achievements and academic records stare back at me, the records of a promising student who dropped out to care for his dying mother, a brilliant mind currently squandering his youth for minimum wage.

Such potential. Such waste. Such beautiful, breakable vulnerability.

No, snap out of it! I have a job for him, nothing more.

Never again will I confuse professional utility with personal connection.

And I absolutely will not fantasize about what Jude would look like stripped bare and tied to my bed, those inquisitive eyes looking up at me like I'm his everything.

Absolutely not.

This is strictly business, a race against time to find my mother's spellbook before my condition deteriorates beyond recovery. My body is in no state to take on any *dependents* right now. I can't trust that I won't lose control; won't kill him without meaning to. And what a travesty that would be.

This arrangement can't be about anything other than finding the Grimoire. Not if I want us both to survive it.

My phone screen lights up with an email notification.

I grab it so fast I nearly drop it.

But it's just another dealer in Estonia. Another dead end. Another red cell for my spreadsheet. *Not Jude.*

𐫱

PERHAPS I GOT my hopes up too soon.

Two more useless book dealers have been crossed off my list since *Morrisons*.

I'm starting to think perhaps this city won't be much help either.

Not a bad place to spend your final moments, I suppose.

It's early evening, and I'm four chapters into a new book I had to force myself to start. Some academic text on preservation techniques that should interest me but doesn't.

The words blur together on the page. I've read the same paragraph three times without retaining a single sentence. But I can't keep opening and closing that damn depressing spreadsheet. The ritual was making everything worse, not better.

At least pretending to read gives my hands something to do besides rearranging pens or checking security footage for the hundredth time.

That's when my phone rings.

Unknown number.

Is it him?

I force myself to wait through the fourth ring—can't seem too eager, too desperate—then answer with a carefully neutral, "Yes?"

"Miss De Crevena?" The voice catches, uncertain and nervous. It's male, young, with a slight breathlessness. "This is Jude. From Morrison's Rare Books? You left your card and I—it's about that catalog you were looking for. I think I found something."

He called!

My grip tightens on the phone. I was right about him; I knew he couldn't resist a good mystery.

Jude is still talking, words tumbling out faster now. "I

went through the acquisition records, cross-referenced with some archives, and I thought maybe if I looked at—" He catches himself, embarrassed. "Sorry, I'm rambling. I thought you'd want to know. If you're still interested, I mean. In the catalog."

I let the silence stretch for a beat, two, three, letting him wonder if he's made a mistake by phoning.

"Jude," I say finally, a smile creeping over my lips. "I'm glad you called."

CHAPTER 6

SUMMER PLACE

(JUDE)

I check the name of the building against the scribble of paper I have nearly worn through with my incessant checking.

Summer Place.

It matches perfectly, but this fact doesn't make my heart beat any slower.

It's been four days since Adriana De Crevena walked into the shop with her unusually specific request, and I've gotten little sleep since.

Every day, as soon as I got home from work, I continued my search, much to the detriment of the rest of my routine.

I wanted to tell Adriana what I had found over the phone, but she replied, *'Not like this. Come over tomorrow night,'* and recited the address I stand in front of now.

The building's glass door suddenly opens, startling me, and I drop the piece of paper.

"Mr. Cole?" the concierge with the white gloves confirms as he holds open the door for me.

How did he know that? I never gave her my surname...

I put the piece of paper back in my pants and smile politely.

"All the way to the top. Miss De Crevena is expecting you." He ushers me into the lift and presses the number thirty-nine.

Inspecting my jeans and sweater combo in the mirror wall as the lit-up orange numbers above the elevator door climb from single digits to doubles, I wonder once more if I'm underdressed. But it's too late to do anything about that now.

With each floor I ascend, my nervousness increases. Something tells me this is about more than finding a book. People typically don't request home visits for information exchange. Not in my limited experience, at least.

The door gives a shrill, electronic chime and pops open, spilling me out into a small corridor at the top. A single wooden door meets me, ajar.

Taking a deep breath, I push inside, right into a space so grand, it could be a movie set.

The double-volume foyer is incredibly luxe, gothic yet somehow modern too. *How much does one need to earn a month to afford a chandelier like that?*

"Jude." The sound of my name draws my attention to the dramatic staircase as the enigmatic host floats down. *Are her feet even touching the ground?*

Dressed in a deep purple dress that reaches to her ankles, her hair is pinned on top of Adriana's head, exposing the pale skin of her neckline that plunges into an ample bosom. My dick jerks uncomfortably as I stare.

"Miss De Crevena," I greet, my gaze locked in hers,

unable to shift, as she closes the distance between us, now less than a yard away.

She's close enough that I can smell her. There's that jasmine scent again. It's as intoxicating as her voice. Like Mrs. Nel, my high school English teacher and first obsessive crush, used to wear jasmine too. I recognize it instantly, just like I did when we first met.

"Please, call me Adriana," she tells me, placing a gentle hand on my shoulder.

"Yes, *Ma'am*," I reply, nodding obediently.

Fuck! Again. It slipped out.

She breaks contact, frowns. "I'm not your Ma'am," she says simply, gliding off to the lounge to the left.

Like a silly puppy, I follow her, grateful that her back is turned to my blushing cheeks.

"You found the catalog?" Adriana asks, eyeing me expectantly, as she settles down on an armchair, pointing to where she wants me to sit, on the leather couch opposite her.

It takes every ounce of control I possess not to close my eyes when she speaks, when that seductive voice rolls over me. So soothing. So mesmerizing.

I simply nod, not trusting myself to speak, to not call her 'Ma'am' again without permission.

"That's good news," she replies, though she doesn't seem at all surprised.

"It's not quite so simple." I finally find my voice, focusing on the book, on the data. "It's owned by a tech billionaire in Italy, and I doubt he'd part with it willingly."

"Oh, I'm not worried. You'll find that I can be quite *persuasive*." She smiles at me with a glint in her eye, and I swear my traitorous cock gets even harder. I shift in my seat, placing one of the couch pillows on my lap in an attempt to hide my shameful desires.

I have so many questions, but I'm unable to vocalize any of them. My mouth appears to have forgotten how to connect to my mind.

"How rude of me; I didn't offer you anything to drink," the host says suddenly.

"I'm okay; I should probably go." I hug the pillow tighter, making no move to rise. "I'll text you the details."

"I don't text," Adriana says simply, getting up. "Tea?"

I stand, ready to go, pillow still in hand. But the words coming out of my mouth are contrary, accepting her offer of tea.

So, instead, I follow her to a kitchen so pristine, it should come with its own private chef. I don't even know what half those appliances are for.

Adriana turns on the kettle, but before she can take out the cups, I reach over on instinct, flinching when our fingers connect. "Let me," I offer, blushing as I jerk my hand away.

Adriana smiles, stepping away from the cupboard to sit down at the marble-top island.

"Tea's in the cupboard above the stove," she directs as she watches me work, and I follow every word, spooning the loose leaves into the antique porcelain teapot as instructed.

Repeating the simple steps in my head, I concentrate harder on the damn tea than I've ever focused on any of my varsity exams. *It has to be perfect.*

"Join me," Adriana invites when everything is arranged on a tray.

Nodding, I take it over to her, gently placing it on the counter without rattling the cups too loudly.

Taking a cup, I sit down across from her, still painfully aware of my semi-erect cock that I hope she hasn't noticed.

"Thank you." Adriana picks up her tea, wrapping both hands around the cup like she's trying to warm them. But she doesn't take a sip. "Such a good job."

The praise nearly makes me drop my cup, but I manage to save the situation and only spill a few drops of tea on the tiled floor.

"Shit." I drop to my knees without thinking, wiping up the mess with my jersey's sleeve.

What the fuck, Jude? Stop acting weird, I scold myself, despite knowing it will have little effect on the outcome.

But she doesn't laugh at me or shout at me; no, Miss De Crevena just watches me intently as I try to mop up the spillage.

When she finally speaks, it's not what I expected.

"I have an offer for you…*Jude.*" She reaches down and tilts my chin up with a single finger, her skin impossibly cold against mine.

Still kneeling on the floor, I look up at her, waiting to hear more. Something about this position feels right in a way I can't articulate.

"You seem to have a good knack for finding lost things," she continues. "And I have an essential 'lost thing' I need to track down. The catalog was only the first puzzle piece."

"What are you looking for?" My curiosity always gets the better of me.

"A book. Of *sentimental* value." She pauses, studying my face. "I'll pay you triple what that bookstore owner gives you. Plus room and board."

"W-what?" I stutter, but she doesn't repeat herself. Just waits for me to process.

The offer seems ridiculous. Doing a side project for someone is one thing, but moving in with a complete stranger?

That's crazy, surely.

But the more I think about it, the more I can't find any reason why not to.

If I accept, it will resolve many of my problems.

I love the bookstore, but the environment itself is beyond toxic. Never mind that the pay is so poor, I'll never be able to move out of the shitty student housing, or have enough money to finally finish my studies and get on with my life.

Though they're reason enough, my depressing circumstances aren't the only consideration.

It's Adriana herself who makes me want to stay. I'm so drawn to her. I know I can't leave, not now. Not when that voice is offering me a purpose, a reason to spend more time with her.

Fuck-it.

I'm not one for being impulsive. Usually, I spend days, weeks, ruminating over something, only to freeze, unable to make a decision. But there is no hesitation when I accept Miss De Crevena's impromptu offer. "Yes," I say without asking for more details.

Adriana smiles, reaching out a hand to help me off the floor.

Despite being much bigger than her physically, she pulls me to my feet in a clean fell swoop.

What the fuck? I stare at her, mouth agape. *How did she do that?*

Adriana gets up, closing the little distance left between us. "I will settle for nothing less than informed full consent, Jude," she informs me in that hypnotic voice that does things to my dick it has no right to do.

I nod, losing myself in that sea-green gaze. This is the part where words would be useful but I simply stare, wordless.

Adriana gently traces a long red nail over my cheek, and my breath stalls altogether. Her touch is startling—not painful, but cold. Impossibly cold, like pressing your palm against winter glass. I don't flinch, just lean into it, closing my eyes. The chill spreads across my skin, raising goose-bumps down my neck.

"There are things you should know about me first." Her voice drops to a whisper. "About what this job really entails."

She moves closer. "You're quite observant, Jude. Tell me, what do you notice when you look at me? Anything unusual?"

I open my eyes, studying her face from inches away. Now that I allow myself to look closer, the details start clicking into place like pieces of a puzzle I've been assembling without realizing.

"Your skin," I start slowly. "It's flawless. Not like makeup flawless. Like...untouched by time." My mind keeps churning as I tally the evidence. "And you don't blink. Or you don't blink enough. Most people blink fifteen to twenty times per minute. You've barely blinked twice since I walked in."

"What else?" she prompts, and there's something approving in her tone.

"You haven't touched your tea." I glance at the cup sitting cold on the table between us. "And the apartment is freezing, but you're not wearing a sweater. You're not cold at all, are you?"

"No," she says softly. "I don't feel temperature. Haven't for a very long time."

The pieces shift, rearranging into a picture I should have seen from the start. For starters, she moves like she's defying gravity. Then there is her casual mention of Renaissance manuscripts as if she'd seen them firsthand. And the rhythm of her breathing that comes and goes, like she's trying to force it rather than a natural rise and fall, that's also super suspicious.

My heart hammers against my ribs as the only logical —yet so illogical—answer surfaces. But I can't say it, can't make it real. There are no such things.

"Do you know what I am?" she whispers, moving close enough that I can see the unnatural gold flecks in her eyes, their shimmer.

"Yes—" I stop myself from adding a 'Ma'am.'

She smiles, and for the first time, I see them clearly: canine teeth just slightly too sharp, too long. I swear they weren't there before!

Adriana licks a broad stroke from my chin to my earlobe, playfully flicking her tongue over my skin, tickling me. My cock jumps in response, pressing desperately against the fabric of my jeans, trapped, thick with need.

"Say it," she challenges me, pressing her body against mine, my erection digging into her stomach. She's almost a foot shorter than I am, yet I want to cower before her. "What am I?" she asks again.

"A...v-vampire." The word comes out barely audible but her devious smile tells me Adriana heard just fine.

"More or less." She rewards me with a "good boy" that makes an uncharacteristic groan rip from my chest without reservation. A groan that makes her smile in the most breathtaking way, a way I want to see again and again.

This can't be, can it?

Years of researching the inexplicable histories of the world, part of me has always suspected there might be other creatures hiding in the shadows.

And now I have proof.

The revelation should surprise me, but my brain doesn't know what to do with the information. Not when she's standing so close and my cock is so hard. I don't dare move.

"If you choose to stay, dearest Jude, there will be rules...I expect your full loyalty and utmost discretion," the Lady of the House lays down the boundaries as her fingers trace the skin along my collarbone.

I'm near delirious with lust, with need. My new employer is dangerous, unmistakably so, yet I've never been more drawn to another person in my life. And I don't even think she's compelled me, if that's even a thing real vampires do. It's merely my own traitorous body and its unconventional desires that are causing this reaction.

"I accept. *Please.*" I don't know why I'm begging. She had made me an offer; the choice was mine.

Every cell in my body is screaming for me to kiss her, to pull her into me, but I wouldn't dare, not without permission.

My heart sinks to my shoes as Adriana moves away, leaving me and my stupid erection standing awkwardly against the wall.

"Come back tomorrow at 8 PM," she calls over her shoulder, and then she's gone, moving faster than my eye can track, the front door left open for me to take my leave.

I should do the smart thing.
Should run for my life and forget we ever met.
But I know I will be back tomorrow.

CHAPTER 7

PAST MISTAKES

(ADRIANA)

L ong after I've sent Jude away, after seeing that look in his eyes, the same trusting devotion that once destroyed me, I'm still pacing my office like a wild thing in a confined space.

Why the fuck did I do that?

Things are moving too fast. This was supposed to just be a first meeting. A test, not a housing offer.

It's a good thing, I rationalize as I crisscross the room.

Time isn't on my side anymore. If *La Famiglia* is stirring, and my powers are failing, my window of opportunity to get out of this alive is closing rapidly.

I need to reclaim the Grimoire, and Jude can help with that.

Beautiful, sweet Jude, who looks at me like I could solve the riddle to life itself; like he wants me to.

Careful, Adriana.

He's here to work. Nothing more. I know this.

Yet I can't stop imagining him in a dimly-lit basement,

those shoulders spread wide instead of hunched, red rope mapping the geography of trust across his skin.

Stop it!

I didn't mean to reveal my nature to him earlier.

But it was simply too tempting to resist. When he kneeled for me, *gods*, the entire fabric of reality seemed to unravel, warping time to slow motion.

When his unmistakable erection pressed into my body, I knew I wasn't the only one who felt the tension. The poor boy was so fucking hard. It took every last bit of restraint not to fuck him right there on the kitchen counter.

Good grief.

Perhaps the nine years alone are finally getting to me.

I reach for my wine glass, intending to refill it, when the crystal shatters in my hand—not from pressure but from cold.

Again?

Ice spreads from my fingertips, flash-freezing the delicate stem until it cracks.

Merda! It's getting worse.

My magic has always been precise, directed. It's never simply *leaked out* like this. And definitely not as ice.

Fire was my mother's gift, passed down through blood. For centuries, witches in my family line wielded flames. At first, I thought it skipped a generation, that I was unremarkable. Until one morning, as a fourteen-year-old, I nearly burned our house down when I got my first period.

Just like that, everything changed.

One day, I was a normal teenager, and the next, I could set things on fire by merely pointing at them.

Well, it wasn't quite that simple. I had to learn how to use my gift, how to tame it.

But when I got it right...

It was incredible while it lasted, while I was mortal.

The vampire transformation changed everything. Death and fire don't mix. The magic inverted, turned cold. Ice instead of flame; a perversion of what it should be.

The Grimoire saved me. Not the book itself but what was added to it. The living spells inside generate artificial life force, the one thing my undead body can't produce but my witch magic desperately needs. A bridge between death and life. With it, both natures coexisted without destroying each other. Now that it's gone, the balance collapses a little more each day.

The ice spreads. The fire dies. And I grow weaker.

What will I lose next?

I try to test my speed, moving from the window to the bedroom in what should be an instant blur. Instead, I stumble, my supernatural coordination faltering mid-step. The world tilts dangerously, and I have to grip the doorframe to keep from falling.

Oh, fanculo.

This is getting ridiculous now.

But there is nothing I can do to stop it.

At this rate, I'll soon have to feed every day to function.

I used to go a week without blood before I risked hibernation. Now, nothing is certain.

Definitely not a good time to bring a human into the mix. Especially not an irresistible human like Jude. The natural submission radiates from him without artifice.

He would make a good familiar.

Careful...

That's not what he's here for.

I don't have a vacancy for a familiar. Never again. Not after what happened last time.

I can't believe I offered him a job.

A live-in position, no less.

What was I thinking?

He'll be here. All the time. In my space. With warm hands, and that look in his eyes that makes me want to—

No.

Focus on the work; that's all that matters.

I should pull myself together before he arrives tomorrow, establish boundaries while I still can.

With a sigh, I return to my desk.

The book on preservation techniques I'd been reading earlier sits there, abandoned. Educational. Boring. *Safe.*

I open it to where I'd left off, determined to distract myself with something that doesn't involve scandalous thoughts about beautiful humans who kneel without having to be asked.

But my mind keeps drifting back to Jude on his knees, how his breath quickened when I got close.

Focus, Adriana.

I force myself to turn the page. Then another.

The technical details about vellum preparation should bore me into stillness, but they don't.

I keep thinking of Jude's hands instead. The delicate way he handled the books at the store, as if they were breakable, made of glass. His hand was so warm when it brushed against mine earlier. Those hands could handle so much more than manuscripts…

Don't go there.

I turn another page, then another. I'm not retaining any of it, but at least it gives my eyes something to do besides closing and replaying that moment he looked up at me from his knees.

The clock on my desk reads 11:16 PM.

I keep reading.

Midnight passes. Then 1 AM…2 AM.

The penthouse is silent except for the whisper of pages turning, the occasional creak of my chair.

Outside, the city's lights begin to dim as late night bleeds into early morning.

I hardly notice, too absorbed with maintaining this fragile pretense of normalcy.

Just keep reading.

Don't think about later.

Don't think about him moving in.

Don't think about—

A key turns in the lock downstairs.

I glance at the clock: 7:04 AM.

Felix.

I'm still in yesterday's clothes, the book open in front of me, surrounded by the shattered remains of a wine glass I never cleaned up. But there is no time for damage control.

Footsteps sound on the stairs, and then Felix fills my office doorway, dressed in his usual dark jeans, button-down shirt, and sneakers, his long blond hair pulled back in a bun that sharpens the quiet watchfulness of his face. One look at me and the concern settles across his face without drama, the way it always does.

Nearly four years later, and I still haven't worked out how he became indispensable to my household. He reminds me of a young Venetian copyist I knew in my first decades, a humanist scholar's assistant named Lorenzo who reproduced classical texts with patient, unhurried hands and grew medicinal herbs on every available windowsill. Felix has never copied a manuscript in his life, as far as I know, but he tends the house and my plants with that same patience and care.

I was fond of Lorenzo too. He lived to sixty-three, which I chose to consider a success.

"Rough night?" Felix asks, stepping inside. His voice carries the slight rasp of a former smoker, though I've never seen him with a cigarette.

"You could say that." I close the book, setting it aside. "I need you to prepare the guest bedroom, please. Fresh linens, the works."

His eyebrows rise slightly, the most surprise I've ever seen on his deadpan face. "Expecting company?"

"A houseguest. He'll be staying for...the foreseeable future."

"*He?*" Now both eyebrows are up. "Should I be concerned?"

"He's a researcher," I answer quickly, too quickly, defensively. "Here to help with a project."

Felix's gaze drops to the shattered wine glass, then moves back to my face. He doesn't ask questions he knows I won't answer.

"I'll handle the bedroom," he says instead. "Anything else?"

"Food." I wave a hand vaguely. "Whatever people his age eat. Coffee. Definitely coffee. I have no idea what else."

"How old is this researcher?"

"Twenty-four."

Felix's expression shifts to something almost paternal. "So, groceries for a growing boy? Got it." He pauses at the doorway. "Adriana?"

"Yes?"

"When's the last time *you* fed?"

The question catches me off guard. Felix knows what I am—impossible not to after four years in my employ—but we don't usually discuss it directly.

60

"Not too long ago." I force a smile to sell the lie. "Don't worry about me."

"You look tired."

"I'm fine."

"Right." He doesn't believe me, but he won't push. That's another thing I appreciate about Felix—he knows when to let things lie. "I'll grab groceries and sort out the bedroom. This researcher arriving today?"

"Tonight, yes. 8 PM."

"Gives me time to stock properly, then." He glances at the shattered glass, my rumpled clothes. "Maybe get some rest? You'll want to make a good impression."

After he leaves, I stare at the closed door for a long moment.

Make a good impression.

Too late for that. I've already pinned Jude against a wall and watched him kneel. Already offered him a job and housing in the same breath. Already showed him exactly what I am.

And he said yes anyway.

Which means either Jude's braver than he looks, more desperate than I realized, or—

Or he wants to explore this further as much as I do.

That last possibility terrifies me.

Because *wanting* is dangerous.

Wanting is how Elijah got close enough to destroy me.

And I'm already wanting Jude far more than is wise.

CHAPTER 8

PACKING UP

(JUDE)

I n a single day, I have undone my entire life.

I'm officially jobless now, homeless too, technically.

I expected to snap out of it before it went too far, before I burned my pathetic world to the ground. But I didn't.

Even now, as I pack my measly belongings into two suitcases, I am certain I will quit this madness and forget all about Miss De Crevena and her unexpected offer.

Yet I keep packing.

Moving in with a vampire is ludicrous!

The fact that they are even real should melt my brain. But part of me has always hoped for more, that the world had secrets beyond our understanding.

All those long nights in the varsity library, combing through ancient texts and forgotten manuscripts, searching for a hint of meaning...

And now I finally have proof that the creatures of the

night extend to the undead. Proof that should make me repulsed by Adriana, not drawn to her.

What's wrong with you, Jude?

Logic has no room in this discussion.

This is the most foolish thing I've done since blowing my first-year English Lit lecturer in exchange for the exam answers I sold to the highest bidders to pay for my textbooks.

Probably *more* foolish.

Definitely more.

But my hands keep folding, pressing neat lines into my clothes, and packing them into the worn leather suitcase my father had left behind when he fucked off the night before my fourth birthday.

The other suitcase turned up on the curb one evening when I was out running, a few weeks prior to my mother getting her diagnosis. I'd considered it lucky at the time.

I fold my leather shoes into a plastic bag and lay them on top of the clothes that barely fill half the case.

The rowing gear takes a moment. Not long, just a moment. Club jacket, river shoes, the shorts I wore the last morning I was on the water, whenever that was exactly. I bag it all up and add it to the bin pile. I haven't needed any of it since before she got sick. I won't need it where I'm going.

Am I actually doing this? I wonder once more as I zip up the bag, surveying the room to see if I've missed anything.

But there is nothing else.

Just a worn copy of Anne Rice's *Queen of the Damned* that I shove into my laptop bag.

For as long as I can remember, I've been waiting for my life to begin. There has always been this sense of anticipation, like something was coming. And now, I have the thread in my grasp.

My life begins here. Finally, a purpose beyond meaningless varsity assignments and unfulfilling days at the bookstore.

How quickly things change. Yesterday, I went to *Summer Place* expecting to deliver the results of my research and be done with the enigmatic gothic goddess who stirs things inside me that haven't been stirred in a long time.

But the visit didn't go according to plan. At least not according to any of *my* plans.

Did I really fall to my knees before her?

Jesus, Jude.

I can almost hear my grandmother's scolding voice, brittle from old age but no less intimidating. *'Why can't you just be normal?'* she asked time and time again while beating the skin off my back with her home-made cane, whittled down from a tree in the backyard.

But I'd be a fool to think there was anything *normal* about me and my desires.

I've always found myself drawn to strong people, to power, to authority…regardless of gender.

It started in high school, with older students, with teachers, fantasizing about them punishing me for my weird fantasies, my unconventional *needs*…I imagined them bending me over the desk and forcing me to pull my pants down and expose my bare bum for them, humiliation coloring my cheeks. They'd laugh at me, ridicule me, and then inevitably beat the living shit out of me. The thought made me as hard in real life as I was in the fantasy.

Inevitably, shame followed when I woke.

I knew it wasn't normal.

The other boys on the rowing team were sharing sneaky, torn-out pages from their fathers' forgotten *Hustler* magazines, but I found these images of women on their knees revolting, completely unappealing.

It didn't get any better with age either.

Why does everyone always assume the big guy needs to be dominant? What if I didn't want to be? What if merely thinking about having to step into that role makes the anxiety press against my chest?

I tried before... She was petite and eager, delicate. But seeing her on the floor like that deflated my dick instantly. I couldn't bring myself to tie her up. Without a word, I left, the ropes still coiled, unused.

That was during my first year of varsity, the only so-called 'girlfriend' I tried to have during my years there. Soon, the rejected sub started spreading the rumors that I was gay. I didn't mind. The sex was fine, mindless... functional.

It never scratched that itch, though. That itch that burned through my skin as I lost myself in my thesis and the wonder of power exchange through the ages. My grandmother would've died all over, probably from shame, if she knew what '*filth*' I was '*wasting*' my education on.

'*Such a little creep.*'

Shut up, shut up! I press my fingers into my temples. *Just shut up.* But even all these years later, I still can't get that mean old bitch out of my head.

Grabbing my headphones off the bed, I put David Bowie on full blast and let the music wash over me. Sometimes, that's all that helps.

I look back at the suitcase sitting on my bed, zipped up and ready.

Moving, again. Always moving. A lifetime of always moving.

With a mumbled "fuck this," I change my mind and repack everything into the plain black suitcase with the missing wheel instead. The leather one, and all its baggage, has been dragged through my life enough. I'm not taking it with me again.

When everything is neatly repacked and my father's old suitcase is empty, I shove it under the bed and leave it there for the next tenant to deal with. Not my problem anymore.

Like I was never here to begin with, I leave my keys at the entrance and pull the front door shut behind me, the automatic latch clicking in place for the last time.

The finality should make me panic but it doesn't.

Just as this morning, when I told Morrison that I am resigning with immediate effect, there's nothing stirring inside me but the restless excitement of anticipation.

Morrison was livid but what could he do?

The foolish old man never renewed our contract when I returned after my mother's death, so he had no leg to stand on; he couldn't make me stay.

For nearly sixteen months, he's exploited the fact that we had no formal agreement, changing my duties and pay at a whim. Now, it was my time to leverage the deliberate oversight.

'You're making a huge mistake,' the old shop owner had told me after I handed in my resignation, wagging a crooked index finger at me. I'd said nothing, let him go off on his tangent about how I was an ungrateful son-of-a-bitch and how he always thought I was worthless.

His words didn't reach me at all. *Water off a duck's back.* My mind was already at Lady Adriana's feet, away from this fucked-up, unfair world where people like Morrison ended up with bookstores so magical.

I had let him ramble on and on until he had no words left to say. Without so much as a goodbye, without the two wage cheques he still owed me, I put my store key on the counter and walked out.

Just like I'm walking out now, keyless, with a single suitcase in hand, my laptop bag slung across my shoulder.

I'm not running away this time; I'm running towards something. Towards my new life.

Sure, I don't know what to expect, what I'm walking into. But I know I will never stop thinking about Miss De Crevena and the impossible knowledge she holds if I don't take her up on this opportunity. I have so many questions!

People like me don't get many opportunities.

You have to take them all.

And one like this? I know I was merely in the right place at the right time.

She won't ask twice…

Besides, what am I staying for?

I have no family worth finding, and the friends dried up as soon as I dropped out, something about not associating with *nobodies.*

They were never my people anyway. I was merely *useful.* I pulled them to victory; I got them results. There's a distinction.

No, there is nothing for me in the past. Nothing but pain and regret, shame…guilt.

Too much guilt.

I force my mind to the present, to the little puddles

from yesterday's rain splashing beneath my suitcase's wheels as I head for the bus stop.

A sleek black car suddenly pulls up beside me, the window rolling down as the driver calls out to me.

Assuming he's mistaken me for someone else, I carry on walking until he uses my full name, and I come to a halt.

I cautiously approach the vehicle. "Yes?"

"Miss De Crevena has sent me. Please get in, sir." The doors unlock with a soft click.

How did she know?

For a moment, I consider walking on. But the next bus isn't for another hour, and the rain clouds overhead have been threatening to break since I left home.

Reluctant but momentarily brave, I reach out to the shiny door handle and slide into the backseat, pulling my suitcase in after me.

No turning back now.

CHAPTER 9

THE CONTRACT

(ADRIANA)

The black car appears blurry in the rain-speckled view projected on the security camera feed on my laptop, fat drops of water cascading down the lens like tears.

Despite the blur, the tall figure crouching as he climbs out, accepting the umbrella from the driver, is unmistakably the young researcher. *Jude.*

Felix has been instructed to bring him up, so I take my seat behind my desk, trying to find some composure before the *guest* arrives.

Felix has been extremely useful to me. Without a familiar, I have to make do with more *conventional* staffing structures. It works fine, for the most part. With obvious downsides, of course.

I refuse to let Felix get involved in the logistics or clean up my feeding, nor any of the shady dealings of the art world. Still, he's invaluable to me. My life may have been significantly longer than most, but it's still too short to bother with doing the ironing.

"Adriana?" Felix's voice follows the familiar knock on the door.

I call for them to enter, sending the housekeeper off with a simple nod he knows well to interpret as his dismissal.

When the door closes again, all that remains is the 24-year-old researcher dripping fresh rain onto my expensive carpet as I silently observe him from behind my desk.

"I'm so sorry," are the first words out of his mouth as he hugs his body tight, trying to contain the spread of the water. His clothes are soaked through, clinging to lean muscle and sharp hipbones, making my mouth water for reasons that have nothing to do with blood.

"You're drenching my carpet," I state the obvious as the boy looks ready to run away. The Persian rug beneath his feet is worth more than most people's annual salary, but honestly, I'm more concerned about him catching pneumonia than any material damage.

"I'm so sorry," he repeats, looking around for something to mop up the water with.

The command comes out sharper than I intended. "Strip," I order, and his gaze shoots up to mine, a single eyebrow lifting in confusion.

"W-what?" Jude stutters, staring at me. Color rises in his cheeks, a blush so vivid I can smell the blood rushing to the surface of his skin. It's intoxicating.

"Lesson one, Mr. Cole. I do not like to repeat myself." I let ice creep into my voice, using a tone that's made grown men weep before. "You're soaked to the skin and dripping everywhere. Those clothes need to come off before you catch your death."

After a brief hesitation, he nods, awkwardly kicking off his sneakers. Water squelches out of the canvas, and he winces at the sound.

Other layers follow suit until he's left only in plain blue underwear that does little to hide the huge bulge pressing against the wet fabric.

Little Jude is gifted. You'd never think a guy with seemingly so little confidence had a dick that big or muscles that toned. That's my first observation. The second is that he is clearly turned on by this little *demonstration*, his body betraying his arousal even as his face flames with embarrassment.

"All of it," I tell him, keeping my voice carefully neutral even as heat pools low in my belly.

The human blushes blood red as he drops the final layer of clothing.

Such a beautiful display of obedience.

His cock springs free, thick and hard. I only get a glimpse before Jude moves his hand down to try to hide his erection.

The scent of his arousal fills the room, mixing with rain and nervous sweat in a cocktail that makes my fangs ache to extend.

He doesn't move as I get up to circle him slowly, to inspect every inch of his warm-blooded body in the dim light of my study. Gods, such beautiful skin. And that constellation of freckles decorating his shoulders...Why do I want to kiss every single one individually?

This is just a test, I tell myself again, trying to snap out of it. To see how he responds to authority, to vulnerability, to being completely at my mercy. *It's research into his psychological profile, nothing more.*

The lie rings off-key, even in my own mind.

"There's a robe in the corner by the bookcase," I tell him as I walk away without touching him, though Christ, I want to. Settling in behind my desk again, I add, "Don't want you to get sick now."

Jude nods solemnly, draping the large black robe around his body before grabbing his wet clothes and bundling them up. He looks around for somewhere to set them down.

"On the drinks cart," I tell him. "Felix will come fetch them later to dry. For now, have a seat." I gesture to one of the two chairs in front of my desk.

Jude does as he's told, pulling the robe tighter around him, as if it could erase the nakedness I had witnessed moments prior.

When I pull the thick stack of papers from my top desk drawer, bound with a paperclip, and put it in front of him on the table, confusion settles over his features once more.

"What's this?" Jude asks.

"Your employment contract."

He eyes the 19-page document without touching it. "It seems awfully long."

"Clear boundaries are important to me. And if you are to take on my employ, we both need to be on the same page in that regard." I learned this lesson the hard way. Assumptions are dangerous, especially when dealing with mortals who don't understand the complexities of the supernatural world.

He picks it up, flips through the pages, skimming the headings. I watch his expression change as he reads: confidentiality clauses, non-disclosure agreements, hazard pay provisions, next-of-kin notifications—legal language that tries to sanitize the reality of what he's agreeing to.

"The long and the short of it is that you belong to me

now, until you complete your mission, until you find the missing book." The words come out possessively.

Jude looks up at me, his bottom lip wedged between his teeth, deep in thought. The gesture draws my attention to his mouth, to those soft lips, straight teeth, to that neck that would look beautiful with my mark on it. *Don't, Adriana, just don't.*

"If I sign this, do I become your slave?"

I can't help but smile at the deep frown indenting his beautiful forehead. "No, *caro*. You are not my slave. You are a salaried employee. You are free to go at any time. You owe me nothing but your time."

"And my blood?" he asks softly.

Oh, sweet boy.

He's thought about this, imagined me feeding from him.

The idea clearly terrifies and arouses him in equal measure.

Some of my powers may come and go, but there is nothing wrong with my scent right now. The desire clings to him, saturating the air between us.

"No, Jude. Our arrangement does not force you to make yourself available to me in any capacity other than professional." Another lie, or at least a half-truth.

He looks back at the document and then to me again. "What stops you from just killing me?"

The directness of the question gives me pause. Most humans dance around the topic of their own mortality, especially when faced with a predator. But Jude meets my eyes steadily, waiting for an honest answer.

"If I wanted you dead, *boy*, you would've never left my house last night. You have my word, I mean you no harm," I say in what I hope is a reassuring tone, despite the fact that I do so desperately want to sink my fangs into that warm skin of his, to drink my fill, to find out what his memories taste like, his fears…

I look away, forcing the need, the hunger, from my eyes. When vampires lose control, humans die. It's that simple.

Control is paramount.

Jude swallows loudly, then looks at me with shaky bravery and newfound determination. "Where's the pen?"

"No, *caro*, this one is signed in blood."

Forgoing the stack of pens on my desk, I reach over to take his warm hand in mine. Putting his forefinger in my mouth, I gently suck on it. I prick it with my fang, just enough to draw a tiny, sweet drop of blood that I savor like it's a line of expensive cocaine.

The taste explodes across my palate: rich, complex, with layers that unfold one after another.

There's the expected copper tang, but there's also more. Youth and vitality sing through every cell, bright and clean. But it's the darkness threaded through that sweetness that makes me want more: his hidden depths, suppressed desires, a hunger that matches my own.

Most humans taste one-dimensional, their blood reflecting simple wants and shallow fears. But Jude's blood is different, *more.*

The taste lingers on my tongue, each molecule suggesting that the human is not as naive as he appears.

Quickly, I pull his finger away from my lips before all control disintegrates, before I drain him dry right here in my office. I press his digit to the page, leaving a single bloody fingerprint above his name. Next to it, I leave my own crimson signature.

"Welcome to the team, Jude," I tell him as I pick up the documents, stacking them neatly.

But even as I say the words, I can't shake the feeling that I've made a terrible mistake.

Not in hiring him; I need his skills too desperately for second thoughts.

No, my mistake was thinking I could keep this professional. His taste, his response to my authority, the look he gives me...it's all too reminiscent of why I swore never to mix business with pleasure again, of why I have been without a familiar for nine years.

And yet here I am, already planning how long I need to wait before I can taste him again.

Oh, fanculo.

CHAPTER 10

ONBOARDING

(JUDE)

My heart is beating in my throat as I press my bloody finger to the page, sealing my fate with Adriana's.

Fuck me. I've just signed a deal with a vampire.

The fact that they are real is one thing. But choosing to live under the same roof as such a dangerous creature? That's plain foolishness. It's decisions like that which get protagonists killed in the Gothic novels I've studied, usually by chapter three.

Then why is excitement the dominant emotion surging through my veins as Adriana dismisses me with a "Felix will show you to your room"?

My cock is uncomfortably perked up as the unconventional housekeeper leads me down the hall with my wet clothes bundled in his arms.

Stripping in front of her was as exhilarating as it was humiliating. My whole body trembled as I stood there while she inspected me like a slab of fresh meat. I suppose that's exactly what I am to her.

After a lifetime of being invisible except for the roles I was useful in, being seen so directly threw me completely off balance. I was one of eight, but another oar in the water, a number on a results board. But she didn't see a number. She looked at me like I was the only one in the room.

The effect Adriana has on me goes beyond my comprehension.

I want to fall on my knees before her every time a single syllable leaves those perfect lips.

Nobody has ever had that effect on me.

I would do whatever it takes to please her. Whatever she needs from me. I crave her praise in the same way my lungs need air to survive.

Stop being weird, Jude.

"After you," Felix speaks for the first time as he holds open the door for me, forcing me to momentarily push my mysterious new employer from my mind.

We're down the hall from Adriana's office, one of many doors in this sprawling apartment that covers two entire floors of the building. The office and the bedrooms are upstairs, with the kitchen and various living areas downstairs. The word *apartment* is deceptive because the place has more rooms than most houses I've ever been in.

I push past the housekeeper with the rigid posture, swallowing down a gasp as I take in my new room. It's at least four times the size of the shoebox I lived in at the commune, complete with an *en-suite* bathroom. No more trudging down the cold hall with my bare feet at night to wait outside the shared bathroom door while my housemate hogged the space.

"Everything okay?" Felix asks after my silence stretches on too long, simply gawking at the high ceilings and luxurious furnishings. There is a double bed *and a* walk-in closet. It even has space for a couch by the large windows with the most magnificent view of the city.

"It's perfect, thank you so much," I manage without taking my eyes off the sprawling view.

"Lady Adriana expects you at dinner in half an hour," Felix informs me with a polite nod before taking his leave and gently closing the door behind him, my wet clothes still in his hand.

Exhaling deeply, I expel the air I've been holding hostage in my chest, falling onto the bed.

Fucking hell, it's so comfortable. Like a fancy hotel. Not that I know what the beds in fancy hotels feel like. My life has been very much *un*fancy. Once or twice, when my gran was sick or away, I went to work with my mom, to the hotel where she cleaned. But I had to hide to make sure her boss never noticed the four-year-old trailing behind her. I was never allowed to sit on the beds, though, definitely not. *'Don't touch anything, Jude. We're not guests here.'*

This is different. This room is mine now. At least temporarily.

I still can't believe I'm doing this.

So far, so good. The contract seemed legit. I nearly choked on my own tongue when I saw the wage amount entered on the allotted line.

It's more than anyone has ever paid me for anything. Definitely way more than the meager stipend I used to get as a PhD student and way more than Morrison's insulting wage.

If I can do a good job and find her book, I might be able

to save enough money to finish my degree, or even my novel.

For as long as I can remember, I've dreamt of having the time and money to write the novel I've been planning for years. Bits of it exist, scribbled on scraps of paper at the bookstore, in the margins of lecture notes, on the back of training schedules during practices. Wherever I could steal a few minutes, I snuck a few words.

But it was never enough. Not when bills need to be paid. Time doesn't wait for you to finish your novel. Survival takes precedence over art, always has, in my experience.

Things are changing, though, so quickly.

Better get ready for dinner.

In the closet, I find an assortment of clothes in my size, which immediately raises the question of how she knew that. Clothes I would never wear, or rather, have never had cause to consider wearing, couldn't afford to consider. The hangers hold crisp shirts with Brioni labels I have to look up on my phone, real leather shoes and belts still wrapped in tissue, trousers with properly tailored hems rather than the folded-and-safety-pinned variety I've been managing with for years. It's the wardrobe of a grown-up, one with money I can't even conceptualize.

I shrug off the robe and step into the bathroom that, in itself, is bigger than my previous lodgings at the commune. Black tile from top to bottom contrasts with the beautiful, exotic houseplants that rain down from hanging pots and counters, a collage of mismatched ornate mirrors adorning the walls.

The walk-in shower is equally massive and the water pressure far superior to anything I've experienced in recent years. As soon as the scorching temperature hits my shoulders, I let out another heavy sigh, relaxing under the water.

My hand finds its way to my aching cock soon enough, finally offering some relief as I stroke the hard flesh to full-mast, the only image behind my closed eyes that of Lady Adriana. The memory of her hand brushing against my skin, the sound of her voice when she called me *'boy,'* it all comes back in vivid detail.

A groan slips past my lips as the mere memory of those green eyes raking up and down my naked body makes my dick shudder.

Fuck!

I come all over my hand within minutes, the sticky liquid mixing with the hot water and disappearing down the drain.

Again? Such a little pervert you are.

Afterward, I scrub my body from tip to toe until my skin is red, properly clean like my grandmother used to demand.

But there is no time for a trip down memory lane. I'm already late by the time I've dried, dressed, and made my way downstairs to the large dining room table that seats twelve but is set for only two tonight.

Adriana is already waiting, smiling approvingly as she inspects the black pants-and-green-shirt combo I chose from my new wardrobe. It makes me look older somehow, more substantial, like I am the kind of person who might actually deserve to sit at this table.

"Apologies, Milady," I tell her as I take my seat. The formal address comes naturally in this setting, surrounded by obvious wealth.

She lets the honorific slide.

"I trust the shower was satisfactory?" she asks, and I avert my eyes to try and hide the resulting blush.

There is no way she could know what I did in the shower, but I still feel exposed.

Maybe she can smell it on me? Do real vampires also have enhanced smell like in books? I silently add the question to the list I've been compiling in my head.

"Perfect," I manage to answer, forcing my eyes back up to hers.

"Well, *bon appétit.*" She snaps her fingers, and Felix appears instantly, carrying trays and trays of delicious roasts and sides.

I can't possibly eat this much, and Adriana clearly has no interest in consuming anything other than what's in her glass, but it doesn't mean that I don't try. It's been a long time since I had a satisfying hot meal, even longer since one with sufficient nutrition.

I eat until I can't fit another crumb, and then Felix appears with dessert, and I find more space. All while Adriana watches me, not speaking, not eating, just watching me quietly, sipping on her wine.

Only when I push my plate away does she speak, calling Felix over.

"That's all for today. Thanks for staying later," she tells him, and with a nod, he's off, not to be seen again until tomorrow morning.

But for now, we're alone as Adriana leads me back upstairs to her office.

My movements are slow, lazy, my body stuffed with way too many delectable treats.

She doesn't tell me to sit, so I don't, remaining standing near the bookcase as she settles behind the desk again.

"We will start tomorrow night," she says as I inspect

the various framed artworks and personal mementos that line the walls. "But I thought it would be good to give you some more background about the research mission…"

I'm only half listening. "Is that a real Picasso?" I ask, stopping in front of a small canvas that has all the hallmarks of his Blue Period work.

"Oh yes." She smiles slyly. "Turn it over."

My mouth falls open as I read the scribbled note on the back:

To Adriana, my muse. Love, Pablo

"No way!" The academic in me is practically vibrating with excitement. "You knew him personally?"

"Perhaps one day I'll show you my full collection."

"This must be worth millions." I'm calculating museum values, figures that exist only in theoretical discussions among art historians.

She smiles. "Actually, it's priceless."

I continue following the wall of artworks, each piece adding layers to my understanding of who Adriana is, or rather, who she's been across the centuries.

I stop at the final frame, a small black square no bigger than a postcard. It's different from the others, less polished, more personal. A watercolor in red, deep red, the color of blood. Perhaps it actually is blood, given what I now know about my new employer.

I can't figure out what the picture is supposed to represent. The abstract shapes might be figures, might be landscapes, might be anything really. But it affects me deeply, for some reason, like I want to cry. There's something raw about it, unguarded.

In the corner, in black, it's signed by the artist. *Cyrus.* Nothing else. Just a first name.

I turn back to her, expecting to make casual conversation about another famous artist I should recognize from my undergrad art history courses. "Who is Cyrus?" I ask.

Adriana visibly stiffens at the sound of the name, her hands balling into tight fists. The temperature in the room seems to drop several degrees.

Oh fuck, I shouldn't have asked.

FORBIDDEN TASTE

(ADRIANA)

The silence stretches between us like a taut wire, ready to snap, as Jude's question hangs in the air, innocent yet devastating: *'Who is Cyrus?'*

My control is slipping, the composure I've maintained all evening cracking at the edges.

"That's enough for tonight," I say when I can no longer bear the weight of the question, my voice steadier than my emotions. "You'll begin your work tomorrow."

Jude's face falls slightly, confusion flickering across his features. He's dissecting my reaction, trying to understand what nerve he's struck. *Too perceptive, this one.*

But there are no answers to be found there. My features are an impenetrable stone wall.

"Of course," he says quietly as he retreats, defeated. "Good night, Lady Adriana."

Lady Adriana. The formality stings. But it's safer this way. Distance, control, these are good things.

I wait until his footsteps fade down the hallway before allowing myself to breathe again, figuratively speaking.

The small painting stares at me accusingly from its frame. That splash of crimson that might be blood, might be wine, might be the color of passion itself.

Fucking Cyrus.

Even thinking his name is like pressing on a bruise that never quite heals.

Not a single day goes by that I don't curse our foolish choices one moon-wine-filled night in the Fae's Between Court. Vampires are not supposed to exchange blood.

But why would we care about what we were 'supposed' to do?

We were untouchable together.

Until we weren't.

Why did I hang it there?

I'll never admit that maybe it's because I still miss him sometimes. Still wonder where he is. When he'll come back. *If* he will—

No, not this time.

I swallow down the nostalgia bubbling up.

The bare space on the wall looks strange when I remove the small frame.

I should've done this ages ago, I think, as I press my finger to the spine of the first edition of James Joyce on the shelf, unlocking my secret library.

The wall of books clicks open, and I push through it like it's a revolving door, Cyrus's painting in hand.

Lights flicker on as soon as motion is detected, illuminating the room and its treasures. Exactly the same size as my office, my secret temperature-controlled library holds priceless artifacts collected over five centuries: books that predate the printing press, paintings that museums would kill for, letters written by hands long since turned to dust. And in the back corner, locked behind glass stronger than steel, sits the collection I can never bring myself to destroy.

Time to put you back where you belong, I think, as I unlock the case with every intention of just dropping the painting inside and moving on.

But I don't.

I set down the painting—a present from Cyrus on our 350th anniversary—and open the glass case.

It's been so long since I even thought about these things, not since I moved in here, and I can't stop the memories that come pouring in as soon as my fingers stroke the edges of the keepsakes I've allowed myself as indulgences.

As tempting as it is to take out the mementos, to lose myself in the memories of what we were for over 400 years of passion and destruction, I can't bring myself to reach for any of the items.

Not the Venetian carnival mask from 1621, the year we met.

Nor the crystalline flower he gave me that night in the Between Court when we forever sealed our fates together.

No, this chapter is done.

Putting the small painting from my office inside, I close the case with shaky hands, the ghost of suppressed memories settling around me.

No good could come from nostalgia.

Cyrus is the past.

He made his choices.

I have work to do.

Pull yourself together, Adriana.

BETWEEN THE PAST thoughts of Cyrus and the future fantasies of Jude, my mind is too tumultuous right now to get any work done.

I sit behind my desk for a few minutes before giving up, closing the laptop.

Perhaps a long, relaxing bath will help me clear my mind.

It certainly wouldn't hurt.

It might even distract me from the hunger gnawing at my gut, the real reason I've been so snappy with Jude today.

I had intended to go out to hunt after sending the human to bed, but it all seems like too much effort right now. *Tomorrow.*

Heading to my bedroom's *en-suite* bathroom, I open the taps of the large footed bath that looks straight out of the Victorian era (because it is).

Many of the pieces in my house are originals, either acquired through nefarious means or legitimate deals. I make no distinction between the sources. I've always been a collector.

Dropping my clothes to the floor in the steamy space, I test the water with my toe. It's too hot. *Perfect.*

But I don't get in, not right away.

His heartbeat thunders outside my bedroom as if it were a bullet train, loud and close.

"What is it, Jude?" I call to the closed door, sighing as I watch it slowly push open to reveal the sheepish-looking house guest.

"I'm sorry, Milady, I—" He looks up, right at my naked body, and instantly, his entire face burns bright red, blush creeping down his neck.

Jude quickly casts his eyes down again. "F-fuck. I'm

sorry. Sorry—fuck." He's mumbling to himself, stuttering, as he looks at his feet, awkwardly shuffling from one leg to the other.

I can't help but smirk at his innocent reaction.

But I don't cover up.

My body and I have lived half a millennium together; I have made peace with every imperfection a long time ago. You'd struggle to find a modest bone in my body.

Jude's reaction is flattering, though.

But it's more than that. Those submissive reflexes, those downcast eyes, are wreaking havoc on my core, twisting it in a need I hadn't felt in too long.

Maybe I'm just hungry.

"Look at me, Jude," I command, squaring my shoulders to stand up straighter.

"S-sorry, so sorry," he repeats as the blushing man looks up and tries to hold my gaze but fails.

"Stop apologizing."

"Sor—fuck." Jude looks down again, flustered.

An amused smirk finds its way to my lips as I close the remaining distance between us. "What are you doing here?" My voice is soft, breathy against his neck as I press my naked body against him.

"I-I...don't know."

His erection is unmistakable, thick and ready, pulsing with life. Without thinking about it, I reach for him, teasingly stroking his cock over the thin fabric of the sweatpants separating our skin.

A string of curses leaves his lips as his eyes close, body rigid, failing as it tries to grasp at some control. *Foolish human.*

His arousal is a scent so strong, it damn near drives me feral with need, clouding my decisions.

It's a dangerous game having him here, especially when I'm this hungry. But I don't send him away; I don't want to.

"Someone is hard," I remark, taunting him further as I slowly pull his pants down and tug his erection free.

Jude nods slowly, looking down at his cock like it betrayed him.

I take it in both hands, testing the skin between my fingers, petting it.

"Do you want me to stop?" I ask as I scrape a single long nail along the underside of his dick, barely touching him.

The human's breathing is heavy, slow, as he shakes his head.

"Words, boy."

"No, Ma'am. Sorry, fuck. No—please. Don't stop." He's cute when he gets all flustered and embarrassed.

"What's your safe word?"

"S-safe word?" Jude stutters, wide-eyed.

"You know what a safe word is, don't you? I know what your thesis topic was." *Power Dynamics in Gothic Romance: From Dracula to Modern Dark Romance.* Public knowledge uncovered during my earlier background check.

More blushing. "Crimson," he finally admits.

I smile as I snake my other hand up to his neck, tilting it slightly to expose the skin. "Good choice."

The slight praise sends visible shivers darting over his skin in little bumps.

But that could also be a result of my fingers wrapped around his thick cock.

I didn't mean to grab him. But his timing made it difficult to resist.

With a sigh, I push him away, breaking all contact to lean against the basin.

A look of anguish crosses Jude's face as he looks up at me with those doe eyes, his exceptionally hard dick still poking out of his loose-fitting pants.

"You should go," I tell him as he moves closer to me again.

"Don't want to," the human replies, momentarily brave in his desperation.

With a single finger, I trace a lazy pattern over his collarbone. "I don't know if I'll be able to stop myself. You look...*delicious*." My fangs grow visible at the mere thought of sinking my teeth into his skin.

Good gods. The fact that he's literally dripping with lust doesn't make it any easier. I want him, in—more ways than one.

"Take what you need, Milady." Jude's eyes are on mine as he tilts his head slightly to the left, exposing the beautifully milky skin of his neck.

It takes every bit of control I have not to pin him to the wall and have my way, drink my fill. But I need him for more than a meal.

"Leave, Jude," I bite out through gritted teeth, as my resistance starts to crumble, my fists clenching by my side.

The final nail in my coffin is when he utters a defiant "no" right before crashing his lips to mine.

I lose it as soon as he kisses me, pulling him closer, into me, devouring his lips until he's panting, breathless, moaning against my cheek. He kisses like his life depends on it, like he's too hungry, insatiable, and my gods, if I don't want to devour every taste from those perfect lips.

When we finally part, my fingers snake through his wavy crop, wrapping around his hair and tugging—hard.

Jude gasps, bites his bottom lip, and there is nothing I can do to stop myself as I bring my lips to his neck.

"Do it," he consents, dropping his hands to play over my naked back, holding me against him.

The animal in me takes over, the hunger, and I sink my fangs into his skin without a second invitation.

Soft, warm, yielding; he offers no resistance.

The moment I pierce his skin, the world explodes into sensation.

His blood carries more than sustenance—it carries *him*.

Every memory, every emotion, every carefully buried dream floods through me like a dam breaking.

5AM starts on the water.

His mother's death.

The old book shop.

Shitty commune.

Our meeting…

The loneliness slams into me, years of it, dragging him down. It's so familiar, so crushing. And threading through every memory is desire, pure, overwhelming want.

Jude's trust is absolute, terrifying in its completeness. Even now, with my fangs in his throat, his hands stroke my skin like I'm delicate. He would give me everything—his blood, his body, his life—and count himself blessed for the privilege. It's all there in his essence.

I had planned on taking a single sip, but I need more.

He tastes incredible!

Every person's blood has its own flavor profile and there is something about Jude's blood that is *addictive!*

My hand finds his needy flesh again, stroking his cock as I drink my fill.

The move elicits a desperate groan from Jude as he squirms in my hand.

I keep caressing his cock as I feed, enjoying the tendrils of desire seeping into his blood. The more flustered he gets, the better he tastes.

I need more!

Drunk on the power of his blood, I keep pumping his dick until the unmistakable shudders of an orgasm start coursing through his body. He's close.

"Please," the human begs, and I know I would give him whatever he asks.

I don't answer, can't, my mouth filled with him, his blood pulsing through my body.

My gods, the moment he topples over the edge, coming all over my hand, the most incredible explosion of desire surges through me. It's not his orgasm but *ours*, and it tastes out-of-this-world. Better than ice cream used to taste even.

It takes everything in my power to stop, to not drain him completely.

But if I don't, there will be no more of this…

I pull back carefully, sealing the small wounds with my tongue, and meet Jude's eyes. They're bright and glassy, entranced.

"Thank you," he whispers, still shaking against me, and I know he is not only talking about the release.

Oh gods, he's perfect.

My dead heart, if it could still beat, would be racing right now.

CHAPTER 12
TRUST

(JUDE)

I don't remember making the decision to leave my room. One moment I'm counting ceiling beams, wondering who Cyrus is, and the next I'm standing outside her door, my hand raised to knock.

The rational part of my brain archives this in the folder labeled 'concerning behavior.' Normal people don't sleep-walk toward dangerous situations. They don't seek out vampires who've just warned them to mind their own business.

But I've never been particularly *normal*, and tonight the academic part of my mind, the part that usually over-thinks everything, has gone strangely quiet.

I tell myself I'm going there to apologize. For overstep-ping, for asking questions I have no right to ask.

The polite thing would be to wait until tomorrow. To approach her formally with a prepared speech about professional boundaries.

But Adriana gives me no chance to change my mind,

her supernatural hearing exposing me before I can even muster up the courage to knock.

Caught, I push the door open slowly.

And then I see her.

Naked, magnificent, and completely unashamed of the body that looks carved from marble and magic.

She's built like a Renaissance sculpture come to life, all elegant lines and perfect proportions that make me understand why artists throughout history have tried to capture the human form. If I had any talent, I'd beg her on my knees to remain like this so I could attempt to paint her. But art has never been my specialty; I'm a words man, and even those are failing me now.

I should look away, should stammer an apology and flee like the embarrassed failure I am. But I don't. No, I remain frozen in the doorway.

When she commands me to look at her, my body obeys before my mind can protest. And when she presses against me, naked and impossibly real, it's like stepping into sunlight after years in shadow. Suddenly, every nerve ending is awake, aware, alive.

The desire isn't just physical, though fuck knows my body responds to hers with enthusiasm that should probably embarrass me. It goes beyond that, like some part of me that's been dormant suddenly opening its eyes.

When Adriana touches me, when her fingers wrap around me with possession, I know unequivocally that I am where I want to be.

And when she asks for my safe word, when she acknowledges that I understand exactly what's happening between us, that I want her to take control, a wave of relief floods through my chest. She knows. She recognizes what

I need and she isn't running away in horror or treating me like I'm broken, like I'm perverted.

I should be terrified when her fangs extend, when the predator beneath the human exterior reveals itself; should remember that I'm entirely at her mercy, far beyond just the physical.

Instead, I feel...honored, *special*.

She's showing me her true nature. And she's trusting me not to reject her, not to treat her like the monster that centuries of literature have painted her species to be.

"Take what you need," I whisper, and mean it with every fiber of my being. Not because I'm being coerced or compelled, but because there is nothing I want more than to give myself to her.

I've spent my entire academic career studying power dynamics, analyzing the psychology of submission and dominance in Gothic literature. I can recite theories about the erotics of the bite, about vampire narratives as metaphors for sexual and social transgression. But all that research means nothing compared to the reality of tilting my head and offering my throat to someone who could end my life in a flash.

It isn't death I'm offering her. It's trust. Complete, absolute trust. Which is ridiculous, considering she's a complete stranger, and I don't even trust people I've known my whole life. But the lizard brain is in charge now. And it wants this, *needs* this, with the same urgency as my lungs need oxygen.

When I kiss her—*oh god, when did I become brave enough to kiss a vampire?*—it's because I can't stand the distance anymore. Can't stand watching her try to push me away when everything in me is screaming that this is right, this is where I belong, this is what I've been unconsciously searching for my entire life.

Adriana's lips are soft and cool against mine, but they warm under my touch. For a moment, she's still, surprised, and then she's kissing me back with an intensity that makes my knees weak.

When her fangs sink into my skin, the pain lasts maybe a second before it alchemizes into something else entirely. Pleasure, yes, but more complex than that, than anything I've ever experienced. It's as if she's opened a direct line between us, a connection that bypasses language and logic, going deeper.

She's in my mind. I feel her, gentle but unmistakable, touching memories I've tried to forget and thoughts I've never spoken aloud.

The years of being overlooked, dismissed, treated like furniture by people who never bothered to learn my name. Coaches who reduced me to numbers on a white-board. Teammates who needed me in the boat and nowhere else. The cold of pre-dawn water and the strange loneliness of moving in perfect synchrony with seven other people while remaining completely invisible to all of them.

She sees it all; she sees everything.

Almost everything.

The feeding itself defies description. Not just the phys-ical sensation—though that's incredible, every pleasure center in my brain lighting up simultaneously—but the emotional component too.

Her hunger floods through me, ancient and consum-ing. It's more than hunger, though.

She's as exposed as I am during the exchange. Through the temporary bond, her memories flicker past like pages in a book: too much, too fast to pick up anything but pieces.

He's there too. Cyrus. I don't know how I know it's him but I do. Different hair, different style of clothes each time, but same age, same mischievous smile. The emotions she carries for him are complex and overwhelming.

As she drinks from me, jerking me off like she owns me, I sink into the euphoria, letting it pull me under, floating away into blissful oblivion as Adriana takes what she needs from me.

When she finally pulls back, sealing the puncture wounds with her tongue, my cum sticky on her hand, I feel different. Like some fundamental part of myself has clicked into place, a puzzle piece that's always been missing.

"Thank you," I whisper, eyes still closed against reality, trying to find my way back.

Thank you, because what else can I say?

When I finally open my eyes, something has changed in her expression. The confident predator who commanded me to look at her is gone, replaced by someone who seems almost...shaken. Adriana's hands tremble slightly as she touches the bite marks, checking that they're properly sealed.

"Is this normal?" I ask but she doesn't answer.

"You should sit," she says instead, her voice gentler than I've ever heard it. "The blood loss...you might be dizzy."

I'm not dizzy. If anything, I feel centered, like I've finally found my place in the universe. But I can see the concern flickering across her face, her hands hovering close then pulling back like she's not sure she's allowed to touch me anymore.

"I'm fine," I assure her, but she's already filling a glass of water from the sink.

"Drink this. And you'll need to eat something soon." She thrusts the glass at me, then immediately steps back, wrapping her arms around herself like armor. "This was...you were convenient. Don't read more into it than—"

Adriana stops mid-sentence when I smile at her.

"What?" she demands, but there's no real bite to it.

"You're worried about me."

"I'm being practical. I need you functional for the research."

But her eyes are still studying my face, looking for signs of weakness or regret that she won't find. And despite her words about practicality, she moves closer again, her fingers ghosting over my neck where her teeth had punctured the skin earlier. Her touch is warmer now, almost human.

"Are you certain you're alright?" The look in her eyes is worth every risk I've taken to get here. Soft, conflicted, almost stunned. Like she's seeing me, really seeing me, for the first time, and isn't sure what to do with what she's found.

As I stand here in her bathroom, watching her process what happened between us, trying to rebuild her walls, I have no second thoughts about what I've gotten myself into.

I didn't expect things to go this way, but I wouldn't have it any other way.

I belong here, with her. Whatever that means, whatever it costs.

I've spent years wondering why nothing felt right,

chasing this contented feeling without knowing what it was. Pure, unfiltered submission.

Once, I thought I'd found it in my final year Modern Fiction professor, years after the fling with the English Lit lecturer. Dominant in and out of the classroom, she took me under her wing and into her bed.

But her dominance was forced, coerced. *'Do as I say and stop asking questions,'* she told me as she tied me up and walked out. I didn't mind being tied. I minded that she disregarded my needs, my safe word, my need for aftercare.

Four sessions later, I broke it off. In response, she threw scalding coffee at my naked body and called me things you wouldn't shout at your worst enemy.

After that, she made sure I never passed another one of her classes. I had to drop the course. Nearly lost my scholarship...

That day, I swore off dominants for good.

Never again, I said.

And now here I am, in a vampire's bathroom, offering my throat and my devotion like it's the most natural thing in the world.

Because with Adriana, it is.

She sees what I need without me having to explain it; takes control with confidence that doesn't require breaking me down first.

This, this is what I've been searching for.

And I'm not letting it go.

Even if it means parting with some blood every now and then.

CHAPTER 13
UNRAVELING

(ADRIANA)

The power coursing through me is intoxicating! Every sense is heightened beyond what I thought possible.

Jude's heartbeat hammers in the space, the lingering scent of his arousal mixed with the copper tang of blood overloading my circuits as the electricity in the air between us grows palpable, tactile.

My supernatural abilities hum just beneath my skin, begging to be used. Right now, I could probably shadow-step across the city like it was a highway, could bend steel poles with my bare hands, command armies with nothing but my voice.

But underneath the rush of power is something far more perilous: the desperate, clawing need for *more*.

Not because I'm hungry. His blood has satisfied me more completely than any meal in a decade.

No, this is different. This is *addiction*. The craving for that connection.

I force myself to step back from the human, wrapping my arms around my torso to keep from reaching out.

The clinical part of my mind, the strategist who has survived for five centuries, scrutinizes his condition: pulse strong, color good, no signs of weakness or distress. He's fine. Better than fine.

But the other part of me, the part that just tasted twenty-four years of Jude's loneliness and hope and desperate desire to belong, wants to gather him up in my arms and never let him go, want to rock him to sleep while reassuring him that everything will be okay.

Inappropriate, Adriana.

"You should sit," I manage, though my voice comes out foreign, soft. "The blood loss…you might be dizzy."

He's not dizzy. I can see it in the alertness of his eyes, the steady way he holds himself. If anything, he looks more alive than he did before I fed. There's a glow to his skin, a contentment in his expression that makes my chest tight with something I refuse to name.

Mine, whispers the predator in me. *He's mine now.*

Don't. I know no good can come from this.

I shove a glass of water at him, using the mundane action to create distance. The words tumble out before I can stop them: "This was just…you were convenient. Don't read more into it than—"

The sentence dies when he smiles at me.

"What?" I demand, but there's no real authority behind it.

"You're worried about me."

I'm terrified, I think but don't say. Terrified of how much I want to sink my fangs into his throat again. Terrified of how right this seems when I should know better.

"I'm being practical," I lie.

But even as I say it, I'm moving closer again, my fingers ghosting over the marks on his neck. They're already fading; vampire saliva heals quickly, but I can still taste him on my tongue, the echo of his trust and devotion still fresh. He was so alive in my grip, so warm... pliant.

"Are you certain you're alright?" The question comes out vulnerable, needy, nothing like the commanding tone I pride myself on.

The human studies my face with those intelligent gray eyes, seeing too much. "I'm perfect," he says quietly. "Better than I've ever been."

The sincerity in his voice dissolves my fear. He means it. He's not afraid, not traumatized, not planning his escape. He's *grateful*.

Dangerous territory, Adriana.

I need distance so I can process what just happened without his pulse calling to me like a siren song.

"I should..." I gesture vaguely toward the tub, though I'm not sure I trust myself to be alone with him in such an intimate setting.

"Let me help," Jude replies, and I freeze, unprepared for the response.

"Help?"

Color rises in his cheeks, but his voice is steady. "Your hair. I could...if you'd like. My mother always said taking care of someone was a privilege."

The request is so unexpected, so sweetly domestic, that I almost laugh. Here stands a young man who just let a vampire feed from his throat, offering to wash my hair like we're lovers instead of predator and prey.

Except we're not predator and prey anymore, are we?

The feeding changed something between us.

He gave me his emotions, his memories, his desires, his conviction that he wants this.

And in return, he experienced everything I've hidden from the world.

Usually, I can shut that door when I feed, close off the flow from my side, but this time, the door was left wide open for him to see.

Perhaps it is another effect of the Grimoire's distance. Perhaps it's something about Jude…

But the exchange has left me strangely vulnerable too, exposed.

"You want to wash my hair?" I confirm.

Jude nods.

"You don't have to," I say, but I'm already moving toward the bath.

"I want to."

Three simple words that shouldn't affect me this much, but they do, because I can hear the truth in them, can smell the lack of fear or obligation. He wants to serve me. Not because he has to, but because it satisfies something deep in his nature.

"Fine then." I slip into the hot water, hyper-aware of Jude's presence as he kneels beside the tub.

The power from his blood heightens every sensation: the heat against my skin, the steam in the air, how his breathing changes when I lean back to give him access to my hair.

Jude's touch is reverent, careful, as his fingers work shampoo through the strands, massaging my scalp with a gentleness that makes my eyes flutter closed.

"This is dangerous," I murmur, though I'm not sure if I mean the intimacy or the way my control keeps slipping around him.

"Why?" Jude's voice is soft as he focuses on his task. "Because I might realize you're not as scary as you pretend to be?"

I open my eyes and turn back to find him watching me with amusement. "I am *exactly* as scary as I appear."

"Maybe." He doesn't stop. "But you're also kind."

"Kind?" The word tastes foreign on my tongue.

"You could have compelled me tonight, made me forget. Could've used me and discarded me." His fingers continue their gentle ministrations. "Instead, you asked for consent. You worried about my well-being. You're letting me take care of you."

Because you make me want to be taken care of, I think but don't say.

"You're not what I expected," I admit, turning away again. It's easier when I don't have to see his eyes.

"What did you expect?"

"Fear. Regret maybe."

He's quiet for a moment as he rinses the soap from my hair with delicate movements. "I'm not afraid," he says finally, with conviction. "This feels...*right.*"

The words land hard because they echo my own thoughts too closely.

I should discourage this, should create distance before we both get too attached. But the power from his blood is singing in my veins, and his touch is so gentle, so perfect, that I can't bring myself to push him away. It does *feel right.*

When he's finished with my hair, he helps me from the tub without being asked, wrapping me in a soft towel with the same careful attention he gave to the washing task.

"You're spoiling me," I murmur as he dries my hair.

"Good." The simple response makes me look at him

sharply. There's no hesitation in his expression, no uncertainty about what he wants. "That's the point."

Mine, the predator whispers again, and this time I don't fight it.

"Jude." His name comes out rougher than intended. "You don't understand what you're getting into."

"Then explain it to me." He sets aside the towel, meeting my eyes directly. "Help me understand. But don't assume I'll run because it's complicated."

The offer hangs between us, loaded with possibility and danger in equal measure. I could tell him everything. About Cyrus, about the centuries of violence, about the enemies who would see a pet human as a weakness to exploit...I could scare him away for his own good.

Or I could trust him. Could trust that the devotion I tasted in his blood is real, that the strength I saw in his memories is enough to handle the truth.

The power from my earlier feeding makes the decision for me.

In this moment, I am invincible, protected. Nothing could touch what's mine.

And he is mine now, whether either of us planned it or not.

"Tomorrow," I decide. "I'll tell you everything tomorrow. But tonight..."

"Tonight?"

I trace the faded marks on his throat, and he shivers under my touch. "Tonight, you should rest. You'll need your strength for what's coming."

He nods but doesn't move away from my touch. "Will you be able to sleep? After...after everything?"

The question surprises me with its perceptiveness. He's

right; the power coursing through me makes rest impossible.

"Sleep is optional for my kind," I say instead of admitting that I'll probably spend the rest of the night fighting the urge to knock on his bedroom door.

"Then I'll stay awake with you. If you want."

The offer is so simple, so genuine. When was the last time someone offered to simply be present, without agenda or expectation?

"You need rest—"

"I need to be where you need me to be." His voice is quiet but certain. "Everything else is secondary."

Looking at him, I see what I missed before. This isn't a frightened boy playing at submission but a man who knows exactly what he wants.

And he wants it all.

CHAPTER 14

EVERY LAST DROP

(JUDE)

It's way past 2 AM according to my watch. I should be exhausted, yet I've never felt more rested.

My veins are on fire but in a good way, like champagne bubbles tickling my bloodstream.

I thought vampires were supposed to drain you, leave you weak and depleted. That's what modern vampire lore usually says, at least.

Whatever happened when Adriana drank from me had the opposite effect.

I know I've lost blood; the mild lightheadedness persists. But there's a new energy rushing through me; it's electric.

"Why do I feel so good?" I ask as Adriana dries her hair with a fresh towel, still standing bare in front of me.

"Energy flows both ways, *caro*," she answers matter-of-factly, turning to face me. "Especially when there's a genuine connection. Plus, my fangs inject euphoric compounds directly into your bloodstream during the exchange. Evolution's way of making prey compliant."

The clinical explanation should disturb me—*prey*, she called me—but it doesn't. If anything, it fascinates me.

She doesn't ask me to follow her as she leaves the towel on the bath's edge and moves to the adjoining bedroom, but I do.

The space looks like something from a Gothic period film. Massive furniture, expensive fabrics, candles everywhere, art that probably has its own insurance policies. But I have eyes only for the subject inside the space.

"How long does it last?" I ask as I reach for the ivory-backed hairbrush she's picked up from the vanity.

"Depends on the person. Usually around four to six hours. Give or take." For a moment, Adriana tightens her grip on the brush, staring at me with something that might be defiance or uncertainty. Then she releases it, handing it over.

I don't reply immediately, just carefully, unhurriedly, gather her hair in my hands, and begin working through the tangles, just like my mother taught me.

Her locks are silky-soft and still damp, and I'm careful not to pull or tug, treating each strand like spun glass even though I'm sure she wouldn't even notice any discomfort I might accidentally cause.

Christ, I'm aroused again just from this simple contact, the intimacy of the task, the trust implicit in her allowing me to tend to her. It's all I can do to resist the urge to press my lips to her shoulder, to trace the elegant line of her neck with my tongue.

Adriana catches my eye in the mirror, that knowing smile playing at her lips. "You may stare, it's okay."

My face goes blood red—again. Caught in the act of admiring her like some lovesick teenager.

"I thought vampires don't have reflections?" I ask to shift the attention away from me.

"There's as much myth as truth in the stories humans tell about us. Each vampire is different. The older we get, the more powerful we become. Well, in theory." She watches me intently as I let my fingers brush over her neck.

"So, you just suddenly developed a reflection at some point?"

Adriana shakes her head, amusement coloring her features. "No, that one belongs firmly in the myth category. The only reason vampires supposedly lacked reflections was because the mirrors in the old days were backed with silver. Modern mirrors use metals that have no effect on us."

I process this information and find myself leaning forward, attention sharpening to a point. Each new piece of truth rewrites what I thought I knew. *What else have I been wrong about?*

The questions multiply faster than I can articulate them, each answer spawning three more inquiries. My fingers twitch with the phantom urge to reach for pen and paper to document it all. "What other myths are actually false?"

"Most of them." She leans into my touch as I work the brush through a particularly stubborn tangle. "Garlic does nothing except make feeding unpleasant; nobody wants to bite someone who reeks. Running water? Complete nonsense. I've never turned into a bat either. Oh, and religious symbols only work if wielded by someone with genuine faith, and even then, they're more irritating than dangerous. Though, holy water does burn."

"Do you sleep in a coffin?"

Adriana laughs. "Have you seen a coffin, *boy*? No, it's a myth. Blackout curtains and treated windows work just as well. Next?"

"What about werewolves?" The question pops out before I can stop it, driven by pure academic curiosity. "Are they real too?"

Her expression darkens. "Were. Past tense. The hunters wiped them out systematically over the past century. Easier targets than vampires. They couldn't hide their nature during full moons, couldn't blend into human society the same way we can."

The casual way she discusses genocide makes my stomach clench, but I push past the discomfort. "But other creatures exist?"

"Fae are real, though they rarely bother with this plane. When they do, they pass as human easily enough; you'd never know. Witches are real too, though not quite the way stories describe them. Most practice with herbs, intention, ritual—slow magic, learned magic. But there's an older kind, much rarer. Fire witches carry their power in their blood. Most spent their entire lives not understanding what they are, writing off the evidence as instinct, as coincidence." A shadow crosses her face. "That bloodline has been largely hunted out now. There are very few of us left."

She lets that sit for a moment.

"Wait? What?" My brain replays the words. "Few of *us*? I thought you were a vampire?"

"I am," she says simply. "Or at least I was...It's

complicated." She crosses her arms, making it clear she doesn't want to elaborate. I don't push.

"Right, so witches, werewolves, Fae, and vampires? Okay…" I catalog the species like the information doesn't break the entire framework of reality I have in my mind.

"There are other creatures too, scattered. Most are very good at staying hidden," Adriana adds. "The supernatural world is smaller than humans imagine and considerably stranger than they'd expect."

I continue combing, the soothing action regulating me. "Tell me about vampires. What can you do?"

Adriana relaxes under my ministrations, her guard dropping as she settles into honest conversation. "Speed, obviously. Strength that increases with age and feeding. Enhanced senses. I can hear your heartbeat from three rooms away, smell your emotions in your sweat, see clearly in complete darkness."

"The feeding enhances everything?"

"Fresh blood is like premium fuel. Everything becomes sharper, more intense. Colors are more vivid, sounds more distinct."

I consider this as I work through another section of her hair. "Do you need sleep?"

"Not the way humans do. I can go weeks without rest, though I enjoy the meditation of it sometimes."

"How old are you?"

Adriana smiles in the mirror. "Don't you know it's rude to ask a lady her age?"

I want to apologize but she continues before I can, answering with a "522 years" that seems impossibly long. I'm not sure what to do with that information, so I continue down my list of questions. "How long can you live? Theoretically?"

"Forever, *theoretically*, as long as I maintain a fresh supply of human blood. Starvation can induce hibernation, but true death requires violence. Decapitation, a stake through the heart, complete destruction of the body, that sort of thing."

The casual way she discusses her own potential mortality should disturb me. Instead, I'm fascinated by the mechanics of eternity, the biological impossibility of her existence made matter-of-fact through experience.

"And it has to be human blood?" The brush moves smoothly through her hair now, the tangles worked out, but I don't stop. The motion seems to calm both of us, creating a bubble of intimacy around us.

"I've tried surviving on animal blood, but it left me weak. The blood bank I raided wasn't much better. Preserved blood lacks the life force that comes from a beating heart. It works but not for long."

"Sounds exhausting," I reply, my hands working independently from my mind now, almost on autopilot.

Her sigh is heavy. "Very much so."

"Are there many vampires?" I ask as I stare into the distance, trying to picture it. "Like communities of them?"

"Not that many," Adriana answers. "Maybe a few thousand worldwide, and most of us are territorial. We don't gather unless forced to. Too many predators in one space tends to end badly."

I've stopped combing, entranced by her voice, her proximity, the fucking impossible hard-on that presses uncomfortably, noticeably, against my pants.

"This probably sounds naive," I say carefully, "but couldn't you all just *coexist*? Find ways to live without conflict?"

Adriana's laugh is genuinely amused this time.

"Spoken like someone who's never tried to share hunting territory with another apex predator. We're not wired for cooperation, Jude. We're wired to hunt, to feed, to survive. Everything else is learned behavior."

She turns around to face me, back to the mirror now. Then she takes the brush from my hands as she pins me in place with that sea-green stare.

My gaze inevitably drops down, raking over her body. I want to be better, but self-control falters. My exploring eyes find the triangle between her thighs, the dark bush at her center.

There is nothing subtle about my staring, about how my breathing hitches, how my dick jumps, the warmth spreading from my cheeks down my neck. But I can't look away.

I bite my bottom lip, forcing my eyes shut. It's all I can do to try and regain control. But the action is futile. My dick refuses to deflate.

Through it all, she watches me; I know she does. Her gaze burns through my skin.

"Jude." Adriana's voice is soft but commanding.

I don't open my eyes, don't trust myself not to stare.

She repeats my name and Christ, if it doesn't sound majestic in that breathy cadence of hers.

Exhaling through pursed lips, slowly, deliberately, I open first one eye, then the next.

"Jude?" The question is as much in the way she says my name as the way she looks at me, demanding honesty.

"Please." The word rolls from my lips unfiltered, volumes of need contained in a single syllable.

"Words. Tell me what you want, darling." It's a command, not a question, and like the good boy I want to be for her, I obey, confessing my need to serve her, to bring her pleasure.

She considers my proposition for an agonizingly long few seconds before a smirk creeps onto her lips and she sits back on the stool, parting her thighs for me. "Eat up, *cucciolo*." *Puppy.* My Italian is rusty but I know that word, know what she called me.

It's all the invitation I need.

Like I'm hypnotized, I sink to the floor. The plush carpet is soft beneath my knees but I don't notice the texture for more than a split second. The space around us has ceased to exist, as has my body. It's just her and that incredibly arousing scent that lures me in as I lean my cheek against a soft, cool thigh.

Adriana snakes her fingers through my hair, massaging my scalp, tugging playfully.

"This is not part of our contract," she tells me in a breathy voice, as she guides my head to her center regardless, disobeying her own rules.

I don't have the words to tell her I don't care about the contract, that I want to give her everything I have and more.

No, I wisely keep my focus on the task at hand, placing a soft kiss on her sex. *Christ, is this a dream?*

When I part her pussy lips to find her clit, Adriana tenses beneath me.

I resist the urge to ask her if she's okay and instead flick my tongue over her hidden bud, testing her sensitivity.

She rewards me with a loud groan that shakes the walls as much as my insides.

Oh god, she tastes amazing.

Grabbing both her thighs, I pull myself closer, reaching

deeper as I nibble at her sensitive skin, scraping my teeth over her pussy lips.

I drink my fill with single-minded intensity, chasing the shudders and shakes as her body responds to my touch.

I want to find every button, learn what it does, uncover the magic combination that will make her feel as amazing as she made me feel, better, if I can.

Nothing matters in this moment except doing a good job, no—an *exceptional* job. It's more important than any exam, more urgent than any deadline.

I'm by no means inexperienced when it comes to anything sexual, but it's never felt this important, this exhilarating…this *significant.*

As Adriana fed from me earlier, I feed on her now.

My lips close around her clit with vigor, and her body responds as if shocked.

I can't help but smile as I play my tongue over her clit, my hands caressing her thighs on their own command.

The space around us comes alive with Adriana's cries of passion as I devour her. Sounds I couldn't imagine her capable of. Magnificent sounds. Raw. Unfiltered.

But I want more.

I want it ALL.

No, not *want.*

Need.

I *need* to know what the Vampire Queen sounds like when she finally loses control, when she lets go, lets me take her over the edge.

My fingers inch closer to my face, to her center…over her inner thighs, closer still.

But I hesitate at her entrance.

I need to see her face, need to know what she's thinking.

Sitting up between her knees, I implore her gaze.

"Do it." The command comes out as a growl, and Adriana pushes me down again with a hand on my shoulder.

I keep my gaze trained on her face as I obey her wish. "Yes, Milady."

Adriana screams when I plunge my middle finger into her, eyes falling shut as she leans back, gripping the vanity for support.

Fucking hell, she's soaked.

The knowledge that this wetness, this obvious sign of desire, of lust, is all for me makes it impossible to think, to breathe.

I swear I damn near come on the spot just at the feel of her, at the thought that I'm the one drawing this reaction from her body.

But it's not about my pleasure now; it's all hers.

I add another finger, slowly pushing inside her as her legs wrap around my back, locking around me, pulling me closer.

Lowering my head again, I seek out the little bundle of nerves, flicking my tongue over it as I pump my fingers into her.

I don't know how long I remain on my knees like that. But when Adriana tugs at my hair, whispering an urgent, breathless "Don't you fucking dare stop" at me, I know she's close.

Making sure to keep the exact pressure, the same rhythm, I lap at her clit while my fingers dance inside her, breathing a secondary function now as I focus everything on toppling her over the edge.

And when she does, holy fuck, it's incredible!

A loud scream rips through the room as the body beneath me shudders and shakes.

I don't stop, just keep going, holding on tightly even as I fear that she might rip my hair from my head.

Heaven, she tastes like heaven.

I lap up every drop of my reward until my lips are numb and my knees are screaming in agony.

"Enough!" Adriana moans in a ragged voice. She pulls me from her pussy by the hair, up toward her.

Kneeling between her thighs, I reach up for her to kiss my dirty lips.

It's messy, it's urgent, raw…but dear lord, it's the most incredible kiss I've ever had in my life.

When we finally part, I'm delirious with need, with lust. All I can do is stare at her, breathless, speechless, as that magnificent smirk returns to her face.

"Thank you, *tesoro*." Adriana licks her lips, regarding me with fire in her eyes. "You did such a good job for me."

The praise sinks into my bones like warm butter on toast, and I almost melt into the floor.

My only response is grinning like a fool as I sit back to study her.

Can't say I've ever given a vampire an orgasm before.

It might be my proudest moment yet.

CHAPTER 15

PRE-DAWN

(ADRIANA)

I t's hard not to lose myself when I stare into the devoted eyes of the beautiful boy on his knees.

Not boy—man, I remind myself.

There is no part of Jude's anatomy that isn't fully *man*. I've seen it, I've touched it with my own hands, made it lose control. But considering the nearly 500-year age gap, he'll always be a *boy* in my mind.

A delicious boy who seems to know exactly what to do with that tongue of his.

Silly me, I thought he'd be inexperienced, awkward, fumble around uncertainly. But oh no, Jude Cole is well-trained in carnal pleasures. Bringing me to climax with such devotion…that wasn't beginner's luck. That was someone who pays attention, who learns, who makes pleasing others an art form.

I've had no shortage of lovers in my long life, but it's never quite been like this. This quiet devotion, this dedication to my pleasure.

When I was human, men took what they wanted and my needs be damned, which is why I was so drawn to Cyrus; he treated me like a Queen.

But it was a different kind of worship. Cyrus was never a patient lover. His passion burned too bright, too feral.

Standing up from the dresser, I finally reach for a robe to cover my skin. Not because I'm cold; I feel nothing of temperature unless I choose to. But more as a measure of protection, armor against the vulnerability threatening to consume me, to stop us both before we go too far.

It's already too late for that.

"You should go to bed," I tell Jude as I reach down to cup his cheek, his skin still flushed.

"I don't need sleep." He shakes his head, defiantly keeping my gaze as he leans against my leg, his cheek pressed to my thigh like he belongs there. Like this is natural, normal, safe.

But nothing about this is *safe*.

"No, darling." I take his hand and pull him from his knees, trying to ignore the electricity his touch sends racing up my arm. "Enough for one night. You have important work to do tomorrow."

His shoulders slump in disappointment, but his arousal remains evident beneath the loose pants.

"Please don't send me away," Jude whines, and the desperate edge in his voice nearly breaks my resolve. He looks so young in this moment, so vulnerable.

"I don't like to repeat myself, Jude. You'll do well to remember that." My voice comes out sterner than intended. But the overriding urge to be alone grows stronger with every second he remains here, every moment that threatens to chip away at my defenses.

I need distance, space to think.

The human doesn't say anything as he stands, exits, rejection coloring his entire presence as he leaves with drooped shoulders and wounded pride.

Part of me feels bad. He looks so pathetic, so genuinely hurt by my dismissal.

But I know it's for the best. I need to set boundaries now, before either of us becomes too invested in whatever this is becoming, before I lose myself as I did with Elijah.

The door closes with a soft click, and the silence is deafening.

The power from Jude's blood still thrums through my veins, making every shadow in the room seem alive, every surface humming with potential energy.

Fresh human blood is always intoxicating, but this feels different, more potent, like he's somehow enhanced the usual effects through the purity of his offering.

You're being ridiculous, I tell myself as I study my reflection in the antique mirror. It's hard to miss the flush that still colors my cheeks, the swollen press of my lips from his kiss. It's the first orgasm not by my own hand in nearly ten years...

Too fast. This is all happening too fast.

I pull the silk robe tighter around my body like it can somehow contain the chaos Jude's unleashed in my usually uneventful routine.

The truth is, I didn't send him away because he was pushing too hard or asking too many questions; I sent him away because of how perfectly he fit between my thighs, how naturally he responded to my commands, how completely right it felt to have him worship me with that devoted mouth.

For a moment, I forgot to be afraid. And forgetting fear

is what got me chained in silver for four weeks while hunters stripped away everything I'd built.

It's all too familiar. Elijah would kneel in almost the exact same position, looking up at me with near identical devotion. *'Please let me stay, Ma'am. Let me serve you.'*

Five years of service. Five years of apparent happiness. Right up until the moment he guided my enemies straight to my door. No, *fuck familiars.*

But Jude's not my familiar…

The smart thing would be to send him away tomorrow. I should pay him for his time and find another researcher. Someone less likely to make me question my boundaries.

But even as I think it, I know I won't.

Not just because I need his research skills, though I do, desperately. He's the first competent, motivated researcher I have found in all my searching. I don't have another nine years to start over.

No, I won't send him just away because some selfish, desperate part of me wants to keep him.

It's an impossible choice. Damned if I do; damned if I don't.

Perhaps work will take my mind off things, I convince myself as I head back to my office without bothering to change out of my robe.

There are business dealings that require my attention, acquisitions that need my approval, all the things that usually consume my evenings.

But my enhanced senses keep pulling me toward the sound of Jude's heartbeat down the hall—strong, steady, slightly elevated with what might be lingering arousal or adrenaline.

He's not asleep; I can tell from the irregular rhythm, the occasional spike of his pulse.

Focus, Adriana!

I force my attention back to the letter in my hands, something from a contact in Greece about a private collection coming up for auction, important business that has nothing to do with storm-gray eyes and willing submission.

But concentration proves impossible. Every few minutes, my mind drifts back to the feeling of his hands on my thighs...

When was the last time someone touched me like that? Not with calculation or agenda, but with a simple desire to give pleasure? To make me feel good, not because it served their purposes, but because my pleasure was reward enough?

I'm already in too deep.

The distance I tried to maintain, the professional boundaries I insisted upon, they're illusions. The moment I allowed myself to taste his blood, to enjoy his devotion instead of simply using it, I started down a path that can only end in disaster.

Because that's what happens when creatures like me try to love mortal things: we destroy them, or they destroy us, or time destroys everything beautiful we try to build together.

Elijah proved that.

Cyrus proved that, in his own spectacular way.

And yet...

I find myself pausing to listen to Jude's heartbeat. Still strong, still steady, still calling to the predator and the woman in me with equal intensity.

Maybe this time will be different.

Or maybe I'm a five-hundred-year-old fool who never learned that some lessons have to be repeated until they finally stick.

Humans have short life spans.

Nothing good can come from this.

The correspondence lies forgotten in my lap as I listen to his pulse and try to convince myself that sending him away was the right choice.

But my body wants more; my *blood* wants more.

Jesus, Adriana. He's going to get you killed.

But that's never been a reason not to want something.

Not for me.

CHAPTER 16
SETTLING IN

(JUDE)

There is no way I can sleep, not after what just happened.

My heart is racing as fast as my breath when I begrudgingly sulk back to my room down the hall.

I wish I knew what I did wrong. Everything was so perfect.

Why did she send me away again?

Did I do a bad job?

My mind is a tumultuous mess as I kick off my pants and slip, naked, under the cool sheets that are smoother than any I've ever felt on my body.

I reach to my neck where she had sunk her teeth into me, drank from me, took more than my blood. But there is nothing there. No holes; not even a little bump.

It's like it never happened at all.

But I know it did. My body knows too.

I'm grateful she let me keep the memory. Just thinking about it makes my cock hard.

Christ, the cries that came from her lips in the moment of orgasm, when she tumbled off the edge, there are no words for the sense of accomplishment that washed over me in that moment. The pride, the *desire*.

If she hadn't pushed me off her, I could've stayed there for hours; for as long as she needed.

"For fuck's sake," I lament out loud to the empty room around me.

This is crazy!

I've been here less than a day, haven't even started on the work I'm *supposed* to be doing, and yet, I am sure this is exactly where I was always meant to be...with her, with Lady Adriana.

Jesus, I sound pathetic.

What is she doing to me?

With a sigh, I reach for my cock, stroking it languidly as I replay the scenes from the past few hours over and over again.

It doesn't take long to reach my climax; I've been hard for so long.

When I come not long after, ribbons of sticky white streaking into my hand, it's with Adriana's name on my lips.

But the climax is empty, unsatisfying.

I head to the bathroom to clean up, falling back into bed with a heavy sigh.

Staring at the ceiling, I'm right back to trying to rationalize my situation, my choices, my desires. But there is no reference book for what one *should* do in the rare instance that one should find oneself desperate to submit to a 522-year-old vampire.

AT SOME POINT, I must have fallen asleep despite my conviction that I'll never be able to sleep.

When a soft knock on the door wakes me, I'm momentarily confused. *This isn't the commune?*

The knock sounds again, followed by Felix's gentle voice, thick with that Eastern European accent of his that I haven't asked about yet. "Coffee, sir?"

The last fog shakes from my brain as I call for just a moment, pulling my pants off the floor.

"Come in," I answer groggily, and the housekeeper enters with a tray that he sets down carefully on the chest of drawers next to the door.

A steaming plunger of delicious-smelling coffee awaits, together with two different kinds of sugars, plus milk and cream.

"Apologies, Master Cole. I was not sure how you took your coffee. Lady Adriana left a note requesting that I wake you at this hour and lead you to the office to begin work. After breakfast, of course." Felix remains hovering by the door, carding his hand through his long hair that he left loose today.

"Please, just Jude is fine." I pick up the plunger and pour myself a cup. "I'm definitely not the master around here." A smirk finds its way to my lips.

"Of course. Whatever you prefer...*Jude*." His smile is genuine.

"Thanks, Felix. What's for breakfast?" I have to admit, I am ravenous. Perhaps it's got something to do with how tired I still am, or the amount of blood and cum I've parted with since my arrival.

"Whatever your heart desires, sir...Apologies, *Jude*," he corrects himself.

"Pancakes?" I chance it as I take a sip of the steaming

brew. Why I said it, I don't know. I've never had pancakes for breakfast in my damn life. But the pancakes the families enjoyed on the TV shows I watched as a kid always looked delicious. My default back then was another dry bread sandwich with only cheap margarine between the slices.

Felix doesn't even bat an eyelash at the request. Perhaps it wasn't as obscure as I thought. "Savory or sweet?" he asks instead.

"Sweet, please." I take the cup in both hands to warm the feeling back into them. "And syrup?"

"The pantry is fully stocked." Felix smiles. "It will be nice to have someone to cook for."

"Lady Adriana not much for regular meals?" I joke, testing the waters. I'm not sure how her arrangement with Felix works, what he knows. Maybe she compels him, or however that works.

Felix shakes his head. "Not really."

Perhaps it's best not to pry, I decide.

"Thanks, Felix. I'll be down in a bit. I need a shower."

With a polite nod, he's off again, the door clicking shut behind him.

The coffee brings *some* life back to my body, but I'm still shaky, wrung out, coming down from the high of last night.

But there were no drugs involved, only something even more addictive: Adriana's attention.

I reach for my long-forgotten phone to check the time but the thing is fully flat. Should probably charge it, but why bother? Nobody has any excuse to be looking for me.

It's still early, before noon, judging from the sun's position when I pull open the heavy curtains to let in the light.

My movements are slow, laborious, as I shower and

change into fresh clothes from the cupboard, forgoing the old suitcase resting on a settee by the window altogether.

Breakfast is incredible and perks me up more, as does a second cup of coffee. The pancakes are perfectly fluffy and a real treat. *I could get used to this...*

By the time Felix lets me into Adriana's office, I'm almost myself again, despite the nagging tiredness that persists in my bones.

The space has changed since yesterday. A second desk now sits in front of Adriana's large oak one.

"And this?" I ask Felix as I lift the lid of the brand-new MacBook sitting on the desk.

"For you, Master Jude."

"Just Jude," I say as I turn it on. "For me?"

"Yes. For your research. Lady Adriana requested it. She's asked that you get started in setting everything up so you're ready when she rises later."

"I see."

Felix continues, pointing to the pile of books resting at the edge of the large desk. Among them sits the De Crevena family catalog I was supposed to track down for her.

Slowly, realization dawns. *It was a test.*

"She also asked that you start working through the background materials."

I look from the books to him. "Wasn't she asleep?"

Felix smiles. "When I arrive in the mornings, there is always a list of instructions waiting on the chalkboard in the kitchen."

"Ah, fair enough. Thanks, Felix. I should be fine from here."

"If you need anything, you can ring the bell." He shows me a string near the door, like we are in some historical movie. "There are water bottles and some juice in there." He points to the mini fridge in the corner I hadn't noticed before, and then he's off, leaving me to orient myself in the space.

The desk isn't the only thing that has changed from yesterday. I can't help but notice that Cyrus's painting is no longer on the wall, replaced by a charcoal sketch of a phoenix.

Next to the door, a large wooden grandfather clock chimes 1 PM, finally giving me the time reference I seek.

Fuck, I'd meant to ask Felix what time Adriana normally wakes up. Definitely not going to ring a bell for that, though.

I guess it's time to get to work.

As much as I want to do a good job for her, do the best job, and quickly find the book she's looking for, I also don't want to outlive my usefulness. I know that as soon as Adriana gets what she wants, she will have no use for me anymore. And then where do I go?

In the end, the need to do good overrides my insecurities, and I pick up one of the large leather-bound volumes sitting on the corner of my new desk. It's heavy and written in Latin.

My ancient languages are not too rusty but I'll need some brushing up.

For the next couple of hours, I lose myself in my chores, installing updates on the computer and logging into all the places I can remember to log in, paging through the ancient books as I wait.

Felix brings me some more coffee and a sandwich for a late lunch, wordlessly leaving them by the door so as not to disturb my work. By the time I notice, the coffee is already cold. But I don't mind.

The books are hard to understand but the bits that I can translate are incredibly fascinating. I don't need the archive look-up on my new laptop to tell me how rare and priceless these volumes are, but I look them up anyway.

How the fuck did she get these? The scholar in me is in awe.

Time moves along quickly until a cramp in my calf reminds me to move.

A book on the shelf draws my attention as I'm stretching my legs, and I walk over to inspect it. It appears to be something about power dynamics in ancient Greece, a book I would've given everything for when I was still working on my thesis.

But when I reach the bookshelf, I forget all about the book.

I don't know how I missed it—blame my tired mind— but when I get closer, I notice that the wall of books is skewed. Not by much, maybe an inch, but unmistakably so.

My fingers curl around the edge, tugging gently. The entire bookcase moves, like I'm in a spy movie, revealing a whole other space behind it, one that lights up as I step inside.

A secret room!

Adriana must have forgotten to close it properly yesterday. I don't ponder that part for long, not when my eyes find the walls and walls of rare books that shouldn't exist but do.

The room contains not only books but also pieces of artwork and hidden cupboards with thick padlocks that give no indication of what they're preserving.

I know I shouldn't be in here, but my curiosity refuses

to let me close the door and return to my duties. I've stumbled upon a treasure trove of forgotten histories.

On the floor, there's a large painting facing the wall, and I almost knock it over when I enter. When I turn it around, I gasp audibly at the striking picture of Adriana and who obviously must be Cyrus, dressed like it's the 1700s, smiling back at me. He's holding her from behind, hands on her hips in an uncharacteristic pose for the era.

She looks amazing. That smile, so radiant.

And him? My god, the glimpses I caught from Adriana's memory when she fed from me did not do Cyrus justice.

What a handsome face.

They make such a striking couple.

My mind wanders to ponder what it must be like when two vampires have sex…

Just thinking about the two of them, of the life they must have lived, the memories they share, makes my heart speed up. Real *forever*.

"You shouldn't be in here." Adriana's voice behind me startles me, and I almost drop the painting.

How does she move so damn quietly?

Caught red-handed, I turn around slowly to face my furious employer.

Fuck.

CHAPTER 17
PUNISHED

(ADRIANA)

My rest was troubled, tormented by unwanted thoughts and memories.

I could smell Jude's desire all the way down the hall.

With my senses still heightened, I heard every muffled groan he tried to suppress, smelled every drop of cum he spilled on my expensive linen.

It wasn't easy to remain in my room, to not go to him. Resisting the urge, I clutched my bedding so tightly that I ripped it in three places.

But I stayed put, stayed in my own room, even as my overactive imagination visualized barging in and impaling myself on that beautiful, thick cock in vivid detail.

If I were a younger vampire, one with less experience in control, there would have been no way to stay away while Jude satisfied himself down the hall.

But self-control is an art. One that I pride myself on having mastered quite well. *For the most part.*

As I stand in my library now, fuming at Jude's guilty face, I'm dangerously close to losing that control.

The temperature in the room drops ten degrees in seconds, my breath misting in the suddenly frigid air.

I had come to my study expecting to find my new employee being a diligent scholar, but instead found him snooping around my forbidden collection. *What is it with this human?*

The rage builds in my chest, and with it comes the ice —wild, untamed, dangerous.

The ice spreads from my fingertips across the nearest bookshelf, crystallizing the ancient leather bindings. "You shouldn't be in here." The words come out rough, almost like a growl.

Jude freezes, guilt draping every feature in anguish. His eyes widen as he watches frost climb across the walls behind me, branching and spreading with unnatural speed.

"I-I'm sorry, Milady," he stutters, carefully putting the painting down. "It was open," he adds like it absolves him of any of his crimes.

As my fury rises, sharp spears of ice begin forming in the air around Jude, pointing toward him like accusations. His breath mists, skin turning pale from the supernatural cold radiating from my body.

He's half a foot taller than me and way more muscular, but none of that matters when I grab him by the shirt and lift him off the floor to push him up against the bookcase, his feet leaving the ground. Ice spreads from where my hands touch him, freezing the fabric, making him gasp as the cold seeps through to his skin.

Fear flashes through his eyes, but I detect his arousal despite it. "This room is forbidden," I hiss between gritted teeth, grabbing his neck and pulling his face down to mine, so close that our noses almost touch.

"S-sorry," Jude stutters, heart beating so loudly, I can't even hear my own thoughts screaming in my head. "So, so sorry—Fuck."

The ice spears drift closer to his throat, sharp enough to pierce flesh, cold enough to kill. One wrong move, one moment of faltering control, and they'll drive straight through his jugular.

I hold Jude up firmly until his lips turn blue from the cold, ice crystals forming on his eyelashes, and I realize I'm about to kill him by accident.

The shock of that possibility breaks through my rage long enough for me to step back. I let go, and he drops to the floor on shaky legs. Instantly, the spears dissolve into mist and the frost on the walls begins to melt.

"I don't pay you to snoop around," I manage, my voice rough with the effort of containing powers that want to lash out again. "Perhaps this was a bad idea after all."

I turn away from the human, from the concern and confusion I can see building in his too-perceptive eyes. He's going to ask questions I can't answer, notice things I can't explain.

But he has no questions, only pleas.

"No, please!" Jude falls to his knees. "Please, Milady. I'm sorry. It won't happen again."

Those sad eyes looking up at me, begging like he means it, humbled—it touches something in me. The sincerity of his regret is virtually palpable.

It doesn't forgive his sins, though.

"Trust is very important," I tell Jude as I pace the small space, fighting to keep my voice steady, to hide the trembling of my hands. "I will not be betrayed again."

Memories of Elijah come back unbidden, but I force them down.

Jude reaches for me, hugging both my legs, his head on my thigh. I can't move. Well, I could if I wanted to. But I don't. "Please, Milady. I'll do anything. *Please keep me.*"

The words, the phrasing of it, they defrost a little part of my icy heart. Enough for the blood rushing in my head to quieten down to manageable levels.

I sigh. "Word of advice, dearest Jude. You should never tell an immortal being you'd do *anything.*" I break free from his grip. "Let's go. Out!" I point to the door, and he shamefully crawls out, not getting up, just staying on his knees as I follow behind.

This time, I make sure I hear the latch click into place when I pull the fake wall shut.

It didn't look like he'd done much poking around, but who knows what he would've found had I arrived any later. The items in this room are priceless, personal, not for anyone else's eyes.

I drop into the chair behind my desk, watching the sorry boy kneeling in front of me, head hung, eyes downcast.

He doesn't say anything, merely waits for his lot.

"I won't send you away…" I start slowly.

Jude looks up, eyes sparkling. "Thank you, thank you so much, I—"

I cut him off with the wave of my hand and a stern tone. "Let me finish."

"Sorry." He looks down again.

"You can stay, *but* I am not one to let bad deeds go unpunished."

His little gasp is audible. "Punishment?" Jude says softly, as if testing the word.

"The punishment should always fit the crime," I say more to myself than to him, as I run the options through my mind.

As much as I want to pull him over my lap and spank him until he cries like a baby, it's not what this situation calls for.

"Lock the door."

Jude gets off the floor to do as he's told.

He comes back, waiting for the next instruction.

He doesn't have to wait long.

"Now, strip!"

This time, Jude doesn't hesitate. He de-layers quickly, folding each item neatly and placing it on his desk until he's standing before me as naked as he was yesterday when I stripped him out of his rain-soaked attire. Except this time, I don't offer him a robe.

"Back against the bookshelf," I order, getting up to pace the space between us. This is risky territory. He's not my familiar. And he's definitely not my sub. Our contract only pertains to research work. Yet it doesn't stop me from punishing him like he's mine.

Jude holds his breath as he finally lifts his gaze to mine, his anticipation palpable in his vital signs.

I take the biggest book from the shelf, a 1621 copy of Robert Burton's *The Anatomy of Melancholy*—all 1,376 pages of it—and place it on his head, balancing it perfectly as he squares out his shoulders to accommodate its weight.

"Now listen to me very carefully, dear Jude," I tell him, my breath whispering against his neck as I press my body against his, his erection digging into my stomach, hard and needy. "You are now my table, got it? And you need to keep this book up, no hands. If it touches the carpet, I will fucking put you in a chastity cage for a week." I grab his cock as I utter my threat, and he shivers in my touch, eyes falling shut.

"Yes, Milady. Thank you, Milady."

Like a good little submissive, he accepts his punishment, breathing heavily as I stroke his cock slowly. There is nothing idle about my threat. I will lock him away so quickly, his head will spin.

His dick is a live animal in my hand, growing, *needing*. A groan leaves his parted lips as I circle the tip of his sensitive head with my fingers, seducing him to full mast.

Cupping his balls in a move that makes him hiss as he bites down on his bottom lip, I tease him until the first drop of pre-cum glistens on my finger. And then I pull away, dropping his cock, and return to my desk.

An anguished cry tears from Jude's chest at the loss of contact, and he nearly drops the book on top of his head, but then quickly straightens out, saving it at the last minute.

I grin as I cross my legs, watching him intently. "I didn't say it was going to be easy."

Jude's breathing rapidly now, chest heaving up and down. His right hand reaches over to his cock, ready to finish the job, but a thunderous "Don't you fucking dare!" from my side stops him dead in his tracks.

Startled, he quickly moves his hand to his side again.

"Nah-ah-ah, darling," I tell him from across the room as I scrutinize every inch of his youthful body, every muscle that ripples under the strain of keeping this posture while so desperately close to release. "No more of that. While you're under my roof, you are not allowed to touch yourself."

He curses under his breath but doesn't protest.

I know I'm being possessive, that I have no right to ask that of him, but I'll go insane if I have to smell his orgasms all day long. No, this is for his own good. And mine.

"Please," Jude whimpers, fists clenching and unclenching by his sides as he struggles to keep from touching his erection. He looks miserable. *Poor baby.*

"Use your words."

"Please let me finish," he complains, blowing a strand of hair from his eyes that settles back in exactly the same place again. "This is fucking torture."

"Punishment is not supposed to be fun, now, is it?" I tsk-tsk at him. "Wouldn't exactly be a *punishment* then." I tear my eyes away from him to focus on my laptop.

"How—how long?" he asks, shaking under the weight of concentration, dick hard, legs spread for balance.

I consider it for a moment. "One hour. When the clock gets to seventeen past again, then, and only then, may you move."

Jude groans, unimpressed. "Please, Milady, I—"

But I cut him off. "Hush now. Tables don't talk."

I don't have time for brats.

CHAPTER 18
LESSON LEARNED

(JUDE)

What the hell happened in there?

The question loops through my mind as I try to keep still while processing what I had witnessed in the secret room.

Ice doesn't just appear from thin air.

But it did; I was there. Those ice daggers were way too close to my throat.

For a moment—one terrifying, crystal-clear moment—I thought she was going to kill me without even touching me.

When did vampires start turning things to ice?

But I don't have time to dwell on that. Not when my punishment is this involved.

How can one book be this heavy?

I'm as humiliated as I am turned on.

When Adriana caught me in her secret room, I was certain it was the end—either of my employment, or my life.

But she showed mercy, offering me a punishment instead.

Or I thought it a mercy at the time.

Stupid me.

Forty-eight minutes and four edgings later, I'm not so sure the word applies anymore.

This isn't mercy; this is hell!

My shoulders are on fire, my neck too.

Trying to keep this damn book up is harder than I thought it would be. Twice, it almost came crashing down. The last time, while she held my cock in her hands, rubbing my pre-cum over my sensitive skin like lube, the book tilted forward dangerously before settling. *So close, so damn close!*

Argh! But then, alas, she once again pulled away at the last second, leaving my skin burning and my shoulders shaky, the book at risk of losing its battle against gravity.

Just twelve more minutes.

But I take no comfort in that fact.

Not when each second brings its own agony.

Twelve more minutes in this position is an *eternity!*

My body is delirious with need, a sensation that overpowers even the pain in my joints from having to remain still for this long.

My mind has lost all capacity to think about anything else. Every brain cell is focused on keeping this position, on keeping the book off the floor.

I don't know what it's like to have your dick shoved in a chastity cage for a whole week but I sure as hell don't want to find out. Not when it feels so good when Adriana takes me in her hands, when she touches me, skin on skin.

No, it doesn't matter how hard it is, how hard *I* am, this fucking book is staying up; I'm determined.

Hopeful, I glance at the clock again.

Eleven minutes left.

What the fuck?!

Move faster!

Meanwhile, Adriana carries on tapping away on her keyboard, never even glancing my way except when she deems it time to torment me again, edging me until I nearly see stars, only to be disappointed—again.

Technically, I know that nothing stops me from walking out right now. I could just drop this book and tell her to stuff her job. This is not normal behavior for something that's supposed to be a business arrangement.

But it was never just an *arrangement*.

It felt like belonging somewhere again.

And now I need to earn my right to stay.

Resolve thickens as I clench my fists again, willing my mind to think of something, anything that isn't my body or the clock.

It's a futile exercise. *How can one think when there are so many sensations?*

My mind goes blank save for the pain and the unbearable need to come. The quiet is a blissful reprieve from the normal chaotic stream of thought that hardly ever slows, not even during my restless sleep at night.

I will only appreciate this fact later. Because right now, I can't think of anything but my immediate needs as the time slowly creeps by in seconds that painstakingly turn to eventual minutes.

When the hands on the clock finally reach four minutes to go, the Lady of the House looks up from her laptop, and my heart sinks and rises at the same time.

There is still time for me to drop that book.

If she would leave me be, I could make it now; I'm close.

Miss De Crevena has no such compassionate intentions, though. No, she pushes her chair out and stalks over to me.

Fuck.

"How's it going over here?" she asks, reaching for my desperate cock that's still painfully hard, neglected. "Learned your lesson yet, little snoop?"

"Yes, yes, Milady." It's hard to speak, and every word costs me. Trying to think of sentences is too complicated when her mere touch sets my skin alight, the book swaying dangerously above my aching shoulders.

Adriana circles the sensitive spot below the tip of my cock, and I swear I'm moments away from spilling my seed right here, on her carpet. But I know if I do that, it would be the last thing I'd be allowed to do in this house.

No, I close my eyes, count to ten, failing even at that. I get as far as seven before I forget what number comes next. My brain is mush.

"P-please, please," I repeat the word, again and again, as she strokes me, teases me. *Please have mercy*, I want to say but can't. "Please."

The clock says three minutes left.

It can't be.

Sorcery! Goddamnit.

Adriana drops my cock and I exhale loudly, relief flooding my body instantly—prematurely.

She reaches for my nipples and twists.

Fuck me, that feels amazing!

But in this situation, that's not a good thing. Not at all. Any stimulation makes it even harder to keep still.

"Don't you dare come without permission," she warns and my anguish turns to despair. It's an impossible instruction in a position this compromised. Especially when she bends down to playfully flick her tongue over my cock.

Oh fuck, I can't hold it. I can't. I can't.

Just breathe, Jude.

My circuits go haywire as I try to retain some semblance of control.

I don't need much. Just enough control to keep the book in position. But even that proves to be a tall ask. Especially when she starts milking my cock again, this time with gusto.

"C-close," I plead, begging her to stop, to wait a minute.

I can't hold it; I need to come!

"You don't have permission," Adriana reminds me cruelly as her fingers touch me like I've always hoped to be touched. Not just random tugging but intentional touches, alternating pressures.

There are no words left in my vocabulary, only whimpers, as the unstoppable orgasm starts to build. She senses it too, reading my body's signs better than I can.

It's happening, I'm going to come, I—

At the last minute, she pulls away, dropping my cock.

No!

I can't contain the loud cry that rips from my chest as the near-pleasure slips away into the slow trickle of an orgasm ruined.

There is no satisfaction to be had, just frustration.

As Adriana watches, the cum drips from my unstimulated cock, decorating the expensive carpet in drops of white.

"Fuck!" I've never had a ruined orgasm before, and it's horrible. Absolutely horrible.

But I know I can't collapse, not yet. *Not yet.*

I'm straining with everything I have, eyes pressed shut with force, fists balled. Every muscle aches, protests. My left leg is cramping for some dumb reason, pins and needles spreading, but I dare not move, dare not open my eyes, dare not breathe.

Fuck, I'm not going to make it.

She's going to put me in a cage.

No, I —

"It's over," Adriana's voice sounds distant, elsewhere. "Open your eyes, darling."

The magic words. *Oh god.*

I slowly open my eyes, exhaling the stale breath, as Adriana gently strokes my cheek.

"You did it. I didn't think you would, but you did it." Smiling, she takes the book from my head and places it on the table next to me. She lifts it like it weighs nothing, like it didn't almost break my body. "You were so good, Jude. So good."

The praise sends me. It's a blow I have no defenses left to counter.

Her smile is radiant as I crumble to the floor, collapsing against the bookcase. The relief of having crossed the finished line, paired with finally being free of the book, is all my body needs to let go, to fall. To collapse into the miserable ball that it is, my thighs sticky from the ruined orgasm.

Adriana's expression changes to concern as she hunches down beside me. "Are you okay?" She lifts my chin to her, wiping a tear from my cheek. Pressing it to her lips, she savors the taste.

I was crying?

I nod slowly, my voice shaky when I finally speak. "Yeah...fine." It sounds inadequate, but it's true, even if my body hasn't finished processing what just happened.

The harsh voice in my head—the one that usually tears me apart for every mistake, every misstep, every moment of imperfection—has gone quiet. For the first time in weeks, maybe months, there's silence where my inner critics usually live.

Adriana's discipline accomplished something I've never been able to do for myself. Instead of the endless spiral of self-recrimination I would have fallen into if she'd simply dismissed my transgression, there's clarity, resolution.

The punishment fit the crime, like she promised, and now it's over. Done.

I don't have to carry the weight of my mistake indefinitely, don't have to replay it endlessly, or wonder if I've ruined everything between us.

"The quiet," I whisper, pressing my cheek against the carpet. "My mind is...quiet."

"Good," is all she says. Her hand moves to stroke my hair, soothing touches grounding me in reality even as it threatens to slip away.

Balance has been restored, equilibrium achieved. There is a way forward that doesn't require me to destroy myself over a moment of poor judgment.

Adriana gets up and returns with a bottle of cold water from the mini fridge. "Here, drink this."

Her whole demeanor is different now. Gone is the furious teacher. In her place, the nurturing matriarch has returned.

She strokes my hair as I swallow the entire bottle down

in large gulps. It somewhat restores my senses. I didn't even realize how parched I was.

"Come, let's get you comfortable." Adriana reaches down and picks me off the floor like I weigh nothing, like the scale doesn't hover around 200 pounds beneath me usually. But for someone with her strength, I probably do weigh nothing.

I don't overthink it; can't—I'm too floaty. My body isn't my own anymore.

She sets me down on the leather couch beside the bookcase, and I'm grateful for the support beneath me, the cool surface of the seat against my warm skin.

"I'm sorry I had to punish you." Adriana's voice is gentle behind me as she presses her hands into my shoulders, hard, forcing the muscles to unclench. "But please don't go in there again." She massages the tension from my body as I sink into the couch, into her touch.

In my mind, I'm tripping, like I've taken too many shrooms, floating away on a cloud, blissful, as endorphins flood my system.

Adriana sits down beside me on the couch and gathers me in her arms, pressing me against her chest, kissing the top of my head sweetly.

I'm confused but also not because I fit here. My naked body against her fully clothed one feels right as he holds me, cares for me. I don't feel ashamed; but forgiven.

My grandmother used to say she only punished me because she loved me. That if she didn't care, she would've thrown me out on the street.

Her punishments never felt warranted. Nor safe.

But this, this is different.

I'm freer, lighter—my guilt has been atoned for.

I exhale loudly against Adriana's chest, nuzzling my face under her arm. "I promise I'll be good," I whisper.

What a ridiculous thing to say.

She's going to laugh at me, I'm certain.

But she doesn't.

Adriana reaches down to lift my face to her gaze. "Don't make me regret keeping you."

My gut wrenches at the mere thought of disappointing her. "No, Milady. Never."

CHAPTER 19

DECISIONS

(ADRIANA)

"**A**re you okay?" I ask Jude as he rests his naked body against me on the couch.

He nods, pulling me closer to him, then smiles, that innocent, youthful smile of his. The one that defrosts my icy heart like he was made of fire instead of flesh. "Just a bit sore."

"We can start work later if you want to decompress a bit first," I offer as I detangle him from my body and get up. *Don't get attached, Adriana.*

"No, I'm good." Jude stretches out then stands. "Lemme just clean up and put some clothes on. I'll be right as rain."

He heads off to the bathroom as I sink back into my office chair, trying to calm my tumultuous mind.

That wasn't supposed to happen.

I snapped.

Punishment shouldn't come from anger. I know that.

When you've been a dominant for as long as I have,

these things become second nature. But it's been too long. I'm losing my touch.

Gods, what a beautiful submissive, though.

Jude wants this so badly. I can sense it in every pore; it radiates from him. He's not even ashamed. He unapologetically wants to be mine, wants to worship me, wants… *too much*. He wants too much.

I'm not sure I still have that to give.

He's young; he's foolish. Time will make him see.

Obsessions are fleeting.

But even as I think it, I know it's a lie. Jude is one of the most serious people ever to step foot into my life. He knows what he wants.

When I sank my teeth into him last night, tasted his blood, his submission, I knew. There was no hiding what he wanted from me. And it wasn't just employment.

The thought of it scared me so much, I pushed it down immediately.

But the feeling still lingers.

It's all too familiar.

Maybe that's why I snapped. Why I made him stand naked, frustrated, cock leaking on the carpet with the book on his head. To test him; to know.

When something seems too good to be true, it usually is.

I expected him to fail, to drop the book. I was ready to show him the door, or the chastity cage—whichever fate he chose.

But he didn't drop it. No, he persisted through the torment.

I didn't plan to be so immensely proud of him.

The aftercare was haphazard at best, but Jude quickly surfaced from his sub-drop again, fighting his way through the haze to regard me with those bright eyes that have the audacity to look grateful instead of disturbed.

Don't dwell on it, Adriana.

This has to stop.

I do my best to center myself, forcing my lungs through breathing exercises I learned from an old woman in the mountains of Tibet, decades before the West discovered meditation and gave it a price tag.

By the time Jude returns from the bathroom, fully clothed in the fancy new linens I handpicked online after sizing him up during our first meeting, we're both more settled.

"I'm fine, before you ask," he offers with a lopsided smile as he takes a seat behind his newly acquired desk, straightening out his posture in the most pleasing way.

"Good. You're no use to me broken." I return his smile, relieved that he seems to be himself again. "Back to work?" It's not an order but a question. I'm not sure what else to do.

Jude nods, opening his new laptop. "Sure, but why do you need this book so badly anyway?"

The question hangs between us, heavier than he realizes. I've been dreading this moment: real answers instead of vague cover stories.

But I promised. And I always keep my promises.

"The Grimoire isn't just a book," I begin, moving to stand behind him, my hands resting lightly on his shoulders. "It's a magical book."

Jude turns his head around to look at me. His muscles tense slightly under my touch, but he doesn't pull away. "What does a vampire need magic for?"

Clever boy. Asking the right questions.

I brush a stubborn strand of hair from his forehead, but

it falls back over his eyes. How can I lie to those innocent eyes? What does it matter anymore anyway? If I don't get that Grimoire back soon, I won't be alive long enough to protect my secrets.

"Remember the first day you came over, when I asked you if you knew what I am, and you said a vampire?"

"Yes…" he answers, face wrapped in confusion.

"Well, that was only half true."

"I don't understand."

Stepping back, I perch on the edge of my desk as I try to figure out where to start this story.

"My mother was a powerful fire witch…" I begin as Jude turns his chair to face me. "A gift she passed down through her blood."

His face lights up. "You're a witch?"

"It's complicated."

"Half witch then?"

"Sort of. I'm a hybrid."

"I didn't know hybrids existed." His eyes are wide in wonder. *Such a curious boy.*

"We're not supposed to." I move to the window, gathering my thoughts. "Vampire and witch, those two natures aren't meant to coexist," I explain, keeping my back to him. It's easier this way. "Witch magic needs life force. A heartbeat. Living energy. Vampires are death. We have none of those things."

Jude doesn't interrupt, just waits for me to continue.

"When I was turned, my fire magic tried to work through a body that had no life force to draw from." The memory still makes me cold. "It inverted. Became ice instead."

For a moment, I'm back there, on the battlefield in Rome, in 1539, where Demetrius found me dying among

160

the corpses and decided I was worth saving, or corrupting. I never got to ask why; he left as soon as the ice spread from my fingertips.

Jude's question brings me back to the present, to those inquisitive eyes. "So, how did you survive?"

"A powerful fire witch, a friend of my mother's, created spells specifically to bridge that gap. Bound them directly into my mother's Grimoire."

"Why a book?" Jude asks.

"It didn't have to be. The spells could've been bound to any object. But the Grimoire already held centuries of my family's magic, residual power from generations of spells. That existing energy made the binding stronger, gave the new spells something to anchor to."

"So, it's generating life force constantly?"

"Exactly."

"Can't you just...not use magic?" Jude asks.

I shake my head. "Being a witch isn't something I *do*. It's something I am. There's no off switch. It's always active, like a second metabolism. Even if I never deliberately use magic, my witch side is constantly functioning in the background, seeking energy to sustain itself. I can't turn it off any more than I can turn off being a vampire."

"What happens without the artificial life force, without the Grimoire?" Jude asks once the information has settled in his mind.

I pause, thinking of my failing powers, the uncontrolled lashing of my ice magic. "Without it, everything becomes *unstable*." An understatement, but he doesn't need to worry.

Jude shifts in his chair, hesitating before he speaks. "Is that what happened earlier? In the secret room? The ice. The cold. That wasn't normal vampire abilities, was it?"

I should have known he'd ask.

"No," I admit quietly. "It wasn't."

Nine years without my Grimoire, and I'm learning just how serious the High Priestess was when she warned me this wasn't a cure, merely a reprieve, that I should never let that book out of my sight. That the spells holding me in balance will eventually degrade...

The silence stretches between us.

Jude doesn't pry further about my condition. "Who has it now?" he asks instead.

I study his face and find no ill intent, no hidden agenda, only curiosity. So, I answer truthfully, "The last suspected sighting was in a private collection about three years ago."

"How do you know it was your book?"

"Misfortune never follows far behind the Grimoire."

Jude leans forward. "What kind of misfortune?"

"The kind that makes underwriters nervous. Sudden business failures, health crises, family tragedies, mysterious accidents." I walk to my desk to pull up a file on my laptop, showing him the pattern I've been tracking as he comes to stand behind me. "At first glance, it looks like random bad luck. But when you map it chronologically..."

"It follows the book." His eyes light up with understanding. "It's cursed."

"Protected," I correct. It was never meant for anyone but me. "There are safeguards built into it. Without a De Crevena to unlock it, whoever possesses the book gradually faces escalating consequences. It's designed to make the book too dangerous to keep."

Jude pauses for a moment. "So, what exactly do you need me to do?"

I stand again, beginning to pace. "I need you to trace

its movement through the insurance claims. Find the pattern of ownership transfers. Dig for a needle in a haystack."

Jude's steady heartbeat is the only sound in the room as he processes the information.

"What happens if we can't find it?" he asks finally, his voice steady.

I don't have to think about answering; I've asked myself that same question too many times.

"My two natures will eventually become completely incompatible," I say quietly.

"You could die?" he asks, gaze unreadable.

"I could cease to exist in any meaningful way." There is no point sugarcoating it. "But yes." I don't elaborate on the details because I can't bear to see him pity me.

"How long do you have?"

I think of my trembling hands, the slowed speed, my ice magic lashing out at him earlier without my conscious control. "I don't know. The deterioration seems to be accelerating."

"And if we *do* find it?"

I smile, but there's no warmth in it. "Then we'll have to take it back from whoever currently owns it. And they likely won't want to give it up voluntarily."

"Stealing it, you mean."

"Reclaiming it," I correct. "It was mine first. It belongs to my bloodline."

He sits back down in his chair, silently weighing up the personal stakes that are higher than initially disclosed.

"You could walk away," I offer, imploring his gaze. "I could pay you for the work you've already done, give you enough money to start fresh somewhere else. No shame in deciding this is too much."

Even as I speak the words, I know that it's not what I want.

But it's not my choice to make.

Jude looks up at me and I see his decision before he speaks it.

"I'll stay." He smiles. "I want to."

CHAPTER 20
THE VISITOR

(JUDE)

It's been almost two weeks since I learned how long an hour can be; how fucking heavy a book can get.

Two weeks of living in Adriana's house, working for her, dressing in the clothes she's picked out for me, eating when she tells me to eat, sleeping when she tells me.

And honestly? It's nice not to have to think about those things and have someone else take responsibility for my health, my well-being.

She's even got me back in the gym, with Felix reporting back to her on my performance. It's the first time since I dropped out sixteen months ago that I have a regular routine again, and my mind is as happy as my body. Someone keeping track of my numbers, expecting me to show up—it's such a small thing, one I didn't know I'd been grieving.

No training this week, though. Felix is off for a few days, gone home for his sister's 50th birthday.

I'm at the penthouse alone, nose deep in research, as I've been all day.

Adriana has been out since sunset, doing work things…whatever it is she does. I know her explanation of being an 'art dealer' is the sanitized version. But it's all I know at this stage.

An unexpected knock on the front door startles me from the screen.

What the fuck?

Nobody is supposed to be knocking.

How did they even get up the elevator? The penthouse button only works with the doorman's fancy keycard.

The knock sounds again, more urgent this time.

Maybe they'll go away.

They don't.

A third knock.

Shit, what do I do?

My brief is to work hard, focus, and not snoop—in that order. Adriana said she might even let me come if I stick to that.

She hadn't allowed me a release since that first night, when she milked my cock dry in the bathroom.

Since then, it's been pure torture on the *release* front.

Just work, eat, sleep, repeat. Routine.

But this persistent knocking is not part of the routine.

"Adriana! Just open up! It's me!" whoever is on the other side of the door demands, as they hammer away.

Okay, so not a stranger.

Someone who knows Adriana lives here.

Perhaps an enemy? Though the familiar use of "it's me" suggests the contrary.

She didn't say she was expecting anyone, but she also didn't say *not* to open the door.

My curiosity gets the better of me. It's been a lonely few days anyway, wandering around the apartment without Felix around to chat to.

I go downstairs with zero intention of opening the door. My initial plan is to just look through the peephole to see who is outside.

Until I see who it is.

Holy fuck!

My heart jumps into my throat as I squeeze my one eye shut to peer through the little hole.

Even in that tiny circle, his features are unmistakable.

It's him! The same man from Adriana's memories, from the painting, from my secret research missions that she doesn't know about.

Cyrus.

Before common sense can enter the chat, my fingers undo the latch, opening the door.

The man outside freezes, mid-knock, deadly stare homing in on me as his eyes narrow.

I forget to breathe as we size each other up.

Cyrus looks me up and down, lips tugged into a sly grin that makes my overstimulated and unsatisfied cock jump with need. *Down boy!*

His dark-brown-nearly-black hair is cut in a modern fade that's longer in front, falling over intense amber eyes that flicker with those same gold cracks Adriana's have. Pierced ears, nose…and those lips—they are full, fuller than a man's should be, kissable.

Christ, get a grip, Jude. Deep breaths.

"Hello?" I dare, as I rake my eyes over his tight, dark jeans and leather jacket outfit, complete with motorcycle boots and a thick belt.

His gaze holds mine when I reach it, and I freeze under it, pinned in place.

"Aha, and who is this fine specimen?" Cyrus asks in a Spanish accent that drips with charm.

He leans against the doorframe as he inspects me, crossing his arms over his chest. He doesn't look more than a few years older than me, but I know age can be deceptive with immortals.

Not knowing what else to do, I reach my hand out in greeting, exhaling slowly to try and regain my composure. "Jude. Jude Cole."

The six-foot-something gothic god before me takes my hand in his but doesn't shake it; no, he brings it to his lips, pressing a gentle kiss to my skin that makes my cock perk up and my breath hitch. *Fucking hell, this man is intoxicating.*

"Aha, the new Elijah," he remarks, holding onto my hand a moment longer.

"I don't know who that is."

He raises a single brow. "Do you know what a familiar is?"

I tug my hand back, offended. "Of course I do," I scoff. "But I'm not her familiar. I'm her research assistant."

Cyrus smirks. "Sure. At least it confirms I have indeed found the right apartment. Though my nose knew that already." He moves even closer. "Where's Adriana?" His question is urgent, a small crack in his overconfident presentation.

"She's not home right now."

"I'll wait."

I hesitate. "Not sure that's a good idea."

"What if I promise I won't eat you, even though you

168

look absolutely delicious?" Cyrus licks his lips, and I swallow loudly, much to his amusement.

He bursts out laughing, a sound so infectious, it's hard not to get sucked into his world.

"I really don't think—" I start, but he cuts me off.

"Come on, 'Jude, Jude Cole,' be a good host. It's freezing out here, and I've traveled a very long way to see her." He shivers dramatically, though I know by now that vampires don't actually feel the cold. "Just until she gets back?"

Every instinct screams that this is a terrible idea, but his smile is disarming, and there's something magnetic about him that makes it hard to think clearly. Plus, he knows Adriana. They have history. Surely it can't hurt to let him wait inside? She kept his painting on the wall after all. She could've thrown it away…

"I suppose…just for a few minutes," I hear myself saying, moving out of the way.

"You're an angel," Cyrus grins, stepping across the threshold.

Too late, I realize what I've done: I've invited a vampire into Adriana's home.

"Fuck," I breathe, the weight of my mistake settling onto my shoulders.

Cyrus turns to me with raised eyebrows, his grin widening. "Language, boy. Though I do appreciate a man who knows when he's made an error in judgment."

"You tricked me into letting you in."

"I asked politely. You said yes. No trickery involved." He shrugs off his leather jacket, revealing a black shirt that clings to his muscular, tattooed frame, seriously hindering my ability to think straight. "Besides, the whole having to

169

invite a vampire into your space thing is bullshit. I didn't have to ask. I was trying to be nice."

He moves through the space like it's his, trailing his fingers along surfaces. "She's got some new pieces. I like it. Very...her."

"How long has it been?" I ask despite myself, following him toward the living room, trying to keep distance between us to give myself time to react if he tries anything. Not that I could do anything if he did. I'm a *mere mortal*, as Adriana likes to remind me.

"How long since I've seen her?" Cyrus pretends to ponder the question. "Oh, maybe a decade. We don't exactly exchange Christmas cards." He settles onto the couch, patting the seat beside him. "Come, sit. Tell me about yourself, Jude Cole."

I remain standing. "I'd rather not."

"Afraid I'll bite?" His voice drops to a husky whisper that makes warm desire coil in my stomach despite my fear.

"Should I be?"

"That depends entirely on whether you're into that sort of thing." His eyes rake over me appraisingly. "And something tells me you might be."

Heat floods my cheeks. "I don't know what you're talking about."

"Of course you don't." He stands quickly, quicker than a human body could move, closing the distance between us before I can step away. "You smell like her, you know. Like she's been *tasting*."

My hand instinctively goes to my throat, where Adriana's bite marks from last night have long since faded.

"Ah, there it is." Cyrus's smile turns predatory. "She has been feeding from you. Lucky you."

"It's not like that," I protest, though my voice lacks conviction.

"Isn't it?" He circles me slowly, like a spider approaching something caught in its web. "Living in her house, wearing the type of clothes she likes, letting her drink from that pretty throat. What would you call it?"

"Research." I swallow loudly. "I'm helping her find something."

"The Grimoire." It's not a question. "Of course. Quite the treasure hunt she's set you on."

My blood runs cold. "How do you know about that?"

"I know a lot of things, *niño*." His grin is all predator as he calls me a boy. "Tell me, have you found it yet?"

I cross my arms over my chest defensively, taking a step back. "What do you want with it?"

Avoiding the question, Cyrus just smiles mysteriously, reaching out to trail a finger along my jawline. "You really are lovely. I can see why she's keeping you around. So full of life. She always did have a soft spot for a pretty face."

I try to step back further, but he follows, backing me up into the kitchen.

My heart hammers against my ribs as I stumble backward. Yet something about the idea of being manhandled by this incredible half-god that oozes sex and charm isn't quite that unappealing.

"She'll be back soon," I manage, exhaling slowly.

"I hope so. I've missed her." His voice turns wistful for a moment before sharpening again. "But that gives us time to get acquainted, doesn't it?"

My back hits the refrigerator with a soft thud. It hums steadily behind me, warm, solid.

Cyrus plants one hand on either side of my head, caging me in with his body. This close, the spice and

171

leather scent that seems to cling to his skin fills my entire orbit.

We're about the same height—he's got maybe an inch on me—and I'm definitely bulkier than him, but he somehow stands taller, larger than life.

"*Please*," I whisper, though I'm not entirely sure what I'm asking for.

"Please *what*, little human?" His voice is barely above a murmur as he caresses my cheek with a light touch. "Please stop? Please continue? Please fuck me senseless? You'll have to be more specific."

Terror and arousal war in my chest as he leans closer. There's an unnatural stillness to him; his chest doesn't rise and fall with breath he doesn't need, just like Adriana's. But he's nothing like her at all.

What's his deal?

He's beautiful and dangerous and completely out of my league. He could literally kill me. Yet I still can't bring myself to put up a fight.

"I can hear your heart racing," he murmurs against my ear. "Are you afraid of me, Jude?"

"Yes," I breathe.

"Good. You should be." His lips brush against my throat, above the spot where Adriana's fangs pierced my skin last night, and pretty much every second night before that. "But you're also turned on. Naughty boy." He presses his body against mine.

I can't deny it, can't explain it. This vampire, this centuries-old beast who could end my life without breaking a sweat, is pressed against me, and my body is responding like he's exactly what I've been craving.

I'm not the only one excited, though. His erection

pressing against mine is so impossibly large, it stills the air in my chest at the mere thought of it.

"She's trained you well," Cyrus continues, his voice honey-smooth and deadly. "So responsive, so eager to please. I wonder..."

His fangs extend as I hold my breath, genuine fear spiking through my arousal.

This isn't Adriana. I don't know him, don't trust him, don't know if he'll stop when I ask him to.

"Don't," I gasp, my hands coming up to push weakly against his chest.

"Don't what?" But there's something darker in his voice now, something that makes every survival instinct I have scream in alarm.

Oh god, this is how I die, isn't it?

CHAPTER 21
BLOOD REMEMBERS

(ADRIANA)

The familiar scent hits me before I even reach the door: sandalwood and leather, and that distinctive undertone of saffron. After nearly four hundred years, I would know it anywhere. *Cyrus.*

But it can't be.

Every step toward my apartment drags like time has stretched itself thin and slow. My supernatural senses are overwhelmed by the familiar presence that shouldn't be here, can't be here, but undeniably is.

A scream speeds time up again. It's Jude.

No!

I crash through the door, rushing to the kitchen.

The scene that greets me is my worst nightmare and deepest desire wrapped into one devastating moment.

Cyrus has Jude pinned against the refrigerator, fangs out, close enough to bite, close enough to kill, to steal the one good thing I've allowed myself in decades.

"Cyrus!" His name tears from my throat like a battle cry. It feels strange on my lips after nine years of pretending I couldn't still sometimes sense him in my dreams.

Grinning, he turns toward me, and time stops altogether.

He looks exactly the same, of course. He still has that mischievous smile that used to make emperors nervous and has never failed to make heat coil in my stomach like a living, hungry thing.

"Let. Him. Go!"

The command carries every ounce of authority I've accumulated over my lifetimes, but it doesn't touch him. It never has. Cyrus bows to no one; he responds to nothing but equal force and matching passion.

"Adriana—" he starts, but I cut him off.

"Leave!" I snarl, taking a step into my own kitchen that suddenly feels like a war zone.

His smile widens, and I see the boy he was when we first met—reckless and charming and completely unafraid of consequences.

"My love," he says, like it hasn't been nearly ten years since he left me to die, like the last words between us weren't accusations and curses, like he has any right to that endearment after what he did…or didn't do.

The affection in his voice stops me cold. It's too familiar.

I shift my gaze to Jude, who's trembling with a mixture of fear and arousal that I can smell from across the room, and fury surges through me again.

"Now, why would I leave?" Cyrus continues, his fangs still out, still too close to Jude's throat. "I've just arrived."

That's it. Enough!

I move faster than sound, crossing the space between us in a heartbeat.

Grabbing Cyrus's shoulders before he can react, I haul him away from Jude with enough force to send him staggering backward.

"Don't touch him," I hiss through gritted teeth, positioning myself between Jude and the unpredictable threat.

Cyrus recovers his balance easily. "Protective, aren't we, Adriana? How *maternal*."

I don't answer him, don't take the bait.

"Jude," I say without taking my eyes off Cyrus. "Go to your room. Lock the door."

"But—"

"Now!"

He hesitates, then the soft sound of his footsteps retreats out of the kitchen. *Good.* It's too dangerous for him here.

"Still giving orders, I see," Cyrus observes, moving closer. "Some things never change."

I cross my arms over my chest and square out my shoulders. "And you're still showing up uninvited and threatening what's mine."

"Yours?" His laugh is sharp, bitter. "Have you started taking in *pets* again, *querida*?"

The casual dismissal of Jude makes something dark and violent bubble up in my chest. "He's not a pet."

"No? Then what is he? Your *research assistant*?" Cyrus's voice drips with mockery as he makes air quotes. "Come now, love. I can smell him on you. You've been feeding from him. Probably fucking him too."

"That's none of your business," I reply too quickly. He

doesn't need to know our intimacy hasn't progressed to that point, that I've been purposefully trying to put distance between us, boundaries.

"Isn't it?" He shakes his head slowly. "When did you become so domestic? So *tame*?"

The words hit their target. I've always prided myself on being untamed, ungovernable, a force of nature that bent the world to my will. But looking at Cyrus now, enveloped in that wild energy that crackles around him like static, I realize how much I've changed in his absence; I'm a mere shadow of who I used to be.

He's winding me up, gaslighting me into reacting. I know his patterns. Yet I'm too worked up after seeing Jude in that vulnerable position to have any defenses against his old tricks.

"Why are you here?" I demand, changing the topic.

"I missed you," he answers nonchalantly, smile widening until his cheeks touch his eyes.

"Missed me?" I laugh, but it comes out hollow. "Is that what you call it? Miss me enough to—"

"To what?" Cyrus steps closer. "To keep searching for you all these years, despite you cutting me off like I'm no one."

"Don't you dare!" The words explode out of me. "You have no idea what I've been through!"

"And me? What about me?" he spits out. "You've never learned how to forgive!"

We're shouting now, circling each other like the animals we are. All the hard-won control I've built is cracking, revealing the raw wound underneath.

"Forgive you?" I snarl. "For what you did? For how you—"

"For being what I am!" His eyes are all black now,

pupils huge. "For loving you the only way I know how. For making mistakes that I can't take back."

"You nearly destroyed me!" I counter.

"And you think I don't know that?" He lunges forward, not to attack but to grab my shoulders, his fingers digging in hard enough to bruise. "You think I don't remember every detail of every choice that led to losing you?"

I try to pull away, but his grip tightens.

"Let go of me." It's a threat, not a request.

"No." His voice drops to a whisper. "I've let go of you too many times. I won't do it again."

Something snaps in me. The rage, the pain, the desperate hunger I've been suppressing, explodes. I wrench free of his grip and strike him across the face with enough force to break a human's neck.

Cyrus's head snaps back, a drop of blood blooming on his lip, but he's smiling when he looks at me again.

"There she is," he murmurs. "There's my Warrior Queen; *mi Reina*."

The possessive claim makes me see red.

I launch myself at him, fangs out.

We crash into the living room, destroying furniture as we go, snarling and clawing.

He's stronger than I remember, faster, but his moves are as familiar as my own reflection. We've done this dance countless times over four centuries: fighting and fucking with equal passion, violence, and love so intertwined it's hard to separate them.

I pin him against the wall, my hand around his throat, but he just grins at me with bloody teeth. We both know his fighting skills have always been superior, more practiced. And without my Grimoire, I'm even more outmatched.

"I've missed *this* too," he gasps.

And then, before I can stop him, his fangs are in my throat.

The world explodes!

Every memory, every moment of connection we've ever shared, crashes into me at once.

The blood bond that I've been fighting for a decade reasserts itself with devastating force, dragging me back into the maelstrom of *us*.

There is no rational thought left in my mind, no thought of any kind, when my fangs extend by their own will and sink into his skin.

My body is on autopilot, the reptilian in charge.

His memories flood through me: the nine years of wandering aimlessly across continents, trying to forget the taste of my blood and failing; the battles fought just to feel something other than the aching emptiness of separation; how he'd stand on rooftops in cities I'd never been to, scanning crowds for a face he knew he wouldn't find; the clawing need that never faded, never dimmed, never gave him a moment's peace.

I drowned him out, but he never closed the connection. He kept the bond open, *hoping*.

I know it's a two-way street; he can feel me too, my memories, my emotions, the truth that I never stopped loving him, even when I hated him, *especially* when I hated him.

We exchange blood with desperate hunger, years of separation trying to be healed in a single moment. The power surge is out of this world, incomparable to anything else. Every sense is heightened beyond reason, every emotion amplified until I fear I might shatter from the intensity.

When we finally break apart, gasping unnecessarily, his forehead rests against mine. For a moment, we're us again.

"I've missed you," he repeats in a whisper against my lips.

"Don't you fucking—"

He silences me with a kiss that tastes like blood and yearning and four hundred years of shared history.

My traitorous body responds immediately, my hands tangling in his hair, pulling him closer until there's no space left between us.

This is what I've been running from. This intensity, this connection that makes everything else pale in comparison. Being with Cyrus is like mainlining starlight: beautiful and addictive and ultimately destructive.

But gods, I've missed it...missed *him*. He makes me feel alive beyond what immortality alone can offer. *But at what cost?*

When we break apart, reality crashes back in.

I'm furious at myself for giving in, for letting my hard-won independence crumble at the first taste of his blood. I'm furious at him for being here, for looking at me like we were still us. But most of all, I'm furious that my body remembers every touch, every caress, every way he used to take me apart and put me back together.

"This doesn't change anything," I say, but my voice lacks conviction.

"Doesn't it?" Cyrus's thumb traces my lower lip, coming away bloody. "You can feel it too."

I do. It's there, the connection thrumming between us like a live wire, his emotions bleeding into mine like they're *ours*. Nine years of separation haven't weakened our bond. They've made it desperate, hungry, impossible to ignore.

"Why are you here, Cyrus?" I ask again, though I'm no longer sure I want the answer.

His expression shifts, becoming guarded in a way that sets off warning bells in my mind. "I told you, I missed you."

"That's not all of it."

For a moment, I hope he might tell me the truth. Then his mask slides back into place, and he gives me that reckless grin that's gotten us both into trouble more times than I can count.

Usually, I would get the answers I need straight from his blood, but today, it's too much to sift through. The surge of memories, of emotions, is too powerful after being apart for so long. I can't pick out anything but snippets, ghosts of feelings in the maelstrom that is this emotional being.

"Can't a man visit his favorite ex-lover without ulterior motives?" His tone is light but I don't buy it.

I step back, ripping myself away, putting distance between us. "We're not doing this again."

"Aren't we?" He licks a drop of blood from his lips. "Because it looks very much like we already are."

He's right, and I hate him for it, hate myself more for how much I want to surrender to this chaotic dance that's defined my existence for centuries.

But I'm not the same person I was nine years ago. I won't let Cyrus destroy my peace—not again. Even if every cell in my undead body is screaming for more of his touch, more of his blood.

No, I can't.

"You need to leave," I say, and this time I mean it.

"I'm not going anywhere, *querida*. Not again."

Growing more flustered, I throw my hands up in the air. "You were never much of a listener." I start to walk away but he grabs my arm, pulling me back with such force that I crash into his chest.

My response is violent, instant, a slap to the face that he intercepts, throwing me against the wall with the mere flick of his wrist.

"You asshole!"

There is no holding back now. I launch at him, clawing at his face, drawing blood across his cheek. All the years of pent-up emotion bubble to the surface, ready to explode.

Cyrus laughs. "Come now, *mi Reina*." He grabs both my wrists, pinning me to the wall, pressing his body into me.

Gods, that scent. That fucking scent. Four hundred years later, and it still makes me want to lean in when I should be pushing away.

He kisses me messily, hungrily, giving me no room to think. "Say you missed me too."

I let out a loud growl as I break free, wrapping my fingers around his neck, squeezing, as he rips my dress out of the way.

There are so many things I've wanted to say to him over the past nine years, but the words are lost in some other part of my brain, a part not in control right now.

How we go from fighting to fucking happens as quickly as it always does, like a comet hurling at a planet, unstoppable, *inevitable.*

Raw passion surges until it explodes in a blinding storm, fully driven by primal desires, no room for conscious thought.

The moment he plunges his cock inside me, my ripped

dress hiked up, panties to the side, my body held up against the wall in those strong arms covered in tattoos and scars in equal measure, the world comes undone at the seams, and I know I'm not winning this battle.

"You fucking asshole!" I repeat but he just grins, thrusting into me again.

I've missed him too.

CHAPTER 22
VOYEURISTIC INTENTIONS

(JUDE)

U sually, I do everything I can to please Lady Adriana. But when she tells me to go to my room, I know there is no way I'm about to obey that order.

Instead, I crouch behind the staircase, hiding around the corner as I watch the vampires damn near rip the skin off each other's bodies.

What the hell is happening?

The question loops through my mind as I try to process my world. One moment I'm researching antiquities databases, the next I'm face-to-face with what has to be the most alluring man I've ever met. And now—this?

Cyrus. The name from the painting. He's here, in the flesh, real.

Only a fool would think they can't sense my presence, yet I don't move, don't leave, don't do anything but stare at them in wonder as my growing erection presses uncomfortably against my pants.

It's a passion I cannot fathom. *So damn intense!*

My breath stills in my chest as Cyrus grabs Adriana by the throat. She fights back, her fangs protruding in threat as they smash through walls and knock over furniture like it's all made of matchsticks.

This isn't the reserved, poised Adriana I know. No, this is something wild unleashed, and watching her match Cyrus blow for blow is stirring fresh, demented desires deep inside me.

When Cyrus pins her up against the wall, high off the ground, I damn near come on the spot.

For reasons I'll never be able to justify, I want to be caught between them, claimed by both, consumed by a passion that transcends mortality itself.

I've never been particularly concerned with gender when it comes to attraction—people are people, desire is desire—but this is the first time I've felt pulled toward two people simultaneously with equal intensity.

Perhaps it's just the effect vampires have on humans, or perhaps it's just the effect they have on *me*.

A moment ago, I was fearing for my life, convinced that all Adriana would find of me when she got home would be an empty husk, drained of all blood. And the worst part? I would've gladly let Cyrus have his way with me and take whatever he needed.

What a devastatingly beautiful creature: dangerous, impulsive, and hungry, in more ways than one.

But then she came back; my Milady came back to save me.

Watching her fight for me, actually fight, does something to my brain chemistry.

And what a fight.

I didn't expect the scene that followed to be straight out of some violent ballet. Or maybe a sequel to that *Mr & Mrs Smith* movie. It's hard to tell the passion of love from the passion of hate, and it's never more unclear than when Adriana flings the tattooed vampire across the room as though he's weightless, his blood dripping down her chin.

Why do I find this so fucking arousing?

What's wrong with you, Jude?

My thesis covered the theoretical erotics of supernatural power but experiencing it firsthand is like the difference between reading about fire and being burned alive.

When they crash into each other, snarling and magnificent, I have to bite down on my bottom lip to keep from moaning out loud.

Any rational person would be running for the door, doing something other than crouching under the stairs, getting harder by the second as two vampires try to destroy each other.

But there is no way I can look away.

Cyrus is magnificent in his fury.

And Adriana? *Christ.*

It's difficult to marry this image of Adriana as the uncaged beast with the version I carry in my mind. My Adriana asks if I'm comfortable, worries about my well-being. This Adriana is pure animal, deadly. I want both, want *all* parts of her.

When Cyrus bites down on her throat, I audibly gasp.

The sound that escapes her isn't pain; it's a sigh of relief.

Moments later, her own fangs sink into his throat as they exchange blood, still destroying the furniture like they're mere inconveniences.

If you didn't know any better, you'd think it's just two people making out, kissing each other's necks. But I know it's more, so much more.

I'm so turned on I can barely think straight.

Should I be jealous?

Because I'm not jealous, not exactly. How can I be jealous of a history spanning longer than my life? No, I want this. Want to be part of this so fucking badly, it hurts.

But why would they want a worthless mortal like me?

I'd be delusional to think I'm anything more than a meal with research credentials. But it doesn't stop me wanting more, doesn't make me leave.

When they finally break apart, the conflict written across both their faces is plain to see.

Adriana's voice when she tells him to leave is steady.

Despite the rational voice in my head screaming that I'm way over my head, I find myself hoping Cyrus doesn't listen to her, that he stays.

I want this, want *them*, even if I'm trapped in the eye of a storm that's been brewing for longer than my lifespan.

He touches her in ways I would never dare, possessively, owning every inch of her body with such familiarity, such intimacy. The confidence in his hands, his certainty in drawing a response from her, makes the blush creep down my neck.

But I don't look away; I can't.

Slowly, I reach down to free my cock from my pants. It's too hard to keep it tucked away. I know I shouldn't, not without permission, but I touch myself anyway, gentle touches, biting down a moan that threatens to draw the attention of the two fighting ancients.

When Cyrus unsheathes his own erection, another powerful ripple of lust rushes through me. Even from my hiding spot, I can tell he's as big as I thought. With confidence like that, of course, he has a big dick. But it's not only the size that's got my breath racing; it's the shiny row of golden piercing bars running down his shaft like a ladder. *Imagine*—

The sound that comes from Adriana's lips when he rips her underwear to the side and fucks her into the wall has my heart stilling in my chest.

How many times have I imagined what it must feel like to bury my cock deep inside her?

Since the day she first walked into the bookstore, I've been unable to shake the fantasy of being inside her.

Not like what is happening with Cyrus; I know I'm not that guy. No, I want to enter her slowly, carefully, deliberately, as she holds me tight, using my body like a flesh dildo, taking what's hers.

But this? This raw primal lust of another immortal being, plunging into her with such force that the wall behind Adriana visibly cracks, this is only for voyeuristic indulgence.

And my god, what an indulgence.

When Adriana screams out in orgasm, my favorite sound in the world, followed by the indecent grunts from Cyrus, I nearly spill my load, joining them in release. But I don't dare. Not without Adriana's permission. I'm already in enough trouble for being here, touching myself.

I freeze when Cyrus's amber eyes find mine across the room, his face contorted in passion. He grins, puckers his lips to blow me a kiss, and then grabs Adriana again, kissing her deeply, like he could fuse them together by sheer force.

I am a kid caught with his hand in the cookie jar: guilty, ashamed, but also a million times more aroused than if my hand were in a cookie jar versus wrapped around my leaking cock, which it is.

Fucking hell, what have I gotten myself into?

One vampire is risky enough, but two? This is madness.

Yet, I can't think of anywhere I'd rather be.

CHAPTER 23

HATE TO LOVE YOU

(CYRUS)

Nobody would believe me if I told them I didn't come here expecting Adriana and I to fall into old habits.

It wasn't supposed to go like *this*.

So much time has passed since the last time I held my Queen, tasted her, had her blood coursing through my veins. *Oh, sweet suffering*, I'd forgotten what her proximity does to me, her scent.

How could I ever have thought I'm better off without her?

I tried to convince myself that it could never be how it was, that our story was a beautiful memory, forever destined to make me sentimental during special songs.

But now, with my cock inside her where it belongs, I know that it was all lies.

She was always the one.

Fuck, how does she feel this good?

I've been trying to move on, to focus on other

relationships, to make something of my life that was just mine, not ours...but it all crumbles the instant she moans my name in that breathless voice I have burned cities to the ground for.

"*Dios mío*, Adriana," I groan, kissing her fervently, urgently, as though a kiss could ever express how much it had hurt me to be apart from her all these years, to have our bond severed, not only physically but completely.

I tried so many countries, so many creatures, but it was never this, never this raw intensity that made my bones ache and my mind race.

She's missed me too. She won't say it, but I can taste the truth when I pull her hair to the side and sink my fangs into her.

Her taste is all vehement lust and fury, mixed with the care and need I know is not for me, but for the human. There is something off too, something worrying her...but it dissipates as quickly as it rises.

The rush is blinding, more exhilarating than the purest hit of heroin. Nothing compares to the blood of a vampire so ancient, so powerful. But it's not just age. It's *her*.

Instantly, I'm delirious with her taste, her presence, her overwhelming emotions.

Holy fuck, the relief.

Hundreds of fucks. Maybe more. But nothing comes close to the intimacy of plunging into the one person who feels like home, who always has. The aching for her had dulled but never left.

Adriana screams my name as we crash through a wall, my cock still inside her.

I'm moments from tumbling over the edge myself, moments from release. I warn her in between rapid gasps as we destroy her living room.

Her precious pet is watching, the one she has all these soft and warm feelings for. I can taste him in her memories, taste her *yearning*.

Knowing he's watching further fuels my need. I want him to see, want him dripping with lust as I fuck the object of his desire.

"I fucking hate you," Adriana hisses moments before she topples over the edge. The orgasm rips through her body, and mine.

"*Mi Reina*—" My Queen. There are no full sentences left in my mind. I'm falling right off that edge with her, repeating her name in broken whispers as I press her tightly against me, inhaling deeply, wishing I could keep this moment forever.

But I know her better than that. Moments like these don't last.

Even as the euphoria of her release bleeds into mine, I know this moment was inevitable but not sustainable.

Less than a minute later, Adriana pushes me off her, face contorted in disgust that I know is as much for me as it is for herself, for her moment of weakness.

And there it is.

It was always hard to come back after a separation period, like she had to get used to me again first. And this time, it's been nearly ten years...

"Go away, Cyrus, before I make you." Adriana's voice cracks over the threat as she pulls her torn dress back in place, Italian curses falling from her lips under her breath.

Fuck, she's beautiful when she's angry. Always has been. Makes me want to kiss her and fight her and claim her all at once.

"I'm tempted to say 'make me,'" I quip.

She doesn't say anything, just glares at me, as I put my

sticky dick back in my pants with slow, deliberate movements, letting her watch. I memorize every line of her face, every curve of her body as she does, because I don't know when I'll see her again. Don't know if she'll forgive me for what I did, what I came here to do, what I was *supposed* to do.

It would've been easier if she had acted like I was a stranger. Or like she didn't care. But her little pet distracted her, made her vulnerable.

If he weren't here, I'm sure things would've gone differently.

I can still taste her desperation in my mouth, remember how she clung to me like I was her last breath. That's not indifference. That's not someone who's moved on.

That's someone who's been as broken by our separation as I have been.

But with Adriana, her wanting something has never been enough.

That mind of hers is steadfast.

"You're thinking too loud," she snaps, running a hand over her hair to try and smooth it out. "Whatever scheme you're cooking up in that head of yours, forget it."

This is my chance to ask, to find out what I came here for. But I can't. Not while my body is rushing with her blood. My mind is empty save for her memories, her feelings. It's too much to process all at once.

This is dangerous.

"I need to go," I say finally, and her expression shifts, relief mixed with something that might be disappointment. Perhaps I'm being too hopeful.

"Good. Don't come back." Adriana crosses her arms over her chest.

"We both know that's not going to happen, my love."

She doesn't deny it. Can't probably. Not with my blood still singing in her veins, our bond reasserting itself after nine years of silence.

I head toward the hallway where the human is hiding. Poor boy probably got quite an education tonight. The scent of his arousal is thick in the air; he enjoyed the show.

"Jude, Jude Cole," I call softly.

He emerges from behind the staircase like a guilty schoolboy, all flushed cheeks and bright eyes. *Angelic almost.* No wonder Adriana's protective of him.

"I—" he starts, but I cut him off.

"No need, *pequeño*. If I had front row seats to that kind of show, I'd watch too."

His blush deepens, and I can hear his pulse racing. Not fear this time, but pure want. *Interesting.*

I step closer. "Take care of her for me."

"I don't understand…"

"You will." I cup his face with one hand, thumb tracing his lower lip.

Before he can ask what I mean, I kiss him—deep, thorough…proper.

He melts into it for a moment and then pulls back with wide, shocked eyes, breath hitched, pupils massive.

I reach for his neck, tilting his head to the side slightly.

So close. I wonder…

"Cyrus!" Adriana's voice stops me at the threshold, pulling me back before I succumb to temptation and sample the thrumming pulse.

When I turn, she's standing in the doorway, fully dressed but still looking thoroughly fucked. "If you're planning something stupid—"

"When am I not?" I grin at her. "But this time, it's the right kind of stupid."

"That's what worries me." She reaches over and pulls Jude from my arms into hers, holding him protectively against her body.

"Trust me, *querida*. Just this once. It will be fine." I smile. "I'm fixing it."

She doesn't answer, but she doesn't need to. It all seeps through the bond. The distrust, the anger, and the faintest flicker of nostalgia.

It's something at least. Something I can work with.

For now, I need to get the fuck out of here so I can think. Which is impossible to do with the proximity of these two.

"See you soon, darlings." Then I step into a shadow and disappear.

This was not how tonight was supposed to go.

They're going to be furious.

I'm so fucked.

CHAPTER 24
CLEAN UP

(ADRIANA)

Cyrus's blood is still rushing through my veins, and with it come the memories. *Our* memories.

The Between Court, 1739. *Why does it always come back to this night?*

Moon wine swirled in golden goblets in all the colors of the universe mixed into one, tempting and forbidden. I should have known better.

'One cup.' Cyrus had grinned at me across the table, that reckless smile that could seduce and infuriate in equal measure, already spelling trouble. *'What's the worst that could happen?'*

Famous last words.

The taboo wine tasted unlike anything I had sampled before, sweet and salty at the same time, prickly with effervescence, yet somehow smoother than any drink in existence. Cyrus said it tasted like the color orange on a cloudy day.

It didn't make us drunk so much as it changed us.

Every sensation heightened until the world became nothing but feeling and want, and *him*. Like the world conspired to be its most breathtaking self, just for one night, sparkling around the edges with a hazy shimmer.

Cyrus plucked a flower from a tree that grew gemstones and tucked it behind my ear with trembling fingers. *'You're magnificent, mi amor.'*

'So are you,' I breathed back, and meant it.

I will never know if he bit me first or I bit him, but the world exploded the moment our blood exchanged, Fae laughter tinkling around us as the soundtrack to our bad decisions.

His blood hit my tongue, and I lost myself in him. Not only his taste but *him*, his memories, thoughts, his very soul pouring into mine while mine flowed into his, our histories intertwining into a single stream, an invisible thread spun between us, binding us with magic older than the Between Court itself.

Unlike with the human blood bags, the connection didn't fade to nothing when we stopped drinking. Cyrus was still there, in my head, while I experienced every intense emotion that passed through his body as he looked at me with fire in those amber eyes.

It wasn't supposed to be possible. Vampires don't blood-bond to each other; we can't. But my hybrid existence already defied every law of the supernatural world. What was one more impossibility?

We damn near destroyed each other after that. We were opposites in too many ways. The bond made it impossible to live apart, but our natures made it impossible to stay together. After a few months or years of harmony, Cyrus would inevitably storm off in a huff again.

He always came back. Couldn't stand the world without me in it, he said, and I knew he meant it.

And I? I was always foolish enough to believe him capable of change.

But we've never been apart this long. It's been nine years since the last time I had him in my head, in my arms, in my blood—an eternity yet no time at all...

I slump against the wall as I watch Cyrus disappear into the night, leaving his scent, his taste, his very essence behind, not only on me and my space, but also on Jude.

What was he doing here?

We stand in silence for a minute or two, my arms still wrapped around Jude from behind, silently thanking the gods that he still has a beating heart. It wouldn't be the first time an impulsive Cyrus has killed one of my lovers.

No, not lover, I correct myself. Crossing that bridge feels insurmountable.

That's the least of my worries, though.

My mind is racing, my blood on fire, as I try to think through the haze, the rush pulsing through my veins in the aftermath of my exchange with Cyrus.

It's Jude who speaks first, voice soft, breaking. "I'm sorry, Milady."

I know what he's apologizing for. He didn't go to his room as instructed; he stayed and watched. His arousal, his need, knowing that he was there, played no small part in fueling my violent dance with Cyrus.

Perhaps it's precisely because Jude was there, because of the tight-wound sexual tension between us, that things escalated. All the feelings I've been suppressing, all the needs I've been pushing down, telling myself it's so I don't get attached...it all flared up the moment I sank my fangs into Cyrus's vein.

There was no stopping that rollercoaster. My body responded instantly, drunk on the rush of vampire blood. And not just any vampire. An ancient. *My* ancient.

No, not mine anymore.

Jude turns to face me.

I stroke a lock of hair from his brow.

"It's okay, *tesoro*. I'm just glad you're safe." It's true. I don't even want to punish him. The post-feeding glow mixed with the aftermath of the violent orgasm that still ebbs and flows in my veins has made me more forgiving than usual.

"He's...he's a lot," Jude remarks, and a shudder passes through his body, his erection pressing against my stomach—hard, ready.

I chuckle darkly. "You can say that again." Normally, I'd completely spiral by now, furious at myself for the lapse in control. But something about Jude's steady, secure embrace makes the moment feel less like the end of the world.

Sure, I'm no idiot; I know if Cyrus has rocked up, it can only spell trouble. But this time, I'm not so worried about drowning. No, I'm more worried about Jude and the unmistakable desire I see flowing between them.

Gods, watching how Cyrus kissed him made my gut twist in need. Despite the fear, despite the anger.

No, I can't think of that now.

"Come, let's go upstairs. I need to clean up." I squeeze Jude's arm, trying to disengage, but the human holds on firmly, his head pressed against my neck like he's trying to hide.

I smile. "Silly boy, let's go."

"Yes, Milady," he replies, bending down to scoop me up with an arm under my ass.

I smack his chest in mock anger. "Jude! Put me down."

He shakes his head as he defies my order, taking the stairs two at a time. "No! What if you leak all over the carpets? Poor Felix." His logic is weak at best, but I let him carry me to my bedroom, suddenly drained, spent.

I hold onto his neck like I'm a new bride being carried over the threshold, resting my face against his chest, listening to that steady heartbeat—the most magnificent sound.

When he places me down on my bed, gently, treating me as fragile despite all the violence he's seen from me, I let out a deep sigh.

This is not the day I had planned. When I popped out to visit an art exhibition, I never expected to find Cyrus pressed up against Jude in my kitchen upon return.

The effect he had on the boy was not lost on me either. But that's Cyrus for you. He's seduced queens and kings in equal measure, tempted the gods themselves with his lust for life, his unmatched passion, still burning bright even after all this time. *Of course, Jude wants him.*

I don't know what to do with that information, with any of it.

The whole experience is a blur. It all happened in less than thirty minutes. One moment, I'm ready to rip his head off; the next, I'm drowning in the familiar pleasure of having him inside me, of his blood racing through my cold veins. *Gods, he fits so perfectly.*

Snap out of it! I reproach my treacherous thoughts with little chance of success.

I'm getting lost in my mind again, and I know no good can come from it.

Cyrus clearly has ulterior motives, and until I know what those are, it's best to stay vigilant.

Jude's soft cadence brings me back to him. "Can I get you anything, Milady?"

My eyes flutter open, staring into a face etched in concern as the human watches me intently from his position next to the bed.

His heartbeat is still too fast; his cock too hard. It's driving my senses even wilder.

"A towel, maybe?" I feel dirty, sticky...*soiled*. Cyrus didn't even attempt to pull out when he came. No, he emptied his cock deep inside me, thrusting so hard, I nearly saw stars as my own orgasm ripped through my body.

"Yes, Ma'am," Jude replies, darting off to the bathroom like the obedient familiar he isn't. I should school him about the honorifics again, but with the lines blurring this much, I don't see the point. He's certainly acting like my submissive. The same way I'm acting like he's mine. *Unethical at best.*

When he returns, warm, wet cloth in hand, I kick off my ruined panties, opening my thighs for him.

The bed indents under his weight as Jude crawls into the space between my legs, gently placing a hand on each thigh to part them wider.

He doesn't bring the cloth down, though. Just stares at my pussy, biting down hard on his quivering bottom lip.

"What is it?" I ask and note his hesitation, the blush creeping over his cheeks. "Speak your words, darling."

"I...may I? No, fuck...never mind." He shakes his head as he stumbles over the sentences that won't form. *So cute when he gets flustered.*

"Tell me what you want."

He shakes his head. "I shouldn't."

"Jude."

He presses his eyes closed, exhales slowly, and whispers what he wants so softly that if I had human ears, I'd never have caught that he wants to eat Cyrus's cum from my pussy.

A smile spreads over my lips as the crimson flush creeps further down Jude's neck. *Such a curious boy.*

"You may," I grant him permission.

A ripple of pleasure shudders up my spine as he lowers his lips to my raw cunt, pounded and spent from Cyrus's urgent thrusts.

By contrast, Jude's touch is so careful, it's more ticklish than anything else. But then he goes deeper, lapping at my center more urgently.

Gods, it feels amazing!

Soon, I'm nearing the edge again, every nerve ending stimulated, alert.

The orgasm crashes over me as I sink into the bed, into the warmth, the sheer bliss tingling through my body.

When I can't take a second more of the overstimulation, I grab a fistful of Jude's hair and pull him up.

Without even thinking, I capture his lips in mine, licking the remnants of my own pleasure, of Cyrus's, from his mouth.

It damn near drives me mad with lust. Tasting us both on him, on those warm lips brimming with life, *gods.*

He kisses me back with fervor, hard cock pressing against my crotch, the only thing between us the thin material of his pants. So close, yet an insurmountable distance.

I lick his lips when he finally pulls away. "Hmm, thank you."

Jude stares into my eyes with an intensity I cannot name. "What was it like?" he whispers, sitting back on his haunches.

I smile, baring my fangs, as I pull my dress back in place. "I can show you."

He nods, cock jumping excitedly at the mere suggestion. "Please." A plea. Always such pretty pleas, irresistible pleas.

My fingers brush over his neck, fluttering over the skin. I tilt his head slightly and I dip my fangs into his vein. The rush is instant, beautiful and warm.

I'm overwhelmed by Jude's intense arousal, his fear, as I share the emotion of what Cyrus's arrival has done to my body.

His breath hitches, gasps, and I can taste how much it all turns him on. He's virtually leaking by the time I've drunk more than a mouthful.

But he's not the only one enjoying the show; I get his memories too.

Seeing the scene play out from Jude's point of view, watching, hidden, aroused but not satisfied...it has me worked up into a fresh frenzy of desire.

Quickly, I pull out, sealing the bites, before I take too much.

"You didn't come." An observation from my side, not a comment.

"No, Milady," he rasps, holding onto me tightly.

"Why?"

"Can't." It's hard for him to speak, but he tries. "No permission."

I don't even mind that he touched without being allowed to. My heart overflows with pride at his devotion, his obedience, and I reach down to reward his good behavior, fishing his erection from the pants struggling to contain it.

Jude groans loudly the moment my fingers make contact with his needy flesh, and it pleases me greatly to find him so responsive to my touch.

"Take it all off," I tell him, snapping the elastic of his underwear against his stomach, and he jumps out of his clothes so quickly that he almost trips and falls.

When he's standing in front of me as naked as the day I employed him, dripping rain on my carpets, I sit up, patting my lap. "Come here, *cucciolo*."

Jude doesn't move, just stares at me with a puzzled look on his face and an impossibly hard dick pointing at the ceiling.

"If the next words out of your mouth are about being too big or crushing me, we are done here," I dare him, baring my teeth in warning.

The human hesitates only for a second before turning his back to me and lowering himself onto my lap carefully.

He's still balancing awkwardly, though.

"All the way." I reach around to wrap my arms around his waist, pulling him down fully on top of me.

Jude shivers against me, body rigid in anticipation, heart beating too fast, as he lets me move him where I want him. A life-size rag doll—pliant, perfect.

"There you go," I coo, and he groans loudly as I reach around to take his cock in both hands, teasing the sensitive flesh between my fingers.

"Christ," Jude gasps when I flick my finger over his slit, smearing his pre-cum down his shaft.

"You have permission, darling," I whisper in his ear, enjoying the gasp that slips from those beautiful lips as my cruel fingers speed up their pace, mercilessly jerking him off to the point of no return. "Come for me."

And when I sink my fangs into his neck again, warm blood flooding my senses with his need, with mine, he does as he's told: he lets go, ribbons of cum streaking over my fingers as a beautiful cry rips from his throat.

Such a good boy.

CHAPTER 25

DISRUPTED RHYTHM

(JUDE)

There isn't a single rational thought left in my mind as I finally find my release, spilling my cum over Adriana's hand.

Fucking hell.

After days of edging, after watching the vampires fuck, and then the audacity of Cyrus to kiss me with such passion that I forget my own name...I'm worked up into a near-delirious state by the time I have permission to release.

'Come for me.' The most beautiful sentence—so perfect, complete. A sentence I've only ever heard in dreams. One usually meant for others.

My body goes limp on top of hers. If it were anyone else, I'd worry about crushing them beneath my bulky frame, but I've seen Adriana's strength. She probably doesn't even feel my weight.

Breath ragged, eyes closed, I lean back against her body as the aftershock of my orgasm ripples on.

The euphoria of her bite mixes with the burning embers of the climax, and all that's left is me in a floaty cloud, content, free.

Holy shit.

One of the best orgasms of my life. No competition.

But I don't have the words to thank her, the words for anything. The overwhelm has turned me stupid.

Adriana holds me against her, stroking my hair gently. "You were such a good boy today," she tells me, and my eyes shoot open.

There it is again. That term.

Nobody has ever called me a *good boy* before.

I've wanted them to. Yearned for it with every fiber of my being. But nobody calls a 6'3" man a good *boy*. Nobody but Adriana, that is…

Fucking hell, in that voice. If I hadn't already melted into a puddle, I would've done so anew. Bliss. Pure bliss.

The comfort of Adriana's bed is everything I want to sink into and never leave. I don't know how long she lets me cling to the moment, lets me savor the feeling. The warm satisfaction seeps through my veins like molten lava.

Her arm is draped across my waist, her cheek against my shoulder, and for a moment, I can pretend that everything is normal. That Cyrus didn't just complicate everything. That I didn't kiss him back when he pressed his lips to mine.

Adriana's command cuts through the memory.

"Up," she says, her voice carrying that familiar note of authority that makes my spine straighten involuntarily. "Now."

I want to protest, want to burrow deeper into the silk sheets that smell of jasmine and daydreams. But her tone doesn't invite negotiation, and honestly, part of me is grateful for the structure. After what just happened, I need something solid to hold onto.

"Is he coming back?" I ask as I reluctantly untangle myself from her embrace.

"Cyrus always comes back." There's something resigned in her voice, like she's stating a law of physics rather than making a prediction. "The question is what he wants when he does." She's already moving, her mind elsewhere, probably thinking of contingencies and plans.

"Kitchen," she commands. "You need to eat."

"I'm not really hungry—"

"I don't recall asking if you were hungry." The sharp edge in her voice stops my protest cold. "If trouble is coming, and with Cyrus, trouble is always coming, you'll need your strength."

In the kitchen, she moves like someone who remembers eating human food, preparing eggs and toast while I sit at the marble-top island in the center of the space.

There's something almost domestic about the scene, if you ignore the fact that she's a centuries-old vampire and I'm her research assistant who's somehow stumbled into whatever complicated relationship she has with another immortal being.

"Eat," she says, placing the plate in front of me. "All of it."

I pick up the fork, ravenous despite my earlier protest. The eggs are perfect—creamy and seasoned exactly how I prefer them. Of course, she knows how I like my eggs. She pays attention to everything, files every preference and weakness.

It's been so long since someone cared about whether I ate properly.

My mother tried, I think, in those early years before the weight of raising a child alone while working two jobs became too much. But mostly I remember her exhaustion, coming home to look at me like I was just another problem to solve, another mouth to feed, another responsibility she hadn't asked for.

"You're far away," Adriana observes, refilling my orange juice.

"Sorry." I take another bite, trying to focus on the present instead of memories that serve no purpose except to remind me of what a burden I've always been, how invisible.

Except to Adriana. She sees everything. When I'm tired, when I'm hungry, when I need structure more than comfort. It should be suffocating but it just feels like being held, like mattering to someone.

My gran was the only other person who ever paid this kind of attention, back when I was small enough to curl up in her lap while she read me stories about knights and dragons. Before Dad left and Mom stopped having time for stories. Before the incident when I was five, the one that sits in my chest like a stone I can't cough up. The one door I don't open for Adriana, not even for myself...

"Finish your juice," Adriana says, and the gentle firmness in her voice pulls me back to the kitchen. "Then gym."

"Gym?" I look up at her, fork halfway to my mouth. "Now?" *Haven't we done enough for one day?* I want to add but smartly don't.

"Exercise clears the mind." Her fingers trail along my shoulder as she passes behind my chair. "Besides, you've been neglecting your routine since Felix left. I won't have you getting soft on my watch."

The casual possessiveness in her tone makes my stomach do a somersault. *My watch.* Like I belong to her.

Maybe I do.

As much as I *really* don't want to work out right now, not in a gym, I know I stand nothing to gain from arguing, so I don't bother.

Twenty minutes later, I'm standing in the gym downstairs, a space I've grown to both love and dread. It was initially a storeroom, but Felix and I spent a couple of days converting it into a gym, at Adriana's request.

It looks nothing like the gyms I frequented at varsity on those 5 AM mornings that used to be my standard—no fluorescent lights buzzing overhead, no smell of disinfectant fighting a losing battle against sweat, no rows of half-asleep athletes going through the motions in companionable silence. Just one well-equipped room, clean and quiet.

I used to be good at this, disciplined, but now it almost feels like learning to ride a bike again: I still remember the action but my muscles are rusty; they protest.

After I dropped out, the gym access went away too. I kept going through the motions in my room, with whatever I could improvise with bags of books for weights, the edge of the bed frame for dips, push-ups until my arms gave out. It was enough to hold the shape of things, but it was never the same.

Now, I have an even better gym and I don't even have to share it.

"Strip," Adriana says, settling into the single metal chair sitting in the back corner of the room.

I hesitate for a moment. Not because I'm modest anymore, but because being naked around her always makes me hyperaware of every imperfection, every soft edge she might find lacking.

Adriana's expectant expression doesn't leave room for self-consciousness, though.

The clothes come off without another thought, my underwear too. She's seen me naked countless times now, has mapped every inch of my body with her eyes and hands and teeth. But I am always so exposed under her gaze, the one that inspects more than my physical form.

"Jump rope first," she instructs, settling back in her chair with a tablet to record my performance. "Twenty minutes."

I pick up the rope, testing the familiar weight of the handles in my palms. This was always my favorite exercise, the one that never fails to quiet the chaos in my head. The rhythmic thud of my feet against the mat as the rope cuts through the air, the burn in my muscles that demands complete focus—there's something soothing about it.

Thud-whisper-thud-whisper-thud-whisper.

I start counting each skip like I always do.

But today, my mind won't quiet.

Nine, ten, eleven…

Cyrus's face keeps flashing behind my closed eyelids. I can't forget the taste of him when he kissed me, dark and dangerous and utterly delicious.

One hundred twenty-three, one hundred twenty-four…

Adriana's reaction to him keeps coming back to me. Her impenetrable shield crumbled the moment she saw him, like he was an activation code, unlocking a part of her nobody else has access to.

Two hundred fifteen, two hundred sixteen…

What if she chooses him?

What if whatever just happened between them reminds her that I'm temporary, replaceable, merely the latest in a long line of humans who've briefly captured her interest?

What if I go back to being invisible?

"Focus," Adriana's voice cuts through my spiraling thoughts. "Your rhythm is off."

She's right. The rope has been catching on my feet for the last thirty seconds, my coordination shot by anxiety I can't quite suppress. I force myself to breathe deeper, to find the steady cadence that usually comes so naturally.

Four hundred eight, four hundred nine...

"Better," Adriana murmurs, her attention burning warm against my skin. "Keep your shoulders relaxed. You're holding tension in your neck."

I adjust my posture, hyperaware of her gaze scrutinizing every movement. This is what I've craved my entire life without knowing how to ask for it: someone who notices the small things, who cares enough to correct my form, who sees value in making me better.

I forget what number I am on and stop counting.

My mother never had time to watch me do anything. Too busy working, too tired to care whether I was eating properly or sleeping enough or slowly disappearing into myself. And after what happened later, she would forever look at me like I was broken beyond repair.

Maybe I was. Maybe I still am.

But Adriana doesn't look at me like I'm broken. She looks at me like I'm a puzzle worth solving. My improvement matters to her beyond simple interest in her employee's health.

"Time," she calls, and I let the rope fall, my chest heaving as I try to catch my breath.

"Good," Adriana says, making a note on her tablet. "Your endurance is improving. But I could see your mind wandering around minute seven. What were you thinking about?"

The question is casual, but I know better than to think she's just making conversation. Everything Adriana asks has a purpose.

"Nothing important," I lie.

Her left eyebrow arches. "Try again."

I towel sweat from my face, buying time while I figure out how much truth she wants, how much I'm willing to give.

"I was thinking about what happens now," I say finally. "With Cyrus back."

"Oh? And what conclusions did you reach?"

"I don't understand what's happening. Where I fit into whatever this is between you two..." The last bit comes out whiny. "...that maybe I don't fit at all."

For a moment, Adriana is quiet, studying me with those intense green eyes that seem to see everything I'm trying to hide. Then she sets down her tablet and gets up, moving toward me.

"Jude." Her hand cups my face, thumb tracing my cheekbone. "Look at me."

I meet her eyes, trying not to lean into her touch like a stray cat starved for affection. Yet every instinct wants exactly that.

"Cyrus's return doesn't change what you are to me," she says quietly. "It complicates things, yes. But it doesn't diminish your value or your place here."

"What *am* I to you?" The question slips out before I can stop it, naked and vulnerable in a way that has nothing to do with my lack of clothes. If I don't ask, I will drive myself crazy.

Her smile is soft, almost maternal, as she answers

cleverly without revealing too much. "Your position doesn't change because someone from my past decides to make an appearance."

The words should reassure me, and they do, *mostly*. Yet there's something in her expression that suggests she's not telling me everything.

There is no room for further discussion, though.

"Now," Adriana says, stepping back and picking up her tablet again. "Push-ups. I want to see if that upper-body work has been paying off."

I drop to the floor, grateful for the familiar routine, for the simple clarity of physical exertion.

Urgh, why is exercise so much harder with an erection?

CHAPTER 26

THE VISE TIGHTENS

(CYRUS)

The fresh night air does nothing to clear my head as I stumble out of *Summer Place*.

Adriana's blood is still flowing in my veins, making every streetlight too bright, every sound too sharp.

Christ, I'd forgotten how intoxicating her essence could be. How it turns the world into something hyper-real, every sensation dialed up beyond reason.

I'm supposed to be clearheaded right now. Supposed to be reporting back.

Instead, I'm stumbling through the city like a drunk, high on four hundred years of connection and the taste of her fury.

Fuck.

As if on cue, my phone buzzes.

It's a text from Julius:

Report. Now.

For a thousand-year-old vampire, he sure knows his way around technology. The ancient bastard probably helped invent half of it. *So damn pushy.*

La Famiglia Eterna doesn't accept delays or tolerate uncertainty. I learned that the hard way. If I don't go to them, they come to me. And they won't be pleasant about the inconvenience.

Accepting my lot, I hail a cab, trying to arrange my thoughts into something resembling coherence as I slide into the backseat. I could shadow-walk to my destination much faster, but I'm exhausted.

The driver eyes me in the rearview mirror, taking in the blood stain on my shirt collar and my disheveled hair. I suppose I'm looking a bit worse for wear after my tangle with Adriana.

But he's a cab driver; he's seen it all. Soon his focus returns to the road as he fights through the busy streets to that eyesore of a building.

La Famiglia's headquarters occupies three floors of a glass tower in midtown, hidden behind the facade of an investment firm. Appropriate, given how they operate. Everything with them comes down to assets, *leverage*, who owes what to whom.

They started as arms dealers, or so the story goes, more than six centuries ago. Now their reach spans continents, quietly steering governments and reshaping the supernatural hierarchy while humans remain none the wiser.

Until recently, I've been quite good at avoiding these ancient pricks and staying off their radar. But this time, they had me cornered.

The elevator rises smoothly to the forty-second floor, my reflection in the mirror-wall showing exactly what I expected: dilated pupils, flushed skin, the telltale signs of a vampire who's fed well and recently.

There's no hiding what I've done, especially not from them.

Cesare is waiting for me at the top. Just like the rest of the Inner Council, he's much older than me and arguably much more of an asshole. Depends who you ask, I suppose.

I've never paid much attention to *La Famiglia*'s fancy preferred titles. It's all made up anyway. More than a millennium old and built like a pro wrestler, Cesare is the henchman, the bodyguard, regardless of the title he insists on. His sole job is to protect that shadow lord asshole, Valerian.

Cesare has never liked me—none of them have—and he doesn't say a word as he leads me to the Sovereign's office. That's the one title Valerian makes sure nobody ever forgets: *Il Sovrano*. Though I prefer 'shadow lord' because he's as shady as the rest of them, definitely more.

Valerian's office is not my style at all, and I hate coming here. Useless ancient artifacts crowd every surface, turning the massive space into a mausoleum of junk. It's probably expensive, but I'm not impressed. *All for show.*

Il Sovrano waits behind his desk, a king on his throne, hands folded in front of him, perfectly still. He's older than most vampires out there, which means he's older than empires. How old exactly, I've never asked; the leader of *La Famiglia* definitely doesn't exactly invite small talk.

Tall and lanky, he's got a face like a classical statue, not because it's beautiful (he's not), but because it's cold and forced. When he smiles, which he does now, it's more creepy than anything else.

"Cyrus." He pronounces each syllable like someone

who learned English from a book rather than at home: too perfect, individual. "You smell *satisfied*."

"Mission accomplished," I lie, settling into the leather chair across from his desk with forced nonchalance.

"Is it?" His pale eyes study me. "Because you smell like her blood."

The two other Inner Council members emerge from the shadows before I can answer.

Here we go.

I force a smile to my lips. "Well, well, well, if it isn't Tweedledee and Tweedledum."

Julius, the second in command or whatever his stupid title is, bares his fangs at me as he stalks closer. He isn't bad-looking for such a cunt. Tall, dark, and handsome; if he had more of a personality, he could've easily been my type. But I don't have time for pompous self-proclaimed *leaders* who treat everyone else like shit. I don't care how much older he is. Besides, I know Valerian doesn't like sharing his *toys*.

Caterina is smaller, deceptively delicate, with platinum blonde hair and milky skin that conceals the soul of a career torturer. She trails behind Julius like a shadow, sly smile on her ageless face, forever young. Operations or something like that; I'm not sure what she does in *La Famiglia*, but she seems to have a finger in every pie.

She looks at Cesare, who's blocking the door behind me with his mountainlike physique, to Valerian, and then settles her gaze on me. "Are you going to deny it?" she challenges, and I know my options are limited.

Time to change tactics.

"I had to get close to her first," I explain, keeping my voice steady as I meet her gaze. "It's all part of the plan. To earn her trust. Build rapport. You can't just demand information from someone like Adriana. She's not some fledgling you can intimidate."

"And what exactly did you two *talk* about?" Caterina asks, circling my chair like a shark scenting blood.

"Loads of things." Another lie, easier now that I'm committed to the path. "She is willing to be cooperative. Adriana has no interest in going against *La Famiglia*. She understands that it would be for the greater good to surrender the book to you when she finds it."

Valerian's laugh drips with malice. "How noble of her. How *convenient* that she should suddenly develop such compliance after centuries of ignoring our authority."

The mockery in his tone makes my fangs ache, but I force myself to remain relaxed. "She's not the same vampire she used to be. Age brings wisdom, even to De Crevenas."

"Does it?" Julius steps closer, too close for comfort.

"Yeah, she doesn't care about the book really. Said she hasn't even been looking for it." Too far, I'm going too far, but the word vomit doesn't slow down; I'm too nervous. "It's of no use to her anymore, apparently."

"Oh?" Valerian asks, as the circle of ancients around me grows tighter, the four of them crowding my space. "Because the information we're receiving suggests otherwise. Suggests she's acquired new *resources*. Human resources."

My blood goes cold, but I keep my expression neutral. "I don't know what you mean."

"The boy," Valerian clarifies, his old Italian accent lending gravity to the words as he leans down to bring his ugly face close to mine. "Young, educated. Ring any bells?"

They know about Jude. Of course, they fucking know.

La Famiglia hasn't survived this long by being ignorant of developments in its territory. They must have been watching her even before they roped me in under the guise of repaying my debts.

"Oh, yes. She has research assistance," I say carefully. "Academic types help her maintain her art-dealing facade. It's hardly unusual."

"No," Valerian agrees, rising from his chair with that weightless grace of the long-dead. "What's unusual is how much she seems to value this particular assistant. He's even living with her."

I scoff, "Since when does *La Famiglia* care about gossip and living arrangements?"

"The boy could be leverage," Caterina observes, a mean grin turning her pretty face revolting. "Threaten him, and she becomes manageable."

"That won't work."

"No?" Valerian's smile is all fangs. "You of all people should understand, Cyrus, how our obsessions make even the strongest of us *vulnerable*."

The threat hangs in the air between us, unspoken but irrefutable. They know about my bond with Adriana. That's how they recruited me in the first place, promising that helping them would keep her safe from more *permanent* solutions.

Well, that was part of it.

I may or may not have broken one of their dumb ancient laws and had an affair with the Fae Prince. The Queen Mother was furious, spouting old racist shit about keeping species separate, blah, blah, blah.

What can I say? The Prince was a handsome fucker.

The Between Court was two seconds away from having my head on a silver platter when Valerian stepped in and said he'd handle it, *'saving'* me from certain death.

But turns out, he didn't give a flying fuck about whether I lived or died. No, he wanted that damn book of Adriana's. Who was I to argue when the options were death or help them locate the book?

The fact that it gave me an excuse to force myself back into her life played no small part in my acceptance of the deal. It was true that I did, in fact, miss her. Perhaps, once this whole mess is cleared up, we could start over, begin anew...

"Speaking of our arrangement," Julius says casually, his tone deceptively light as he pulls me to the present. "Do you have anything useful to report, or was it all fun and games?"

The accusation hits its mark. They're right, of course. I was supposed to be professional, detached, get close enough to find out how the Grimoire search is going, then report back with actionable information.

Instead, I lost myself in her the moment our blood mixed.

It's the human. He complicated things. The proximity of his blood, the intensity of his desires...it messed with the circuits of my brain, even before Adriana's blood hit my tongue. But I'm not telling them *that*.

Thank fuck vampires can't really read minds like in some movies.

"I gathered what I could," I lie, trying to keep my voice steady as I shift in the chair.

"Did you?" Valerian's smile is razor-sharp. "Because from where we're sitting, it looks as if you spent the evening *reconnecting*. Rather thoroughly."

Heat rises in my cheeks, embarrassment and anger

manifesting physically. I hate having to answer to anyone. But even I know how badly I've fucked this up.

"The bond makes it difficult to maintain objectivity," I admit, which is at least partially true.

"Clearly," Caterina purrs, then sighs dramatically. "It's better for everyone if you do as we ask, Cyrus."

"Is it? What if I refuse?" I ask, though I know the answer.

Caterina's laugh is bitter, cruel. "Then we stop viewing Adriana De Crevena as a manageable inconvenience and start treating her as the threat she actually is." She runs her nails over my neck, sending shivers down my spine, and not in a good way. "Ancient vampires rarely die peacefully in their sleep, don't you know?"

The walls of the office seem to press closer.

"She doesn't know anything yet," I say desperately.

"Then you have time to rectify tonight's lapse in judgment." Valerian's tone suggests this is my final warning. "Get close to her. Report back. And Cyrus?"

"*Sì*?"

"Next time, try to remember that her life, and yours, depends on your ability to maintain professionalism. Sentiment is a luxury neither of you can afford. I have no problem sending you back to the Fae Queen."

Fucker. "I understand," I say finally, my nails digging into my palms as I try to restrain myself. No good can come from pushing my luck. And I definitely shouldn't give in to the urge to call *Il Sovrano* a cunt to his face.

"Excellent." Valerian's smile is all teeth and no warmth. "We knew you'd see reason. Family is so important, don't you think?"

I stand on unsteady legs, sobered up, the euphoria

from Adriana's blood completely evaporated now. "That all?"

"For now." Valerian's voice stops me at the door. "Next time you report, do bring something useful. Our patience isn't infinite."

I nod and leave, walking calmly to the elevator, waiting until the doors close before allowing my composure to shatter.

Fuck! Fuck, fuck, fuck.

The elevator descends, carrying me back toward street level and the impossible situation I've helped create.

Those old farts have me trapped.

Unless...

No, there's no unless. Not this time. There's no clever solution, no way to outmaneuver vampires who've been playing these games since before human civilization learned to write.

I need a drink. Several drinks. Maybe an entire distillery.

What a fucking mess.

CHAPTER 27

TRUTH OR ELSE

(ADRIANA)

The satisfaction of a job well done settles into my bones as I watch Jude towel the sweat from his body, his chest still rising and falling from exertion.

His form is improving, his endurance building exactly as I've planned.

"You did well today," I tell him, making notes on my tablet. Anything to avoid his eyes on me, all earnest devotion and barely concealed need dripping from his naked form.

"Thank you, Lady Adriana."

The formal address stings more than it should. We were so much more informal mere hours ago, when I let him eat Cyrus's cum from my pussy.

"Tomorrow you'll focus your search on the insurance records," I say, my voice deliberately crisp as I switch over to work mode. "Start with the northeastern corridor. New York, Boston, Philadelphia."

"Of course." Jude's voice carries a note of confusion, probably wondering why I'm suddenly treating him like a stranger. "Should I prepare a report on what I find?"

"Brief summaries will suffice. I don't need exhaustive analysis, just patterns and anomalies." I close the gym door behind us with more force than necessary. "You should rest. Goodnight."

His disappointment is unmissable in every feature, especially the slight slump of his shoulders at my dismissal. But I force myself to look past it, to keep strong.

Part of me wants to explain, to smooth the sudden distance I'm creating between us. But explanation would require admitting how seeing Cyrus made me realize exactly how much I have to lose.

It's better this way.

"Good night, Jude."

"Good night," he echoes, those simple words laden with the questions he does not ask.

Heading straight to my office, I wait until I hear his bedroom door close before allowing myself to let go of composure. My hands are shaking when I sit down behind my desk.

When was the last time that happened? When was the last time I felt this off-balance, this uncertain about my own reactions?

Cyrus. It's always Cyrus who fucks up my peace.

But it's not only his presence that has me rattled. It's what I tasted in his blood during our exchange, the memories and emotions that bled through our connection…

Something is making him anxious, desperate, guilty beyond what he should be atoning for.

Only when Jude's heartbeat finally slows to a sleeping

rhythm does my mind clear enough to solve the puzzle, to home in on the piece that's been bothering me.

La Famiglia Eterna! That's what I tasted, what I saw. It was only a brief flash, but it was there, hidden in plain sight among the other memories in his blood. Cyrus has been with them. Recently.

Why though? Cyrus hates *La Famiglia* as much as I do. Something doesn't add up.

What would they want with him?

La Famiglia doesn't involve itself in individual vampire affairs unless those affairs threaten its interests. And the only thing that could be of *interest* to them is a particular missing spellbook.

But why now? Do they know about my deterioration?

My chair scrapes against the floor as I stand abruptly, ice spreading from my fingertips across the desk surface in crystalline patterns that look like spider webs.

Did they send Cyrus to test me, find out how much time they have until I'm weak enough for them to move in?

Fuckers. Surely not.

What made them think I'd let him back in that easily? After what happened? After all this time.

Yet that's exactly what I did.

I caved—instantly.

You're a hypocrite, Adriana.

But I can't dwell on that now. If I could take it back, I would.

There's no way to purge his blood from my system, though. What's done is done.

I'm pacing now, the ice spreading from my hands to everything I touch. Frost forms on the window glass, on the leather chair, on the antique letter opener that belonged to a Grand Duke once. My office is turning into a winter landscape, magical and deadly and completely beyond my conscious control as I imagine every possibility that could've led Cyrus to The Family of Devils.

What are they planning?

I need to know what Cyrus told them; how much they know.

My hands are still trembling with a mix of ice and anxiety as I grab my coat from the closet.

Fuck-it.

I've spent nine years telling myself I never want to see Cyrus again. Nine years of convincing myself that I'm better off without the chaos he brings to my life.

But if he knows what *La Famiglia* is planning and how to counter it, then my personal feelings become irrelevant.

I can hate him and still need him. I can despise what he's done while recognizing that he might be the only source of intelligence I can access quickly enough to matter.

I have to know what Cyrus has gotten himself, gotten *us*, into this time. I'll drive myself insane with the possibilities if I don't know what to brace for.

Last time I left him to his own devices, he damn near got me killed.

I won't be caught off guard again even if it means tackling this bull by the horns.

I need to find him. And, in this city, there's only one place Cyrus goes when he needs to think.

With a sigh, I head for the door.

Might as well get it over with.

Before I can change my mind, I step into a shadow and head out.

❧

WITH CYRUS'S blood pulsing in my veins, my powers are more stable than they've been in months. It's a short trip to my destination and the shadows let me slip through without hassle.

The *Blue Moon* is exactly as I remember it: dim lighting, exposed brick, and a smoky atmosphere that makes secrets feel safe under the low ceilings.

Tonight, the stage hosts a jazz trio with piano, bass, and trumpet, weaving something melancholy that suits the morbid expressions around me.

I claim Cyrus's usual booth in the back, settling into the worn seat that has carried the smell of smoke and spilled liquor for decades now. We used to frequent this spot in the 70s, drawn by the music. *Always the music.* The world was a different place then.

For nostalgia's sake, I order an Italian wine, a vintage from the hills where I was born. It might as well have been food coloring and water as far as the taste goes, but the familiar writing on the bottle is pleasing to look at.

I don't have to wait long.

When Cyrus appears twenty minutes later, I'm struck again by how little he's changed. Things happened too quickly earlier for me to get a good look at him. But he still has that same smile, the same confidence in that stride.

He spots me immediately, his face cycling through various emotions as he approaches. Surprise. Excitement. Anxiety. Always such an open book that man; terrible poker player.

"Adriana." Cyrus slides into the booth across from me without meeting my gaze. "How did you find me?" The question comes automatically, though we both know it's pointless. I've had lifetimes to grow familiar with his routines.

I swirl the wine around in my glass. "Why are you here?" I ask, not bothering with preamble.

"To get a drink, of course." He tries to lighten the mood but fails.

"Not the bar. *Here*, in this city, in my life." I study his face in the low light, noticing the tension in his jaw, his tired eyes. "What do you want, Cyrus?"

Instead of answering immediately, he signals the bartender, who brings over a second wine glass.

"To see you," he says simply, pouring wine into both our glasses. "To remember what it felt like when we were good together."

"We were never good together." The words come out harsh, venomous.

"No, I suppose," he agrees, raising his glass in a mock toast. "But we were something."

I take a sip of my wine to gather my thoughts, letting my eyes wander to the musicians on stage.

"I haven't forgiven you," I say quietly.

"I wouldn't have expected you to." His acceptance is matter-of-fact, devoid of the dramatic self-pity I might have expected. "I fucked up, plain and simple."

But that's not what his blood told me earlier. During our exchange, beneath the desperation and desire, I tasted something else. *Hope.* The fragile, desperate hope of someone who hasn't given up on redemption. Someone who believes there might still be a chance.

I lean forward, studying his face in the candlelight. This close, I can see the micro-expressions he's trying to hide, the tells that four centuries of intimacy have taught me to read.

He's lying. Not about wanting to see me, that much is genuine. But about his reasons for being here.

It's Cyrus who breaks the silence, who tries to reach for me. "How many times must I say I'm sorry? I've changed, Adriana. I'm different now."

I shake my head, pulling my hand away. "You can't just say you're different, Cyrus. Actions speak louder than words."

"But I really am sorry."

I sigh, leaning back. "Sorry isn't always enough. You can't undo everything that happened in the past with some grand declaration. This isn't some Hallmark movie with a guaranteed happily ever after."

His shoulders droop from the heavy exhale. "Please give me another chance."

"Why, my reckless one?" The endearment slips out before I can stop it, carried by frustration and something dangerously close to tenderness. I haven't called him that since our Prague days, hundreds of years ago, during the honeymoon phase, when his impulsiveness was charming rather than terrifying.

The effect is immediate and devastating. His composure crumbles like ancient parchment, and I find myself looking at raw pain instead of the rehearsed nonchalance.

"Christ, Adriana." His voice breaks on my name.

"Tell me why you're here." I reach for my glass to give my restless fingers something to hold on to. "No games, no deflection. Just truth."

For a moment, I think he might actually tell me, might trust me with whatever secret is eating at him from the inside. Then his walls slam back into place, and he's looking at me with that familiar mix of desire and regret that's defined us for centuries.

"I missed you," Cyrus says instead, persisting. "Every day for nine years, three months, and seven days, I missed you. Is that not reason enough?"

"No." Ice creeps into my voice. "Because I tasted *La Famiglia* in your blood, Cyrus. Saw your memories. Stop lying to me."

His face goes pale. "Adriana—"

I cut him off. "So, I'll ask again, and this time I want you to be honest." I lean closer, letting the full weight of my attention settle on him. "Why are you here, Cyrus? What does the Family of Devils want with me?"

"It's complicated." He looks away, emptying his glass.

A frustrated sigh leaves my lips. "What did you promise them?"

The silence stretches between us, loaded.

Finally, he closes his eyes and speaks the words I knew would follow: "The Grimoire."

Oh, Cyrus. What have you done?

Ice spreads over the wine glass as the fury sears through my veins. "How could you?" I hiss, despite having no reason at all to be surprised.

Cyrus empties the bottle into his glass and waves it in the direction of the bar, calling for a refill, then turns his attention back to me. "It's just a book, Adriana. Is it really worth all this trouble?"

"Such a fool." I shake my head. "You still don't get it."

It's never been *'just a book'*...

CHAPTER 28

INSECURE ATTACHMENT

(JUDE)

My sleep is riddled with weird dreams of demons chasing me down dark paths.

After my late-night gym session and the evening's activities preceding the workout, you'd think I'd be exhausted, sleeping like a baby. But I slept like a real baby—one that wakes up every few hours, yearning for something I cannot voice.

Twice, I almost went looking for Adriana. But she sent me away with such indifference, like I was no one, that I knew she'd be less than happy if I disobeyed her direct order to get some rest.

So, I stayed, continued my fight with the sheets, rolling around in my sweat as I sprinted through my dreams, prey to faceless pursuers.

At exactly 05:37 AM, I give up, slipping into some pants and a t-shirt to sneak downstairs under the guise of pouring myself some water in the kitchen. It's just an excuse to run into Adriana. Perhaps I'll muster up the courage to ask her the question repeating in my mind: *What's wrong with me?*

I've been here for two weeks now, serving her, servicing her, letting her drink as much as she wants from me, whatever she needs. But we still haven't had sex, not in the traditional, penetrative sense of the word.

Not from lack of trying. God, it's all I think about: what she'd feel like on the inside, with my cock buried inside that magnificent pussy that tastes unlike anything I've ever tasted. The mere thought is enough for my half-erect cock to tent against the flimsy pants as I pad down the hall.

But every time, she stops at the last minute, pushes me away. As soon as I get close, the door slams shut in my face, and she retreats.

I've been patient. Figured she had good reasons. *Maybe she doesn't like sex,* I reasoned. But then that tattooed god of an immortal with the black earplugs and slutty little nose ring shows up, and she lets him fuck her senseless.

Must be me. The toxic thought repeats in my head as it always does. The things I want are often meant for others only...

I knock softly on her office door, pushing it ajar when I get no response.

But Adriana's not there.

She's not in her bedroom either, nor anywhere else in the apartment.

Guess she's gone out.

Sulking, I saunter off to the kitchen for the glass of water I supposedly came downstairs for.

The place is still a mess from the damage caused by Adriana's run-in with Cyrus earlier, with broken furniture scattered on the floor amid drywall fragments. Poor

Felix will have his work cut out for him with all the clean-up work, but I don't spare much thought for the future.

There's a note pinned to the fridge, and I groan in annoyance as I read the message addressed to me.

At the top, there is no warm greeting, no endearment, just *Jude*. She doesn't waste any words as she outlines my chores and tasks of the day, as if I'm merely another employee. Maybe I am.

It's formally signed, with her full name and signature at the bottom. Nothing personal. No hint that I might be more than a human blood bag with good research skills.

I crumple up the note and toss it in the bin. Forgoing the water, I head upstairs to the office.

Just like the rest of the house, the space is warm despite the late autumn chill raging outside. The underfloor heating does a great job. Not that Adriana needs it. But I appreciate the luxury of walking around without needing to dress up in more layers.

Plonking down in my desk chair, I stare at the laptop without turning it on. My brain is still fuzzy from the lack of sleep that's been accumulating since I moved to *Summer Place*.

It would've been better if I switched over to being nocturnal like Adriana. But her insistence on keeping distance between our routines, of clinging to her solitary early mornings, has left me in this weird limbo.

I should go to bed, but she keeps me up. I should be awake, but I'm too tired to keep my eyes open. And through it all, the burning need in my blood for *more* never goes away.

For the umpteenth time since he barged in last night, I find myself wondering what it would be like to have

Cyrus feed from me. Would it be the same as it is with Adriana? The kiss wasn't the same...

I want them with the same intensity, but in different ways. It's impossible to explain, even to myself. But it doesn't stop my analytical mind from trying, churning and churning, only to produce nothing except another loop.

This is not the first time I've found myself obsessed with a confident man with a sadistic streak and a dark past, but everything predating my discovery that vampires are, in fact, real feels lesser somehow, muted.

My mind cycles through my largely uneventful sexual history that mostly comprises six years of bad blowjobs for 'straight' team mates after practice, a lecturer I had no business messing around with, and exactly two women— one in my final year at school; one at varsity—who convinced me I was 'the perfect boyfriend material' but in fact wanted nothing from me but a buff body to show off and a supporting cast member to their mundane lives.

Not that it has ever bothered me much. I learned a long time ago that it's better to suppress your needs, your curiosities.

'Deviants like you should have their willy cut off!' my grandmother shouted that day, that day when I fucked everything up for good...I have never forgotten that line. It keeps coming back to me. Even now, despite how much I fight it.

The memory sinks into my tired mind as I slouch in my chair, and I lack the energy to push it down. I'm exhausted from all the years of having to keep it buried, hidden. The shame of it all...

I was five. He was a few months younger.

Nate was my best friend. He lived next door. He had been around to play since before he could walk.

I was supposed to *'know better,'* my gran screamed at me when she discovered us in the bathroom, playing doctor-doctor like curious children do.

It all went to shit so quickly after that.

I never meant to be naughty, to do anything wrong. I was just curious.

That day, we got caught in the rain at the park and came back drenched. We discarded our clothes on the bathroom floor and jumped in the bath as instructed.

But his little worm looked different I noticed when we stripped down. I was too young to know about circumcision, cut and uncut. Growing up without a father, in a house full of women, I hadn't seen any other male genitalia other than my own…

The extra skin was fascinating. So squishy. *Was he wrong, or was I? Did my skin fall off? Was he born with extra skin?* I had so many questions, none of them sexual in any way. Too young for anything other than innocent curiosity.

That would be the day all innocence died.

When my gran swung that door open with such force that it shook on its hinges, screaming profanities as she dragged me out of the bathroom by my ear, naked and crying, dragging me out into the yard in broad daylight…

No. I force my eyes shut, humming softly to myself until the memory sinks down where it belongs.

I don't want to think about what comes next. *I can't.*

Rubbing my temples, I exhale slowly, counting my heartbeats until they slow down to a steady pace.

When the world finally stops spiraling, I turn on the laptop in the hopes of getting to work. Instead, I find myself falling down a rabbit hole of chasing Adriana and Cyrus's lives through history.

The immortal couple shows up in unexpected places.

Adriana has been subtle, mostly avoiding notice save for some art dealings. But Cyrus? God, jazz historians still write about 'the great Cy Roman.'

That's the juicy part I don't expect to find. In the 50s, it seems Cyrus became a jazz musician, doing quite well for himself before 'dying' in a 'mysterious accident' at the advent of the 70s.

This whole era predates YouTube entirely, and only fragments of his work remain, but I play what I can find, despite the poor sound of the laptop speakers and the grainy quality of old recordings.

It's the perfect distraction to ease my mind as the shards of broken memories settle back into the dark corner of my mind where they usually live, locked away. Anything not to think, not to remember.

The temperature drops suddenly, and I know she's here, even before she commands me to *"Turn that trash off"* in a stern tone.

Fuck. My heart speeds in my chest as I apologize, quickly slamming the laptop shut. She's always sneaking up on me.

The dread of being caught red-handed, again, sits uncomfortably in my stomach, stealing my breath until I am dangerously close to hyperventilating. *You fucked up again, Jude.*

Adriana looks exhausted as she sinks into the chair behind her desk, dawn fading into daylight outside.

"Aren't you supposed to be asleep?" Her voice is tinted with annoyance as she opens her laptop without looking at me directly.

"Where were you?" I counter, wringing my hands.

Adriana looks up, glaring at me over her laptop like I've insulted her bloodline or something.

"None of your business," she replies simply, dismissing me.

I stand so fast, I almost knock my laptop off the desk. "I'm not a child, Adriana. Jesus."

"I beg your pardon?" Her voice rises an octave and I know I'm in dangerous territory. But the frustration, the insecurity, the guilt that has been bubbling inside me has gone from simmering to damn-near exploding. "Compared to the lifetimes I've lived, you *are* a child."

"That's not fair, and you know it." I bang my fist on the table. "I have lived as well."

She laughs, a cruel, mocking sound. "Ha! What do you know? The pain and suffering I've had to endure—"

I cut her off. "You're not the only one with darkness."

"Oh, really?" she challenges.

My hands are shaking as I stare out the window, avoiding her fiery gaze. "Perhaps this isn't working." I don't mean the assignment; I mean everything. I know when I'm not wanted.

"Perhaps." Adriana doesn't react, which pushes my buttons even more. I don't even matter enough to get a proper reaction out of her. *Foolish, Jude. Thinking anyone could care about trash like you.*

'*I wish she aborted you,*' my grandmother said. Not just that day when I was five, eyes blurry with tears as she chased me through a field of stinging nettles with the home-made cane in her hand, but often.

Maybe she was right. Perhaps it would've been better for everyone if my mother had aborted me.

I'm barely keeping it together, repressed emotions rising to the surface. "This is not a one-sided thing. I can't keep putting my heart, my life, on the line for you, only to have you stomp all over it with those fancy shoes."

Adriana looks at me with a challenge in her eyes but doesn't even bat an eyelid when she says: "Then go."

I'm momentarily frozen by the cruelty of her words.

But I will not beg, won't plead.

I storm out of her office without another word, slamming the door behind me.

She doesn't try to stop me, doesn't even call after me.

Guess she has Cyrus now; she doesn't need me anymore.

Fuck this!

CHAPTER 29
FAMILIAR BETRAYAL

(ADRIANA)

The sound of the door slamming echoes through my office as I rake my hands through my hair, my shoulders slumping in a sigh that weighs as much as the universe.

I didn't mean to take my frustration out on Jude but he caught me off guard. I thought he'd be asleep when I got back.

Speaking to Cyrus was more unsettling than reassuring. He says he did it to protect me, but all that matters is that he did it. He promised *La Famiglia* the Grimoire in exchange for my life, for his freedom. *The road to hell is paved with good intentions.*

Idiot. I sigh. They're just using him. Once they get what they want, both of us will be on the strike list.

I still don't know what The Family of Devils wants with that damn book but it can't be anything good. Destroy me, use it against me, or use it to bend me to their side—none of those options end well for me.

Cyrus never did understand what the Grimoire was to me, not entirely. Even after all our time together, I couldn't trust him with that secret, that vulnerability. Yet I spilled it all to Jude so effortlessly. *Circumstances change...*

We're in a world of danger, and the liability of getting attached to a fragile human does not escape me.

But it's not Jude's fault. I shouldn't have taken it out on him.

He's been nothing but helpful and obedient since he trusted my unconventional offer of employment.

It takes eleven minutes to convince myself to follow him down the hall.

Despite the urge to throw the door open uninvited, I knock gently. "Jude?"

For a long three seconds, there is nothing but silence, but then he replies. "It's open." His voice drips with resignation.

I push inside slowly.

He's sitting on the bed, back against the headboard, a notebook on his lap. Lines of neat black scribbles fill half the page with whatever he was writing. It's not work stuff.

Not sure where to start, I stand in the middle of the room as he quietly regards me with suspicion.

He doesn't snap, doesn't lash out, even though he's got every reason to; he just waits.

"Jude," I say softly, keeping his gaze. How easy it would be to just compel him into compliance, to make him forget yesterday. I could make him forget everything, including what's happening between us.

But I do no such thing. I just stand there awkwardly until he shifts, making space for me.

The bed indents as I sit down on the edge. I turn to face him, regarding the intensity in those perceptive eyes that are looking at me like they have too much to say but will never spill their secrets.

"I'm sorry, *tesoro*." I keep his gaze in mine as I reach for his hand, squeezing.

His fingers are limp in mine, unresponsive. "It's fine." His tone makes it clear that he doesn't mean it.

"No, it's not." I sigh. "I got overwhelmed and took it out on you. It's not fair."

Something in his face softens, not a lot, but a little crack in the stone exterior. *It's a start.*

Jude doesn't reply, just waits for me to continue, setting his notebook down on the bedside table.

"It's been almost ten years since I last saw Cyrus. It threw me a bit…" I look away, trying to hide the emotion from him, but Jude reaches over, pulling my face toward him to keep my eyes on his.

"Yet you had no problem fucking him." The innocence dissipates from his expression, replaced by an icy cold glare that turns my dead insides to lead.

I hang my head in shame. "I shouldn't have. There are no excuses." How does one explain the rush of an eternal blood bond to a human, the potency of such an exchange? Does it even matter? I could've had *some* semblance of self-control.

"What is wrong with me?" Jude's next question catches me off guard. I search his eyes but find no explanation.

"What do you mean? Nothing is wrong with you. You're perfect." I reach for him, stroking his cheek. "Why would you even ask that?"

This time, it's Jude's turn to look away. Even with my enhanced hearing, I miss his answer the first time. The second time is barely any louder, but the words finally form an audible sentence. "You never want to be with me…Not like that, like with *him*."

I sigh. *There it is.* "It's complicated."

Jude rolls his eyes. "Sure, such a cop-out."

He's right. He deserves more. "I could tell you it's not you, it's me, which is true. But I'm afraid that is no less of a 'cop-out,' as you call it."

When he meets my gaze again, it's winter in those gray eyes. "Then tell me something real."

I consider it for a moment, then admit, "I'm scared."

"Of what?" he asks, surprise on his face. The honesty of the answer surprised me too.

"Of the past repeating itself. Of hurting you. Of getting hurt. Any and all of the above."

He's quiet for a while before asking, "Is this about Elijah?"

My body stiffens at the name. "What do you know about Elijah?" I snap, too quickly, and then catch myself. "Sorry, I suppose it is…Partially at least." Despite the passage of time, the wound is still too fresh.

I sit back against the headboard beside him, shoulder to shoulder, so I don't have to face him.

"Cyrus called me the new Elijah."

"*Porco puttana.*" I shake my head vehemently as I curse. "You're nothing like him." But even as I say it, I know it's not the truth. The similarities are undeniable…

Jude places a gentle hand on my thigh. "Tell me, Adriana."

It's strange to hear him use my name without honorifics now.

"It's not all that exciting."

He puts an arm around my waist and nestles his head against my chest, not saying another word as he waits for me to continue, giving me the permission to spill the hurt that's been slowly poisoning my veins over the past nine years.

I don't know why I tell him. I've never told anyone the full story.

After it happened, after I got free, I shut myself off from the world and built a fortress around my heart, my life. *Never again*, I promised myself. *I'll never be made weak, made blind, by so-called love.*

"Elijah was my familiar..." I begin, the word hard to say, heavy.

I don't look at Jude when I speak, staring right ahead. Perhaps the confession is more for me than for him. But every word costs me, cuts deep.

"At first, Elijah was compelled. Cyrus's doing, not mine. But I've never liked keeping someone against their will, so I gave him a choice—stay or go. He wanted to stay." My voice drops. "Or so I thought."

I pause, focusing on Jude's steady breathing against my ribs. His presence grounds me, gives me the courage to continue.

"For five years, he was everything I thought I wanted. Devoted, eager to please, protective. It felt genuine."

Jude's hand finds mine, squeezing gently.

"I loved him," I whisper, the admission scraping my throat raw. "Not the same way I love Cyrus, but...differently. Softer. I was ready to give him everything, to start a life anywhere he chose, when—"

I stop, the memory cutting into my flesh like a shard of glass, even after all these years.

"When what?" Jude's voice is soft, patient.

"When I discovered it was all performance. Every moment of devotion, every gesture of care was calculated.

Fake. He'd been in contact with vampire hunters for months. And I was too obsessed to even notice. They wanted a supernatural genocide, and little dear Elijah bought into the dream, the mission: a world only for humans."

I close my eyes, but the memories play behind my eyelids anyway.

Such life in that deceitful boy, matched by a temper that kept things interesting. He cared for me, or performed care so perfectly I couldn't tell the difference. Once trained to my preferences, he could have me screaming in pleasure with nothing but his tongue.

We fucked everywhere: kitchen counters, library floors, against the floor-to-ceiling windows overlooking the city.

He was beautifully masochistic, craving pain in the same way I hunger for blood. I gave him what he needed with careful cuts, blooming bruises...the sweet violence that quieted whatever demons drove him.

After each session, he'd go calm and loose-limbed, like he'd finally found peace. But there were rooms in his heart I could never enter, shadows I couldn't illuminate. Even when I drank from him, tasted his memories, his emotions, something felt closed off.

I never saw it coming.

"They came at noon. During my rest," I tell Jude, the memory so vivid, it could've happened yesterday. "Elijah let them in. Poisoned my wine. And then had the audacity to tell me it was the right thing to do."

I can sense Jude's tension, the change in his breathing. But he still doesn't interrupt, just gives me the space to figure out which words come next.

"They took me to a warehouse outside the city. Wanted me to break the lock on the Grimoire. I refused. Even death would be safer than having those spells in hunter hands."

The words come faster now, venom I need to purge from my system, as I finally unclench my fists around the pain I've held so tightly that it became my entire identity these past few years.

"For nearly a month, they…" I swallow hard, the words sticking in my throat. "Let's just say they were *thorough*. Creative. Silver burns differently. It doesn't only hurt; it prevents healing."

I still had my fire magic then, but it was no use to me. They'd thought of everything, sucking all the air from the room, creating a vacuum. I didn't need air to breathe but fire needed oxygen to ignite. There was no fighting science.

Trapped. Fully. In a hellish nightmare with no escape.

The worst part wasn't the pain; I'm used to pain. But Elijah's betrayal, the knowledge that I let it happen, let myself be weak, that's what destroyed me.

Jude's hand tightens in mine. "Why did they want it?"

I sigh. "They thought the Grimoire was the source of my powers, and that they could reverse-engineer it into a weapon against vampires. But the idiots had it all wrong. Half a story. It never *gave* me any powers…"

Jude nods, taking it all in. "How did you escape?" he asks.

"Patience. Planning. I bided my time, managed to break free when they let their guard down. One night, they sent in a newbie who neglected to seal the airlock properly. Amateurs."

I don't elaborate on the details of what I did to my captors. Don't describe the warehouse painted red, the systematic way I hunted down every person involved in my imprisonment, tearing their limbs from their bodies piece by piece without remorse, getting stronger with each body I drained.

"What happened to Elijah?"

"I saved him for last." The words come out flat, emotionless.

The traitorous familiar Elijah didn't die by the hands of the vampire hunters; he died by mine. In the month since my capture, he'd run away, changed his name. But there was nowhere he could run where I wouldn't find him. He was marked, *mine*.

Jude lifts his head and looks at me expectantly, like I'm telling him some dark fairy tale instead of my personal trauma. "What did you do?"

"I made sure he understood the consequences of his actions," I say simply. Jude doesn't need to know the pleasure I got from the begging, the crying, the miserable sound Elijah made when I crushed his pathetic cock under my heel.

The traitorous familiar had broken in seconds, pleading, promising me anything and everything I wanted. But it was too late. My heart was iced over, a little bit more charred than it was before.

When I dug my nails into his eye sockets, he screamed, but nobody came to save him. Just how nobody came for me in that torturous cell they kept me in for four weeks, stripping me bare of my skin, my powers, the will to live.

There was no satisfaction to be had for the justice finally served. I didn't take a drop of blood from him that day; I didn't want to be left with that bitter aftertaste. No, I just ripped his throat open and watched him bleed out on the pavement like a nobody.

I felt nothing. No remorse, no regret, nothing except

maybe the conviction that I would never be caught in the same vulnerability again.

"Tell me...I want to know," Jude insists, and after hesitating briefly, I do; I tell him all the details without sugarcoating any of the horrors of my revenge.

The words are sharp, cutting as they leave, but there's also something healing about finally releasing them, letting go of a burden I've carried so long I forgot what it felt like to stand upright without its crushing weight.

When I finish my tale, when I have no more words and Jude has no more questions, for a moment, we sit in silence. Time feels suspended, fragile.

If I still had working lungs, I'd be holding my breath right now. The vulnerability sits heavy in my throat, stuck.

This is it, this is when he realizes his mistake, when he leaves.

With a heavy heart, I meet Jude's eyes, expecting to see horror, revulsion, the moment when he realizes exactly what kind of monster he's gotten involved with.

But there is none of that in his eyes. There is no judgment or fear, just Jude listening to the worst parts of my history and staying exactly where he is, holding me.

When he speaks, his voice calm and certain: "Good. He deserved it."

The simple acceptance hits me harder than any declaration of love ever could.

"You're not horrified?"

"Horrified that someone who claimed to love you sold you to people who tortured you for weeks?" Jude's voice carries an edge I haven't heard from him. "The only thing that *horrifies* me is that you had to go through that alone."

Something cracks open in my chest. The world unpauses, exhales.

"This is why…" I whisper, unable to find the words to complete the thought. But Jude doesn't need any more words.

He hugs me tighter, threading his fingers through mine.

"I'm not him," Jude says firmly. "I'm not pretending. What you feel from me, what you taste in my blood, it's real. All of it."

"I know." And I do know, intellectually. But knowing and trusting are different things. "It doesn't calm the storms in my mind."

I also thought I *knew* with Elijah. Yet he still managed to fool me, to manipulate me, to hide enough that I never suspected the truth, not even when I drank from him. I just thought he wanted to keep some things private. Never suspected the things he kept private were his real feelings and intentions. He was so good at managing his act, at making me believe that he loved me, even his heart rate didn't spike when he lied. Nothing gave him away.

Fuck Elijah.

Jude shifts beside me, turning so he can meet my eyes directly.

"Let me earn your trust," he says simply. "Please, Milady."

The earnestness in his voice makes me want to believe that maybe this time will be different, that he will be different.

I don't answer, just wrap him in my arms as we lie down on the bed, holding each other, my head on his chest, the rhythm of his heart regulating me.

Don't get attached, Adriana. Don't.

But I know it's already too late.

CHAPTER 30
FALLING APART

(JUDE)

L ittle over an hour ago, I was ready to pack it all up, to leave for good. But now I can't imagine being anywhere but here with Adriana.

She feels so right in my arms, vulnerable but not weak, *safe*.

"Where was Cyrus when this all went down?" I ask quietly after the silence between us stretches for a minute, two.

The question has been turning over in my head since the start of Adriana's gruesome tale of how she lost her Grimoire. *How could he let this happen to her?*

Adriana sighs, lifts herself off my chest to sit against the headboard again. "Cyrus was gone. He'd left a few days before the hunters came, stormed out after one of our infamous fights."

I know I ask too many questions. My grandmother tried to beat it out of me many times with that unforgiving homemade cane of hers. But I can't help it; I want to know more. "What were you fighting about?"

The laugh that escapes Adriana's throat is hollow, bitter. "The same old thing. I called him reckless. He called me controlling. But this time, he *did* fuck up."

"By bringing you Elijah?"

"No, he had no way of knowing. I think he was genuinely trying to help. As much as the two of them didn't ever get along. Elijah was way too homophobic for that. Another red flag I should've seen a mile away."

This Elijah guy sounds like a royal cunt. But I don't say anything. I don't want to risk her shutting down. Not when she's finally opening up, finally letting me in. Seeing this side of Adriana makes her seem almost human...

My mind cannot fathom how someone could do this. After five whole years together? I've never even had a relationship that long.

Adriana doesn't deserve being hunted simply for who she is, something she has no control over. *No better than a bunch of bullies.*

The anger is bubbling in my veins as I pull her back against my chest while she continues her story, listening closely, despite some of the words being difficult to hear.

"For hundreds of years, I lived as a hybrid without having to look over my shoulder," Adriana narrates as she runs her fingers lazily over my arm in repetitive infinity patterns. "Nobody suspected I was anything other than a vampire. Only Cyrus knew what I was, as much as he didn't really comprehend the mechanics of it. The coven knew but nobody survived long enough to tell anyone."

The pieces slowly fall into place. "He told someone, didn't he?"

Adriana sighs. "Indeed. Slipped out in a moment of

passion, or so he claims. All I know is the information got out, and suddenly I had a target on my head."

Asshole. No wonder Adriana was pissed.

I stay quiet as she tells me about the months that followed, about the running from one hideout to the next, the list of pursuers growing faster than she could deal with them.

"He kept apologizing, but it was too late," she says. "The damage was done, the secret out, my safety shattered."

And instead of staying to help fix what he'd broken, Cyrus ran away and left her to face the consequences alone. He didn't even come back when she was captured.

"I kept expecting him to sense my distress through our bond, to come for me. But he never did." Her voice breaks slightly and it damn near rips apart my heart. I try to comfort her, to hold her tighter, but I know the damage has already been done long before I came around.

"Maybe he was too far away to feel your bond," I offer, though even as I say it, I don't believe it.

But Adriana shakes her head. "No, he chose not to come. Decades, centuries, I've bailed him out of every imaginable situation. And the one time I needed him, he disappeared. Fucking coward."

Just thinking about it makes me furious. *What kind of person does that?*

"Did you ask him why?"

"No, I didn't want to hear his excuses, his hollow apologies. I needed time for myself, to..." Adriana trails off, but I can fill in the blanks.

The silence that follows is heavy with implication.

I have no words of comfort to offer, nothing that could

erase years of pain and betrayal. All I can do is sit here, holding her, witnessing her emotions.

Adriana suddenly stiffens in my arms, her hands flying to her ears as she lets out a sharp cry of pain.

"What's wrong?" I ask, but she doesn't seem to hear me. Her eyes are wide, unfocused, like she's hearing something I can't.

"Too loud," she gasps, pressing her palms harder against her ears. "Everything's too loud, I can hear—"

Then, she's straining forward, eyes darting around the room. "It's gone, all gone. I can't hear anything. Like cotton in my ears, but—"

There's panic building in her expression as another wave hits. Her supernatural hearing is glitching, fluctuating.

She cries out again, the sound echoing off the bedroom walls.

"Adriana, hey, look at me." I take her face in my hands. Her skin is cold, colder than usual, frost forming at her fingertips where they grip the sheets.

"It's my emotions," she manages through gritted teeth. "It's destabilizing my powers."

Without thinking, I tilt my head, exposing my throat. "Take what you need."

Adriana shakes her head furiously. "Jude, no, I can't—"

"You can," I insist, pulling her closer. "You said fresh blood helps, right? So take it."

Her eyes meet mine, and I can see the internal war playing out across her features, her body's needs fighting the will of her convictions.

Seeing her like this is too much. I am helpless, useless. *"Please,"* I whisper. "Let me help you, Milady."

That breaks her resolve. Her fangs extend, and she bites down on my throat.

I brace for impact, but it doesn't come.

It's not working how it should.

Something is wrong.

Adriana coughs, shaking as her fangs retract and extend at their own will, making it impossible for her to pierce my skin, to drink.

"Adriana?" I ask, but she doesn't respond, her eyes rolling back in her head as her fangs retract again.

Fuck, fuck, fuck!

I jump up and rush to the bathroom, my mind bouncing all over.

She can't die. Not now.

Ripping open cupboards and drawers, I sweep through the space to find something, anything, that can help.

But my search comes up empty, my desperation becoming unbearable.

There's only one option left that my overwhelmed mind can see.

The shattering echoes off the tiled walls as I smash my fist into the large oval mirror hanging over the basin.

I feel nothing, even as blood fills the scrapes on my knuckles; nothing as I grab a large shard, gripping it so tightly that the edges dig into my fingers, slicing them.

When I return to the room, Adriana's body has gone still, eyes wide, staring at the ceiling.

"Stay with me, please," I beg, as I climb back on the bed, pulling her toward me, hugging her close.

She's unresponsive as I bring the jagged shard of glass to my left wrist with steady hands. It doesn't sink into the skin smoothly as a blade would but rips through my flesh like the piece of broken mirror it is, the white lines filling with crimson until the cuts are brimming, overflowing with blood that drips onto the bed sheets.

The pain doesn't register in my mind. My thoughts are on loop: *'don't die, don't die, please don't die.'*

Sitting her up against my chest, her body limp like her bones are made of Jell-O, I force her lips open, letting the blood drip from my wrist.

"Too slow, fuck," I mutter under my breath as I bring the shard down again, cutting deeper this time. But I misjudge the pressure, and the shard sinks in further than anticipated, blood falling freely onto Adriana's lips now.

Pain floods my circuits, but I push it down, keeping my focus on Adriana.

At first, she remains unresponsive, body soft, a rag-doll in my arms.

No, please no.

I'm shaking her now, desperate, as blood splutters all over her face, the sheets, my shirt. But I notice none of these details, only how her body seems to be freezing over, a thin layer of ice forming on her lips, spreading.

For a painful eternity, nothing happens.

Too late, I'm too late.

And then Adriana sputters, gasps.

"Thank god," I mutter, as she grabs my wrist with both hands to hold it in front of her lips, drinking desperately, nearly choking.

Slowly, the life comes back to her pale skin, the ice melting around her as she drinks her fill, drinks until I'm lightheaded but relieved.

I'm about to pass out when she finally regains control and pulls away, licking a broad stroke over my gashes. The blood coagulates as soon as her saliva touches it, the wounds beginning to seal over, healing.

"Better?" I ask softly, touching her cheek as I offer a small smile.

Adriana nods, looking around bewildered. "Thank you. I—I don't know what happened."

"It's okay," I tell her, holding her close. "We'll figure it out."

"You didn't have to—" she starts but I cut her off.

"I wanted to."

"You should go. I'll be okay. Don't worry about me." Adriana tries to untangle herself from my embrace but I hold on for dear life. "It's only going to get worse."

I shake my head vehemently, refusing to move.

"I'm not going anywhere, Milady," I whisper against her hair, and I've never meant anything more. "Whatever happens, I want to be here, with you."

CHAPTER 31

THE RIGHT ORDER

(ADRIANA)

I slip from Jude's room without a sound, closing the door carefully so as not to wake him. His breathing has finally evened out, deep and steady with mortal sleep.

Outside, the early morning sun is painting the horizon in soft gold hues as I head to my office, the echo of Jude's blood still rich on my tongue.

Gods, I can't believe he just did that.

The mere thought that he'd cut his veins open willingly to save me makes my black heart ache.

It's also a lot to process.

My mind feels fractured, like a mirror with too many cracks to count. Too many emotions are hitting at once: the vulnerability from sharing my history with Jude, the gratitude for his sacrifice, the terror of my own instability. And that's not even considering Cyrus's unexpected return after all these years. I don't know which feeling to trust, which impulse to follow.

Trying to rest now would be futile, I know that. So, I don't even bother.

I should get some work done, I tell myself as I head to my office instead, knowing that is unlikely.

I'm so behind on assignments; the messages have been piling up. But those rich assholes can wait a bit longer for their artifacts.

Once the office door clicks closed behind me, I select a record from my collection, Chopin's nocturnes, something to soothe the chaos in my mind. The needle settles into familiar grooves as I turn to my bookshelves, suddenly unable to tolerate their current organization.

They've been arranged by author for years, but now I need them by title.

I pull out the first stack, appreciating the lack of dust. Felix is doing a good job at keeping things pristine. *Maybe I should keep him.* But it's not just Felix I want to keep…

Stop it!

I force myself to focus on the titles, on the patterns, on something I can control when I can't even control my own mind, my own reactions. The familiar task soothes the hypervigilant part of me that's screaming danger at every shadow, every sound.

Anna Karenina fits before *Atlas Shrugged*.

Beloved next to *The Bell Jar*.

The repetitive motion calms me, but it can't fully quiet the tumultuous thoughts assaulting my mind. They keep returning to Jude, to the memory of his selfless offer when he cut his own wrist without hesitation when he saw me fading.

The metallic sweetness of his blood lingers on my palate, and with it, the memory of how naturally he'd submitted to my need. Without being asked. Of his own free will.

'I'm not going anywhere,' he'd whispered, and the weight of those words threatens to crush me as I pull another stack of books from the shelf, dumping them on the desk.

He trusts me too much: with his life, his blood, his safety. *Foolish boy.*

Trust is such a fragile, precious thing…And so easily destroyed.

I slide *Crime and Punishment* between *The Count of Monte Cristo* and *David Copperfield*, remembering the last time such a level of trust broke through my armor. *Remember how that ended?*

Elijah damn near destroyed everything, and now I want to bash my head against the same stone again? *You never learn, Adriana.*

An immortal lifetime of betrayals has trained me to expect the worst, even when logic tells me Jude isn't Elijah.

I know they're different, as much as my mind insists on finding similarities like this is some spot-the-difference game. Yet part of me keeps waiting for the other shoe to drop, for Jude to reveal some ulterior motive, a hidden agenda.

Don Quixote fits neatly after *Doctor Zhivago,* as my mind continues to pit them against each other.

Where Elijah had been calculating, ambitious beneath his devotion, Jude is genuine, almost raw. When he kneels, there is no performance in it, no manipulation; only instinct, like a flower turning toward sunlight.

He's perfect, the submissive I've always wanted. He actually wants this rather than wanting to want it, like Elijah did.

And that scares me.

Because Jude is mortal. Beautifully, tragically mortal.

The mathematics of our situation is brutal and inescapable. If I survive this, and that's a big if, what's the best-case scenario here? In the span of Jude's lifetime—another sixty, maybe seventy years if he's lucky—I'll barely notice the passage of time. He'll age and change and eventually leave me, if not by choice then by the simple progression of years. His hair will gray, his hands will wrinkle, his mortal body will fail him.

And I'll be left with another collection of memories, another locked case full of artifacts from a love that couldn't survive the weight of immortality.

The thought of watching him grow old, of seeing vitality fade from those expressive eyes, makes something inside me revolt.

How do you open your heart to someone whose heart-beat has an expiration date? When you know every kiss, every touch, every shared moment is borrowed time?

The English Patient slides between *Emma* and *Ethan Frome* without conscious thought. It belongs there.

I can't turn him into a vampire either. I would never do that to anyone else. Vampirism isn't salvation; it's a curse dressed up in promises of power and eternal youth.

The guilt of carnage from my first feeding never leaves. Twenty-three people, including seven children, all dead because I couldn't control the monster I'd become.

It was not the future I had worked so hard for.

When I still had a beating heart, my own natural life force to draw from, there was no ice, only fire and purpose.

It took me years to control the flame burning in my veins, but once I did, I was unstoppable. Well, as unstoppable as a bastard female child born out of wedlock in the 1500s could be.

My father contributed little except a surname and some sperm. One night of passion, then back to his *real* family. Everyone in the village knew; it was an open secret, but it granted me no favors. When I pleaded at his door at fifteen, the smell of my mother's burning body still thick in my throat and nowhere else to go, he laughed. Called me *'impure'* and threatened my life if I ever dared show my face again.

The coven took me in and helped me master my magic, my flame. Back then, it burned bright and ferociously. I took what I wanted, built the world I craved, and nobody dared try to stop me. I was untouchable!

Until Demetrius discovered me amongst the dead, moments from expelling my final breath.

My sire never bothered to ask what I wanted—just forced his blood down my throat and disappeared, another disappointing father figure, while my fire inverted to ice and the insatiable hunger for blood ripped through my insides like poison.

The transformation tried to tear me apart, vampire and witch natures fighting for dominance. I couldn't control either one, especially not with the endless hunger, the all-consuming need for more blood.

By dawn, there was nothing left of that village but silence and the weight of what I'd done, ice spreading over the corpses of the innocent children, life snuffed out before they even had a chance to live.

Desperation drove me back to the coven I swore I'd never return to, back to the High Priestess who created the magical spell in the Grimoire to stabilize what should never have existed. She gave me back my fire, even if she couldn't save me from the fate of the undead.

The memory makes my hands shake as I reach for the next book. That village was my first lesson in the true price of losing control. Innocent people died because I was too weak, too new, too overwhelmed by what I'd become to maintain even basic restraint.

What happens when I lose control again? Because I will. My powers are failing, my grip on both my vampire and witch natures loosening with each passing day.

When the Grimoire's stabilizing influence finally fails completely, when the ice tears me apart from the inside, what collateral damage will I leave behind?

What about Jude? What if he's there when it happens?

The image flashes through my mind uninvited: Jude's body frozen solid, his trusting eyes wide with betrayal and terror as ice spreads from my fingertips to destroy him, just like those children in the village nearly 500 years ago.

My hand brushes the shelf, leaving frost in its wake.

Ice, always ice now.

The English Patient finds its place before *Frankenstein*, Mary Shelley's masterpiece about the hubris of creation and the responsibility we bear for our monsters. *How fitting.*

What good could come from keeping Jude? I'm creating another attachment, another beautiful disaster waiting to unfold. I'm drawing an innocent man into my orbit, letting him offer his blood and his devotion, knowing that proximity to me will eventually ruin him.

It's inevitable.

History speaks for itself.

I couldn't bear it if Jude were the one paying the price for my weakness.

But the alternative, pushing him away, feels impossible now.

He's only been here for a few weeks, seconds in the context of my existence, yet the thought of him leaving, of returning to my former routine, is more depressing than I care to admit.

I've sampled true devotion, and I'm not sure I'm strong enough to give that up.

The record cascades through another nocturne as the spiral continues.

More books on the desk. More what-ifs I don't want to consider.

The *Handmaid's Tale* slides in between *Hamlet* and *Heart of Darkness*. I'm no longer just organizing books but attempting to arrange my thoughts, my emotions, the chaotic tangle of want and fear and longing that Jude's simple act of sacrifice has unleashed. But there is no alphabetical system for my inner struggle.

I should send him away, I know I should, for his own safety. But I can't; I won't.

The truth is, I want him. Not only his blood or his submission or his research skills. I want his laughter in my kitchen, his questions about my past, his absolute faith that I'm something more than the monster I know myself to be. I want to deserve the way he looks at me, even knowing I never will.

That wanting scares me. Because wanting leads to taking, and taking from mortals always ends the same way: with silence and blood and the weight of another death on my conscience.

But Jude isn't just any mortal. He cut his own wrist to save me, offered his life force without hesitation or condition. There's something about that level of selfless devotion that cannot be ignored, cannot be stomped out.

It's an impossible choice. One that has no win-win solution. Sacrifices will have to be made.

One problem at a time.

Step one is surviving, finding the Grimoire, dealing with *La Famiglia Eterna*, regaining control over my fractured nature. Whatever feelings are involved will have to wait until I'm stable enough to examine them without the risk of losing control and destroying everything I touch.

But first, *War and Peace* needs a new spot on the shelf.

CHAPTER 32

MASTER PLAN

(CYRUS)

Two months of stalking Adriana and her pet human have left me restless.

La Famiglia Eterna grows more impatient with each inadequate weekly report I deliver. They want results, want the Grimoire, want Adriana broken and compliant.

But she's proving more resilient than any of us anticipated, even weakened as she is.

I haven't dared approach her directly again. Not after having to confront the disappointment on her face at the *Blue Moon*.

No, I carried on, followed in the shadows, pleaded with some goddess up above that a solution would present itself.

But so far, nothing.

Tonight's debrief with Caterina was particularly tense. The rest of the council members no longer bother coming to the check-ins.

'The Family is questioning your methods,' Caterina had said earlier, her fingers trailing along my jaw in that way that used to distract me from her words but now makes me want to throw up in my mouth. 'Perhaps a more direct approach—'

'Give me more time,' I interrupted. 'She's close to finding it. The human is proving useful.'

Caterina smiled, but it didn't reach her eyes. 'Time is a luxury we may not have, caro. The preparations are nearly complete.'

Preparations for what, she didn't say. She never says.

That's why I'm following her now, twenty minutes after she dismissed me from our usual meeting spot at La Famiglia's headquarters.

The Inner Circle thinks I've returned to my surveillance of Adriana, but something in Caterina's tone tonight set my teeth on edge. Her tone spelled nothing good. I had to know.

Caterina is a woman on a mission as she slips through the city's shadows, weaving through the industrial district.

I keep my distance as I trail her deeper into territory that feels distinctly unwelcome.

After months of stalking Adriana, this role comes almost naturally now.

The warehouse that Caterina approaches looks abandoned. Broken windows gape like empty eye sockets, surrounded by weeds that have grown as tall as a teenager through cracks in the concrete. But that's not what's wrong with the picture.

The shadows around the building move oddly, and there's a hum in the air that makes my supernatural senses itch. There's magic here.

Caterina surveys her surroundings and disappears through a side entrance.

I wait thirty seconds, then dissolve into a shadow and slip through a crack in one of the broken windows.

It shouldn't be this easy, but I've always been notoriously good at slipping in and out of places undetected. Blame four centuries of forbidden loves and stolen moments, sneaking through the shadows to avoid scorn. Sorcha used to say that some men are made for the front door but I was made for the window.

Inside the warehouse, I materialize behind a stack of crates.

The area is dimly lit and the repugnant smell hits me immediately: blood, chemicals, and something vile that makes my dead stomach turn. *What is that?*

The large space has been converted into some kind of laboratory complete with surgical tables, medical equipment, and glass containers filled with substances that could be anything. Rows of tables stretch back into the dark, each one holding a shape under a white sheet that can only be one thing.

Forty-three of them. I count to make sure, and then I wish I hadn't.

I lift the nearest sheet. A woman, eyes open, stares at nothing. Her chest has been opened and sewn shut again, the stitches small and even. I drop the sheet and don't lift another.

My sensitive ears pick up voices from deeper in the warehouse, and I move closer, using the shadows to disguise my presence. The overwhelming scent of death and magic in the air must be masking my own supernatural signature, because no one seems to notice my approach.

I stay hidden in the shadows, far enough from the voices so they don't see me, but close enough to hear every word.

"—the latest batch?" Caterina's voice is coming from what appears to be an observation area overlooking the main floor.

"Complete failures again, I'm afraid," replies a male voice, unfamiliar, with a slight German accent. "The subjects didn't survive the transformation process. Their nature still rejects the serum too violently, even with the modifications."

She swears under her breath, the Russian unintelligible to my ears, but I've heard those curses before.

I creep closer to the observation window, staying low. Through the glass, I can see Caterina standing beside a gray-haired man in a blood-stained lab coat.

"This is very disappointing." Caterina starts to pace.

"We've tried every variation of the turning process we can think of." The man consults his clipboard. "Slower introduction of vampiric essence, magical suppressants during transformation...Nothing works. The fire witches keep dying."

I duck low as Caterina moves to the window, surveying the rows of sheet-covered bodies below with detached interest.

"*La Famiglia* wants progress," she says in that same tone she uses to threaten me. "Why can't you simply replicate what was done for Adriana? You're supposed to be the best."

"Because it's not as simple as just copying the Grimoire's spells," the man replies, frustration creeping into his voice. "It's an active magical system. The spells inside generate life force constantly, bound to her blood.

We'd need to understand not just what the spells do, but how to bind them to operate autonomously."

"So, we still need her Grimoire?" The irritation in her voice is unmissable.

"Unfortunately, yes. We need the book *and* the subject it was created for. We need to understand it, deconstruct how the spells generate and sustain life force in an undead body, then adapt the mechanism for mass production."

Mass production.

I have to steady myself against the wall to keep from staggering as the words sink in.

Fuck. That doesn't sound good.

"And if we get everything we need, get it all working, how quickly can we scale up?" Caterina asks.

"Conservatively? We can make hundreds of hybrids within the first year," the German answers. "We could turn entire covens, create an army of beings with vampire strength and witch magic."

"More powerful than the Fae?"

The man's smile is visible even from my hiding spot. "The Fae may be individually more powerful, but they can't stand against those numbers. We'd be unstoppable."

Caterina nods, satisfied. "Then perhaps it's time to apply more pressure. Cyrus is not proving as useful as we had hoped."

The sound of my name makes a shiver run up my spine.

"What did you have in mind?"

"The human boy, the one she's grown attached to. Perhaps he will finally be useful. As leverage." She's speaking to herself more than the guy now, staring off into the distance.

"Shall I have him taken?" the man asks, pulling my full attention back to the conversation.

"Not yet. Let's see what Cyrus comes up with. But prepare contingencies. If Adriana won't come willingly, we'll give her an additional *incentive*."

I've heard enough; too much.

Keeping low, I step back, desperate to put distance between me and the fucked-up conversation. The mere thought of the future they're planning is making me sick to my stomach.

The casual way Caterina discusses threatening Jude, an innocent human who stumbled into this nightmare, makes me want to smash my fist through the glass. The rage is immediate, visceral, catching me off guard with its intensity.

I slip back the way I came, through the broken window, my mind reeling with the implications of what I've discovered.

La Famiglia isn't only interested in Adriana's power; they want to weaponize it. They want to create an army of hybrid creatures using her blood and her mother's spellbook.

And I've been helping them.

For two months, I've been tracking her movements, reporting her weaknesses.

I thought I was part of a simple acquisition, bringing a rogue vampire back into the fold, keeping her safe. They said the Grimoire was too dangerous for one vampire to keep, that they would protect the species by putting it somewhere safe.

Instead, I've been helping them to lay the groundwork for genocide.

Even the all-powerful Fae stand no chance against an

army of vampire-witch hybrids. *La Famiglia Eterna* would become the undisputed rulers of the supernatural world, the top of the food chain.

And Adriana...Christ, what they have planned for her doesn't bear thinking about. They need her alive to unlock the Grimoire, to explain its secrets, but after that? She becomes redundant, a potential threat to their new order.

I wish she had told me what the Grimoire really did, that it was more than just a power booster. I guess I never gave her any reason to trust me with that secret. It doesn't matter anymore anyway.

I emerge from the warehouse into the cold night air, bile rising in my throat. My hands shake violently as I lean against the building's exterior wall, fighting the urge to vomit blood onto the cracked concrete.

Forty-three bodies. Forty-three witches who died the most painful death, human bodies torn apart by opposing forces.

And I helped make it possible.

Every report I've filed, every detail about Adriana's life, it's all been feeding into this nightmare. *La Famiglia* has been using my intelligence to prepare for the moment when they can take everything from her.

The weight of complicity crashes over me like a building collapsing.

I slide down the wall until I'm sitting on the filthy ground, my head in my hands. How many more will die when they perfect the process? How many covens will they slaughter to build their hybrid army?

Christ, what have I done?

For months, I've told myself that *La Famiglia*'s methods were harsh but necessary. That supernatural order required strong leadership, even if that leadership made difficult choices.

But this isn't order. This is butchery with a political agenda.

The memory of Jude's shy smile flashes through my mind. He has no idea what he's gotten mixed up in. No idea that simply being near Adriana makes him a target.

The bond between us means I can taste echoes of him sometimes, when Adriana feeds. Sweet, willing, completely devoted. It should make me jealous—and it does—but more than that, it makes me protective. He's part of her now, even if he doesn't fully understand how much.

I may be a monster, but the suffering of innocents has never been something I can stomach. Especially not innocents who love Adriana better than I can. Who makes her happy, as happy as her immortal heart could be. *No, he's no use to anyone dead.*

There's something about Jude; I recognize something in that boy, something that cuts too close to home. He looks at Adriana with wonder, like she's the most magnificent creature he's ever seen. *Oh, sweet suffering,* I know that look; I've worn it for centuries…gladly.

I don't know why her. There's something about Adriana that defies all explanation. A pull that goes beyond the physical, beyond even the blood bond. She's more extraordinary than most people will ever know, and those who do recognize it, we become satellites in her orbit, pulled in by her gravity.

Nothing has been the same since she decided to keep me all those years ago.

Even though I gave her little reason to do so.

Back then, I had nothing to offer but passion and promises.

The role of the last-born son of four doesn't come with many advantages, no matter how well off your family is. Actually, I can't think of any. Just another mouth to feed, another disappointment when you're not the heir, not the spare, not even particularly noteworthy. A pitiful lifetime of being overlooked, dismissed, invisible until the night Adriana smiled at me like I was worth something.

Jude never mattered until he mattered to her. And perhaps it was the same for me. Even if I'll never admit it out loud.

I push myself off the ground, legs still unsteady. The smart play would be to run. To disappear into the night, find some distant corner of the world where *La Famiglia*'s reach can't follow, and let Adriana and Jude face whatever's coming alone.

But I know I can't walk away.

Not again.

I have to warn her.

How though? I know Adriana better than to assume she'd let me into her apartment willingly, that she'd listen to reason from me. Too much history, too much hurt between us.

No, I'll have to try another way.

Jude.

CHAPTER 33
THE DISCOVERY

(JUDE)

After that initial surprise visit, Cyrus stays away for two months, during which Adriana and I fall into some semblance of a regular routine.

I'm allowed to stay up until 1 AM, sometimes 2 AM, depending on how my research is going.

Felix has come back after his nearly three-week holiday, and by the time I wake up, usually around 10, my coffee is ready and waiting.

Next up, exercise, on Adriana's insistence, outsourced to Felix.

A few days each week, I go for a run instead, though. Mostly to get out of the house. Plus, it clears my head; always has.

Adriana has become more paranoid about me leaving the house, but if it's during the day while the sun is out, she usually lets me go, albeit reluctantly.

She tried to keep me inside all the time, but my legs grew restless. I *need* to run.

When I was still in school, I could outrun any bully. If I got half a chance to run, that is. Useful, you'd think. But more often than not, I never got a single step in, outnumbered before I could flee. *'Run faster, maggot.'*

Nobody is chasing me these days, but I do still enjoy the rhythmic sound of my feet hitting the sidewalk. Long before rowing became an escape, before I even knew I could hide out on the water, running was my only solace.

Every part of my day is mapped out now. Breakfast is usually a smoothie of some sort; lunch is eggs and normal breakfast foods; and for dinner? A feast.

Felix is a formidable chef, and he keeps telling me how grateful he is to have a stomach appreciative of his talent. It's not out of the ordinary to have restaurant-quality steak on a normal Monday night. Not in Felix's kitchen.

He usually leaves after making my dinner, returning sometime before I wake up in the mornings.

The rest of the time, Felix manages the household tasks: laundry, cleaning, etc. I am grateful that I don't have to do it all alone, because despite my grandmother trying to beat it into me, I never cared much for domestic chores. That's not the kind of *service* I'm into.

Afternoons are mostly spent researching, doing what Adriana actually hired me to do. It's fascinating work, following the Grimoire through history, tracing the destruction it's left in its wake.

I used to wonder why Adriana didn't just do the work herself, but for one, she's always busy with some or other art thing, and also clearly doesn't have the patience for detailed work. Well, that, and her aversion to daytime activities, of course.

I don't think she sleeps much; I know she doesn't have to. Still, Adriana spends most of the daylight hours in her room. I've learned not to bother her during this time unless explicitly invited in.

In the early evenings, I usually brief her on my work and what I've found, and we'll work together for a few hours until dinnertime, which she makes me have around 9 PM.

There is nothing special about the routine. But the moments outside of it are what've been giving me a reason to get up in the morning. The moments she lets me worship her the way she deserves, the way I want to.

It's not uncommon for me to kneel at her feet, under her desk, eating her out before she starts work. Sometimes, I stay down there for a bit, even as she works. It's safe down there.

I know I'm lucky.

Lady Adriana takes care of my sexual health in the same serious manner as my physical health. She meticulously keeps track of when I come, making sure I am *serviced* regularly to keep my *'pipes clean and the juices flowing,'* as she calls it.

I sure don't mind. It's fucking hard not to come by any hand other than hers, but it's become impossible to finish without her explicit permission. I crave it. *Need* it. I can't even touch myself anymore without her permission.

But that's a good thing, a relief, something I don't have to think about, feel shame for.

She still feeds from me regularly, an exchange so powerful that it leaves me delirious with euphoria for hours after, despite the blood loss. Apparently, I taste better when I'm in the throes of climax, so I'm often rewarded with a hand job at the same time. Though, she doesn't always let me finish.

Sometimes, the Lady of the House edges me for days

before letting me come over that cool hand with the sharp nails that completely undo me when they're scraping my skin, marring it in beautiful red lines.

Mere months in her care and I'm fitter and healthier than I've been in sixteen months, since my days at the rowing club.

But I know my use to her is temporary. Part of me can't help but worry that when we find the Grimoire, all this will end.

But I push that thought out of my head as quickly as it surfaces.

Not finding it is worse. I can't watch Adriana fall apart in front of my eyes and not do anything about it.

Even though she's been mostly stable, thanks to the regular feedings, there are still times when the fear in her eyes is unmissable, when it all feels dangerously close to unraveling completely.

It's best not to think about that part, I find. It only makes me anxious, freezing me over in fear. It's better to focus on the research, on the pleasure I'm giving and receiving.

Our contract has an addendum now. The living document continues to evolve as we explore this dynamic. I told her we don't need a contract for the kink stuff, but Adriana insisted, making me sign my safe word in blood.

She says it's for my safety, but I never feel safer than when I am in her care. Not only because she is physically the strongest person I know and could probably take out any human who tried to harm me. But she's emotionally safe too. She always asks for consent.

My heart still breaks for her every time I think about the story of what Elijah did to her. Of how Cyrus abandoned her in her time of need. *The fuckers.* How could they? How does one abandon a Queen? A Goddess like Adriana?

No, I'm glad Cyrus has been staying away.

This routine existence is something I can get used to.

But only a fool would think moments in-between could last...

§

THE BREAKTHROUGH COMES at 4:17 PM on a Tuesday, buried in a footnote of a footnote in an obscure insurance journal from a year ago. It's a dead-end most researchers would skip over as irrelevant, one Adriana probably glanced at and dismissed months ago.

I've been staring at my laptop screen for six straight hours, cross-referencing claim numbers with auction house records, building connections through insurance databases Adriana doesn't have academic access to. That's when I finally spot it: a single line mentioning *'unusual atmospheric disturbances'* at the Romero estate, fourteen pages after the brief note on *'miscellaneous Renaissance manuscripts.'*

Most people would read 'miscellaneous Renaissance manuscripts' and move on. But I spent two years cataloging manuscript collections for my thesis. I know that term is a red flag. Real collectors are specific. 'Miscellaneous' means something in that lot is being kept deliberately vague.

My heart starts racing as I dig deeper into Rafael Romero, a Spanish collector from a private estate two cities over.

I pull up my old university database access and dig deeper through mundane institutional archives, academic libraries, public records. It's a boring bureaucratic paper trail that most people (and vampires) have no patience for. But I am used to finding needles in haystacks. Or in this case, not needles, but insurance claims.

It's all there. Not in one place—that would be too easy —but scattered across three different insurance companies over eighteen months.

Pattern recognition is my specialty. Where others may see each claim as a separate data point, I see the pattern.

"Holy shit," I breathe, grabbing my notebook to scribble down everything I can find:

A kitchen fire started in an empty room. Three car accidents in the estate's driveway within a month. A groundskeeper who developed sudden, severe migraines whenever he approached the main house. Two maids who quit without explanation, both claiming they felt *'watched'* by something in the library.

This is exactly the sort of clues Adriana hired me to find.

Losing all sense of time, my fingers fly over the keyboard.

Every piece of evidence is mundane. There is nothing supernatural, just careful documentation and obsessive cross-referencing that got me called 'intense' by every professor I've ever had.

This is what I'm good at. Not the flashy stuff, but this: connecting dots across disparate systems, recognizing patterns in noise...

It's all right there, hidden in plain sight.

"Jackpot!" I jump out of my chair when I find the underground auction listing hidden on a private Discord server. It's scheduled for next weekend: an invitation-only viewing event for serious collectors, held at the estate itself. It's the perfect cover for infiltration.

"Adriana!" I call out, practically bouncing in my chair. "Adriana, I found it!"

She appears in the doorway so quickly, I wonder if she was already on her way. "Found what?"

"The Grimoire. I think I know where it is." I gesture excitedly at my screen, pulling up the relevant documents. "Romero. He's had it for two years. It's been making his life hell, but he's holding onto it anyway. There's an auction this weekend—"

"Slow down, *tesoro*."

Adriana moves behind my chair, her hands settling on my shoulders as she studies the information I've gathered. "Show me everything."

Taking a deep breath, I walk her through the research, pointing out each connection, each piece of evidence that led me to this conclusion.

Her grip on my shoulders tightens as I tell her about the upcoming auction.

"Next weekend?" she asks.

"Saturday. Very exclusive. The Grimoire won't be for sale; it's not on the list, but it'll be there, I imagine. In his private library, probably." I turn to look at her, suddenly aware of how close she is, how her scent makes my pulse quicken.

"This is perfect, Jude. Absolutely perfect." She leans down to kiss the top of my head, and the praise makes warmth spread through my chest. "You did such incredible work. I knew you would find it."

In this moment, I don't even care about the money, my fee. *This*, pleasing her, makes it all worth it; doing something right for once in my miserable life.

A broad smile spreads over my cheeks. "So, what's the plan? How do we—"

"*We* don't do anything. *I* will handle this part." Adriana straightens, already shifting into calculating mode. "You've given me everything I need."

The indirect dismissal stings. "But I could help. I—"

"Jude." Her tone makes it clear that the discussion is over. "This isn't an academic exercise anymore. It's dangerous, and you're human. I won't risk it."

I want to argue, want to point out that I'm the one who found the damn thing, that she's unstable. But the set of her jaw tells me it would be pointless to push.

"Fine," I say simply, trying to keep the disappointment out of my voice. "So, what do *I* do now?"

For weeks, this has been my sole mission: find the spell book. Now what?

I've outlived my usefulness...

"Now, you get some exercise, darling, that's what you do." Adriana's expression softens slightly as she runs her fingers through my hair, a gesture that makes me lean into her touch despite my frustration, my anxiety. "You've been sitting at that computer all day. Go lift some weights or something."

Shaking my head, I pull away. "I don't want to work out right now. I want to help plan—"

"Jude." The warning in her voice is clear. "You found the Grimoire. You did your job beautifully. Now let me do mine."

The praise helps, but not enough to completely ease the sting of being sidelined just when things are getting interesting.

Still, I know better than to push when she's in this mood.

"Yes, Milady," I say, closing my laptop with perhaps more force than it needed.

"Don't sulk," she chides, but there's affection in her tone. "You did well."

She's trying to cheer me up, and it's working a little. Especially when she places a tender kiss on my forehead.

I stand, stretching muscles that have been cramped over the keyboard for hours. "You're sure you don't want backup?"

"I'm sure you have none of the skills required, boy." Adriana cups my face, forcing me to meet her eyes. "The most helpful thing you can do is stay here and stay alive."

"Alright," I concede. "But you'll tell me if there is anything you need, right?"

"Deal." She kisses me, quick and warm, then steps back. "Now go work that body. I'm not asking you again."

"Yes, Milady."

CHAPTER 34

OLD FAVORS

(ADRIANA)

It's been two months since the unstoppable whirlwind Cyrus appeared in my apartment, since Jude cut open his wrist to save me, changing everything between us.

Two months of waiting for the other shoe to drop, for ancient politics to come crashing back into the fragile peace I've built with Jude.

Fragile peace—that's all it's ever been for me, isn't it? Moments of stability between catastrophes, brief respites before the next loss.

I'm tired of losing things, tired of having to fight this hard just to survive.

But it's always been like this: having to fight for what others received as a birthright or privilege. *'Women should know their place,'* they threw in my face every time I dared open my mouth, dared ask for a spot at the table. Anyone who thinks the patriarchy is bad now has never lived through the Renaissance as a woman. Add being an orphaned bastard, and I had no hope of finding the power I craved.

Except my mother gave me hope anyway. Five centuries later, I can still smell her burning flesh on the pyre, still hear the jeers of the men who lit the flames, as I watched, powerless and afraid. They reduced her to smoke and screams because she dared to be powerful, burned her to ash as a warning to the other witches. What kind of last memory is that for a fifteen-year-old to have of her mother? But even as the flames took her, she'd already given me something they couldn't burn: the belief that bastard daughters could rise above their birth, that women didn't have to accept scraps.

So I built something with it. For nearly two decades, networks of women spread across Florence, invisible webs of influence. I started schools where girls could learn more than needlework; funded female merchants; arranged marriages that gave women autonomy instead of transferring them between owners like property. All I wanted was a world where women like my mother wouldn't burn for being extraordinary. And I was making progress...

Until Demetrius found me and took all of it away. The transformation didn't just steal my mortality; it stole my purpose, my networks. Two decades of painstaking work were rendered irrelevant the moment I woke up with fangs and a hunger I didn't know how to control.

That's when the lesson finally settled in for good: don't build anything you can't afford to lose, don't care about anything more than survival.

And then Jude walked into my life with that innocent smile and a mind that was anything but, breaking every rule I'd built my survival around. He gave me something to lose again, something worth protecting beyond my own survival.

This time, unlike the night Demetrius turned me into a monster, I won't go down without a fight.

The only question that remains is: what now?

I lack resources, lack allies. All I have is a mounting list of foes and a growing attachment that's becoming my greatest weakness.

And a thread—importantly.

Jude found it, just as I knew he could.

Such a brilliant boy.

His achievement makes my chest warm with pride.

It's been so incredible to watch him grow these past couple of months. He's become more confident, more vocal, letting himself take up more space. It's a good look on him.

He fits into my solitary world so easily. It makes no sense. I'm used to having things my way, to routine... peace. Yet, having Jude around doesn't disturb any of those things; it makes them better. He slotted into my world as though the space had always been waiting for him, a puzzle piece meant to fit.

It has been nice to have something to care for, a purpose beyond my own needs. Though having Jude around has been incredible for my needs too. When he services me...*Gods*. There is just something about a man who takes direction, who listens.

What I wouldn't give to continue this peaceful existence, to see how his submission evolves.

But we're not out of the woods yet.

Until I lay my hand on that book, our situation remains as desperate as it's always been.

Settling in behind my desk, I open my laptop to dig in.

The Romero estate is infamous, it seems.

I pull up everything Jude's compiled, cross-referencing it with my own databases.

Rafael Romero. Sixty-three years old. Made his fortune in pharmaceuticals before transitioning to 'cultural preservation,' which is a polite way of saying he collects things that were never meant to be collected.

The fact that he's held onto the Grimoire for almost two years, according to the trail of insurance claims Jude tracked down, means that he has no idea what the source of his misfortune is.

Silly humans.

They're so closed off to the supernatural world sometimes, they won't believe what is right in front of them.

But that's a good thing. Humans, I can handle. Even in my weakened state. Even with their weapons. I need to be careful not to alert any of the more powerful beings, immortal ones.

Zooming into the satellite map, I trace the estate's layout on the screen, memorizing the details that will matter when I need to move through shadows that may or may not obey my commands.

The irony isn't lost on me that I'm planning a heist while my powers flicker like an old neon sign.

A year ago, I could have walked into that estate, compelled everyone to forget they saw me, and walked out with the Grimoire before anyone noticed it was missing.

Now, I'll have to rely on more conventional methods like strategy and planning.

Reaching for my phone, I dial the familiar number, leaning back in my chair as I wait for it to ring.

A voice I haven't heard in ages answers almost imme-diately.

"Adriana." Angelo Beaumont's English accent sounds tired. "I was wondering when you'd call."

"I need a favor."

"I assumed as much. It's been, what, three years since our last conversation, darling? You only contact me when you require something *inconvenient*..."

Angelo and I have a history that involves too many shared secrets to ever be completely comfortable with each other. Human, in his 60s now, he runs the most exclusive auction house in Europe, where objects change hands without ever appearing in official catalogs.

"There's a private auction next weekend. Spanish collector named Rafael Romero. I need an invitation."

"Ah." He pauses. "And I suppose you'll need docu-mentation to support whatever identity you're planning to assume?"

"Let's go with Dr. Adri Crevan. Art Authentication Specialist. I'll need a portfolio, client references, the full package. Just add it to my tab."

"That can be arranged. What's your interest in Romero's collection?"

Angelo doesn't know about the Grimoire, doesn't know what I am beyond a wealthy woman with expensive tastes and flexible morals. He's not completely in the dark about the supernatural world. But there is nothing to be gained from adding another liability to the list. It's better that I keep my cards close to my heart. *Trust no one.*

"Let's call it a family matter," I answer simply.

"Ah. One of those." His tone suggests he understands more than he's saying. "I'll have everything ready by tomorrow evening. Though I should warn you, Romero has a reputation."

"What kind of reputation?"

"The kind that suggests you shouldn't go alone." Angelo pauses, choosing his words carefully. "I could arrange for additional security, if you like? Someone with experience in *unusual circumstances*."

"No." I don't even consider the offer. "This has to be clean, quiet. No outsiders."

"Your funeral." He says it lightly, but there's genuine concern in his voice. "The documentation will be delivered to your usual drop box. Try not to get yourself killed, darling. You still owe me an expensive bottle of wine."

The line goes dead, leaving me staring at Jude's research. Floor plans, catering details, a guest list—everything I need to plan what might very well be a suicide mission.

Because Angelo is right: I shouldn't go alone. Especially not now, when my abilities are weaknesses instead of strengths.

But that's exactly why I can't take anyone else. My powers are unreliable at best. Any human backup I bring becomes a liability if my abilities fail at the wrong moment.

And Cyrus...Cyrus is still reporting to *La Famiglia*, no matter what pretty words he promises. I know he's been stalking us; I've sensed him near a few times.

No, this has to be a solo operation. Get in, find the Grimoire, get out.

If you want a job done right, you need to do it yourself.

Gods, I could use a drink right now. Not the alcoholic kind. The bloody kind.

But Jude's not around, and I don't drink from Felix.

That boundary is important to me, one of the few moral lines I've managed to uphold over the centuries. Employees deserve protection from their employers, even when those employers happen to be apex predators.

Okay, maybe I have broken my own rule once or twice, when there was an emergency. When I *desperately* needed blood and had no other options. But I felt like shit having to compel him to forget afterward. The weight of violating his trust still sits with me, even though he'd never remember it.

I try my best, though.

No, I'll wait for Jude to finish his workout.

With a sigh, I pour myself a glass of wine instead and settle in to memorize every detail of his research.

The wine is tasteless, bland, but I finish it anyway. *Dutch courage*, they call it now. Though I suspect what I need isn't courage, it's luck.

And luck has never been something I could rely on.

Outside, the setting sun paints the skyline in beautiful hues of orange and pink against the gloomy December backdrop of fluffy clouds after fresh rain. But I don't notice the weather or the light, not until it's fully dark out there and Jude has yet to report back from his workout.

My eyes shift to the clock on the wall. He should've been done by now.

I call Felix to my office and he appears moments later.

"Please tell Jude he doesn't have to overdo it. Send him here when he's done."

Felix looks at me, eyebrow raised. "Jude?" he asks, confusion etched on his forehead as he shifts from one foot to the other.

"Yes, I thought you were overseeing his workout downstairs?"

His face goes pale as he stares at me, shaking his head. "No, Jude went out for his run. Didn't you send him?"

"What? This late?" My eyes dart to the darkness outside, anxiety gripping my throat. "He was supposed to go lift some weights, not run. What was he thinking?" I'm talking to myself more than Felix now as I start to pace the space. It's not safe outside. Not in the dark. He knows that.

Foolish boy.

What if they get to him?

What if—

CHAPTER 35
NIGHT RUNNING

(JUDE)

*J*ust a quick one, I tell myself as I sneak out the front door before Felix notices.

I don't usually go running this late. But I really need a run. My mind is a mess of insecurity and 'what nows.'

It's well-lit and busy outside; I will be fine, I rationalize as I step into the street and stretch.

Shoes laced, heavy rock playlist blasting in my ears, I get fully into the zone. Streets blur by as I work up a sweat, focusing on the rhythm of my feet, on the beat of the songs.

That's when a brick wall appears in front of me—seemingly nowhere.

That scent! Leather and lust with a hint of spice that I now know is sandalwood. It's such a masculine scent.

It's *him.*

"Why are you here?" I ask, catching my breath, as

Cyrus blocks my path, leaning nonchalantly against a lamppost while pretending he didn't materialize from literal shadows to get in my way.

He doesn't answer my question, just grins as he rakes his eyes up and down my sweaty body. "You know, for a subby, you're built like a football player."

He has no idea how close to the truth he is.

But it was never football; it was rowing.

I never expected a life of sport. I had zero interest in physical activities beyond their ability to clear my mind and provide an excuse not to go home after school; anything was better than sitting in that depressing apartment as the walls pressed closer and closer.

That, and all those naked men in the shower after practice was a great perk for a bisexual teenager fighting with his hormones and desires.

Nobody cared what I wanted anyway. *'You are built for it,'* they kept saying, taking one look at my naturally broad shoulders and deciding my future before I'd opened my mouth, pushing me toward sports when all I wanted was to be left in peace with my books. Eventually, I had to pick something, just to shut up the nagging teachers, and rowing made sense. It was punishing, but at least it didn't come with the locker-room dynamics of football.

Though the real reason I picked rowing probably had less to do with any of that, and more to do with Nick Masterson, captain of the first team. He was the real star of our crew, the poster boy with his long-term cheerleader girlfriend in tow. But I'd be the one getting railed after practice, bent over a chipped wooden bench behind the bleachers as I bit my own cheek to try and contain the scream that wanted to escape the moment he came inside me with that beautiful cock attached to an absolute cunt of a human being.

He never talked to me in public, not beyond the minimum requirements expected of teammates. I'd lost my virginity to Nick Masterson. And that fucker never even acknowledged me.

The sex wasn't even good; he was just using me. I hated myself for it because I knew better. But it didn't stop me from giving in, from wordlessly following him to the bleachers each time.

It would be the same pattern repeated for two years, until I went to varsity on a rowing scholarship I didn't want but could use to study any field of interest as long as I kept performing. I never saw Nick Masterson again, but the varsity rowing teams had no shortage of that type…

My mother kept pushing me about why I didn't have a long-term girlfriend. She never knew about the disasters I did try and date. Instead, I told her I was focusing on my sport. Nobody could argue that; I was a reliable asset to the team.

But even reliable assets have needs and weaknesses, especially around irresistible immortals with amber eyes and sadistic smiles.

"What do you want?" I hiss at Cyrus, not bothering to address his dumb comment about my build.

He circles me, sniffing in my direction, as I stand perfectly still. "Why are you being so grumpy, *niño*?" The hairs on the back of my neck stand upright as he whispers in my ear, so close, too close.

"Fuck off, Cyrus." I don't have patience for his bullshit. Now that I know what kind of guy he really is, how he abandoned Adriana in her time of need, I feel less inclined to swoon.

"Now, now," he chides, grabbing me from behind, arms locking around my waist like we're posing on the hull of the Titanic.

My breath hitches as the shape of his large cock presses against my ass.

"Don't be rude, *pequeño*."

I spin around, trying to push him off me. "Or what? You're going to eat me?"

He laughs, a loud and hearty sound, fangs growing visible in the well-lit street. "I might. Don't tempt me." He touches my cheek affectionately.

"What do you want?" I ask again, eager to get away from him.

This is dangerous. Very dangerous. From what I've learned, Cyrus is unpredictable at best. If he chose to bleed me dry right now, Adriana would never get to me in time.

"So direct." He crowds my space, refusing to let go. "No time for foreplay. Tsk-tsk."

"Cyrus." My tone is firm, the annoyance bleeding into the syllables of his name, as I pull myself from his grip, stepping back.

"The book. The Grimoire," he asks finally, exhaling loudly, "What have you found?"

I cross my arms over my chest defensively. "I'm not telling you shit."

Cyrus moves quick as lightning, pinning me against a nearby shop window so fast, I don't even see him coming. His breath is warm on my cheek as he whispers. "I don't believe you have a choice, *niño*."

His fangs are maybe two inches from my jugular, and I should be praying or running or something useful. Instead, I'm mesmerized by how his eyes shift color, the perfect symmetry of his face...how this is too similar to the dark, fucked-up fantasies I've never admitted to having.

I'm probably about to die, and all I can think of is how magnificent he looks doing it.

Christ, Jude. Still as fucked up as always.

I take a deep breath. "Go to hell," I hiss.

"Why the sudden animosity, *niño*?" he growls, dangerously close.

"You fucking abandoned her when she needed you." The accusation is loaded with venom. "How could you?"

Cyrus lets me down but holds on to my shirt so I can't run away. He sighs. "What are you on about now?"

"Nine years ago." I try to pull free, but it's no use. "When Adriana lost the book."

Realization sets in, and his shoulders slump, a look of defeat washing over him. Cyrus breaks character only for a second. But in that second, I see everything: the regret, the hurt, the guilt...

"It's not that simple." The mask snaps back in place as quickly as it slipped.

"Really? From where I'm standing, it looks pretty simple. You left her for dead. The woman you supposedly love?"

Cyrus swipes his free hand over his face as he admits, "I was an idiot."

Back away, Jude. Don't engage.

I know what I *should* be doing.

Instead, I bite back: "No shit, Sherlock."

"I was going to save her. Really. But she beat me to it."

"What the fuck is that supposed to mean?"

Cyrus lets go of my shirt, turning his back to me as he speaks. "I thought I could be the hero. Barge in and save her at the last minute. Live happily ever after."

I scoff, "You sure don't look like the hero from where I'm standing."

"I got *distracted*..."

"Distracted how?" I demand, desperate for answers that I know I have no right to, but want nonetheless.

"I was in the Fae realm, drowning my sorrows and pretending I didn't miss her every fucking second, when I felt it through our bond." His voice drops to barely above a whisper. "She was hurting."

"But you didn't come back."

"No, I didn't." The admission seems to physically hurt him. "I was still angry, still convinced she'd overreacted about my slip-up. I thought maybe she was just...I don't know, having a bad feeding or dealing with some business complication. The bond doesn't always transmit clear information, especially across different planes."

"When did you realize it was serious?"

"About a week in. The pain and fear were constant, unrelenting. That's when I knew something was wrong." He looks up at me with haunted eyes. "But instead of rushing to her immediately, I had this...fantasy. This stupid, romantic notion that I could swoop in at the last minute, save her from whatever was happening, and she'd be so grateful that she'd forgive everything. Forget our fight, take me back, realize she needed me after all."

The narcissism of it is breathtaking, and my expression makes no surprise at how ridiculous I find his excuse. I had expected more...

"I know how it sounds. Believe me, I've had nine years to understand exactly how selfish and pathetic it was. But at the time, I'd convinced myself I was being strategic, giving her time to need me before making my grand entrance."

"What happened?" I don't want to ask but I have to know the rest.

His expression darkens further. "By the time I convinced myself to look for her, she was already gone. Time moves differently in the Fae realm. I thought it had been days, but weeks had passed. The warehouse was empty, burned to the ground, nothing left but ash."

"You never even tried to save her?"

"I tried. Just...too late. Always too fucking late." He starts pacing with agitated energy, looking away, as he confesses his sins.

"And you never tried to explain?"

"I was too ashamed." Cyrus's voice cracks slightly. "The message was pretty clear: she'd saved herself, cleaned up the mess, and moved on. Without me."

"Is that why you're here now? Still trying to be the hero?"

"Maybe."

I have more questions, but Cyrus is done speaking.

Within milliseconds, he's closed the distance between us, crowding me with his imposing frame.

Before I can protest, he devours the next words right from my lips, kissing me with such ruthless passion, I nearly forget my name.

I can't contain the groan that presses from my lips as Cyrus grinds into me, his hardness outlined against my own.

"You like this, *niño*," he observes, his breath warm against my neck.

"Y-yes," I confess as he presses the palm of his hand over the tent in my running shorts. There is no point in denying it. Adriana has been edging me for so long that even the smallest contact sends me near delirious with lust now.

Cyrus pushes me back against the shop window with such force that all the air is expelled from my lungs, leaving me breathless as he places his fingers in my mouth to muffle my whimpers.

"Such pretty sounds you make." His voice is gruff, a low bass that ripples through my whole body.

I can't help but stare. Cyrus is beautiful the way dangerous things are beautiful, like standing at the edge of a cliff, or watching lightning split the sky. He's the kind of man who would look at you like you were simultaneously the most interesting thing in the room and potential prey, and somehow make you grateful for both forms of attention.

Fucking hell. When he looks at me like that, zooms in on me and me alone, nothing else in the world exists anymore.

My heart stops as a jogger passes us while Cyrus's hand is fishing my cock from my shorts.

I'm exposed on the sidewalk for all to see.

My traitorous cock grows even harder in Cyrus's grip as he chuckles darkly at my distress.

"Such a dirty little slut," he whispers in my ear, and all I can whimper is a pathetic "Don't."

I don't mean the word; I don't want him to stop. My racing heartbeat betrays me as Cyrus holds me captive against the wall, my dick in his hand, hard and ready.

This is the part where he kills me.

The thought repeats in my mind as fear spikes through my body, adrenaline fueling the raw lust coursing through my veins.

"Such a big boy, aren't you?" Cyrus whispers as his nimble fingers play along my length.

"Fuck," I rasp, melting into his touch, nearly coming on the spot.

Where Adriana is gentle, careful, Cyrus is the opposite. He's brutal, rough, and dear god, if it doesn't turn me on even more.

When he wraps his free hand around my neck, squeezes, my eyes fall shut involuntarily, my body reduced to sensations and need.

I am so exposed, so vulnerable, my cock out on a well-lit street as the occasional person strays past at a hurried pace, avoiding eye contact with the two men pressed up against the shop window.

He's jerking me off right there, out in the open. *Fuck me.*

Nobody stops us. Nobody saves me from the moment I don't want to be saved from.

I know I can't last long like this.

I'm a whimpering mess, shaking, as I try to delay the inevitable release I don't have permission for.

But there is no way I want to stop, not now, not this close to toppling over the edge.

"Let's make a mess of you, *pequeño*," Cyrus whispers against my neck. He flicks his tongue over the sensitive lobe of my ear, reducing me to a puddle of need.

I have no words left, only grunts and whimpers as he jerks me to completion, my lungs on fire as they reach for air but finding none. But he doesn't let go of my throat. Doesn't stop pumping my cock.

When I finally come seconds later, the world goes dark and then bright again, an explosion behind my eyelids, the pleasure ripping through my body along with the hoarse scream of ecstasy that Cyrus kisses from my lips when he finally releases my throat as I choke for air.

He reaches for my cheek when our lips part, smearing my own cum on my face, in my hair, making as much of a mess of me as he promised. And I let him, licking my lips to catch a taste.

"Christ, Jude Cole." Cyrus laughs, a boisterous sound that escapes into the night.

He steps back and I have to hold onto the wall to stop myself from falling to the dirty sidewalk. My knees are weak, every system overstimulated.

Bewildered, I stare at him as I try to process my world. My heart is pounding in my throat as I stuff my cock back into my now-soiled shorts.

What was that?

It all happened in fast forward.

I didn't have to think; didn't have to do anything. I could just let go, let him take charge, let him have his way with me the way Nick Masterson used to do, somewhere we were not supposed to be, somewhere we might get caught.

"Cyrus—" I start, still breathless.

"No," he cuts me off, closing in again. "I'm sorry, *niño*, but I can't let you keep this one."

I've never been compelled by a vampire before. I trust Adriana when she tells me she would never, has never. But when Cyrus's amber eyes start glowing red at the edges, his voice steady and rhythmic, I know I'm about to expose all my secrets.

Despite not wanting to, I can't stop myself from answering all his questions and telling him what I found out about the Grimoire. *Fuck.*

"It's been a pleasure, Jude Cole," Cyrus tells me when I

have nothing left to spill, stroking my sticky cheek with a mischievous grin playing on those beautiful lips that kiss me like they want to steal all my air forever.

And then he's gone, as if he was never there in the first place, disappearing into the shadows like a complex dream that only leaves behind a feeling, no details.

CHAPTER 36

IMPOSSIBLE CHOICES

(CYRUS)

The shadows embrace me as I slip through them toward the docks.

Jude's scent still clings to my clothes: clean soap, sweat, and that underlying innocence that makes my fangs ache.

He won't remember our encounter but I'm not sure I'll ever forget it. It's made the hunger in my veins worse, the restlessness in my blood clawing at me like a living thing.

He's found the Grimoire. That's good *and* bad news.

No more limbo. No more waiting. But also no more stalling, hoping the situation with *La Famiglia* will resolve itself. Something needs to be done *now*.

A cold shudder passes through me, forcing my mind to pay attention to my body.

I need to feed. *Desperately.*

It took every ounce of self-control not to sink my fangs into that boy's delicate neck, not to taste the pulse pounding its invitation against his throat. So young, so healthy, he was a feast waiting to happen.

But Adriana would know if I had so much as a sip.

I'm trying to get in her good graces, not fuck up even more spectacularly than I already have.

No, Jude is off limits. No matter how every instinct screamed at me to devour him right there under the streetlights. It was hard enough to stop when I did.

Forget about Jude.

The neon glow of the strip club cuts through the darkness ahead, casting everything in garish pink and blue. A steady stream of potential meals flows in and out of the building they'll never admit to visiting in daylight, chasing desires they can't name in polite company.

I'm tempted to go inside, to pick up more than dinner. A good fuck would help with the tension coiled in my shoulders, perhaps distract me from my cock that still strains against my jeans from my encounter with Adriana's not-so-little pet.

But it's too much effort tonight. I don't feel like playing the familiar games of human sin and seduction.

Instead, I grab the first man who makes the mistake of wandering into the deserted parking lot alone. He barely has time to register my presence before my fangs find his throat.

When I've drunk my fill, I slip away unnoticed, leaving his alive but weakened body crumpled beside his rusted Honda. Anyone who finds him will think he's just another drunk incapable of holding his liquor. Nothing suspicious...

He tastes of poor decisions and an even poorer diet. Sour memories of underage prostitutes and a deceitful marriage settle in my chest like heartburn as I make my way back to what I laughably call home.

Jude would've tasted way better; I know it.

§

MY APARTMENT, OR 'THE SHITHOLE,' as I call it, squats two blocks from the neon district. The building reeks of mold, its brick facade stained with decades of neglect.

I climb three flights of stairs past doors marked with eviction notices and muffled sounds of domestic disputes. The key sticks in the lock, as always. I have to jiggle it just right while applying pressure with my shoulder to get the warped door to open.

I hadn't expected to need this place for so long. The plan was simple: get *La Famiglia* off my back, convince Adriana to take me back, live happily ever after in her silk sheets and comfortable embrace. Maybe I could even finally start that damn club I've been thinking about, obsessing over, for decades.

Things have very much *not* gone according to plan. *Story of my life.*

The darkness inside is absolute as I enter my apartment, broken only by neon bleeding through heavy sheets hung over every window. It casts a purple hue over the furniture that came with the place, lighting up the torn couch with its generations of bedbugs and the television from the previous decade that I've never turned on.

Without turning on a light, I head to the kitchen. I grab a glass from the sink full of glasses I don't care about enough to wash, pouring three fingers of whiskey from the bottle that's become my most reliable companion.

What a fucking night. The couch groans under my

weight, springs poking through the fabric, as I stare at the water stain on the ceiling.

Two months since the *Blue Moon*. Since I told Adriana everything, and she walked out, leaving me with an empty bottle of wine and a lifetime of regret.

Well, almost everything.

I'd wanted to explain, to make her understand that I was trying to save us both, that I had changed, but she just shook her head at me with that particular brand of disappointment reserved for someone who's let you down too many times to count.

'*Stay away from Jude,*' she'd said, standing abruptly without finishing her drink. '*Stay away from me. I'll fix this myself like I always do.*'

I'd called her selfish. She'd returned the insult. Just like that, we found ourselves at the familiar impasse.

And then she was gone.

In the two months since, we haven't spoken another word. She knows I'm stalking them—she must know—but Adriana has made no move to acknowledge my existence.

She's blocked the bond, walled me out of her head while I bang against a locked door, yearning to get in. The connection that used to burn between us now sits behind bulletproof glass. I can sense her there but can't touch her, can't reach her.

The tasteless whiskey burns down my throat as I throw back the contents of my glass.

Four centuries on this earth, 419 years to be exact, and I've collected lovers in the same way some people collect stamps. Yet none of it satisfies the specific hunger I have for that brilliant, bitchy vampire Vueen with the sea-glass eyes and blood like pure heroin.

Everyone else is *predictable* now.

They throw themselves at my feet with or without compulsion, begging me to own them, to claim them, to make them feel something, *anything*.

It's flattering, I suppose, but ultimately hollow.

Adriana's my ride or die. Always has been. Since she saved me from my maker all those lifetimes ago.

I pour another whiskey, watching the golden liquid catch the sliver of light bleeding through the windows' sheets. It does little to settle the restlessness in my bones.

When we were good, we were fucking brilliant. Her mind and my strength were complementary skillsets. We did whatever we wanted, reshaped the world according to our whims. Afterward, we'd fuck until the sun came up.

It was beautiful and bloody and perfect, a montage of love and lust epic enough to entertain the gods themselves.

But look at us now, broken, possibly beyond repair.

I used to fantasize about the day we reconnected. About the crazy make-up sex we'd have. How we'd rebuild our lives; reclaim our spot at the top. But as the years of silence drew on, I slowly lost hope of that fantasy ever becoming a reality.

The glass makes a satisfying crack as I slam it down on the folding table, whiskey splashing across the charred surface.

I wish I had done things differently. I should've tried harder to find her, to save her from the hunter's fucked-up plans. But I was too proud, too hurt, too ashamed, any and all of the above.

Instead, I fled back to the Fae realm, where time moves differently and moon wine flows freely. I drowned myself in intoxication for months, becoming a curiosity to the Between Court. A heartbroken vampire made for interesting entertainment, and I was willing to trade anything for temporary oblivion.

The affair with Prince Lyros began as a physical release only, someone who didn't know my history and didn't pity me. But I could never be his, not with my cold heart pining for the only person who could make it feel warmth again.

It was easy with the prince. He never asked for more than I could give. We both had our own demons we were trying to bury with his cock in my ass. It was a convenient arrangement.

Except for the Queen, his mother. She had it in for me from the start. She showed no mercy, just locked me up like a common criminal when she found us together one reckless night, my execution scheduled along with a grand festival to celebrate my misfortune.

The imprisonment forced sobriety, and all my suppressed trauma and guilt came flooding back. As the days stretched on in that miserable cell, I made peace with my sins, convinced it was finally the end. *This is how I go,* I remember thinking.

By the time *La Famiglia* 'rescued' me, I was physically free but spiritually broken, sober for the first time in years, and now indebted to dangerous ancient vampires who knew exactly how to use my bond with Adriana against me. They offered me what I'd been searching for: a chance to find her, to explain, to make things right.

But I should've known better than to trust Valerian and his entourage of ancient assholes. They never cared about anything besides their own bullshit plans for world domination.

Those fuckers know how to get what they want and have no problem sacrificing individual pawns for what they call 'the greater good.' And that's exactly what I am to them: a stupid, expendable pawn. A pawn that now needs to make a decision, and soon.

I can't stall much longer. Jude has found the Grimoire. The auction is next weekend.

I know I have to tell *La Famiglia*. That was literally our deal.

But how can I? Now that I know what they want it for and what their plans mean for Adriana, how could I possibly continue playing my designated role of accomplice?

No.

I stand abruptly, sending the folding table wobbling.

My fists clench at my sides, resolve hardening.

Fuck that. I'm not telling them shit. Not this time.

I can be the villain in everyone else's story, but not in hers. Not anymore. Adriana's my queen, has always been, and without her, I'm nothing but a listless wanderer who's already proven hedonism loses its appeal.

There has to be a way out of this mess. A way to protect her without getting us both killed in the process.

Even if Adriana never forgives me, I'm not going to sit around and watch it all fall apart. Because without her, there's no life worth living anyway.

One week, that's all I have.

What the fuck am I going to do?

CHAPTER 37

SCENT OF MISTRUST

(ADRIANA)

When Jude's still not back half an hour later, my restlessness spikes to overdrive levels.

I'm pacing my office, my brain cycling through all the horrible things that could have happened to him without me there to protect him. *What if he's been kidnapped, or worse, killed?*

I try to use my enhanced hearing to monitor the building's sounds, as I always do. Instead of the usual crystal-clear symphony of heartbeats and whispered conversations, I get...static. All that comes through is muffled noise, like listening through cotton.

It's all wrong.

When did I become this person? I've never been someone who paces and worries and checks the time obsessively when their pet is out of their sight.

It's Jude's fault. That's the only logical answer; the only variable that has changed.

The human with the stormy eyes and the endless

curiosity has somehow wormed his way past defenses to a heart I didn't even know I still possessed.

I've gotten accustomed to having the human around, to the sound of his heartbeat racing and slowing around the apartment, the incredible taste of his blood that's keeping the deterioration at a manageable level. (On most days, at least.)

Despite my best efforts, the boundaries I established on his first night have eroded rapidly, inevitably.

Professional distance becomes impossible when someone offers their devotion so completely, so genuinely. Especially if it's what you've been searching for your entire life: someone who would literally cut open their veins for you.

Get a grip, Adriana.

I force myself to sit down and return to the Romero estate schematics.

But focus doesn't come. Not when my mind repeats a single thought on loop: *Where's Jude?*

I look up at the clock again. He's forty-five minutes late now.

If he's not back in ten, I'll go look for him, I decide, scrolling through the schematics on the laptop without paying much attention.

When I finally hear the soft click of the door downstairs eight minutes later, relief floods my circuits. *He's back.*

"Jude!" I call down, summoning him to my desk.

He jogs in, sweaty and smiling. "Yes, Milady?"

I shouldn't be this happy to see him. But the vise around my heart loosens the moment he steps into my office.

I'm about to reprimand him for sneaking off so late when that unmistakable scent hits me. It clings to the boy like he's bathed in it: Sandalwood and spent lust with a hint of saffron, as distinctive as a fingerprint.

"What did *he* want?" I get up and move closer, confirming my suspicions as I sniff Jude's neck.

The human eyes me with confusion, crossing his arms over his chest protectively. "Who?"

I grab him closer, breathing in the odor that shouldn't be there. "Cyrus," I hiss.

"When?" Confusion pulls his face into a frown. "I didn't see him."

"Doesn't mean he wasn't there." My voice comes out as a growl.

Jude is still looking at me like I'm the one who owes him answers and not the other way around.

There is no deceit in his eyes, nor the pulse thrumming steadily under my fingers. Just a slight delay in his answers, a missed beat so faint, anyone else would've overlooked it. But I don't miss any detail about this boy, never.

All evidence points in the same direction: Cyrus compelled him.

Stronzo! (*Asshole!*)

Jude tries to shrug it off, acting way more nonchalant than he normally does. "Sure it's nothing serious."

But I don't let go, even as he tries to slip from my hold.

"There's cum on your pants, Jude." The scent of his arousal is as overwhelming as Cyrus's signature on him, fanning the rage burning me up.

Jude freezes as he follows my gaze down to the unmissable wet patch on his shorts, the sticky smear that wasn't there when he left.

"I didn't—"

I don't let him finish. He calls out in surprise as my

fingers grasp his semi-hard cock barely hidden by those flimsy running shorts, tugging him toward me with force.

"Fuck...Christ," he hisses, flinching.

I grab a fistful of sweaty t-shirt and pull him down to my eye level, my other hand still around his cock that's rapidly grown stiff between my fingers.

"I don't remember giving you permission to cum," I bite out as I struggle to control my emotions.

The fury in my veins is largely for Cyrus. For the fucking audacity. But I know Jude made his choices willingly.

Cyrus may be foolish and too passionate for his own good, a reckless dreamer who wants too much from the world...but he would never do anything without consent.

No, Jude may not remember, but he wasn't an unwilling participant. I'd bet my deteriorating life on it.

Just the thought of the two together does things to my insides, churning them in need. The image is as infuriating as it is arousing. *How dare he touch what's mine?*

"I didn't do anything," Jude insists, pulling me from the mental frenzy induced by Cyrus's familiar scent. It's the same smell that's been burned in my memory since that night we first met on the rooftops in Venice, that night our lives became forever entwined.

"You stink," I spit out between pressed lips, squeezing his cock until he bites down on his quivering bottom lip.

Jude lets out a flustered huff. "Yeah, that's how running works."

The fucking sass.

"Take off those pants," I reply simply, dropping his cock and stepping back.

Jude sighs and kicks off his running shoes. "You're overreacting, Adriana. I said I didn't see him."

I'm on him before he even finishes his next breath. "Not another fucking word." My fangs extend as the threat whispers against his skin.

"Yeah, or what?" Jude drops his pants and kicks them away. When he comes back up, my hand is around his throat faster than he can even blink.

"Careful," I warn, my voice dripping with venom. "You know I don't have time for brats."

Jude's pulse spikes beneath my fingers, whether in fear or excitement or both, I don't know.

"Oh? And why is that?" He's taunting me, asking for it. The defiance in his eyes is as infuriating as it's inviting. He *needs* this, needs me to pull him back in line, to familiar ground.

"On your knees." The command comes as naturally as Jude's response.

As soon as I release his neck, he slips to the floor with a soft thud, knees bent.

"What if I wanted to spank you for your bad behavior?" I ask as I grab a fistful of hair and tug his head back, eyes up.

Jude swallows loudly. The corner of his lip tugs to the side as a smirk spreads over his features. "You always do what you want anyway."

He's trying to see how far he can push, but there's no winning this game. "Get up," I order.

But Jude doesn't move, just looks me dead in the eye and says the two words that will be his entire undoing: "Make me."

You little shit!

I don't react, despite every instinct screaming to smack his defiant face. No, I calmly straighten out my shoulders, pressing air through my lips. "Upstairs," is all I say, pulling him to his feet by his ears.

Jude's body suddenly tenses, his breathing shallow and deep. All the bravery from a moment ago evaporates as quickly as it appeared.

The tension is uncomfortable as I march his bare ass to my bedroom, dressed only in his shirt like some human Winnie-the-Pooh. It's a ridiculous look but it only adds to the humiliation that's burning deep red on his cheeks, down his neck. *If he wants to act like a child, I'll treat him like one.*

The trip is silent save for Jude's pounding heart as I follow him upstairs, pushing him ahead of me.

He halts when we reach my bedroom door, fists clenched by his sides, erect cock pointing to the ceiling.

Pushing past, I walk in ahead. "Come here," I call, snapping my fingers in command as I sit down on the bed.

Jude drops to his knees, as he's been trained, and crawls to me, eyes lowered.

There he is. There's my good boy.

Instantly, my anger ebbs.

Discipline was marked with a big red X on the kink list I printed out for Jude a few weeks back. While I watched from my desk, he sat quietly as he completed the lengthy document, pausing from time to time to consider the options. Once or twice, he pulled up his browser to look up some terms, his cock visibly straining against his zipper as he got more and more turned on the further he got down the list.

Some of the answers, the things he was into, surprised me. Primal play. CNC. Pet play. Cuckolding. Exhibitionism. The introverted human was hiding a delectably kinky side, a side I've been enjoying exploring as much as he has.

Humiliation was also marked as a clear turn-on for him. But not pain so much; not like Elijah or Cyrus, the latter who used to last hours as I ripped the skin from his back with a spiked whip straight out of a Medieval torture chamber. The only way to calm his demons, he used to say.

But pain won't calm Jude's demons. Not like that.

No, Jude needs a gentle but firm hand, structure. He needs someone who cares enough to make rules and see that they are followed.

It's not just about his needs though. What is it about the idea of disciplining him, correcting his behavior, that is such a turn-on?

Because, my gods, I swear Jude has never looked more beautiful than now, crawling towards me like he trusts me more than he trusts himself. Like he'll take whatever punishment, whatever discipline, I dish out and thank me for it.

He reaches my feet and heels, waiting, heart beating like a runaway train.

Reaching for his hair, I absentmindedly massage his scalp, dragging my fingers through the brown strands of hair curling at the tips. It's getting long. *We should get it cut soon.* I ball my fist around the strands and tug upward, forcing his gaze to meet mine.

"On my lap with you," I order as my fingers trace the edge of his jaw, enjoying the shiver of anticipation that ripples over his skin. "Disobedience is such a nasty thing. Better nip that in the bud, don't you think?"

CHAPTER 38

ATONEMENT

(JUDE)

My heart is pounding like a jackhammer as I sit down on Adriana's lap with my bare ass. Dread swirls in my stomach, refusing to settle, like I'm five years old again, caught in the act, punishment inevitable.

I feel ridiculous with my bulky frame balancing on her knees, her arm supporting my back as I sit sideways, legs together. It's such a vulnerable position.

"Let's see what you are hiding from me," Adriana says as she tilts my head to gain better access to my neck. She trails a nail down my throat, barely touching my skin, and I swallow loudly as anticipation prickles my skin.

As soon as she sinks her fangs into my vein, euphoria and forgotten memories flood my circuits.

In a flash, it all comes back: Cyrus interrupting my run; telling him everything; him pushing me up against the wall in public and jerking me off right there, smearing my cum on my cheek, on my shorts.

325

Adriana pulls out almost instantly again, only taking a single sip. But it's enough to break the compulsion.

Christ. My heart stills as I try to process it all. My cock is rock hard, a fact that's impossible to hide as I blush blood-red on Adriana's lap. *I can't believe I did that.*

She doesn't say anything at first. When I dare steal a glance at her expression, she seems as affected by the moment as I am, flustered almost, like it turns her on too.

But she quickly recovers, expression icing over as the stern teacher returns.

"You told him about finding the Grimoire." A confirmation, not a question.

Slowly, I nod, the guilt making my muscles stiff as it holds me in its grip, winding tighter and tighter.

"Oh, Jude." She sighs. The tone of her voice crushes me more than any physical pain could. Disappointing Adriana is the last thing I want to do.

Why do I want to cry? Like I'm twenty years younger again, incapable of escaping the consequences of my own actions.

The familiar darkness settles in my intestines like it wants to consume me. *You fucked up, Jude. Again. 'Why can't you just be normal?'* It's my grandmother's voice in my head, relentlessly cruel as always.

"Do you know what you did wrong, Jude?" Adriana asks, voice steady.

Shame sinks to the pit of my stomach as I force the confession from my lips. "Yes, Milady. I told him things I shouldn't have…and I came without permission." The last bit comes out softer, barely audible.

My ears are burning. I'm exposed beyond my naked skin, laid bare under the bright light that is Adriana's scrutiny as she tells me how much I disappointed her.

The words are hard to hear. I wish she would beat me instead. I deserve it. Pain is easier to handle than this patronizingly sweet talk that cuts deeper than any whip ever could.

Adriana reaches over and wipes a tear from my cheek.

"You trust me with your care, Jude, and that means all of your body. It's displeasing when you don't listen to me."

I'm crying freely now, the anticipation of my punishment making my skin crawl. She hasn't even touched me yet. But I'm ready to fall apart.

I fucked it up. *She's going to throw you away now, Jude. 'Nobody wants naughty boys.' You never learn. Tsk-tsk.*

"I'm sorry, I-I'm sorry," I whimper on repeat as Adriana shakes her head at me slowly.

"You understand why I have to punish you, right?" she asks, and I nod, swiping at my tears with the back of my hand. "Words," she insists, and I find a "Yes, Milady" somewhere in my jumbled mind.

She gently taps my bum with her hand, springing me into motion with her command to "Bend over."

I'm shivering, visibly shivering despite the heated space, as I do as I'm told, bending my large body over her lap like an arch, feet on one side, hands down on the other.

So exposed, so vulnerable, there are no words to describe the maelstrom of emotions and hormones rushing through my system as I wait for her to begin, my ass in the air, hard cock squished on her lap.

I'm as aroused as I am ashamed. Just thinking back to Cyrus in the street…it fuels fantasies I shouldn't have. Of *things* I shouldn't want. Things like Cyrus doing the most depraved, fucked-up things to me and compelling me to forget after, so I don't have to live with myself for wanting it…

'What's wrong with you, Jude?'

I shudder as Adriana runs her bare hand over my ass, pulling my attention back to the present.

She smacks me lightly, as if testing my skin, and I almost jump up, the anticipation, the dread, making me jittery.

"What's your safe word?" she checks, reaching over to the bedside table to retrieve her implement of choice, placed there upon entry.

"Crimson," I answer, even as my breath hitches.

She doesn't give me a "good boy," despite how badly I want those words from her lips. I know I don't deserve them.

Fuck knows why I provoked her. Bratting is not normally my style. Perhaps to see what she'd do, if she'd even care, or just ignore me, like I'm a nobody.

But Adriana clearly has no intention of ignoring my actions. No, when the hard bristles of her ivory hairbrush run over my bare skin—the same one I combed her hair with that first night here—I know I'm in for the hiding of my life.

Keeping the bristle side down, she runs the brush over my thighs, over my ass, up my back, as my skin shivers beneath her.

When she turns it over and lands a gentle but firm smack on my butt with the smooth side, I exclaim in surprise, despite expecting it.

"You're going to count to ten for me, okay, *Jude*?" I wish she wouldn't say my name in that way. Like I have been so bad. Like I have fucked everything up beyond repair.

That stings more than the first smack of my punishment that lands on my ass with a loud thud, pain radiating from the center outward.

"Count," Adriana reminds me, and I find a "one" somewhere in the tangle of my mind.

The second smack lands firmly on top of the first, burning even more, and the tears are back, blurring the world around the edges as I fall deeper into my shame, the guilt that has defined my existence.

'Why, Jude? Why do you do these things?'

It's not Adriana's voice but my grandmother's.

I press my eyes closed, my ears burning as much as my ass. I'm five years old again, crying so much I can't see where I'm running as I try to escape my inevitable punishment. My grandmother is screaming profanities at me, calling me horrible names, names I won't fully understand until I learn the big words later.

I can't slow down; she'll catch me, and then she'll punish me. For looking at Nate's little peepee, for touching it. *'Bad, Jude. Such a bad boy.'*

Somewhere in the distance, Adriana's voice breaks through, insisting that I count.

"T-three," comes out ragged, breathless, as I clench my fists into balls, nails digging into my palm, the pain radiating throughout my whole body now.

Grandma dragged me out of that bathroom by my ears. That's how I knew I was in deep trouble. It hurt so much, but she wouldn't let go, no matter how I cried. *'You should know better, you filthy boy!'*

Adriana's number four lands on my ass louder than the first smacks, and I whimper like a puppy, crying wildly now. *I deserve this. My punishment for being bad.*

When Grandma dragged me into the courtyard, still

naked, still by the ear, I knew there was no escaping my punishment. Just as there is no escaping now, as I struggle to find the "five" to follow Adriana's next strike.

Grandma finally let go for a second to reach for her stick, but it was all the gap I needed. I sprinted toward the back of the yard, where the thickness of nature started. *Freedom*, I foolishly thought.

Until the first sting of the nettle set my skin on fire.

The pain was blinding, but I couldn't stop, couldn't turn back. Grandma was right behind me, her home-made cane in hand, ready to skin me alive, she promised.

I kept running, through an entire field of stinging nettles, my naked skin ripped and welted from all sides, tears blurring the path as thorns stung the undersides of my feet.

"Jude, give me the number," Adriana insists and I don't know how many times she's asked. "Jude," she repeats softly when my only response is another anguished cry.

I sniffle a "six," and she moves on, lifting the brush high again as she runs a cold hand over my flaming skin to soothe the burn.

But there was no soothing the sting all those years ago, when I finally ran out of space to run to, when Grandma finally caught me, dragging me back to the house by the ear as she whipped me while I walked, breaking open the fresh welts the nettles burned into my skin with her merciless cane.

The pain was unbearable!

It was clear as day that I needed medical attention, proper care. But my grandmother threw my sobbing, naked, bleeding body into the washroom and locked me in until nightfall, when my tired mother came home to look at me with more disappointment on her tired face.

'I work too hard to deserve this, Jude.' I will never forget those words.

They left me there for the night like a common criminal. No dinner. Nothing. Just an empty washing powder bucket should I need to use the bathroom.

My mother never looked at me the same again.

The painful welts eventually faded, but never the shame.

Adriana's next smack pulls me into my body, but I'm unable to give her the "seven" she demands.

I should answer, I want to, but I can't. The word, language, feels too far away.

My eyes pressed shut, I brace for the impact that doesn't come.

Adriana puts the brush down but I barely register the sound. "Are you okay?" she asks, gently touching my shoulder.

The question catches me off guard. My grandmother never used to ask if I was okay when she beat me. She never cared about whether I was or not.

"Jude?" Adriana strokes my hair as she helps me into an upright position. I almost lose my balance, but she steadies me, keeping me from falling. "Open your eyes, darling."

She caresses my cheek and I force one eye open, winching in the light that now feels too bright. I expect disgust, anger, revulsion, disappointment…but her eyes hold only care and concern as she wipes the tears from my cheek.

"Am I hurting you?" she asks, and I shake my head, no.

Adriana's brow furrows in concern as she studies my features. "We can stop—"

"No, please!" I finally find my voice, cutting her off. I don't want to stop. I want to take my punishment; want to repent for my sins. "Don't stop."

She stares deep into my eyes, searching, before agreeing. "You have your safe word, right?"

I nod, looking away, unable to bear my own vulnerability.

"Good, now back in position," she tells me as she picks up the brush again.

Getting up from her lap with shaky legs, I bend over her knees again.

"What number was that?" Adriana gently taps my ass with her hand, bringing my attention back to her, to the sensation on my skin.

"Seven, Milady," I answer, bracing for the rest.

Eight follows closely, and by nine, I'm all but lost to language. There is only the sting, the red-hot burn on my ass blurring out everything else, taking over my mind, forcing the darkness from the loop it's repeating on. I sink into the pain, letting it flood my circuits like ink spreading in water, coloring everything in sensation.

Adriana soothes my behind with a cool hand when I finally croak out a nine. "One more, can you take it for me?"

I nod, knowing I could call my safe word at any time and stop this. This time, I have control; I have the power. But I don't want to stop. I want to take it all. Take what I deserve.

The final smack is the loudest, stinging my raw skin as my walls crumble to rubble.

It's not the pain I'm fighting. The pain is comforting;

the endorphins are flowing. It's the shame, the guilt, the fear that rips through my body like torture.

This is the part where she throws me away, where she tells me to pack my shit up. *Nobody wants you, Jude.*

Instead, Adriana puts the brush down and runs her cool hand over my ass again, her voice even more soothing than the temperature change. "All forgiven now." Her tone is gentle, maternal. "Such a good boy for me. You took your punishment so well. Look how pretty this ass looks in red."

The praise sinks into me, warm, wrapping me in a blanket of comfort I don't want to trust, don't want to need.

Adriana helps me up and into her arms again, enfolding me in a tight embrace. "I hope you learned your lesson, darling," she says as she kisses the side of my head. "I only did it because I care. I want you to be the best boy you can be. Rules are important."

I can't look at her, so I bury my shameful face against her chest as the tears continue to flow. I'm too scared to let go. What if I never get to hold her again?

"It's okay, *tesoro*." Adriana strokes my back in soothing patterns. "You're safe, I've got you. Let go."

"J-just leave me...leave me, I deserve it," I beg, my voice sounding young, fragile.

But she does no such thing. She doesn't leave, just holds me closer as she starts to sing an Italian lullaby, rocking me on her lap like I am a baby.

I sink into the solace of her voice, of the song, trying to ride the rush of adrenaline, of endorphins, overflowing my circuits.

"I'm not going anywhere," she promises when the song finishes, tilting my face to look at her.

God, I must look like such a pathetic mess.

I swipe at my tears. But she takes my hand away, kissing my fingers.

I'm shattered from the release and don't know how I manage to stand on my shaky legs, but Adriana supports me throughout as she helps me onto the bed. Then she lies back on the pillow and opens her arms for me.

"Do you want a bedtime story?" she asks, and I nod, nestling my head between her breasts.

"You okay?" she asks as silence stretches.

I nod again.

"I will be better," I promise, even as she kisses my head and tells me I'm already the best.

I don't remember anything about the story she tells me. Don't remember anything but the lightness in my chest, the relief, as she holds me until I fall asleep, allowing me to stay in her bed.

I'm a good boy again—that's all that matters, even if my ass still stings like a motherfucker.

My sins have been atoned for.

CHAPTER 39

GUNG-HO

(CYRUS)

Six days of pacing my apartment like a tiger in a cage, and I'm still not certain this isn't the stupidest thing I've ever done. And I've done many, *many* stupid things in my life.

La Famiglia will be furious when they realize I'm going against them, that I'm trying to help Adriana.

But fuck them.

Even as a mortal, born in Castile, Spain, in 1587, the youngest son of a duke whose bloodline stretched back to the Reconquista, I always had trouble with authority, with the weight of *expectations*.

Noble, devout, unquestionably loyal to 'God and Crown,' my family embodied everything Spain was supposed to be at the time. My father served the king with unwavering dedication and my three older brothers followed perfectly in his footsteps, each one a mirror of ducal expectations.

And then there was me: *Don Carlos Diego de Mendoza y Zúñiga*. A name I didn't choose, a title I didn't want.

Even as a child, the weight of tradition was a noose around my neck. While my brothers studied politics and military strategy, I was drawn to the poets whose work the Church condemned, to minds that dared to think beyond the suffocating, rigid orthodoxy.

My father called it 'rebellion.' I called it living.

It was a constant battle. Father arranging marriages to strengthen political alliances, me finding ways to sabotage each engagement. Him threatening disinheritance, me calling his bluff with increasingly scandalous behavior.

I wanted more than the world had to offer at the time. Wanted nobility to be about more than bloodlines and political marriages. Wanted love to be a choice, not a transaction. And above all, I wanted meaning.

Instead, I found myself born into an age where everything I valued was being controlled by institutions that cared more about power than purpose, about appearances than feelings. There was no room for individual expression, for passion.

My father never understood. He just thought I was 'being difficult on purpose.'

The final confrontation came on a winter night in 1614. He'd delivered his ultimatum with the coldness of a man accustomed to absolute obedience: enter the monastery or be disowned completely. No more chances, no more compromises.

'You've always been a disappointment,' he'd said, twenty-seven years of accumulated frustration unmissable in his voice. *'I'm just glad your mother never had to put up with you.'*

The words cut into me, jagged and deep. My mother had died bringing me into the world, and while I'd never been explicitly blamed, the implication had always lingered.

That night, I walked Toledo's dark streets until I found a tavern where no one knew my name or cared about my lineage. I drank until the wine finally numbed the conviction that I'd been born into the wrong century, wrong society, wrong life entirely.

That's where he found me.

Aureliano: my Maker, my Sire.

Unlike most vampire turnings, he offered me a choice. He explained exactly what he was offering: eternal life at the cost of my humanity.

I accepted without hesitation, offering him my blood, my companionship. Even drunk and furious, I knew I wanted out of the cage mortal life had built around me.

Nearly four centuries later, and I finally understand that the cage had nothing to do with mortality and everything to do with who holds power over you.

La Famiglia thinks they own me.

Just like my father did.

Like Aureliano did.

They're about to find out just how wrong they are.

I'VE BEEN WATCHING the estate since sundown, noting guard rotations and camera positions.

The hedges here are as pristinely trimmed as my father's estate used to be. Different country, different century, same suffocating perfection.

The auction is still a few hours away, according to Jude's intel, but the catering staff and some others are already on-site.

Nothing appears amiss. Just another wealthy estate with pretentious hedges.

The plan, if I can even call it that, is simple: get inside, find the Grimoire before the auction starts, and steal it outright before *La Famiglia* even knows it's here. With everyone running around getting the house ready for the auction, one more body shouldn't draw any attention.

It's a terrible plan. Adriana has always been the strategist between us; I'm usually the doer. But right now, the time for doing is running out fast, and this half-baked idea is all I have.

Still, even a terrible plan is better than watching her walk into an ambush.

I dissolve into the shadows and slip through an open upper window I spotted earlier. It leads to a guest bathroom in the east wing, all pristine with shiny surfaces and lavender smells.

Peeking my head into the empty hallway, I scan both ways, listening for any sounds. *All clear.* I try the first door on the right.

It's surprisingly quiet out there, but I'd be stupid to let my guard down. Even if this is merely a human residence and their silly guns don't scare me, not when I can compel them...

But nobody stops me as I work my way through the various rooms in the wing. It's mostly bedrooms and bathrooms.

The furthest door leads to a massive library, one lined with books on three sides. Perhaps the Grimoire is hidden here? It wouldn't be the first time something valuable has been hidden in plain sight to protect it.

I start searching through the top shelf, but I don't get very far.

Too late, I notice that I have company.

"Well, look who we have here," a familiar voice purrs from the shadows. "Such dedication."

Of course, she's here.

I spin around to find three figures emerging from the darkness like nightmares materializing for the living: Caterina in the center, flanked by Julius and Cesare.

Fuck.

Caterina is slow-clapping as they corner me. "*Bravo*, Cyrus. Though I have to say, your technique lacks subtlety."

I sigh. "You knew I was coming." *Why am I not surprised?*

"Of course we did." Cesare takes a step closer, and I notice the thick silver chain wrapped around his gloved hand. "Did you really think we wouldn't notice you sneaking around?"

Julius chuckles, the sound grating against my nerves. "We've been testing you all along," he says, his voice laced with that sickening confidence of someone who's never doubted their own superiority. "*La Famiglia* needed to know where your true loyalties lay."

I laugh, though there's no humor in it. "And now you know."

"Indeed." Cesare begins uncoiling the silver chain. "Though I admit, we expected something more dramatic. This reconnaissance mission is rather *disappointing*. Did you really think you could save her?"

"How long have you been watching me?" I ask, ignoring the rage bait.

"We're always watching," Julius replies, pinning my wrists behind my back; I let him. "You really should pay more attention to what is following in the shadows."

I consider my options.

If I fight, I might take one, maybe two down before they overwhelm me. But what would be the point? There is no winning here for me, not against three ancients. Their plans would proceed, and Adriana would still walk into their trap with no warning.

You're a fucking idiot, Cyrus.

"So what now?" I ask. "Torture? Interrogation? Or do you just kill me and move on?"

"Oh, we won't be killing you. Not yet." Caterina glances at her companions. "I'll handle our little wayward spy while the others take care of your *'Queen,'* as you call her."

"Where are you taking me?"

"Somewhere you can contemplate your poor choices without interfering with our plans." Her smile turns predatory. "The warehouse should provide adequate *motivation* for cooperation."

The warehouse. With all the dead witches. *Of course.* Where else?

Not like it makes any difference where they take me; there is no one left who'd save me. Adriana made it clear she was done with my bullshit and even Sorcha would just let me perish, I'm sure. *Can't blame either of them.*

"Why not just kill me?"

"You're far too valuable as a demonstration of what happens to those who defy us," Cesare continues, silver chain glinting in the moonlight streaming through the library windows.

The first blow catches me across the chest, silver searing through my clothing to burn the flesh beneath. The pain is immediate and intense, but instead of crying out, I find myself laughing.

"Something amusing?" Cesare asks, raising the chain again.

"Just thinking about how fitting this is." I meet his eyes, letting him see my genuine amusement. "Four hundred years of being in the wrong place at the wrong time. My father always said I had a talent for it."

The second blow strikes my ribs with enough force to crack bone. Silver burns like acid, but still I laugh. Because what else is there to do? Beg? Plead? Promise to cooperate if they spare my worthless existence?

"She won't come for me, you know," I say as the third strike tears across my face, splitting skin. "Whatever leverage you think I represent, you're wrong. Adriana would probably thank you for doing what she's been too civilized to do herself."

"We have no shortage of leverage; don't you worry about that." Cesare wraps the chain tighter around my throat, the silver searing into my skin, coloring the world in pain.

Vision blurring from the silver poisoning, I let my thoughts drift back to that night in Toledo, far away from here, when Aureliano offered me a choice...

If I'd known then what I know now, known how my life would turn out, the pain I'd endure, would I have chosen differently? Would I have accepted my father's ultimatum, entered the monastery, lived out my days in quiet submission to forces beyond my control?

No. Never. There is no doubt in my mind that I would have made the same choice, would've chosen the burden of immortality over and over again.

Because it led to her, to Adriana. To the one person in four centuries who made existence worth maintaining. *Mi Reina.*

As consciousness begins to fade around the edges, I find myself oddly at peace with what's coming.

My last coherent thought is a prayer to whatever gods might still listen to creatures like me, that somewhere, Adriana will find a way to survive what's coming.

Even if I won't be there to see it.

Even if this is how it ends for me.

CHAPTER 40
ENEMY LINES

(ADRIANA)

The Romero estate sprawls across thirty acres of manicured countryside, all ivy-covered stone and understated wealth.

As I navigate the winding approach road, I might as well be walking into my own execution. But I continue forward anyway; I have no choice.

Each day I'm separated from the Grimoire, my powers destabilize further. This morning, I accidentally froze my entire bathroom when I turned on the tap, ice spreading across every surface until I could barely recognize the room.

At this rate, I have weeks at most before my opposing natures tear me apart completely.

And Jude...Gods, he doesn't deserve to be caught up in all this. Cyrus compelling him still makes rage bubble up in my chest. But there is also fear. If *La Famiglia* knows about the auction, which I have to assume they do, thanks to Cyrus's intel, they know about Jude's research. They know he matters to me.

I should have left him somewhere safe the moment I realized they were watching us. But nowhere would be safe from *La Famiglia*. Their network is vast.

No, my only hope is to play the cards I've been dealt and pray for some divine intervention.

I present my credentials at the gate. *Dr. Adri Crevan*, it says on the forged ID Angelo dropped off at the lock box earlier this week. According to my business card, I'm an independent art authentication specialist, here on behalf of a private European collector interested in Renaissance manuscripts.

The guard's face doesn't move as he notes the Bentley I'm driving—stolen, naturally—and waves me through without a second glance.

Half a millennium of experience has taught me that confidence and expensive clothes open as many doors as compulsion does. Useful, considering my compulsion has become virtually useless, like the rest of my abilities.

But I can't think of that now. There is no room for weakness. Not today.

The circular driveway is lined with vehicles that collectively represent more wealth than most small nations possess. Maseratis and Aston Martins are parked beside an armored Mercedes, while a helicopter sits on the estate's private helipad to the right.

The guards stationed at various strategic positions throughout the property don't escape my notice either. There is too much firepower for a mere auction.

But it's not the guards that concern me. It's the unmistakable vampire signature that permeates from every corner of the estate as I make my way up the stairs to the entrance. It wafts past in waves as my sense of smell toggles between heightened and useless.

This is a trap, and I'm walking into it with my eyes wide open because the alternative—slowly disintegrating while *La Famiglia* closes in anyway—is worse.

My powers are failing, Jude is in danger, and this might be my last chance to reclaim what was stolen from me. Everything to lose; everything to gain.

Inside, the mansion's lobby has been transformed into an elegant showroom.

Taking off my coat, I hand it to the butler and straighten my dress.

Show time, Adriana.

Around me, priceless artifacts rest in climate-controlled cases, lit up with museum-quality lighting.

The auction catalog lists forty-seven lots, ranging from a supposedly authentic Stradivarius to a collection of Aztec gold that most likely wasn't acquired through official channels.

The influence required to acquire these pieces must be extraordinary.

You're not here for the art, I remind myself. Though I wish I were.

Making an effort to blend in, I accept a glass of champagne from a passing server with no intention of drinking it. My hands are steady but unwanted frost creeps across the glass stem as soon as I touch it. I set it down quickly on a nearby table.

"Magnificent collection, isn't it?"

The voice beside me belongs to an impeccably dressed man in his sixties, silver-haired and well-poised.

"Remarkable," I agree, taking in his expensive suit, the

shimmer of the RR-inscribed cufflinks. He looks the same as in his pictures. "Rafael Romero, I presume?"

His smile is pleased but carries an odd quality, like he's performing a role he doesn't quite remember rehearsing. "Indeed. I don't believe we've had the honor of meeting."

I smile politely, shaking his hand firmly. "Dr. Crevan. Representing the Venetian collector Conte di Castellane."

Angelo did a great job with the fabricated identity. If anyone were to look up Castellane, all they'd find is that he is a wealthy recluse, with impeccable taste and unlimited resources. *Perfect.*

"Welcome to my home." He looks to the collection behind me without really seeing it. "Anything in particular that Mister Di Castellane is interested in?"

Not wanting to seem too eager, I take my time to answer. "Ah, yes, he's inclined to medieval manuscripts and early printed works, in fact."

"How unfortunate." His tone carries confusion rather than menace. "I have several pieces that might interest him, though they're not part of tonight's auction."

The compelled look in his eyes confirms what I suspected: he's being used, manipulated. Someone else is pulling the strings tonight, and Romero is merely another human puppet.

"I see. Perhaps you could show me around your private collection later?" I lay it on thick with my most non-threatening, seductive smile.

Romero's expression grows distant for a moment, as if he's trying to remember something just out of reach. "Perhaps. Let's discuss after the auction concludes."

"Of course," I murmur. "Thank you for your hospitality."

He nods and moves away, disappearing into the crowd.

Scanning the room, I square my shoulders and stand up straight.

Too late to turn back now.

✿

THE AUCTION BEGINS PRECISELY at eleven, with Romero taking the podium to welcome his guests.

His opening remarks seem scripted, empty, the words of someone who's been told exactly what to say but doesn't understand why.

I position myself near the back of the room.

The bidding is aggressive and swift, with million-dollar transactions concluded in minutes.

During the intermission, I excuse myself to use the powder room but instead slip down a corridor marked 'Private' that leads toward the estate's family quarters. Now would be a good time to do some snooping, while everyone is distracted and chatting away.

The hallway is lined with family portraits spanning generations of Romeros, each face bearing the same aristo-cratic air.

There's something wrong with the silence around me as I continue down the hall. It's too silent. *Where are all the guards?*

The ice in my veins responds to my rising tension, frost forming on the wallpaper where my fingers brush. My flickering powers are more unstable than ever, fed by adrenaline and the proximity of genuine danger.

At the end of the corridor, a door stands slightly ajar.

Its position is too deliberate, too inviting, a trail of bread-crumbs leading exactly where they want me to go.

I don't slow down, though. I'm almost to the door when footsteps sound behind me, moving with a rhythm that is way too graceful to be human.

"Lost, *Dr. Crevan*?"

I turn with a curated look of surprise on my face, though my heart sinks when I see who's speaking.

Standing in the hallway, impeccably dressed in a char-coal suit that screams old money, is Cesare. I would recognize that sinister face anywhere. A fucking thug, that's what he is. Everyone knows *La Famiglia*'s enforcer is the last person you want to meet in a hallway—or anywhere.

I can't believe I didn't hear him sneak up on me or even smell him. But the ancients have always been good at concealing themselves, even if my powers were behaving as they should.

"Cesare," I say, less than pleased. "Always *such* a plea-sure. Though I have to admit, your timing could be better." Sarcasm drips from every word.

His laugh is genuinely amused. "Oh, *cara mia*. Our timing is absolutely perfect."

"I was looking for the powder room," I say smoothly, though I know he won't believe it for a second. We both know I have no use for a bathroom.

"Were you?" His Italian accent makes the words sound deceptively sweet. "How curious. I was under the impres-sion you might be looking for something else entirely. Something rather more *specific* to your current interests."

"I'm afraid I don't follow," I lie, calculating distances to exits and weighing my chances of reaching them before he can react. But even in full control of my body and my powers, I'd have a tough time winning a showdown with

Cesare. Beyond the sheer physical size of him, he's nearly double my age, making him notably stronger, more powerful. No, my only hope is to outmaneuver him mentally.

"No? You don't follow?" Cesare takes a step closer, otherworldly power radiating from him like heat. "Then perhaps I should remind you of your recent *research* activities. Your human assistant has been asking some interesting questions about insurance claims and private collections. Questions that suggest a particular urgency about locating something that's been missing for...oh, what was it? Nine years?"

My blood turns to ice, literally, as frost spreads across the wallpaper behind me in fractured patterns, cracks branching outward toward the ceiling.

"You see, *cara*," Cesare continues, his voice dropping to an intimate whisper that makes my skin crawl, "*La Famiglia* has been watching for a long time. We're always watching."

Behind him, the soft sound of multiple footsteps approaches as more vampires move in like a hunting pack, trapping me.

The enforcer's smile widens, revealing his fangs, as he pulls on his gloves and slips a silver knuckle duster over his right hand. "Oh, you'll see it soon enough. Though I'm afraid the viewing conditions won't be quite as comfortable as you'd hoped."

One of the approaching vampires produces a set of silver manacles from his coat, the metal shiny in his gloved hands. My vampire nature recoils instinctively from the sight.

"*La Famiglia* has been so patient," Cesare continues conversationally, as if we're discussing the weather. "So many years of searching, of watching, of waiting for you to lead us to your mother's little spell book. And here you are, gift-wrapped and delivered right to our door. And it's not even Christmas yet."

The manacles click shut around my wrists before I can react, sending searing pain through my body. The agony is immediate, but there is nothing I can do to fight it, to stop the blow as Cesare's silver-knuckled fist connects with my cheek.

The silver burns through my flesh like acid, eating away at the thin veneer of strength I've been clinging to.

This is it, then. The end I've been running from since the Grimoire was stolen. Not a glorious final stand but captured and shackled like a fucking criminal.

My mind skitters through possibilities, searching for escape routes that don't exist.

The silver burns deeper, and I can feel consciousness trying to slip away, offering escape from both physical pain and the crushing weight of failure.

My last thought, as unconsciousness claims me, is not for myself or my mission...

Jude.

Gods, I hope he's safe.

CHAPTER 41

ON LP

(JUDE)

The silence is deafening.

I'm standing in the hallway where Adriana kissed me goodbye moments ago, still tasting the lingering sweetness of her lips as she promised me she'd come back for me.

Yet this feels like the beginning of the end. Like everything is about to change. And I don't want it to.

These past three months have been the most stable, purposeful period of my entire adult life. The routine we've established has given my existence a structure, something I didn't realize I've been missing all this time.

I have a place here, a function, a reason to get up each morning that goes beyond mere survival. It's the first time in too long, perhaps since I learned to read, that I prefer reality to books.

But now, I've completed the task Adriana hired me for. And the possibility that she might not need me anymore sits in my stomach like a cement brick.

What happens now that I'm redundant?

Where do I go?

What do I do?

My old shitty room at the commune is probably long since rented to someone else. Morrison definitely doesn't want me back at the bookstore after my dramatic exit. Even the university is unlikely to give me another chance, despite finally being able to afford returning, thanks to the money Adriana has been depositing into my bank account without comment.

My wages have been accumulating week by week but I haven't spent a cent of it. I haven't needed to; Lady Adriana's been taking care of my every need.

But what good is the money?

If Adriana dismisses me now, I'll have more money than I've ever possessed and absolutely nowhere to go.

The thought is terrifying, and not for any practical reason about housing or employment. It's the prospect of returning to invisibility, to being forgettable and disposable, that makes my chest tight with something approaching panic. I don't want to be *Mister Cellophane* anymore.

I've gotten addicted to mattering, to having someone who notices when I'm twenty minutes late, who worries about my safety, who insists I drink more water and go for my damn workouts.

Adriana has become my entire world, and I'm not sure she realizes it.

I move through the empty penthouse like a ghost, running my fingers along surfaces that have become familiar over the recent months. Every room now holds memories that will turn painful if I'm forced to leave them behind.

The apartment is massive and empty without Adriana's presence. Too quiet, too still. Without her, I'm unmoored. Purposeless. I don't even have the Grimoire to search for anymore; no work to distract my mind.

Mission accomplished.

Why doesn't it taste like success then?

Academically, I should be rejoicing. I found the impossible find. I 'did good.'

But did I?

I settle into the chair behind Adriana's desk, surrounded by the artifacts of her various business dealings. Art catalogs, correspondence with collectors, insurance documents related to pieces she's acquired through methods I've learned not to ask about too much. It's all there: evidence of a life that's complex and dangerous and entirely separate from the domestic routine we've established between us.

I don't know what I'm looking for but anything is better than wandering aimlessly around the house.

My phone sits silent on the desk beside me. I look over to it again, checking *just in case.* But nothing has changed. There are no missed calls, no evidence that anyone outside this penthouse is aware of my continued existence.

The social isolation that once comforted me now drives another nail into my coffin. If something happens to Adriana tonight, if she doesn't return, who would even care that I am here?

The thought sends a chill through me that's 100% unrelated to the apartment's temperature.

I've bet everything on this arrangement; put all my eggs in one basket.

But what choice did I have?

When someone offers you purpose after a lifetime of

drifting, when they give you structure and meaning and the addictive satisfaction of being genuinely useful, you don't hedge your bets; you dive in completely.

Even if it means I'm moments from drowning now at the mere thought of losing it all again. Now that I know what I'd be missing, how fulfilling this particular brand of servitude could be, how could I go back to *before*?

Oh, Adriana. There is none like her. Could be none like her.

My mind returns to the gentleness of her caress when she touched my face before leaving tonight, the sadness in her eyes as she stared into my soul without saying anything. The kiss tasted so final...

What happens when she comes back?

Or when she *doesn't*?

The questions circle through my mind like vultures, picking at insecurities I've tried to ignore during the blissful routine of recent weeks.

The grandfather clock in the hallway chimes ten o'clock.

She's been gone for two hours.

The auction probably hasn't even started yet, but I find myself straining for sounds of her return: the elevator opening, her key in the lock, footsteps in the hallway that would signal everything went according to plan.

Instead, there's only silence and the weight of questions I'm not brave enough to ask directly.

The one I keep returning to is: *What if she compels me to forget we ever met?* I would never know what I'd lost, that it could be like this.

I'm one of the few mortals who know the truth, who's been permitted behind the curtain of supernatural existence. It's a privilege I don't want to lose; a knowledge I don't want to live without. But wanting something desperately doesn't guarantee you get to keep it. I learned that lesson the hard way too many times.

The only difference is that for the first time in ages, I have something to lose again.

These months in Adriana's care have taught me who I am when someone sees value in my service and offers genuine appreciation for my efforts. Take that away, and what's left? The invisible boy who settles for scraps of attention from people who barely remember his name?

I can't go back to that; won't go back to that.

But first, Adriana has to come home with her head on her shoulders and her spell book in her hand.

The clock chimes again. Quarter past ten.

It's going to be a long night.

❧

MY GRAN USED to be a firm believer that *'cleanliness is next to godliness.'* She would make me scrub the splintered wooden floors of her creaky house with a worn brush, on my knees, until either my fingers bled or the wood shone. It didn't matter to her which came first. I was six.

She used to tell me that *'no woman would want a useless man,'* a man who couldn't clean up after himself. She refused to raise another useless man in a world full of useless men, she said. All I could do was nod.

I'd scrub and scrub, scrub until I was crying. But it was never enough. The house remained *'too dirty,'* according to her. As did I.

Just like back then, I can't scrub the chaos spiraling in my mind from my thoughts, no matter how hard I try.

Adriana has been away for less than four hours, and

I'm already going insane, overthinking, worrying about how I would know if she were dead?

What would I do if they caught her? What could I possibly do?

'*Just a human,*' she'd called me. And it's true.

I can't even fight a mortal to protect myself. How am I going to fight a supernatural army to protect Adriana?

Useless.

My fingers are raw, bleeding in places, from the hour I've already spent on my knees, scrubbing the floor in Adriana's office.

The more I stared at her computer, the more my mind unraveled until I didn't know what to do except make myself useful.

She didn't put me to work. What work was there for me to do anyway? I'd already found the one thing she needed me for.

Felix cleaned in here this morning, like he always does. But it was all I could think to do to calm my spiraling mind.

The walls are too close, the sounds of the city bustling outside, too loud. I can't breathe; it's like someone is standing on top of my chest with heavy boots.

Anxiety, familiar and crippling, seeps into every corner of my existence until it's as murky as the water in the bucket beside me.

In vain, I keep scrubbing, trying to wash it all away, wash away my thoughts and my fucked-up memories, the cycle of doom repeating on loop in my brain. '*Make yourself, Jude,*' my gran chides in my head.

As much as I try to stop it, my mind drifts to the auction again, to Adriana's present predicament, alone across enemy lines.

They've probably caught her by now, torturing her, like last time. And I sent her away, to face the firing squad, so to speak.

I'm no better than Elijah.

The thought cuts deep.

I never wanted to disappoint her. She's become the most important person to me. More important than the extended family that never wanted anything but money from me. More important than the two friends I have in the whole world, who haven't checked in since I dropped out. More important than all the fictional villains and heroes I've idolized throughout history and literature. *She's everything!*

And I might have just lost her.

'Useless Jude.'

I dip my hands back into the dirty water, wringing out the cloth.

I've never been more complete than these months in Lady Adriana's care. She cares, she nurtures, corrects…it feeds a part of my soul I thought could never be fed. A part I thought would shrivel up and die, untouched.

Before meeting her, I thought submission was a sacrifice, but now I know it's a gift. She's taught me that, showed me how to care for myself, given me a voice.

And how do I return the favor? I send her to her death with a single goodbye kiss like a modern-day Judas. Except I have no pieces of silver to show for my betrayal.

Body slumped over in defeat, I take the bucket to the bathroom in Adriana's room to continue the scrubbing, my knees aching on the hard tiles. The brown water sloshes over the floor as the anguish in my mind bubbles over to panic.

It's too much. All too much.

I can't breathe!

Stripping off my clothes, I press my entire body against the cold tile, my cheek against the floor, in the hopes of grounding myself, of making the world stop spinning. But the walls are still getting closer and closer.

What if she doesn't come back?

What if she doesn't come back?

What if—?

The thought repeats on a loop as the shivers burn across my skin from the freezing tile. But I don't move, can't. My body is heavy.

Where would I go?

What would I do?

What would my purpose be?

No, there is no after without her.

Please, please, be okay, I beg to no deity in particular as the tears drip onto the tiles beneath my shivering, naked body. *Please, please.*

Curling up in the fetal position, I hug myself as I cry, past and present blurring into a nightmarish hell that imprisons me in my mind, its dark claws digging into me, refusing to release.

What if she doesn't come back for me?

CHAPTER 42

POWER PLAY

(ADRIANA)

Consciousness returns in waves of agony.

The silver chains bite into my wrists and ankles, the first sign that I'm still alive.

It takes me a moment to get my bearings.

I can't tell how long I've been out for.

My senses have been dulled to a human level. I can't even hear the chatter of the auction from here.

I'm suspended from the ceiling in a way that keeps me upright but helpless, my ankle chains bolted into the floor. My arms are stretched above my head, shoulders already screaming from the strain. Each link burns against my flesh, sending jolts of pain through my entire nervous system.

The room around me is sterile, windowless. It's some kind of converted basement or bunker, but I can't tell for certain. I'm surrounded by concrete walls and fluorescent lighting that make everything look sickly and pale. And there, arranged on a table like a doctor's surgical instruments, are tools I recognize from my nightmares, designed for torturing…torturing a vampire specifically.

It's too much like the first time, nine years ago, when the hunters strung me up in silver under similar conditions, with the same end goal in mind.

No, this is different. Last time, the foolish hunters didn't know what the book was capable of. Unfortunately, *La Famiglia* doesn't suffer from that same handicap.

Despite the aching, I turn my neck as far as I can.

Every muscle tenses at the sight of my mother's Grimoire sitting on a pedestal just out of reach. After nine years of searching, of slowly dying without its artificial life force, and there it is, right there, so close I can almost taste the magic radiating from it, but I might as well be looking at the moon.

"Ah, you're awake." It's Cesare. "We were beginning to worry the silver had damaged something important."

A second figure emerges from the shadows, and my heart sinks further. *Julius.* We've never had the displeasure of meeting, but the reputation of the Inner Circle precedes them. All vampires know about the four ancients who pull the strings at the top.

His dark eyes study me with detached interest.

Of course, he's here.

No sign of Caterina, though.

Nor Valerian.

None of Cesare's thugs either.

It's just the two of them.

Such foolish confidence.

"Lady De Crevena," Julius says, his voice carrying the cultured accent of pre-Revolution France. "How delightful to see you here. Though I must say, your current circumstances are less than favorable."

I try to speak, but my throat is too dry. The silver is doing more than burning; it's sapping my vampire strength, making even basic functions more difficult.

"Thirsty?" Cesare asks with mock sympathy, watching my every move. "I'm afraid *refreshments* will have to wait until after you've fulfilled your *purpose*."

He gestures toward the Grimoire. "Your mother's little spellbook has been quite the prize, though unfortunately useless without the proper *key*. Your blood, of course."

I don't say anything. There's no point in responding to someone *mansplaining* my own property to me, as Jude would've said.

They don't have it quite right, though. But why would I tell him that technically it doesn't need my blood, only my touch? Cyrus got it wrong all those years ago when he let my secret slip...

"My purpose," I repeat, forcing the words out past the dryness in my throat. "You want me to unlock it. To what end?"

"All in good time."

"You've gone to considerable trouble for a spellbook." My voice is steadier than I expected. "What's in that book that's worth all this?" I've been wondering all along.

Julius's smile flickers, but he doesn't answer the question. Instead, he crouches slightly, bringing himself to my eye level. "Tell me, Lady De Crevena. In five centuries, how many others like you have there been? How many of them survived?"

Where is he going with this?

"None," I say slowly, watching his face for a reaction. "I'm the only success in five centuries."

"You give yourself too much credit, *ma chérie*," Julius

says. The dismissal is too quick, too smooth, the sort of thing said to close a door rather than open one.

And then everything clicks into place.

"You don't want one hybrid." The words come out flat, disbelieving even as I say them. "You want to replicate it. You want an army."

Neither of them denies it and the silence is answer enough.

Fuck.

All this time, I thought they either wanted me as a weapon or to destroy me before I became one. I had never even considered that they wanted to force more hybrids into existence.

"You think you can mass-produce what took centuries and a High Priestess and pure luck to achieve once." A laugh escapes me, brittle and humorless. "Do you have any idea what happens to a hybrid without those spells? What happened to every other attempt?"

"We're aware there were difficulties," Julius says smoothly.

"Which is precisely why we require your cooperation," Cesare adds, producing a ceremonial blade that sparkles in the harsh light. "You're going to bleed on that book, unlock its secrets, and teach us how it was done correctly. The process shouldn't take more than a few hours."

"And then?" I manage to croak out, refusing to give them the satisfaction of a reaction. "What happens once you get what you want?"

Julius smiles, revealing fangs that have tasted the blood of kings if legend is to be believed. "Then you become redundant, *ma chérie*. I'm sure you understand."

Of course I do. They're the ones who don't understand.

"But first," Julius says, moving to a control panel built into the wall, "let me explain your current situation. See these symbols carved into the walls?" He gestures to intricate runes that I now notice covering every surface of the room. "One of our *subjects* was kind enough to help us with a containment spell." I doubt that any kindness was involved.

"If you attempt to use the Grimoire's power against us, the entire room detonates," Julius continues. "Silver shrapnel, fire, the works. Quite spectacular, really."

My blood runs cold, but not from my ice this time.

Oh, fanculo!

This makes my situation significantly more complicated.

"The spell is specifically attuned to the Grimoire's magical signature," Julius adds with satisfaction, touching what appears to be a golden pendant hanging around his neck. I notice Cesare is wearing an identical amulet.

"Any attempt to weaponize that book's power will trigger instant destruction. Of course, our protection charms will shield us from the blast, but you..." Julius shrugs elegantly. "Well, you won't be so fortunate."

I'm not surprised at all. Of course, there are contingencies. *Merda.*

They think they have me completely trapped. The silver chains suppress my vampire abilities, while the threat of a magical explosion keeps me from using the Grimoire against them. The perfect defense.

This is the part where he expects me to play the helpless victim, defeated, ready to trade my life for a few more minutes of existence. And I damn near do.

The pain from the silver is becoming unbearable,

making it hard to think clearly. My vampire healing can't function properly with the metal touching my skin, and my strength is ebbing with each passing second. Even if I could somehow get free, how could I fight two ancient vampires in my current state?

I have only one chance, and if I fuck it up, the only certain outcome is death.

"Shall we begin?" Cesare asks, approaching with the blade.

I look at the Grimoire, so close and yet impossibly far away.

Focus, Adriana.

I let my breathing grow even shallower, as if weakness has completely consumed me.

Both vampires move closer, confident in my help-lessness.

Julius lifts the Grimoire from its pedestal, bringing it within reach of my chained hands.

But there's something they don't know. Something I've been carefully keeping hidden since the moment they chained me up.

They don't know that the ice in my veins is still there; the silver only affects my vampire nature…

The containment spell remains the biggest risk. It was specifically designed to detect the Grimoire's magical signature, but I have no guarantee it won't be triggered by *all* magic.

It's my only chance, though, even if the odds are stacked against me.

"Your blood, if you please," Cesare commands, bringing the blade to my palm.

But instead of complying, I do something they don't expect.

I'm counting on science, the only card I have left as I channel all that I have into those single contact points. Frost spreads along the links faster than either vampire can react.

The silver chains are strong, but metal becomes brittle when flash-frozen to subzero temperatures.

The symbols on the walls flicker briefly, and for a second, I think it's all over, that the containment spell is going to activate. But then the lights stabilize again, the wards settling.

"What—" Cesare starts, but he doesn't get to finish.

I wrench my limbs apart despite the pain, and the frozen silver chains shatter like glass.

The sudden freedom sends me stumbling forward, but I manage to grab the Grimoire before Julius can pull it away, still too dumbfounded to react.

The moment my fingers close around the ancient leather binding, everything changes.

It recognizes my signature, and the stabilization spells activate instantly. No blood needed. Artificial life force surges into my body, and the shock of it nearly drops me to my knees.

My vampire nature recoils, every dead cell screaming in protest as something that feels horrifyingly like living floods through my veins. I haven't felt warmth in my chest in over nine years. Now it burns there, foreign and invasive, like swallowing something that was never meant to fit inside a body like mine.

I bite down hard, tasting blood, as the spells continue their work, forcing my two natures back into alignment.

The repair is agony. It takes only a second, not long enough for anyone to react. To me, it stretches on, every fraction of that second its own small catastrophe.

The artificial life force spreads through my circulatory system, following pathways that haven't carried anything but cold blood for nearly a decade.

That's when the real pain begins.

My magic ignites with brutal force. For nine years it's been drawing from a well that doesn't exist, inverting itself into corrupted ice. Now there's fuel again, and heat explodes in my core, my magic lurching toward fire the way it was always meant to be.

But the ice is still there. Nine years of corrupted magic, threaded through every nerve, every cell, refusing to yield. Fire and ice collide inside me, neither willing to give ground.

I can't breathe. I don't need to, but my body tries anyway, an old reflex triggered by the life force's return. My lungs expand, and the sensation is wrong, painful, like breathing in broken glass.

This is going to tear me apart.

It doesn't.

The ice holds, and then it shatters. Not gradually, not gently, but all at once, nine years of corruption fracturing inside me like a glacier calving into the sea. I feel every splinter, every jagged edge, as my power rebuilds itself from the inside out.

My nerve endings catch fire. Not figuratively. They *are* fire, flames crawling under my skin, through muscle, wrapping around bone.

The scream that tears out of me doesn't sound human.

My knees finally buckle, but I don't let go of the Grimoire. *Never again.*

Fire consumes the last of the ice, and for one moment I am burning, truly burning. Flames erupt from my pores, racing across my skin in patterns that leave no mark behind.

The heat is transcendent, all-consuming, pain so total it whites out thought entirely.

Then, like a bone snapping back into place, everything settles.

Gods, there it is.

That feeling.

For the first time in nine years, I am whole. I am me again.

Power floods back into me, dizzying in its intensity, and fire erupts outward from my body in a single blinding flash, flooding the room with light.

Cesare, standing closest to me, doesn't even have time to step back. The flames consume him in seconds, his ancient form reduced to ash before his protection amulet can react.

The magic happened too fast, too close. No charm could have saved him.

Julius staggers backward, his clothes singed, his perfect composure finally cracked. The amulet around his neck glows desperately, trying to shield him from the residual heat, but there are burns along his exposed skin where my fire found him.

"Impossible," he gasps, staring at me with something that might actually be fear. "The containment spell should have—"

"You should've thought it through, old man. The containment spell is attuned to the Grimoire's power," I interrupt, advancing on him with feet that don't touch the ground. Fire dances around me like living jewelry, responding to my will instead of fighting against it. "Time to pay the piper, *mon chérie.*" I throw his patronizing endearment back in his face, and the French tastes bitter in my mouth.

I don't give him time to recover. Julius has centuries of experience, but he's injured now, his amulet damaged by the initial surge. And I finally have my powers back.

The fight is brief and futile.

"Please, Adriana," Julius begs as I rip the cracked amulet from his neck and throw it on the floor. "Have mercy."

I don't bother wasting my breath explaining to him why mercy is wasted on cunts like him. No, I just sink my fangs into his neck, letting the ancient blood flow into me.

He struggles, tries to claw at me, but my strength increases with every ounce I drain from him. The weaker he gets, the more powerful I grow, more than a thousand years of secrets and sins flooding my senses.

Good gods, I've never tasted blood like that. It's incredible! Like it's irradiated, lined with sparkles, fizzing on my tongue. It tickles down my throat, warming my stomach.

So much killing. So many fucked-up things he's done. It all flows into me along with his blood as Julius's life drains from his body.

My eyes grow wide as I near the end of his memory loop, when I catch up to the events of tonight.

Cyrus. Fuck!

They have Cyrus.

The last image I see before I pull out, careful not to drink the last drop, is Cesare's silver-wrapped fist smashing into Cyrus's face as the beautiful disaster I've never stopped loving just laughs at his captors.

He never told them about the Grimoire. Instead, he

tried to help. Without any reward or motivation, he risked it all to try to stop this. *Oh, Cyrus,* you fool.

I feel nothing when I rip Julius's throat out and throw him to the ground beside Cesare's ashes, stepping over the carnage with my heels dirty but intact.

This ends tonight.

CHAPTER 43
FOUND

(CYRUS)

I've lost track of how many hours I've been at the warehouse. Time stopped mattering somewhere around the second time Caterina walked back into the room with a scalpel and some holy water.

The silver at my wrists and ankles keeps me strung up, burning steady and constant, a pain so familiar now it's almost background noise. *Almost.* When it spikes past that, when she gets too close, I go somewhere else in my mind, somewhere happier…

Memories of Venice are all I cling to now. I always go back to 1621, to the first time I laid eyes on the magnificent being that is Adriana De Crevena.

I'd been hunting that night when I caught movement on a rooftop above the Grand Canal.

I should have gone straight home to Aureliano's palazzo with our dinner like the dutiful servant I'd been raised to be.

Instead, I found myself following the hooded figure across Venice's labyrinthine rooftops, fascinated by the woman who moved like she never asked permission for anything.

When she finally turned to face me, I expected the usual: dismissal, maybe irritation, the casual cruelty older vampires tend to reserve for anyone younger.

Instead, she smiled. *'Are you going to follow me all night, or are you going to introduce yourself?'*

Four centuries later, I still haven't fully recovered from that smile.

Adriana changed everything.

For seven years, I'd existed in Aureliano's shadow. I was grateful for his rescue from mortality yet trapped by his expectations of what a good companion should be: quiet, devoted, and content to bask in his reflected glory while my own fire dimmed to embers. By his side, I'd become the opposite of everything I'd spent my life fighting to be.

But when Adriana looked at me that night with a spark of mischief, that fire roared back into my veins.

Despite the places we both had to be, our first conversation lasted until dawn: philosophy, poetry, the weight of immortality, topics I'd been trained to approach with caution. She challenged every assumption, turned every certainty on its head, and by the time the sun came up I'd said more true things than I had in seven years combined. *Christ*, she was incredible from the start.

The pain pulls me back to the present, Caterina's shrill voice cutting through my reverie with its usual venom.

"Had enough yet?" she repeats, but I do not answer.

Instead, I retreat again, deeper into 1621. What I wouldn't give to relive those years.

Those stolen nights in Venice became everything to me. We met in secret. I knew Aureliano wouldn't understand. He'd become possessive, clingy, all the things that make no sense for an immortal being with forever ahead of them.

I should've nipped it in the bud before I grew too attached to Adriana, but there was never such a time. From the first night, I was hooked on her.

By then, she'd been living in Venice for almost two decades and knew all the good spots. She showed me parts of the city tourists never saw, hidden places where we could talk until dawn without interruption.

She never tried to change me or quiet my nature as Aureliano did. Adriana encouraged the parts of myself I'd learned to suppress, like my tendency to question authority, my impatience with arbitrary rules, my need to live passionately rather than safely.

'You were born to burn bright,' she told me one night as we watched the sun rise from a bell tower. *'Don't let anyone convince you that dimming yourself is a kindness to them.'*

For the first time since my transformation, I felt like myself again. Not a reflection of someone else's desires, not a project to be shaped and molded, but a person worthy of being known and chosen for exactly who I was.

We had three months of perfect stolen moments before Aureliano inevitably discovered our affair. Frankly, I was surprised it took him so long.

I expected anger from him, maybe violence, the blind rage vampires were known for. Instead, I found something worse: heartbreak.

'Choose,' he said simply that night he discovered the truth. *'Her or me. You cannot have both.'*

But it wasn't really a choice, was it? He'd already made

the decision for me by demanding I prove my loyalty through abandonment of the one person who made me feel like the world had meaning.

When I refused, when I told him I couldn't give up Adriana, his heartbreak hardened into something colder.

'Then kill her,' Aureliano demanded. *'That's the only way.'*

I stared at him in disbelief. There was only one answer to his ludicrous request: *'No.'*

'You will do this, Cyrus. You are mine, created by me, bound to me by blood and oath. You will—'

'No!' The word came out stronger this time, carrying all my suppressed rebellion. *'I won't.'* I couldn't. How could he ask me that and still claim to love me?

That's when I understood the true nature of the cage I'd been living in. How did it become so impossible to escape the subtler bonds of gratitude and obligation that made resistance feel like betrayal?

I stormed out before he could say another word, straight to Adriana's comforting embrace.

As she held me tight, I told her everything. About Aureliano's ultimatum, his demand that I prove my loyalty through murder, the impossible position he'd forced me into. I expected her to run, to decide I wasn't worth the complications that came with an ancient vampire's possessive fury.

Instead, she took my face in her hands and said, *'Then we kill him first.'* No hesitation.

'I can't.' The words came out broken, desperate. *'You know we cannot kill our own Sires. It's impossible. The blood connection—'*

'You can't. But I can.' Her voice was steady, certain. *'And I will.'*

She didn't do it for revenge or anger. She did it for me, for us.

The night she killed him was the first time I experienced the terror and exhilaration of complete freedom. No more obligations, no more balancing between gratitude and selfhood. Just the vast, terrifying possibility of becoming whoever I chose to be.

Adriana saved me that night.

And now...

Now I can't even return the favor.

You fucked it all up, Cyrus. Still a disappointment.

AROUND ME, the laboratory continues its grisly work as bodies in white sheets are wheeled past, their experiments continuing. But in my memories, I'm elsewhere, in Adriana's arms, safe.

Caterina visits regularly. Sometimes she brings others.

They ask questions I don't bother answering, make threats that have lost all meaning. What can they do to me that they haven't already done? What's left to take when you've already lost everything that mattered?

"Still with us?"

Caterina's voice cuts through the fog of memory and pain. I force my eyes open, though the effort it takes is monumental.

She's standing just out of reach, twirling the scalpel in her gloved hands.

"The auction was quite successful," she continues conversationally, as if we're discussing the weather. "Your little witch walked right into our trap. So predictable, really."

I try to speak, but my throat is raw. The sound that emerges is far from human.

"What's that? You'll have to speak up." She moves closer, close enough that I can smell the old blood on her breath. "Are you concerned about her welfare? How touching. I'm afraid there's nothing you can do. It's too late."

The words hit with brutal, flattening force.

They have Adriana. They probably have the Grimoire too. Everything I tried to prevent has happened anyway, and my futile gesture accomplished nothing except landing me here as entertainment for Caterina's sadistic pleasures.

I close my eyes, unwilling to give her the satisfaction of seeing my despair.

"Nothing to say? What a waste. You used to be so much more entertaining." Caterina sighs dramatically. "Perhaps you need motivation. Would you like to see her? I could arrange a reunion. Let you watch as we—"

She doesn't get to finish her sentence.

Light explodes through the laboratory, blinding and absolute. The temperature rises so fast that a nearby metal table begins to warp.

Through the glare, a figure emerges in a torn emerald-colored dress and heels.

Adriana.

But not the weakened, desperate woman I remember from our last encounter. No, this is Adriana the way I've always known her: radiant, glorious, the Grimoire safe in her hand, where it belongs.

Sweet Jesus. Even after all this time, she still takes my breath away.

"Hello, Caterina." Adriana holds up her hand, flame

dancing on her open palm. "Can't say it's nice to meet you."

Caterina recovers from her shock with admirable speed, producing a wooden stake from the hidden pocket in her dress. "Come to rescue your worthless ex-lover? Never pegged you for a romantic." Her voice drips with sarcasm.

Adriana doesn't bother responding. She takes a step forward, and I swear I can see the air itself catching alight around her. "Did you really think you'd get away with this?"

"Fuck you." Caterina lunges, stake first.

Adriana doesn't even flinch, just catches the wood mid-air. It combusts the moment she touches it. "My turn."

Even from here, chained and useless, I can tell Caterina is already dead. She just hasn't caught up yet.

She comes again anyway, teeth bared, all pretense of control gone. Adriana catches the strike and twists. Bone cracks, audible even over Caterina's scream.

"You only ever cared about power," Adriana says, her voice steady as she lifts Caterina off her feet by the throat. Flames crawl up her neck where the fingers grip, blackening the skin. "Funny how that works out."

"You bitch—" Whatever else Caterina means to say dies on her lips as Adriana's hand ignites, her whole fist becoming fire. She drives it into Caterina's stomach, and the smell of burning flesh fills the lab. My torturer convulses, mouth open in a silent scream, smoke pouring from the wound.

"This is for taking what's mine." Adriana reaches into the charred hole in Caterina's torso and closes her hand around the heart.

One pull, and it's over.

Adriana stands, Caterina's heart crumbling between her fingers. She lets the ash scatter. Within seconds, there's nothing left of the ancient vampire but dust, drifting on superheated air before settling across the laboratory floor.

Then, and only then, does she turn to me.

The flames still wreath her body, casting dancing shadows across her face. Power radiates from her in waves that make the air shimmer.

"Hello, love," she says, her voice almost gentle as her face softens.

"*Mi Reina*," I manage to croak, my voice breaking on the words.

She approaches the chains holding me, fire dancing along her fingertips. The silver melts away without burning me, and I collapse to my knees as circulation returns to my limbs.

"Drink," she orders, kneeling beside me and offering her wrist.

I don't argue.

Her blood flows into me like the purest drug I could ever imagine, warm, incredible. Surging through my body, it undoes the damage Caterina has done, restoring my strength.

"I can't believe you came for me," I whisper against her wrist after I've drunk my fill.

After everything I've done, every way I've failed her, every reason she had to leave me to my fate…she still came.

"Cyrus." Adriana cups my face in her free hand and smiles. "Did you really think I would leave you here?"

"I thought—I hoped. But I couldn't be sure. Not after—"

"I could never leave you, my reckless one," she says simply, certainly, pulling me into a hug. "Not then, not now, not ever. You should know that by now."

Good god, is this a dream?

Please be real.

CHAPTER 44

QUEEN'S VENGEANCE

(ADRIANA)

From the moment he told me his name, one warm autumn evening in Venice, I knew Cyrus was unlike anyone I'd ever met.

A pagan name, chosen in rejection of his predetermined fate, there was something familiar in his rebellion, in his hunger for a different world. He gave my dark existence color again, injected meaning into a world rendered meaningless by the weight of eternity.

Cyrus never treated me as anything less than equal or made me fight for my seat at the table. He just pulled out the chair for me as if it were the most natural thing in the world.

My father rejected me for my bastard blood. Demetrius rejected me for the chaos my hybrid nature caused. But Cyrus? He never saw me or my blood as less. In his eyes, I was always more. *'Everything,'* he'd whisper as we danced in the moonlight, weaving his fingers through mine.

It was the first time in my existence, mortal and undead alike, that I felt as if I belonged somewhere. That's when I knew I would keep Cyrus for life, for better or for worse.

When I killed his Sire to free him, I swore I'd always fight by his side, always protect him. Even after all this time, I still mean it.

Despite everything that's happened between us, I can't imagine my life without my beautiful, reckless fool.

When I found Cyrus strung up in this decrepit makeshift laboratory earlier, chained and broken, I knew that I would burn this entire building down, and everyone in it, before I let anyone harm him again. It was the same feeling I had centuries ago when I realized what Aureliano was doing to him—this brilliant, passionate creature being slowly dimmed until nothing remained but coerced submission.

He doesn't deserve this.

Sure, Cyrus isn't perfect. He made mistakes, kept secrets, played both sides. But he ultimately tried to do the right thing; I saw it all in Julius's blood. He never told *La Famiglia* about the auction and instead tried to save the Grimoire himself, knowing it would more than likely get him killed.

Yet he still risked it all, for me.

"You ready, my love?" I ask as I crack my knuckles, preparing for the wave of vampires and compelled humans I can hear filing through the warehouse corridors toward us.

He reaches over and squeezes my hand. "Born ready, *mi Reina*."

I can't help but smile, shaking my head. Even after everything, he's making jokes. *Some things never change.*

"You take right and I take left?" I suggest, and Cyrus nods, pushing a strand of hair from my forehead. The simple gesture makes my heart clench. So familiar; so intimate.

"Like old times." He yanks me toward him for a kiss that leaves me figuratively breathless.

I smile against his lips. "Let's do this."

Gently, I place the Grimoire on one of the surgical tables beside me. With a short incantation, fire rises up around it, a cage of flame that doesn't reach the valuable pages but leaves the spellbook untouchable to anyone but me.

The first attackers come fast, two vampires and a handful of compelled humans, the remnants of La Famiglia's forces. But there is no force behind their movements, no structure. They're scrambling to make a stand, not because they think they can win, but because they have nowhere left to run.

I catch the nearest vampire by the throat and slam her into the wall hard enough to crack the concrete, the sound sharp in the sterile space. She's strong, but I'm faster, and faster wins. My fangs find her throat before she can even scream properly, and her blood floods through me, young and frightened and electric. When I drop her, she doesn't get back up.

The rush is incredible, fueling me forward.

Gods, I'd forgotten what it felt like to move through the world without something inside me pulling in the opposite direction. Nine years of fighting my own body just to function, and now there's nothing left to fight, just me and nearly a decade of pent-up rage.

And I'm in the mood to make someone pay for it.

Beside me, Cyrus moves like he always did when we

hunted together, like Caterina's torture never happened, like his body simply remembers what it's for. He has a compelled guard in a chokehold, the man's face going purple, and a moment later the human goes still in his arms.

Cyrus looks over, checking on me even as another vampire closes in behind him, always watching out for me even when he should be watching his own back.

"Focus, *idiota*," I call out, though there's no real warning in it.

He grins at me with that crooked grin I love so much, and turns just in time to catch his attacker's wrist and snap it.

I get back to the fight, bodies and faces blurring until nothing matters but destroying it all.

"Have mercy," one of them whispers, a female vampire with olive skin and pleading eyes. "We were just following orders."

"That's what they all say." I'm on her before she can respond, sinking my teeth into her throat. Her blood tastes of cowardice and desperation, and I drain her quickly. There's no satisfaction in it, just one less thing standing between me and the rest of them.

More reinforcements follow the first wave, charging into the lab.

I lift my hands, and my fire answers immediately, effortlessly, like it never stopped being part of me. It floods across the laboratory floor, catching the nearest vampire mid-stride, blistering his skin as his screams fill the space. Even as the flames spread, part of me is still marveling at them, half expecting this to be some trick of adrenaline that will fade at any second. It doesn't fade. It's just there, warm and steady under my skin, exactly where it's always belonged.

My vampire strength recedes as the flames take hold, pulling back the way it always does when I draw on magic instead, leaving me slower and heavier than a moment ago. I know this, should expect this: I can't use both natures at once, never could. But I'm so caught up in the moment that for one crucial second I stop paying attention to my blind spots.

An older vampire breaks from the chaos, a stake raised, aimed for my heart. I sense him half a second too late, and even as I try to turn, I know I'm not going to make it in time.

Cyrus is faster.

I turn in time to see him catching the vampire's wrist, snapping it before driving his other hand straight through the man's chest. "Nobody," he snarls, "hurts my Queen."

The vampire gasps, blood frothing from his lips as Cyrus's hand finds his heart. He tears the heart free like it's not attached to anything, and the vampire crumbles to ash.

Good gods. I'd forgotten what he looks like when he's not holding back.

"Behind you," he says simply as he wipes his ashy hands on his pants, as if saving my life cost him nothing at all.

The rest fall quickly, torn apart and scattered across the floor. I know I'm exerting more power than the Grimoire can sustain, even with Julius's ancient blood in my veins, but I'm not ready to stop, not yet. So I keep drawing, indiscriminate now, pulling life force from anything close enough to give it. The compelled humans charging at me with stakes never get near. They're drained before they hit the ground, their energy flowing into me.

"For you, *querida*," Cyrus calls me over when I run out of attackers to destroy, gesturing at the pile of wounded vampires, offering me the kill like it's merely a side of fries on a plate.

I smile, cracking my knuckles. "Don't mind if I do."

I kneel beside the first one, a young vampire, maybe fifty years old, with expensive clothes and terror in his eyes. "Please," he whispers, but I'm already biting down, his blood flowing into me without resistance.

I drain him slowly, savoring every drop while his two companions watch in horror. When I'm finished, I move to the second one, then the third, taking my time, letting the power build inside me until I'm on the brink of bursting from the sheer intensity of it.

"Just like Prague," Cyrus says, wiping blood from his mouth, and I know he's remembering the same night I am, when we tore through an entire nest of feral vampires and didn't stop until the streets ran red.

"Better than Prague," I reply, taking his outstretched hand and getting up.

And then it's over.

Silence falls over the space, broken only by the steady drip of blood from the ruined walls. Bodies lie around us like discarded dolls, broken and drained and utterly still.

I reach for Cyrus, and he comes to me without hesitation, his arms wrapping around my waist as I stand on my toes to press my forehead against his.

"We did it," I whisper.

"We always do," he replies, crushing my bloody lips under his.

Every cell in me thrums with life as I kiss him back with everything I have.

Four centuries later, and he's still the only one who can match my violence, my hunger, who sees my fire and wants to burn brighter instead.

Gods, it's good to be me again.

CHAPTER 45

RECONNECTING

(CYRUS)

The warehouse is eerily quiet and it's the most glorious sound.

I know the war is far from over, not with Valerian still at large, but for now, the battle is won. We are both alive and Adriana has her Grimoire back. That's all that matters.

The carnage around us tells its own story. It's a masterpiece of violence that would make Jack the Ripper weep with envy.

That's my Queen, I think as the grin spreads over my face. *My magnificent, terrifying, absolutely unstoppable Queen.*

It's been years since I've felt this incredible. Decades even. My blood is on fire! Not only from everything I've consumed and drained, but from Adriana's power, seeping through our bond.

She's always amazing but with the Grimoire back where it belongs, with her fire magic restored, she's on a whole other level, virtually glowing with power. And I've never wanted her more.

Our bloody kiss turns to desperate groping as the primal urges surge through my body, wild and feral.

When I sink my teeth into her throat, when she lets me, my world explodes in color and power. A rush unlike any I've known swirls my mind into near-delirium.

Grinning with bloody fangs, she bites down on my skin seconds later. The bond between us flares up like a physical thread as we both drink, exchanging blood, exchanging *everything*.

Fuck, I've missed her so much.

Every single day of these past nine years has been gray without Adriana, colorless, like living in a world where someone has stolen all the light, all the music, the poetry, the very reason for existing.

"Cyrus," Adriana breathes against my throat when we finally disengage, and the sound of my name on her lips in that tone after all these years nearly brings me to my knees. Her voice is rough with power and bloodlust, and when she pulls back to look at me, her eyes turn white, reflecting the overhead lights.

"I know," I whisper, because I do; I know what she's feeling because I'm feeling it too. This overwhelming, desperate need to reconnect. It's consuming me.

I lean my head against hers, breathing in her scent: death and magic and jasmine, and something uniquely Adriana that's haunted my dreams for centuries. "I'm sorry, *querida*—" I start to say, but she silences me with another kiss.

"Don't," she says against my lips. "Not now. We have forever to reconcile the past."

Forever. What a beautiful word coming from her.

Adriana runs her fingers through my hair, and I lean into the touch.

It's been nine years of wondering if I'd ever taste her blood again, if I'd ever see that particular smile she saves only for me, the one that's equal parts affection and desire.

"You still fight like a god." There's wonder in her voice. "Incredible."

"For you, *mi Reina*, I would raze empires," I tell her, and I mean it with every cell in my undead body.

The bond between us flares, bright and hot and undeniable. It's been there since the moment we first exchanged blood in the Between Court. Nearly four hundred years later, that feeling hasn't dimmed even in the slightest. If anything, it's gotten stronger.

I hold her close to me, my fingers intertwining with hers, as the new memories, new emotions, reorder themselves in my mind.

The silver chains have left marks on her wrists that have all but faded, but I can sense the echo of her pain through our connection, taste the distress in her memories. They hurt her. Those *Famiglia* bastards chained her up and hurt her, and I wasn't here to stop it. Again.

The rage that thought brings is so intense, I can barely see straight. I want to hunt down every last member of that fucked-up *Famiglia*, make them suffer the way they made her suffer, and listen to them scream until their voices give out.

But whoever is left is long gone now. Valerian didn't even show his face, just fled like the coward he is, leaving his subordinates to die. *Spineless cunt.*

"I can sense your anger, darling," Adriana murmurs,

her thumb tracing the line of my jaw. "Don't. They're not worth it."

My fists clench at my side. "They hurt you."

"They tried to." Her smile is sharp enough to cut glass. "Emphasis on *tried*. Besides, look how it ended."

She gestures at the massacre around us, and I have to admit she has a point.

I unclench my fists and smile.

"What are you thinking about?" she asks.

"Prague," I tell her honestly. "That first winter we spent there. When you figured out how to boil blood in someone's veins."

Her laugh is music, wind chimes dancing in a Fae forest. "You thought it was the most romantic thing you'd ever seen."

"It was." I cup her face in my hands, marveling at how she leans into my touch. "You are. The most beautiful, most terrifying, most perfect creature I've ever known. And I've spent nearly all my life trying to be worthy of you."

"Foolish man," she says fondly. "You've always been worthy. Impulsive, sure. Infuriating at times, undeniably. But never unworthy, my love."

Adriana's fingers trace the line of dried blood on my throat where she bit me, and the touch sends electricity racing through my entire body. "I missed this," she whispers, finally admitting it out loud.

"Never again," I promise her, taking her hand in mine again. "I'm never deserting you again, Adriana."

She smiles. "You know I never minded you leaving, Cyrus. You're a child of the world, not mine to keep. The stormy fights and lack of communication, though? That I can do without."

"Yes, Ma'am." I kiss her fingers, one by one, even the bloody ones.

Adriana shakes her head at the honorific, playfully pushing me off her. "Don't start. I'm not your Mistress."

I pull her closer again. "No, you've got your little pet human to fill that need."

She's quick as lightning, impossibly strong, as she jumps up and pins me to the wall, blood-red fangs punctuating her predatory smile. "Don't touch him," she growls like the beast she is.

I'm only playing; she knows that. But it's fun to push her buttons. "Not without permission, *mi Reina*. Don't worry."

"Good boy," she teases, and then the time for words is done.

She fists my bloody shirt, ripping it clean off me, her eyes never leaving mine.

I'm impossibly hard as I pull her to me. My body needs her like it needs blood to survive; my dick is ready to burst!

With a grin spreading over her face, she scratches me across the chest, deep cuts slicing through my skin as the beautiful pain bleeds into my circuits.

Growling, I catch her hand mid-air when she goes in for a second strike, scratching her across the face with the other in retaliation.

Her only response is a laugh so pure, so genuine, it cuts through the shadows of my immortal dark heart.

The cut on her face heals almost instantly, but not before a streak of blood trails down her cheek in a crimson tear. My tongue flicks over the bloody drop, savoring the taste of her. Then I crash my lips into hers.

She kisses me until time loses its meaning, until

everything speeds up and slows down at the same time. We have no need for breathing, no reason to stop. Adriana's nails dig into my back as I devour her lips like I can make up for the missing years. Perhaps I can.

Grabbing her by the throat, I slam her into the solid concrete wall with enough force to crush a mortal. Adriana just laughs, wrapping her arms around my neck.

"Enjoying yourself?" I whisper against her ear as I flick my tongue over the lobe, biting down gently, nibbling on her skin.

"Maybe." Adriana grinds her hips into my straining erection, teasing me.

A loud groan rips from my core as my cock jumps at the friction, threatening to rip my pants from all the strain.

"You'll pay for that," I threaten, grabbing her breast roughly over her dress, squeezing, pinching, until she moans breathlessly against my chest.

"We'll see." She pulls my face back to hers for another kiss, ripping the belt from my pants without bothering with the buckle. The leather band snaps in two, then falls to the ground.

Words have become inadequate, violence the only expression left for the sheer intensity of the lust and desire coursing through our veins. Kissing and scratching, biting and hugging, we're tearing at each other's skin like we could separate it and wear it as our own.

Both dominant, both unyielding, we're grabbing the reins at alternating intervals. It's a negotiation of power so brutal, so natural, a primal dance as old as time itself.

"Just fuck me already," Adriana growls as I slam her through another wall, and I don't have to be asked twice.

I don't bother trying to get her out of her dress, just

bunch it up at her sides, ripping her panties off in a clean sweep. They fall to the bloody floor.

My desperate fingers find her clit, and I bask in the magnificence of the moan it draws from Adriana. When the pad of my thumb swipes over her swollen bud, she gasps loudly, digging her nails deeper into my back.

Moving lower, I slip a single finger between her pussy lips, enjoying the whimpers that flutter from her in little gasps. When I pull it out, my finger is slick with her desire.

"You're soaking, *querida*." I shove my sticky finger into her mouth, grinding into her as she sucks off every last drop of her own need.

Adriana spits out my finger again, grinning mischievously. "All your fault."

I grab her hair, pulling hard, forcing her gaze to mine. "Do you expect an apology?"

Her fingers trail over the tent straining in my pants, teasing me as she slowly tugs the zipper down. "No, I expect you to do something about it."

Grabbing her hand, I pin it above her head, ripping my zipper down with my other hand. I've waited long enough.

The moment my cock sinks into her, our bodies merge into one, power flowing in all directions like a single entity. Everything else falls away, ceases to exist. It's only her and I and this dance of love and power until the end of time.

"Gods, Cyrus." Adriana's voice is raspy, needy, as she grinds her hips down on my cock.

She ends up on top, pinning me to the floor, the blood staining my pants as I wrestle her to the bottom again, driving my cock into her with such force, it would've ripped a human body in two.

But Adriana has no problem taking it, taking all of me. Even at my roughest, at my most brutal, I never have to worry about breaking her. I know she can hold her own.

Dios mío. The devil knows, I will die a happy man if this is how I go, fucking her in a river of blood, the corpses of our enemies scattered around us like a buffet of carnage.

CHAPTER 46

THE REUNION

(JUDE)

Time stretches, slow and warped.

I don't know how long I have been lying on the cold bathroom tiles. My entire body has been reduced to shivers and goosebumps, tear tracks drying on my cheek.

It's all over. Adriana's not coming back.

Every second she's been gone has become its own eternity. There are no clocks in here, but enough time passes to fuel my despair into a raging wildfire of misery.

She didn't make it. They got her.

There isn't a single positive thought left in my mind. It's all dark, worst-case scenario conjurings that make my muscles contract in another dry heave.

I sent her into a trap. It's all my fault.

I should get up off the floor but what's the point? There's nothing I can do that will make this better.

Why were you even born?

The thought arrives the way it always does, unbidden,

in a voice that isn't quite mine and isn't quite anyone's. It's lived in the back of my skull since I was seven years old, since I cut my knee badly enough that it should have been stitched and hid it for three days rather than tell my mother, because I'd already learned what it cost when I needed things. By the time she found out, it was festering, and the doctor's bill meant two weeks of nothing but stale bread.

After that, my mother took a night shift at the hotel for better pay but longer hours. I saw her less, and some small, shameful part of me was relieved, because every time she looked at me I could see the calculations running behind her eyes, what I cost, what she had left. Watching her age in fast-forward, lines carving into her face like a countdown, taught me everything I needed to know about my place in the world, about how to stay small, invisible.

This darkness isn't new. I've been here before, flat on my back, powerless, watching someone I love suffer while I do nothing but take up space.

And now here I am again, lying on bathroom tiles, too weak to do anything but wait.

Useless, fucking useless Jude.

When the front door opens downstairs, I don't immediately register the sound. It's distant, elsewhere.

But when Adriana's familiar voice echoes through the apartment, calling my name, I bolt upright, heart racing.

Is it real? Or merely a hallucination devised by my desperate mind?

But there it is again. *"Jude!"*

Slowly, the world around me becomes real again, but it's still blurry around the edges of my swollen eyes. I don't need a mirror to tell me I look as shit as I feel.

Adriana's calls get more urgent, closer, until she finally

rips open the bathroom door before I manage to find even a single syllable of speech.

My breath catches as my Goddess comes into view, towering above my naked, pathetic body on the floor.

My eyes blink a few times until she comes into focus, but all I see is red.

She's hurt. Oh god, so much blood.

"Oh, Jude," Adriana's tone turns soft as she sinks to her knees and gathers me in her bloody embrace. I've never been so damn happy to be enveloped in that familiar jasmine scent I've come to associate with safety.

She's real. She's here!

Like a blind man reading braille, my hands roam all over her, searching for the source of the blood, searching for the wounds. But there are none, just a few fading marks on her wrists.

"It's not mine," Adriana assures me, pulling me close again.

Relieved, I clutch at her, burying my face in her blood-smeared chest, holding her so tightly, I fear I might squeeze her rib cage to pieces.

"It's not mine," she repeats as I cry against her chest.

She's okay.

Fresh tears flow as Adriana rocks me, her body wrapped around mine on the cold floor. There are still no words close enough for my tongue to reach, only the broken sobs tearing through my body.

"It's okay, *tesoro*. Shh, it's okay," she coos softly as she presses kisses to my forehead. "Let's get you up."

Adriana gets up first, reaching down to help me off the floor.

My knees buckle when I try to stand, and I begin to crash back down, but Adriana catches me, effortlessly pulling me upright with that superhuman strength of hers.

Oh god, I'm so happy she's here, in one piece. I was so sure I would never see her again, that I would be lost forever, alone again, invisible.

Despite the murder in her eyes and the deep purple veins pulsing under her skin, Adriana remains gentle as she leads me to the walk-in shower and opens the taps.

She sits me down on the edge of the bathtub and starts stripping the bloodied layers from herself, baring that beautiful pale skin I long to touch.

I've rarely seen Adriana fully naked before, aside from that first night I washed her hair in the bath. She usually remains clothed during our sexual exploration of my submission, during our games. Sure, I've had my face in her pussy many times, but she's always kept her dress or skirt on, hiding me under the folds of the fabric while I drew the moans of pleasure from her lips.

But today, she rips it all off without ceremony.

Mesmerized, breath caught in my chest, I keep her gaze as she discards her bloody, torn clothes onto the floor.

Holy fuck, those breasts. Five hundred years old and still perfect. *Magnificent!* Those perfect little nipples that accent the heavy half-moons I have fantasized about nearly every night as I lie in bed with an impossible hard-on I'm not allowed to alleviate by my own hand without permission.

Adriana's hips sway gently as a grin creeps over her lips.

I must look like a complete idiot, blatantly staring at her body. But I don't even care. I don't want to miss any of it.

Part of me is still convinced this is a dream. That she

isn't really here. I can't look away; what if she dissipates like the steam fogging up the mirrors?

But she remains solid.

My Lady Adriana walks over to me and pulls me to her, pressing my face between her breasts. I inhale deeply, nearly smothering, as I pull her even closer, my hands resting on her hips, fingers digging into her skin.

"I—I was so worried," I finally manage a sentence when she steps back, tipping my chin toward her with her index finger.

"I know, darling. But it's all over now." She strokes my cheek affectionately and my cock instantly jumps to attention. It's been growing harder with every layer of clothing Adriana removed, nearly at full mast now.

"Come." She steps into the shower and I follow her.

As the water returns some feeling to my ice-cold limbs, my brain slowly flickers back to life like an old computer that needs time to boot up. "Did you get it? The Grimoire?"

Adriana smiles. "Oh yes, darling, all thanks to you." The praise warms me up even more than the steaming water easing into my cold crevices with relief. "You did such good work."

All the tension inside me sinks down, draining out with the red-stained water, as Adriana slowly lathers up a sponge and starts washing me with delicate movements.

My erection grows to painful hardness levels between us when she takes it in both hands, lathering it in soap, and starts washing it.

A soft moan slips from my lips uncontained, and Adriana smiles. "There's my good boy. Louder," she encourages me.

But a sudden gust of cold air against my back pulls me from the fantasy to the half-opened door.

For a second, my heart stills, terror knotting my stomach as I swing around, expecting the worst: enemies that have followed her home...

But a familiar laugh freezes the terror before it creeps too far up my spine.

"Well, well, well," Cyrus announces as he closes the door behind him again, that devious grin coloring his face. "Looks like you started without me."

His torn-up clothes are as bloody as Adriana's, the fire in his eyes raging just as furiously. Whatever they did, they did it together, and something feels different. But in a good way.

"Want to join us, my reckless one?" Adriana's voice is sensual, seductive as she calls to Cyrus.

Gone is the ice she usually reserved for him, the tension eased.

Cyrus rips the already-buttonless shirt off his body with ease. "I'd love to, *querida*."

The rest of his clothes suffer a similar fate, reduced to shreds on the bathroom floor until the beast with the bulging muscles and hard, pierced cock stands naked in front of us, covered only in blood and tattoos.

My body stiffens, frozen, as Cyrus slips into the shower behind me, his front to my back like I'm a little spoon, his erection pressing against my ass. The little bulbs of his piercings are cold against my skin.

Reaching over my shoulder to kiss her, he presses me against Adriana, her magnificent breasts to my chest, sandwiching me between their bloody bodies.

Trapped between them, I hold my breath as they make out like the long-lost lovers they are.

Holy fuck, it's electric!

It's Cyrus who reaches around to stroke my cock, whispering Spanish sweet nothings in my neck as I shiver in his grip. The moment completely overwhelms everything that came before, the miserable loop in my mind shattering as pure primal need replaces every conscious thought.

"It seems you've left this one on edge, *mi Reina*," he mocks, and Adriana grins in response, pressing a kiss to my lips.

"You know I like a good edging."

Her hands roam over my chest, touching, testing, pinching my skin as she explores. Meanwhile, Cyrus's hands are filling in the gaps, his nails scraping over my back, my ass, my stomach, my desperate cock.

It's incredible to be touched, be held, caressed until I'm moments from spilling my seed right here. Slowly, it brings life back into my body, driving the cold from my bones, anchoring me in the present, in them.

My breath hitches as Cyrus licks my earlobe. "Please," I beg. A plea for permission in a single word containing all my desires.

"Seems your pet *wants* something," Cyrus teases, playfully smacking my bum.

Adriana pulls me in for another kiss, deep, slow, yet urgent, her tongue dancing with mine as my breath grows increasingly strained, Cyrus's body imprinted against mine. "Seems so," she whispers against my lips. "Tell me what you want, *cucciolo*."

I don't even have to think about the answer. "You. *Please*. I want you, Milady."

She looks up, exploring my gaze as the words hang between us. For a terrifyingly long second, I fear she doesn't understand what I'm asking, or worse, that she's about to reject me.

But my fear is unfounded.

She smiles, nods.

"Not here." Adriana reaches over and turns off the water, stepping out of the shower without bothering to reach for a towel.

Leaving Cyrus behind, I follow the wet footprints from the shower, adding new ones of my own, as she leads me to the bedroom.

She doesn't look back to see if I'm still following. Not once.

She doesn't have to.

I'm right behind her.

CHAPTER 47

RELEASE

(ADRIANA)

Seeing Jude curled up naked on the bathroom floor, tear-stained face twisted in despair, ripped into my cold heart with a tear so painful, it felt physical.

He seemed so small, so fragile, broken.

To be driven that mad at the fear of losing me? He undeniably cares. Not only for performance or because he's compelled. No, that's real emotion.

Even when I was broken, the most incomplete version of me, he looked at me like I was his universe. And now, he still looks at me like that.

Coming home, to him, with the Grimoire back in its place, with Cyrus here, it's like the broken pieces of my world are slowly being mended together in uneven stitches. Imperfectly perfect.

I crawl onto the bed now, curling my forefinger to call Jude. The awkwardness is still there and I'm not sure how to bridge it, but gods know, I want to try. Because I want him, *need* him, inside me.

Jude starts toward me but Cyrus grabs his arm, holding him back, as he whispers in the human's ear. *"Let me warm her up for you."*

"You know I can hear you, right?" A smile spreads over my cheeks as Cyrus tells me he's counting on it.

Then he kisses Jude with such passion, a twang of lust coils warm and needy in my belly.

Oh gods, watching the two of them together. Is there anything more arousing?

Jude is flustered when Cyrus finally pulls away, smacking the human's ass playfully before stalking over to the bed.

"Watch and learn, *niño*." He grabs me by the ankles and pulls me to the edge of the bed.

I squeal in delight at the unexpected action, giggling as he flips me over onto my stomach, manhandling me like a piece of meat. I let him.

When was the last time I giggled? I thought I had outgrown the reaction centuries ago. But today, I'm light, weightless, and it flows from me with ease.

"On your knees, *mi Reina*," Cyrus orders, guiding me where he needs me.

On all fours, ass in the air on the bed, with my back to them, a loud growl rips from my chest as Cyrus grabs my ass, pushes my cheeks apart, and sinks down between them, licking me slowly from top to bottom.

"Jesus," I hiss, digging my fingers into the sheets beneath me, my eyes falling shut as Cyrus flicks his skillful tongue over my puckered hole, rimming me.

My back arches on its own accord as he moves lower, lapping at my pussy.

"Hmm, so wet already, aren't we?" he growls against my cunt, the vibrations making my skin tingle.

I nod, biting down on my bottom lip to swallow a gasp. "Your fault."

"Well, let's see what we can do about that." He flips me over onto my back again, legs flailing as I let him reposition me. I don't try to control the movement. Don't give any instructions. No, I relax into the bed, slipping an arm under my head as I stretch out. There are only a few things I fully trust Cyrus with, and my pleasure is one of them.

Jude is still standing in the doorway. Frozen, naked, *hard*—he watches us intently with his hands at his sides, not touching. *Good boy.*

Cyrus calls him over, and the aroused human statue moves toward us, climbing onto the bed on instruction.

I pull Jude toward me for a kiss, slow and deep. His cheeks are a deep shade of red when we separate, and he whimpers softly, like a real puppy.

"What is it, *tesoro*?" I ask, smiling, as I wipe a damp lock of hair from his forehead.

Jude sighs. "How are you this perfect?" There is nothing but wonder in his eyes.

I laugh. "Hardly."

Cyrus joins us on the bed, the mattress indenting beneath his large frame. He kisses me hungrily, messily, cupping a breast as he swallows a moan from my lips.

"Like the boy said, *perfect*." He leans down to kiss my nipple, sending shivers rippling up my spine, and then he's moving down, a trail of warm kisses leading to my center. But he stops before he reaches my pussy, leaving me wanting.

"Please." My voice is hoarse, desperate.

Cyrus nips at my inner thigh, and I gasp. "Words,

407

querida. See how difficult it is?" He plants a kiss just off center, so close, but still so damn far.

I grab him by the hair and pull him into my cunt. "Enough words. Make me scream already."

His gaze is pure mischief and desire, that growing grin shifting his expression to pure sin. "Be careful what you wish for, Your Majesty," he teases. When he lowers his lips over my clit, a moan sticks in my throat, tearing through me but never quite releasing.

Holy fuck, I'd forgotten how good that man was with his tongue. Four centuries of experience must count for something. There is no one who knows my body like Cyrus does. He knows every button, every trigger, every little nerve that makes me pant like a rabid dog as he licks and sucks and nibbles at my swollen clit.

Jude's face is pure wonder as he regards me with such intensity, you'd think he's trying to see through my skin to the skeleton beneath.

I pull him closer so I can kiss him.

Starting soft, the kiss grows more desperate as Cyrus works his magic between my thighs.

When Cyrus plunges a finger inside me, I accidentally bite down on Jude's lip. A single droplet of blood beads on his bottom lip, and I swipe it up with my tongue.

Gods, his heart is beating so fast, every note echoes through the space like a hammer on a metal pot.

I reach for Jude's cock, and his entire body jerks like it has been shocked, touched by a live wire. My fingers trail over his skin without me having to concentrate, without having to try to control them. They play over his skin, exploring, as Cyrus continues his assault on my pussy, driving a second finger inside me, pumping at increasing speeds to match the rhythm of his tongue's patterns over my clit.

Jude is watching me through heavy, hooded eyes that fall shut whenever I stroke a sensitive spot. I pull him in for another kiss, my free hand tugging at his chest hair, twisting. This time, I'm the one rewarded with moans, which I hungrily devour from his lips.

The boy grows bolder, reaching for my breasts, squeezing, and I melt into the bed, touched, wanted, by both.

The pleasure builds slowly, then becomes more urgent, tugging at my seams, threatening to burst.

I pull away from Jude's lips only for a second, only long enough to tell Cyrus in a raspy voice, "I'm close."

His "Come for me" is inaudible to human ears, muffled by my pussy as Cyrus continues his mission, picking up speed. But I hear it. It vibrates against my skin, every syllable from that gruff, deep voice prickling my oversensitive clit.

I do exactly as instructed, falling into the sensation as it takes over my body. It starts at my center and ripples outward like rings in water, spreading, tingling, consuming me.

The climax builds and builds until I scream into Jude's kiss, my nails digging into his chest. I come apart beneath the two of them.

Cyrus doesn't stop. He laps up every single drop of my release until my legs shake and my vision blurs.

I'm only brought back to the mortal plain by Jude's desperate cry, a whimper. A familiar sound. *Puppy needs to come.*

I had forgotten that I was still stroking his cock through it all, holding onto him, owning him with every movement.

My grip goes lax, as does my entire body, sinking into the bed like I could fall through it, my veins surging with post-orgasmic euphoria.

Cyrus places a sweet kiss on my mound that makes my legs shake in aftershock, and then he guides my knees down onto the bed. Gods, like I'm made of Jell-O.

He licks his lips and then shares the taste of my release, first kissing me, then Jude.

"May I finish off your pet, *mi Reina*?" Cyrus asks, teasingly running a finger along the underside of Jude's shaft. A single drop of pre-cum glistens on his finger as he circles the tip, and he feeds it to me.

Sucking it off his finger, I look to see Jude's dilated pupils, his speeding heartbeat as loud as a siren now.

"If the pet consents, his Lady permits it."

Jude nods furiously. "Please, Milady." Desperate. Needy. *Beautiful.*

"You have permission. Let me see you come for him."

Jude shudders against me as Cyrus takes his cock between his lips. "Fuck," the human hisses, nestling his face between my breasts.

Good gods, watching them together as the tingling slowly subsides inside me, could there be anything more perfect?

It doesn't take long. Only a few minutes. Cyrus knows what he's doing, and Jude has been on edge for a long time.

When the familiar shakes start tensing Jude's body, I pull Cyrus off his cock by the hair. "I want that cum on my tits," I tell them, and the mischievous grin on Cyrus's face spreads.

"I like your thinking," he responds as he exchanges his lips for his hand, fisting Jude's erection.

"Fuck, fuck." Jude's voice is but an urgent whisper as he nears the edge, his breath warm against my breasts.

"Do it, *cucciolo*. Come on my tits."

On command, he lets go, ribbons of white streaking over my chest, over Cyrus's hand.

A loud groan follows the release, Jude collapsing against me as Cyrus milks him dry, then licks his fingers.

When he kisses me, messily, hungrily, I taste both my own release and Jude's. And it damn near drives me insane with need.

I'm slick with desire again when Cyrus parts my thighs and presses his hardness against my opening, wordlessly asking permission to enter.

Lifting my hips in response, I shiver as his head breaches me, then the first piercing, the next, my pussy swallowing each of them level by level, until all four metal bars are buried deep inside. Good gods, each one scrapes against my insides, making my toes curl from the delicious friction.

Still holding onto Jude, my arm cradled around his back, I let a loud cry rip from my throat as Cyrus pushes all the way inside, burying his cock to the hilt, his piercings pressing against my inner walls.

His pace is punishing as he fucks me hard and fast, giving me little warning before pumping me full of his cum, his roar of pleasure so loud, I swear it echoes off the ceiling beams.

When he collapses on top of Jude and me, I accept him into my embrace, holding them both against me as his cum slowly leaks out of me.

What a beautiful mess.

CHAPTER 48

PERMISSION

(JUDE)

I have never heard Adriana laugh out loud, let alone giggle, and it's the most beautiful sound in the world. Correction, the *second* most beautiful sound. First place belongs to her moans, her cries of passion, the sharp intakes of breath when her face contorts in pleasure.

I've heard many of Adriana's orgasms in the three months since I accepted her unexpected employment offer. But I've never gotten to watch them up close, to study her reactions.

When Cyrus devours her pussy, I am tuned in to every micro-expression, every gasp.

I'm right there, my naked body pressed against hers, my fingers toying with her nipples, as the orgasm rips through her.

As Adriana loses herself in the throes of passion, I stare at her like the voyeur I am, committing every twitch, every gasp to memory. I never want to forget how she looks in

413

this moment; how exquisite the most beautiful woman I know is when she lets go and gives in to the pleasure.

Usually, I'm the one with my tongue buried in her pussy, losing my mind to delirium as I chase her high, chasing that sweet taste of my reward. But this time, I can watch. Unashamedly watch. And it is *exhilarating*!

They are having such an intimate experience, yet somehow I'm not intruding, not the third wheel. No, I'm a part of the moment.

Christ, afterward, when Cyrus kisses me, when I taste my Goddess's spent lust on his lips, I damn near come on the spot.

What is it about that man that screams sex? Like he has desire and wanting dripping from every pore. It's difficult not to get swept up in the frenzy of need when Cyrus is around. I want to *be* him and *have* him all at the same time.

Fucking hell, and those tattoos? They're extraordinary, an entire universe in black sprawling over his left side from neck to hip. I'm so tempted to run my tongue along those inked lines, following their path over those lean muscles. But I don't dare move lest I disturb the perfection of the moment.

Eventually, Cyrus detangles his limbs from the pile of sticky bodies on the bed. "Clean-up time," he declares jovially, then heads to the bathroom.

I'm not focused on him; it's hard to think straight when you're draped over a naked woman who's lazily stroking your back like you're a real pet.

Emboldened, I look at Adriana, my cock hard and my mind buzzing. "May I..." I know what I want, but the words are impossible to say out loud.

"Tell me, *tesoro*," Adriana encourages, tracing a finger over my hipbone seductively.

Closing my eyes, I want to sink into the bed from the humiliation as I finish my sentence. "May I clean you up, Milady?"

When I get no response, I slowly open one eye, then the other, to find Adriana grinning at me.

"You're only allowed to use your mouth, though," she tells me, and I swear my dick jumps at the mere thought.

I've never tasted my own cum before, but I don't think twice about reaching down to lick a broad stroke across her breast, lapping up the salty-sweet taste of my own release drying on her porcelain skin.

Adriana strokes my hair, entangling her fingers in the messy, now-dry locks as she praises my work, making my cock even harder.

When I've licked her torso clean, she pulls me up by my hair before I can go lower and clean up the rest.

Glassy sea-green eyes trap me in their gaze as she speaks those magical words that reduce me to a bucket of goo: "It makes me so happy when you are such a good boy for me, Jude, do you know that?"

My whole body stills as the praise sinks in. When she says my name in that raspy voice…

"Oh fuck." I gasp.

Cyrus laughs as he returns, a loud, hearty sound that bounces off the walls.

"That, little *niño*, is what I call pussy-whipped," he declares and kisses me again.

I don't even try to deny it. It's true. "So lucky," is the only response I can muster, drawing a smile onto Adriana's lips.

"Why don't you get us some wine, my reckless one?" She kisses Cyrus deeply and sends him away with a wink.

Leaning against the door, he gives her a knowing look,

so many unspoken words passing between them. And then he's off, strolling down the hall without bothering to cover his perfect, naked ass.

And then it's just us, alone.

Adriana pulls me back down beside her, propping herself up on an elbow to look at me intently. "Hey, you," she whispers, a soft smile tugging at her lips.

My own smile is dreamy, content. "Hey."

Her lips seek mine, and I part them for her, let her in. The sweet kiss turns urgent as my hands fan out over her stomach, her breasts, touching her everywhere I can reach, growing more needy for her.

The moment grows more desperate, and soon I'm panting again, dripping with *wanting*, my cock painfully hard between us.

I'm not the only one who notices.

Adriana smiles. "You want me?" she asks, despite the obvious answer written in my body's every response.

"Yes, Ma'am. More than anything." My voice is shaky, but I know she hears me just fine; she always hears everything. *"Please."*

Adriana cups my cheek, gently kissing my eyelids. "Gods, so pretty when you beg. You have no right to be this pretty."

The praise makes me squirm, giddy almost, a hit of dopamine to the brain so strong, I almost purr like a cat as my skin dots in goosebumps.

"Please, Milady. I *need* you." A grown-ass man of 6'3", but I have no issue begging. For her, I'd give her everything if she only asked.

Fast as lightning, faster, Adriana's on top of me, pinning me beneath her thighs, straddling me.

Holy hell, she looks incredible from this angle, breasts

resting heavy against her waist. Like the shore to the moon, my hands are drawn to her, reaching for her nipples despite my lack of permission.

Adriana catches my wrists, and for a second, my heart stills as I wait for her to push me away again. But then she smiles and kisses my fingers, biting down gently to draw a single drop of blood from my index finger.

She throws her head back, savors the taste, and squeezes my finger to catch another drop of crimson.

A thigh on either side of my waist, Cyrus's cum leaking out of her, the wetness is unmistakable on my abs as Adriana slides further down, down, until she reaches my hardness.

My heart freezes like it's been touched by her ice, breath trapped in my throat, as she grabs my cock and lines me up.

Fuck. The feel of her so wet, so close, knowing that Cyrus's cum is still inside her, lubricating her for me...I damn near lose my mind!

Adriana smiles, a devilish grin spreading, as she moves her hips slightly to test my reaction.

"Please," I beg again.

I know what her next line will be even before she speaks it but still I struggle to fulfill her request to speak my words.

She asks again, pushing back a bit further, my head perfectly lined up with her entrance now, so close, but not yet.

"Fuck." I gasp, pressing my eyes closed to try and concentrate but it doesn't make it any easier. I'm so aware of her heat, of how close I am to where I've never been before.

"Words, *tesoro*," Adriana insists again, swirling her

hips and creating just enough friction to push me to the brink of tears as I try to keep my restraint. "What do you want?"

"To be...to be i-inside you," I finally manage in a whisper that mumbles half the syllables. But it's enough for her. She lowers herself onto my cock, taking me slowly, inch by glorious inch, until she's impaled all the way, her ass resting against my balls.

I inhale sharply as her pussy clenches around me. *How the fuck is she that tight?* Magic, divine intervention, genetics? It doesn't matter. What matters is how incredible it feels to finally be inside my Goddess, how correct. I could die a happy man now.

"Open your eyes, sweetheart," she tells me, stroking my cheek.

I don't know how long we've been like this, interlocked but not moving, simply enjoying the feel of each other, the intimacy of the connection.

When I look at her, I am met with pure wonder. But also something more, something I can't name. I dare not hope for love. Even as I love her with everything I have. Who am I to deserve it in return? Especially not from an immortal Goddess like this.

"Oh, Jude." When she says my name like that, it melts away all the insecurities, pulling me into the moment, out of my head.

We stay like that, connected but still, watching each other.

I've waited so long for this. Didn't think it would ever happen...

"Well, look at that." It's Cyrus who shatters the tension as he places the wine bottle on the dresser and stalks over to us. He leans over to kiss Adriana, grinning widely. "Took y'all fucking long enough."

She grabs him by the chin and kisses him furiously, my cock still buried deep inside her as I watch them, surely the luckiest human alive right now.

When they part, he looks down at me and caresses my cheek affectionately. "Good luck." He takes his wine to the armchair in the corner, which he pulls closer for a better view. Glass in one hand, the other is lazily stroking his cock as he watches us, that sexy smirk permanently etched on his lips.

There's no invasion, no intrusion. No, there's something about him being here that makes this moment easier, more natural. There is no room for overthinking in Cyrus's hedonistic world of blind passion and lust...

Adriana trails a single long nail over my chest, pulling my attention back to her, and we both watch the thin line of blood form in its wake.

The hunger in her eyes flashes in feral gold as she licks her lips.

I don't dare move as the Lady of the House leans down to lick the blood off my chest, and I shudder at the friction between us, my eager cock desperate for *any* movement.

But I know I'm not the one in the driving seat. No, not in this house. It's the most freeing realization.

When Adriana kisses me, the copper taste tickles my senses. I surrender to her fully, matching the intensity of her kiss, gasping when we finally part.

Her face is close to mine as she asks for permission to drink from me.

I consent, bracing for impact.

It doesn't hurt, but the moment her fangs break my skin always comes as a shock.

The connection is instant!

The slight sting fades as quickly as it appears, replaced only with euphoria and emotion, as Adriana drinks from me.

When she lifts herself off the bed slightly, letting my dick slide out almost completely, before plunging down again, I let out a guttural scream that sounds more animal than human.

Holy fuck, it feels incredible, like I'm on drugs.

Through the connection, her memories flood me, her feelings, and for an eternity and a half, I'm suspended, overwhelmed, overstimulated and blissful.

When the events of tonight, what transpired at the auction, seep through our connection, I experience her pain like it's real, like it's mine. It locks tightly around my heart, squeezing.

They hurt her. The fuckers hurt her.

She's letting me see, letting me in. It all flickers through me like a dream, or maybe a movie.

I'm halfway between the present and the downtown warehouse, as she rides my dick, her energy surging through my veins as she gives as much as she takes.

So many bodies. So much carnage.

But the image doesn't last.

It's quickly replaced by one of her fucking Cyrus in the pool of blood, and *holy fuck,* as depraved as it is, it's the most erotic visual.

It's like I'm there. Like he's entering *me.* Like it's my body exploding in orgasm instead of hers. The rush of the memory mingles with my present reality as Adriana digs her nails into my chest, grounding me, anchoring me.

I'm delirious with passion, feral with euphoria as Adriana fucks me into the bed like I'm a mindless doll.

My mind empties from everything, releases, and then I'm falling through space toward oblivion.

Oh fuck.

I don't know how much longer I can last.

When Adriana reaches down and squeezes my throat before slamming her lips on mine, bloody with my taste, I'm moments from toppling over the edge.

My plea for permission, nothing more than a breathless grunt, is granted in a shaky voice as Adriana struggles against the throes of her own passion, her rapid breaths coming in faster now, her free hand that's been circling her clit speeding up.

I can't hold it. Don't have to. *Fuck, fuck, fuck!*

The release rips through my body like a tear in the very fabric of the earth, breaking me open, shattering me, as I repeat her name until my voice is hoarse and her body filled with my cum.

Bliss. Pure bliss.

The reality of it exceeds every fantasy I've ever had of this moment.

When Adriana opens her eyes and shares a tired smile, kissing me sweetly, I know that I'm exactly where I need to be: with her; with *them*.

Cyrus claps his hands with a *"bravo"* that pulls my attention to him in the chair, to the thick dick he's still stroking leisurely. "Great show," he announces.

I'd been so lost in Adriana, I'd almost forgotten he was there. Almost, but not quite. Knowing he was watching, touching himself as our Queen fucked me senseless, it added to the intensity of the build-up, to the high of the climax.

Smiling, I let my eyes fall shut for a second as I bask in the afterglow of the moment, cataloging every detail of my first time inside Adriana, saving it for later, preserving it.

Worth the wait, one hundred percent!

CHAPTER 49

CIRCLE COMPLETE

(CYRUS)

Watching Adriana take what she needs from Jude warms my heart as much as it hardens my dick.

I was hoping they would find their way to each other eventually. But I didn't expect to find Adriana straddling Jude when I returned with the wine.

Dios mío, what a sight.

There is no jealousy in my blood as I sink into the chair to stroke my cock while watching them.

Jude's taste, his feelings, pulse through me as my bond with Adriana brings him closer to me. There is no jealousy in the exchange. Just pure joy at seeing how happy they make each other, how fulfilled.

Compersion. Still one of my favorite words in the English language. One I never understood properly until now.

In this moment, I am not worried about losing Adriana, of being second-best, no. I'm glad she's found Jude, that he can give her this gentleness, this care that seems to go against my very nature.

Jude.

Bloody hell, I underestimated the boy. Thought he'd never close the deal. But there he was, getting impaled by the Queen of Darkness herself.

Complete submission is a good look on him. It radiates from every youthful, human pore and echoes through my blood as Adriana drinks her fill of the boy.

When her fangs draw his blood, I feel everything!

The amount of self-control it requires not to storm the bed and rip Jude's veins open myself is unfair. But somehow, I manage, digging my nails into my free palm to ground myself in the pain.

Only when Adriana's final scream of ecstasy dies down, Jude's body limp and spent beneath her, do I approach the bed, my cock still in my hand—hard, ready.

She reaches for me, and I greedily kiss Jude's blood from her lips. It's just a taste, but it's enough to drive me ravenous!

My Queen smirks. She must have noticed the lust flaring in my eyes. If not, she definitely felt it pulsing through the bond.

"What is it?" she asks against my lips, holding me close, still bent over.

"Mind if I have a turn with the human?" I ask, flicking my tongue over her bottom lip to catch the last of that sweet, coppery taste.

Jude gasps audibly, and Adriana smiles as she tells me, "Ask him yourself."

I turn my gaze to the man now perched on his elbows, regarding me with such fiery desire that I damn near lose control and take what I want without asking.

But I hold it together, raising an eyebrow in question instead. "And what does the human want?" I ask him, enjoying as he squirms under my gaze.

"Please." There it is, that beautiful plea of his, containing volumes of desire in a single word. "Please use me."

"See how pretty he begs." Adriana smiles as she finally gets up, lifting herself off his impressively large cock. When she stands, Jude's cum slowly leaks out, mixed with mine, trailing down her leg. "He's all yours. But play nice, Cyrus."

Reaching out a hand to help her off the bed, I kiss her deeply when she lands in my arms, running my finger through her cunt when we part to lick the slick coating from my digit, appreciating the taste.

"I always play nice," I say, despite nobody in this room believing it.

Fuck, she tastes delectable.

I turn my attention back to Jude, who hasn't even blinked. He's staring at us with large eyes, his lower lip trapped between his teeth like the needy little sub he is.

Calling him over to the edge of the bed where I stand, I order him to "wet it for me," and he does exactly that, bringing his pretty face closer to wrap those kissable lips around my dick.

"Christ," I hiss as he starts sucking, swiping his tongue over my sensitive head, teasing the bulbs of my piercings as he takes more. "That's it, *niño*, take it all. I want you to choke on my dick."

He grunts in response, but doesn't let up.

My fingers find his hair as I pull him closer, forcing him deeper, until he does choke, until tears stream down his face.

He has his safe words, I remind him; he can tap out any time. But he doesn't. No, he takes me so well, persisting, enduring, as I become more ruthless, punishing his mouth with my cock.

Meanwhile, Adriana has stretched out on the bed next to Jude, on her side, to get a good view, watching her pet suck me off like a pro.

He's good. Too good. An innocent face like that has no right being this good at sucking dick.

There is no way I can last like this.

A loud growl rips from my chest as I pull Jude off my cock before I empty myself down his throat. That's not where I want this cum to go.

He looks up at me with such wide eyes, tears tracking down that youthful face, spit dribbling from his chin. And *good lord*, has there ever been a more beautiful man beneath me?

Meanwhile, Adriana traces little circles on his arm, moving up to his neck, to the spot where she had her fangs dipped in not too long ago.

I know what she's thinking, but I dare not ask for it, dare not hope. I want it too badly. But she has my blood pulsing through her veins; she knows what I want.

"How are you feeling, Jude? Do you still have some energy left?" she asks him, and I know that's not what she's really asking.

Surely not?

She's not going to let me.

He won't…

He smiles up at her. "Fucking incredible."

"Not dizzy?"

"No, Milady." He shakes his head from side to side, eyes dreamy but alert.

Adriana is quiet for a painfully long second as I stand frozen, not daring to move lest she change her mind.

And then there it is. The words I've been dreaming of since he first let me into the apartment. "Should we let Cyrus over here have a bit of a taste?"

Fuck me. My heart jumps like it's been shocked, resuscitated.

A wicked grin spreads over Jude's face as he sits up, reaching for my hips and pulling me closer. He tilts his head slightly, giving me full access to his neck, pulsing with life. "All yours," he offers.

I look at Adriana to make sure she's okay to share, but she's smiling, nodding, hand outstretched as she hands me the lube from the bedside drawer.

She sits back on the bed, legs crossed, as she pulls Jude into her lap. Sliding a pillow under him, she repositions him for me, letting him lie back against her chest, so they're both facing me, his ass at the edge of the bed.

That's all the permission I need.

I order him to hold his legs for me. Knees pressed to his chest, Jude does as he's told, looking up at me with so much blind trust, it nearly thaws my cold heart.

"Stop looking at me like that if you don't want me to break you," I threaten as I squeeze the lube onto my finger.

Jude just grins, puckering his lips. "Make me."

"You little brat!" He squeals as I kiss that smug look right off his face. "You ready?" I ask against his cheek when I break away, and he nods, begging me to fill him.

Don't need to ask me twice. My reputation has taken on many myths and legends, but never once have I been accused of being a man of patience.

Reminding him to breathe, I slip my forefinger inside him slowly, coating his hole with lube as I go.

Jude hisses through his teeth, holding onto Adriana as his eyes fall shut.

"First time?" I ask, wiggling my finger inside him.

He shakes his head, eyes still closed. "No...*Sir*."

Sweet mother of Christ, that word undoes me, unlocks the feral beast that's never hiding far away. "What did you just call me?" I ask as Adriana just laughs.

Jude bites his lip, fluttering those impossibly long eyelashes at me, as he repeats, *"Sir."* The little devil knows exactly what he's doing to me.

"Don't start," I growl as I slide in another finger.

Fuck me, the human moans so prettily for me as I stretch him, preparing him.

"How does that feel?" I ask, seeking out his prostate.

"Hmm, good...so good." He places a hand on my chest, above my heart's cavity. "More."

Not so innocent after all, are we? I think as I soak up the moans that adding a third finger to his ass elicits.

With my other hand, I reach for his balls, fondling them in my palm while I devour the symphony of sounds slipping from his lips in a long, slow kiss.

"You ready for me?" I whisper when we part, and he nods, pulling me closer.

"Ready...*Sir*."

I growl at him as I pull my fingers out, enjoying the little gasp it draws from him. "Careful with that word, dear Jude, Jude Cole."

I reposition myself to line my cock up with his hole.

"And you, my love?" I look to Adriana, who has as much desire etched in her features as the human in her arms. "Ready for the show?"

She smiles, pulls me closer by the neck, and presses her

lips to mine. "I'm ready, my reckless one. Make a mess of him."

There is so much she isn't saying but she doesn't have to, not in words. I feel it all through the bond. She wants this as much as I do.

Taking my time, I lather my dick in lube as they watch, Jude still clutching his knees to his chest.

"Please," the boy begs as I continue to leave him empty, exposed, waiting.

"Patience, pet." I press my hardness at his entrance. "Now breathe for me. Inhale."

He does as he's told, and I push inside, slowly at first, watching him intently.

"There you go." I push deeper, inch by inch, piercing by piercing, until my cock is buried to the hilt inside him. "You take me so well."

Jude winces, still holding his breath, as I stretch him around my cock, the lube easing the path for me. *Fuck, so tight.*

Adriana's face is pure wonder as she watches us. "Such a good boy," she tells Jude, and he shudders beneath me, goosebumps breaking out over his skin.

Dios mío, what a beautiful specimen.

He still hasn't said a word, hasn't breathed.

"Exhale, *niño.*" I gently touch Jude's cheek, and he lets his chest deflate, slowly expelling the air from his lungs before filling them up again. "You okay?" I add as I search his eyes.

He nods despite the unmistakable signs of pain on his face.

"Don't lie to me."

"Just a bit sore. You're big." His voice is breathless, almost a whisper. "I'll get used to it."

429

I trace his perfect collarbone as I slowly slide out of him again, almost all the way, keeping just my tip still inside. "Let me help you with that."

Jude's eyes grow wide even as he nods, turning his head to bare his neck for me, literally handing it to me on a silver platter. *Well, luckily, not on real silver.*

The world reduces to only this room, this bed, to the two of them, the anticipation coursing through my veins like hot lava racing down a mountain.

"Just breathe," Adriana tells Jude as she reaches for his hand. "You're safe. I won't let anything happen to you."

Jude visibly relaxes, and I take it as my cue, my fangs protruding.

Holy fuck!

The moment his blood hits my palate, I know unequivocally why Adriana keeps him.

He's delicious!

But it's not just the taste of his blood. It's everything! It's his emotions. His memories. His feelings for Adriana. His desire for me. Pure devotion. Grateful surrender. Lust. Their bond. Ours. *Everything.*

The rush infiltrates my blood faster than a virus, mixing, dancing. Euphoria ripples over my skin as the red liquid warms me, giving me power, giving me life.

I plunge my cock back into Jude, and I'm instantly rewarded, not only with a loud cry from him, but the most incredible surge of pleasure in his blood. *That taste!*

I need more.

Jude puts his hands behind my neck, pulling me even closer, as I fuck him hard, pressing down on his bent knees to ram my cock deeper into him, again and again, while I drink from him.

All time stops moving. Reality is on pause. There is only this feeling. This feeling and his warmth.

I can't tell how much time passes in this beautiful delirium, Jude's blood flowing through me as I punish his asshole. I want to stay like this forever.

"Enough, my love." Adriana's touch is gentle as she taps my shoulder, bringing me back to the present.

Reluctantly, I let go, the little puncture holes in his neck sealing almost immediately. Thank fuck for her, because I'm not sure I could've stopped, despite everything I promised.

I pull her closer for a kiss as we share Jude's blood on my lips, his need between us, before she returns her attention to the human.

"You good, *tesoro*?" She kisses Jude's hair.

His eyes are dreamy and his smile wide as he replies, "Yes, Milady. In heaven."

"Hmm, let's get this good boy some more rewards, what do you say?" She reaches for his neglected cock.

Grinning, Adriana turns to me, "Fill him to the brink, my love."

I've never been one for taking orders, but I gladly oblige, picking up my pace until Jude is nothing but a shuddering mess beneath me, my cum leaking out of his ass, his own decorating his chest, a Jackson Pollock display in creamy white over all our bodies.

Fuck, he's perfect.

They're perfect.

CHAPTER 50
HINDSIGHT

(ADRIANA)

There is something so beautiful about experiencing Cyrus and Jude together in such close proximity.

They're two magnificent beings, opposite in nearly every way, but somehow a beautiful storm together. It's as arousing as it is heartwarming.

I love how gentle Cyrus is with him, that he asks permission; it makes me believe that maybe you can teach an old dog new tricks. I didn't think he had it in him, but clearly I have underestimated his capacity for growth.

And Jude? His trust, his want of us in equal measure, his blood singing in our veins—gods, it makes it impossible to imagine ever letting him go again.

It's nearly 6 AM when the boy falls asleep in our arms, cradled between our bodies, sticky and spent like the rest of us.

"Wine?" Cyrus mouths, and I nod with a smile as I detangle myself from Jude's warm, slumbering form.

The human will need a lot of fluids and nutrients once he wakes up. But for now, the best thing for his body is rest.

My body doesn't need rest. Neither does Cyrus's. And we have nearly a decade of lost time to catch up.

"White or red?" he asks, kneeling before my collection in the kitchen.

I scoff, tying the black satin robe around my waist as I enter. "You know the answer to that."

Cyrus smiles, grabbing the red and collecting the appropriate glasses from the cupboard. "White is for desperate housewives."

"You remember." It's the little things that remind me why I always had so much time for him, why I'm letting him back in, yet again, despite my promises to be done with him for good.

But it feels different now, more balanced. I don't need everything from him anymore. I have Jude too. They complement each other so well.

For so long, it has been just me. I convinced myself it was by choice. I have Felix. And Dimitri. And a chatty doorman. *What more do I need?*

But as Cyrus pulls the cork from the wine bottle with a satisfying pop, I allow myself to dream about more, about having a family again.

It's just a momentary indulgence; I'd be a fool to get comfortable.

Cyrus always leaves. He has to. It's in his nature.

And Jude? Jude's body comes with an expiration date. As much as we are all avoiding that fact, you can't fight the laws of nature.

But that's tomorrow's problem. *Not now.*

"Mi alma." My soul. Cyrus hands me a glass and settles

on the wooden highchair beside mine, facing the large window overlooking the city as morning starts to claim more territory over the night. The tinted windows cast the world in a charcoal hue that saves us from the sunrise. Not that I need to worry about the sun anymore, not with my Grimoire back.

I inhale the wine and take a slow sip. "Good choice."

He's sitting so close that his knee touches mine as he samples the wine. "You bought it."

I let the silence linger before I speak. "You haven't called me that in a long time." *Mi alma.*

"Ah, never thought I'd live to see the day Adriana De Crevena asked for *more* Spanish." He smiles as he shifts his gaze from the fading city lights to my face.

"You used to drive me crazy with that poetic shit." I sigh with mock drama.

Cyrus chuckles.

"I see why you keep him, by the way." He changes the subject as he returns his eyes to the view.

I know who he means, but still ask, "Jude?"

Cyrus nods, gaze still faraway.

"I mean, he's human. So, this doesn't exactly have permanence written all over it," I try to joke, but Cyrus is serious. What a reversal of roles.

"He's not Elijah."

"I know."

"That shithead didn't deserve you." Cyrus swirls the wine in his glass as he speaks. "I curse myself every day for bringing him here."

My face softens as I gently lace my fingers through his. "You meant well. How were you to know he'd turn out to be a deceitful little cunt?"

Cyrus squeezes my hand. "You deserve better."

"So do you." I push a strand of hair from his forehead. "I'm sorry too, darling."

He looks at me with one eyebrow raised. "Whatever for? I'm the one who fucked it all up."

I shake my head. "No, I played my part. Let him drive a wedge between us. Fell for his empty promises, his lies." A heavy sigh presses from my chest.

"I won't let anyone hurt you again, I promise." Cyrus clenches his fist, fury burning bright in those expressive eyes. "I was a fool back then. For leaving. For not saving you. I failed you." Cyrus looks away, but I pull him back to me.

I shake my head. "A fool, yes, on that we can agree. But you still don't get it, do you?"

The dumbstruck look in his eyes tells me he doesn't. "What?"

"I was never pissed that you didn't save me, you beautiful fool." I cup his cheek, keeping his gaze trapped in mine. "I was pissed that you didn't come back after. A bit of emotional support would have been nice after the traumatic event of being betrayed, tortured, and then having to rip out your lover's heart."

"Fuck." Cyrus lowers his head. "When you put it like that…"

"I just needed *you*, Cyrus. I don't know if you've realized, but I don't exactly have an abundance of friends or family or anything. You're it. You're my person, my home."

Silence stretches out in the space as dawn breaks outside.

"I'm a fucking idiot." Cyrus sighs heavily as the information sinks in. "I was too ashamed. For failing to rescue you."

I squeeze his hand. "Men and their fucking savior complexes. I never needed saving. I needed you to be present. Emotionally available. Actually show up, you know? Not just pretending that I'm nobody to you."

How long have I waited to say those words out loud? I've repeated them over and over to myself, growing more resentful with each repetition. But I never thought I'd get to finally have this conversation with Cyrus; I couldn't imagine him being receptive to my reality.

But the Cyrus sitting beside me, filling up my wine glass, is not the same Cyrus from nine years ago.

"You're not a nobody to me. You're *everything*. Jesus, Adriana." He gets up, slamming his wineglass on the counter with such force that a small crack forms in the base. "Don't you see? That's the fucking point. I'm petrified of how much I feel for you in this cold, dead heart of mine. The thought of losing you? Last time, I came so close. I couldn't risk it again. You are the strongest person I know, but I made you weaker. And I didn't want that for us. It's better for you if I stay away. That way, I can't hurt you again."

The kitchen feels too small for his restless energy as he speaks, stomping around while carding his hand through his messy hair. If we were still in the 60s, he'd be chain-smoking now.

"Cyrus, slow down." I reach for him, pulling him into a hug. "I don't want you to stay away."

He sighs against my neck, kissing my skin. "I'm sorry, *querida*. I should've talked to you instead. And not just run away like I always did. I'll be better."

For a long time, we just hold each other, sitting with the heavy feeling pouring through our bond.

"That's very mature of you." I finally say, breaking the

tension as I reach for a kiss, smiling against his lips. "Have you been going to therapy, my love?"

"Not the right kind," Cyrus says, grabbing my hand and spinning me out like there's music playing, but there's none.

I laugh and quickly put my hand in front of my mouth, muffling the sounds so as not to wake Jude. He needs rest.

Cyrus catches me and pulls me against his chest. "Does drowning my sorrows in moon-wine count as therapy?"

I shake my head. "Probably not."

"Maybe it was my time in prison then." His tone is light but I feel the anguish through our bond, snippets of memory flashing by.

"Good thing the Family of Devils made you a deal for your freedom then," I joke.

Cyrus stops dancing. "It wasn't just for my freedom; that's not the only reason I agreed to help them."

"Why then?"

He sighs. "Because of you, Adriana. What else could it be? I would literally give them my immortality rather than think of failing you again. Never again. They gave me a reason to seek you out again, a way to protect you, or so I thought."

"Oh, Cyrus." Even after all this time, for all his faults, still loyal to the bone.

He turns serious, gaze holding mine as he tells me, "I want to be worthy of you. Because the gods know there is no me without you. I've tried everything to forget you. Every drug, every fuck, every trick in the book. And do you know where it got me, dearest Lady Adriana Isabella De Crevena?" He pauses, the sadness unmistakable in his features. "Nowhere. The void only ever grew, never shrank. Chaos and pain, the same circle, over and over, with no door out. But not here. Not with you. When our blood bonds, I stop drifting. For the first time in a decade, there's a direction. A reason. You."

He sinks to his knees before me, still holding my hand, stripped of every defense he usually hides behind. The move completely disarms me.

"For the record, you're still a fucking idiot," I say as I lean down to kiss him.

"Yes, *querida*." He takes my face in both hands. "Please let me spend eternity making it up to you."

It's hard not to default to pessimism. "That might not be very long if Valerian has anything to say about that."

"Let him come. It will be their funeral."

I want to argue, to preach caution, but Cyrus gets up off the floor and crashes his lips over mine, silencing the insecurity with a kiss that burns through every argument I was about to make.

Maybe he's right. Maybe this time we can have it all...

CHAPTER 51

BEACH DAY

(JUDE)

ll my life, I have been invisible, desperate to be seen but petrified of getting my wish.

And now, with my bare toes digging into the soft beach sand, clutching the towel around my waist with white knuckles, I'm about to take my wish to a previously unimaginable level.

Adriana squeezes my other hand, pulling me into her embrace. "You ready for this, *cucciolo*?" she asks for the umpteenth time since we left the house, crossing the small distance to the beach that starts at the east end of the property.

"Yes, Milady." My voice sounds braver than I feel as I shiver in anticipation, despite the warm sun baking on my skin.

We've been staying at Adriana's beach house, lying low. Turns out she's got properties all over.

I don't know how she managed to find a house this private. Only four other properties share this stretch of coast, and most of them are vacation homes, empty outside of summer. For most of the year, we might as well have the beach to ourselves. I've seen another person out here exactly once, a couple on a distant dune last month, gone within the hour.

But there *could* be people. Someone *could* see me like this. The possibility is always there.

Four months have passed since Adriana returned with the Grimoire, since sharing me with Cyrus, and nothing around here has been the same.

For one, she can walk in the sun now. As can Cyrus. Something to do with having the Grimoire back and all the vampire blood they've consumed at the auction estate. Not for long—they can't stay in the sun the way humans can—but long enough to be life-changing to our routine.

Today, Adriana's wearing a navy-blue tunic that flutters in the soft breeze paired with a sun hat and sandals. It's the most casual I've ever seen my Lady.

"This is probably going to be very humiliating." She releases me from her embrace to start uncoiling the thin metal leash wrapped around her wrist.

My cheeks flush in anticipation as my cock jumps traitorously. *Down, boy!*

All I can do is nod, my bottom lip wedged between my teeth, as she reaches over to clip the chain into the collar around my neck.

Oh, fuck.

It's all becoming extremely real now.

We've discussed the scene in detail before, defined every boundary, walked through what I need, what I want, what I desire. But now that we're here, at the beach, my heart is pounding so loudly in my throat, I fear I might forget how to breathe.

Despite my fear of her sending me away, that hasn't even come up as an option. My *'What now?'* question was quickly met with *'All I know is I'm keeping you. We can figure out the rest.'* Good enough for me.

She's been putting my research skills to use to help her track down some artworks and rare books. But most of the time, she encourages me to work on my own projects. Such as turning my thesis into a book, like I've been meaning to do for ages. I'm finally *inspired*.

Cyrus stuck around for a bit, making sure my body got some proper *workouts*. My favorite is still when we double-team it to service Adriana. It's like having an accomplice, a partner in crime. Plus, bonus, it makes Adriana come so hard, she damn-near screams the roof off the house. I could never get enough of that reward.

Cyrus inevitably left again but recently joined us at the beach house for two weeks.

It's been nice having him drop in. But I also enjoy the moments in between, when it's only Adriana and me.

There was one week where Adriana disappeared—'work stuff,' she said—and it was just us guys. A literal fuck fest where days blurred together in the delirium of passion spent. Don't think we bothered to get fully dressed once that week.

Cyrus didn't think twice about strutting around butt naked on the beach. I always pulled on some shorts or boxers at least.

But not today. Today, that changes. I'm not wearing anything under this towel. *Not a single thing.* Just a dog collar and an untimely, but predictable, erection.

I couldn't even sleep last night in anticipation of what was to come today.

The date had been set for more than a week now, days counting down to this exact moment.

Oh god, my heart.

Adriana cups my cheek, kissing me sweetly.

When we separate, her face is pure sin. "Shall we, *tesoro*?"

She tugs my leash playfully, and I gasp as the collar tightens around my throat.

"Yes, Milady."

"What's your safe word?" She knows the answer but she still asks. She always reminds me before a scene, ensuring the word is within easy reach, even when my brain goes quiet and mushy.

I repeat the word, and I know what the next command will be even before she gives it. "Strip for me, darling."

I make the mistake of extending my gaze beyond her to the sand stretching out along the shore. There are no actual people but my mind still conjures up the shadows of watchful eyes.

Initially, my fantasy was playing out the scene on a real nudist beach, in front of real people, but Adriana quickly shut down the idea of doing anything in front of people who did not consent to being part of the scene. Fair enough.

"Jude?" Adriana's voice is gentle but firm.

I take a deep breath and slowly undo the towel, a chill running up my spine as the breeze flickers over my exposed ass.

The smile on her face spreads as I hand her the towel, cupping my hand over my junk in a feeble attempt at modesty.

But that's not what we're here for.

Adriana squeezes a butt cheek and smiles. "My

beautiful *cucciolo*, you are doing so well. I'm so proud of you." The praise warms my skin as much as the blush on my face. "We can leave at any time, okay?"

I nod. "Yes, Milady. Thank you."

She pulls me into her embrace, holding me against her as she kisses me slowly, intently, her tongue dancing with mine. I know she can hear my heart thundering between us.

"On your knees," she whispers in my ear as we pull away.

This is it.

This is what I asked her for.

Closing my eyes for a moment, I take a deep breath and sink onto the warm sand, the little grains grating against my knees as they instantly cling to my skin.

I'm so aware of my nakedness, my body, my erection pressing against my stomach as I look around at the expanse of the beach; I have nothing to hide behind now.

"Let's go, pet." Adriana tugs on my leash as she ruffles my hair.

I do not have words, no more. Digging my fingers into the sand, on all fours, I start crawling beside her, ass in the air.

Fuck me!

Humiliation burns on my skin, warmer than the summer sun, as Adriana walks me to the shore, my leash wrapped tightly around her fist.

My desperate erection is on full display in the harsh light, as is the leash, the collar…the obedience. There is no mistake that I'm *owned*.

My heart is pulsing like a techno club as she leads me through the warming sand, making my cock uncomfortably hard as I crawl awkwardly, slowly, beside her.

It's the most exciting thing I've ever done. It feels dangerous somehow. Like I'm being bad. Yet, I am safe. With Adriana on the other end of that leash, I know nothing could happen to me. She'll protect me. Good luck to anyone who tries to fuck with us. She's the strongest being I've ever encountered.

And she's made it quite clear that she'd never let anything happen to me.

I believe her.

Fucking hell. I'm so self-conscious as we cross to the water, my naked ass in the air. There is no one around—I know that—but with my eyes trained on the ground, my imagination easily fills in the blanks, covering the bare sand with towels and watchful eyes.

Every sense is on high alert, still buzzing from when she drank from me earlier, during the slow sex under the fan, listening to the waves crashing outside.

"Such a good pup. You're doing so well for me," Adriana tells me as the sand turns damp beneath me, the waves drawing nearer.

Her voice grounds me, anchors me, as she leads me to a more secluded part of the beach.

My thoughts slow down to only *hand-knee, hand-knee,* as I concentrate on crawling over the sand, like I'm a real animal. There are no thoughts in my mind, just instincts and *needs.*

Adriana tugs sharply on my leash, and I look up at her. All I see is wonder in how she looks at me—*Christ.*

She's embarrassed by me, not inconvenienced. She's not simply enduring this silly game for my sake. No, she looks at me, this version of me, naked, in the sand, fully devoted to her, and all I see is warmth, love, *acknowledgment.*

446

All my life, I've been scared to bring up my fantasies, but not with Adriana. She sees me, even the weird parts and the dark parts, and she wants more, wants everything *from* me and *for* me.

She pulls my face toward her as she leans down, wrapping the chain around her knuckles, shortening the leash. And then she kisses me so messily, leash still taut, I almost choke.

"Come, let's build some sandcastles, *cucciolo*." There is mischief in her eyes as she hunches down to playfully tug at my cock. "I see the perfect shape to poke windows with."

Oh god, that can't be sanitary.

But I don't give a single fuck.

I follow her, naked, on my knees, like the good pet I am for her and only her.

CHAPTER 52
GOOD DOG

(ADRIANA)

I am dripping with pure need by the time I've led my beautiful pet behind the dunes, his kneecaps red from crawling on the gritty sand.

For so long, I've hidden from the world, hibernating in the shadows, barely existing. But as I walk the naked human like he's a real dog, in broad daylight, I'm no longer hiding. This is a different kind of power that has nothing to do with my physical strength.

Jude isn't my slave; he is my trophy, my pet...my power. Young, built, ethereally beautiful, and crawling unashamedly beside me like I'm the only person who exists to him, this is what true worship looks like.

And my gods, if I don't feel more alive than when I was still mortal. I'm rushing with energy as I lay out the large blanket for us, tugging Jude toward me.

"Heel," I tell him as I reach over to unclip the leash, dropping it onto the blanket.

Fuck, how can a simple piece of leather make such a big

difference? I don't think I'll ever tire of seeing a collar around his neck, seeing how proudly he wears it, like he's mine and he doesn't mind admitting it.

"Open up," I tell him as he remains kneeling before me, sitting on his haunches. Jude opens his mouth obediently, and I squirt some water into his mouth. "Hydration is essential."

He swallows loudly as I feed him, excess water running down his chin, his chest, drops glistening in the sun.

The sun. I can't believe we're out in the sun. Previously, when I had the Grimoire, I could probably have spent more days outside, but I never had the desire for the light. Nothing but judgment and regret happens once you leave the shadows for the sobriety that comes with the exposure of illumination.

But not this time. This time, it's different. Jude is different. So am I.

I'm not foolish enough to think this is our happily ever after. I know that somewhere out there, *La Famiglia* is regrouping. We may have done a lot of damage, wiped out most of the Inner Council, but *Il Sovrano* remains, hiding, licking his wounds. Cyrus brings back snippets of news whenever he comes home. Nobody has seen or heard from Valerian, but it doesn't mean he's not out there.

But for now, we have this moment in between. And it's ours.

Cyrus will probably be back next week or so. He's serious about this opening a new club thing. I don't try to dissuade him anymore. It's been nice to see him focused like that again.

It's been great for our relationship to have Jude around. Cyrus doesn't have to be everything I need, and I no longer ask it from him, which, in the past, inevitably only led to disappointment and friction.

Yet, I'm always happy when he comes home. As is Jude…And Felix. I'm pretty sure Cyrus has been fucking the help, but honestly, good for him. I'm sure Felix could use some fun too.

It's not like Cyrus and I have ever been exclusive. Monogamy didn't even make sense to me when I was mortal, with a limited lifespan. Now, with forever stretching impossibly long, promising exclusivity would be a selfish act, dooming all involved to endless disappointment and betrayal.

I wouldn't be able to choose between Jude and Cyrus. Luckily, I don't have to. They speak to different sides of me, bring out different parts of me. Neither takes away from my relationship with the other. They enhance it.

I am whole, more so than I have been in a long time. I'm no longer fighting for scraps from Cyrus, wanting more than he can give. It's done wonders for our relationship. Our fighting has been cut down drastically.

I'm slowly letting go, working on being less controlling.

These past two months have been incredible for experimenting to find the boundaries of Jude's submission.

It's been as much about my needs as his. I've lived for half a millennium and never did the work to find the limit of my own desires, to voice the needs I feared would be seen as *too much*.

But for Jude, I can never be too much. He wants me all the time. All of me. Even the mean parts and the dark parts; the parts that still have to spill blood every few days to function.

Caring for Jude isn't a chore any more than his service

and devotion are obligations. We simply exist this way, like he was made for me, and I for him.

Hell only knows, the sex is incredible. Jude's insatiable in a different way from Cyrus but no less so. And much easier to train in what I like.

It's been only a few months, but Jude's skills with that mouth of his have leveled up to god mode. I make sure he gets lots of practice.

Like now.

Sitting down on the blanket beside him, I bunch up my loose-fitting dress, widening the distance between my legs, as the ocean waves keep crashing peacefully in the distance.

I don't say anything, just keep Jude's gaze as I do so. Like Pavlov's dog, he starts panting as soon as he realizes I'm not wearing any panties under the dress.

He whimpers like a real pup, words beyond his grasp now. But I know he's not lost. He has non-verbal safe words and signals too. We can stop at any time.

"Good doggies get rewards," I tell Jude as I slowly reach down my hand to leisurely stroke my clit, my gaze still pinning him in place, despite how he's squirming, restless on his knees. "Are you a good doggy?"

Jude nods eagerly, virtually salivating now. He's no longer looking at my eyes; his gaze is locked on my pussy, on the movement of my fingers as I tease my clit, tempting him.

An anguished whine leaves his trembling lips as I taunt him.

The look on his face turns desperate as I hold up two fingers, halting him wordlessly. He's been well trained. He knows the signals.

I make him wait. Even as I see the strain on his face, the pre-cum glistening on the tip of that huge cock of his.

He doesn't move, doesn't disobey, just whimpers softly, pupils huge, as he waits for the signal with his palms pressing firmly on his thighs.

How am I this lucky? To find a sub this good? This devoted?

I know it can't last. He's only human. Cyrus likes reminding me of this. But I can't turn him. I will not curse him with the burden of being a monster. No, we have here and now. And that's enough. It's precisely the fleeting nature that makes it more precious.

My two-finger signal drops a finger; only one remains now. When the final finger falls, so does Jude, face-first into my pussy.

I moan loudly as his warm lips close around my clit, sending instant sparks of pleasure rippling over my body.

I feed him gentle praises and increasingly louder moans as he seduces my clit into release, my hands roaming over his head, his neck, tugging on his hair when the climax starts building to its crescendo.

"Just like that, *tesoro*. Don't stop," I encourage him, my voice breathy. "Make me come."

Like the good boy he is, Jude does as he's told, not letting up until I'm growling in pleasure, my body shaking as he laps up every last drop of my orgasm.

When he emerges from under my dress, he looks proud, almost smug, victory written all over his lips. I pull him up for a messy kiss, licking my climax from his lips.

"Thank you, *cucciolo*," I whisper as I lick his neck, kissing where I want to bite instead. But not here. Later, at home, when I can drink from him in private and at my leisure, devouring his emotions and pleasures like intravenous drugs.

Jude hugs me tightly, squeezing like he could crush me if my bones were weaker, human. "No," he says, mumbling into my chest. "Thank *you*, Milady."

Gods, how I love the sound of that title. But only from his lips. I've never had any intentions of playing the part of any 'lady,' but this is different. The honorific feels correct, proper.

I smile, tugging playfully at Jude's collar. "Flattery will get you everywhere, little pet."

Jude goes quiet as he looks at me with such intensity, I fear something has gone wrong.

"What's it?" I ask as I take his hands in mine, holding them.

He starts to speak but only gibberish comes out. Stops again.

"Breathe, darling. Slow down. It's okay." I encourage him, squeezing his hand. "Take your time."

Jude takes a deep breath as he stares into my eyes so deeply, I swear he's looking for my soul. "I love you, Milady."

Something in me stills as he repeats the words, as if testing them.

Imploring his gaze, I know he speaks only the truth. I've tasted it in his blood, felt it in more ways than one. But to have him say it out loud, to bravely make it real...

The longer the silence stretches, the more uncomfortable Jude gets, fidgeting with his hands, looking down, until he finally says, "I'm sorry, I shouldn't, I—" Dejection colors his entire posture as he pulls away from me.

But I cut him off, pull him closer again. The shock has finally worn off enough for me to reply. "Oh, *tesoro mio.*

Don't apologize." I tip his chin toward me with a single finger, until his eyes are back on mine. "I love you too, Jude Cole."

He jumps on me like an excited dog, and we both tumble backward on the towel, laughing, tangling our bodies together, everything light despite the gravity of the moment.

I kiss him sweetly, kissing his neck, his chin, that space between his eye and his ear, everywhere. *Mine.*

Playfully, I tug at his cock, wiping some sand from the tip I had him bury inside our sandcastle not too long ago. "Come on, *cucciolo.* Let's go home. I have a surprise for you."

CHAPTER 53

DOMESTIC BLISS

(CYRUS)

My keys jingle as I hang them up by the door, kicking off my shoes in the designated spot. I don't want to track dirt into Adriana's beach house. She's schooled me about that enough.

"It's me," I call out, setting the warm coffee beans down on the kitchen counter.

The Mistress of the House appears in the doorway, hair pulled back, reading glasses perched on her nose. "You didn't have to—"

"I was in the neighborhood." It was an hour out of my way, but that's not the point. I know how much she likes the smell. "The Ethiopian you like was on sale."

She picks up the bag, inhales. A small smile. "Thank you."

"Anytime, *mi Reina*." I pull her closer for a kiss, pressing her body against mine, the lingering scent of roast coffee mingling with jasmine as I flick my tongue over hers.

My cock instantly springs to life, just from being near her.

Six months back in Adriana's life, and I could get used to this.

Smacking her ass playfully, I let go before I succumb to the temptation to bend her over the counter and take her right here. I don't want to ruin her kitchen. Not again.

"Cyrus!" Adriana scolds, but I don't miss the slight wrinkle of the smile she tries to hide.

"Where's that little pet of ours?" I lean back against the counter, looking around. "Jude around?"

Adriana shakes her head. "No, he's at the library. Something about research for his book."

My heart clenches. "Is that safe?"

"Who's being overprotective now?" She laughs. "Who are you and what have you done with Cyrus?"

"You know what I mean," I scoff. "Valerian is still out there."

"Just teasing, my love. Jude's fine. It's daytime. And I sent Felix with him just in case. They'll be back before dark."

"Great, two humans. So secure."

She takes her hand in mine, squeezing my fingers. "It's cute how possessive you've become over him."

I pull my hand away. "Ha! Cute? That's a first. I've never been called *cute*." She's right, though. Over these past few months, Jude has crept into my black heart unexpectedly.

I wish Adriana would turn him. Or better, let me do it. Just to still this stubborn fear that keeps flaring up, the fear of losing him. But she has made up her mind. *'No means no.'*

458

Adriana smiles. "Never thought I'd see the day we finally found someone we both wanted."

"Another first, for sure," I agree. "Certainly don't mind. He's so…" I trail off as the front door opens.

Jude's face lights up as he drops all his books on the table and rushes over into my arms.

Christ, like a real puppy, he's always so happy to see me.

I hug him tightly, planting a kiss on his lips.

Felix shoots me a wink and I grab his ass as he passes, before returning all my attention to the warm-blooded human in my embrace.

"You staying?" Jude asks hopefully, his fingers brushing over the tent straining in my pants. *Such a tease.*

I smack his hand away. "Don't start. I've got work to do. The grand opening is two weeks away," I protest even as every cell in my body screams to give in, to stay. But I know that if I do, I'll lose days again, wrapped in the haze of passion and lust. And I really do have work to do. I'm determined to make this club work, to build something long-term.

Jude whines, bottom lip quivering as I reject his advance.

"Don't sulk, *niño*." I pet his hair. "I'll be back tomorrow."

His eyes light up. "You will?"

"Uh-huh, of course," I tell him, kissing his forehead. "Now be good, and I might even bring you a present."

Jude leans into my touch as I pull him closer for another kiss, his erection pressing against mine, making it damn near impossible to pull away, to resist.

Adriana leans against the doorway as she watches us, a warm grin spreading over her face. I don't miss the affection coloring her expression, nor the way she clenches her legs together. Miss De Crevena has always been as much of a voyeur as I am.

"Tomorrow," I repeat, reaching out an arm to Adriana too, inviting her into our embrace. She presses her face to my chest as Jude crowds her against me. A single heartbeat races between the three of us.

Dios mío, how good they feel.

After four centuries of running, of doing the wrong thing at the wrong time, I'm finally doing something right. And I have zero intent of fucking it up again.

How could I ever have been so stupid to think I could live without Adriana?

There is nobody I'd rather come home to. Every time. Until the end of time. I am the best version of me when I'm with her. With *them.*

"Fuck-it," I breathe, my teeth scraping against Jude's neck. "I'll stay."

THIS IS FAR from the end for Adriana, Jude, and Cyrus. Want to read the bonus epilogue where the throuple celebrates Jude's birthday with all the spoils and spice? Join my newsletter for bonus content & art: https://mkaynoir.com/newsletter

Acknowledgments

I could not do this alone. Really, not a chance.

It really takes a village to publish a book. Suppose it makes sense, considering books are pretty much our babies.

This book initially started as an idea for a Halloween novella. It was 2022. Hubby and I were living in Cusco, Peru. And I wrote this note on my phone that just said, *"What We Do in the Shadows* but make it femdom." The note grew, as did the story. And here we are, more than three years later. I didn't write what I set out to write at all; the story changed so much…but it could not be any other way. I love these characters so much.

A massive thank you to my editor, who read it first and didn't tell me to burn the manuscript. Thank you for asking the questions, for catching my silly mistakes, and for encouraging me to keep going. Mostly, thank you for fighting with my tenses and forcing them into shape.

To my beta reader team—Clary, Daisy, Caz, and Claudia—I'd be lost without you. Thank you! Thank you for reading a manuscript that isn't fully perfect yet. Thank you for picking up on things I missed, for all the funny notes, and for the excitement. I'd be lost without you. After spending so much time with a manuscript, it's hard to let anyone else read it. But I know I am safe with you, so thank you for that. I am also eternally grateful to Cynthia for helping me improve the second edition.

To the ARC readers: thank you for trusting me with a new genre and a completely new direction. And thank you for taking the time to read and review the story. Every review means a lot to me.

To my cover designer, Erika, you are so damn talented. I am in awe of your work, every time. Thank you for your patience and for putting up with my perfectionist tendencies. I am absolutely in love with this cover; it's exactly what I wanted. Thank you for making my dreams come true. I still can't believe I get to have a cover this shiny!

I also want to thank my artists for all the character art that has kept me excited throughout this journey. Thank you for bringing my characters to life (with and without clothes, hehe). To Bernie and Casta, thanks for making it look so good. You really captured the characters and the moments so well. I can't wait to share all the art I commissioned for this book.

A special shoutout to my husband, who had to listen to me freak out about this book for months, brainstorm countless ways out of plot holes, and talk me down every time I wanted to rip it up. I am lucky to have a partner as supportive as you. Thank you for always believing in me and for your infinite patience—and for being so good with action sequences.

Also, to my friends, who've had to listen to me talk about "that vampire book" for months now. Thank you for your support and for indulging me in all my weird and wonderful little side quests.

Caz and Daisy, you deserve another shoutout for listening to all my panicked voice notes and freak-outs about this book. Having author friends and a community has made such a difference. Thank you for being my biggest cheerleaders and not letting me fall too deep into a rut. Y'all are true friends.

Last but definitely not least, to the incredible Meg Kelly, thank you! You are an incredible PA and you've really helped me elevate my brand. Thank you for believing in me and my stories, and for making everything so pretty. It's been amazing to have you in my corner, especially for the ARCs.

I feel truly lucky to have so many people who believe in me and support my work.

Thank you!

-Kay

ABOUT THE AUTHOR

M KAY NOIR is a South African queer romance author and journalist obsessed with moments of desire (blame Lacan). Most of her stories are kinky, queer-friendly, polyamorous undertakings with neurotic characters who are often their own worst enemy. If you expect any regard for traditional gender roles or power dynamics, you will be disappointed.

Kay has been penning steamy moments for more than 15 years now, from fanfics to ghostwriting and now finally her own stories. Her day job also involves a lot of writing, albeit a different kind—mostly sustainability things. When she's not writing (or reading), she enjoys making her husband look at yet another sunset and watching live music concerts. Oh, and snuggling with her diva of a Siamese cat, Aetherius, who is just the cutest (a biased opinion).

**See mkaynoir.com for the long version.

MORE BY M KAY NOIR

COVERT DESIRES, *Chapter 1*

Nobody knocks at 2 AM.

Not during the off-season.

And definitely not during a tropical storm.

Yet there it is again—urgent pounding that cuts through the howl of wind and rain, forcing my paintbrush to halt mid-stroke.

Every instinct, honed from years I'd rather forget, screams danger. The smart play would be to keep painting my black flowers, to let the storm swallow whoever's out there.

But something about that frantic rhythm stirs a dormant part of me. An itch I thought I'd buried along with my past life. When was the last time my heart raced with anything but morning cardio?

The hammering grows more insistent. A voice carries between thunderclaps—male, desperate, demanding.

Fuck-it.

I set down my brush, dark paint dripping like blood onto the newspaper-covered floor.

"Hold on!" I call out, flicking on lights as I move through my sanctuary to the inn's adjoining door. The storm throws shadows that dance like enemy combatants across my walls.

When I unlatch the door, the wind nearly tears it from my grip. And there he stands—six-foot-something of trouble, drenched to his bones.

In the dim yellow glow of the porch light, the unannounced guest looks like an unsettling mix of serial killer. He's handsome by any standard, but I'm way past the age of letting dangerous men with haunted looks upset my entire world. *Fuck that.*

His raven hair is plastered to a face that belongs in a fashion magazine, all sharp angles and dangerous beauty. But it's his eyes that give me pause—arctic blue and feral, like a wolf's in winter. They lock onto mine with an intensity that sends electricity down my spine.

"About fucking time," the man snarls, trying to shoulder past me. His expensive suit, now ruined, clings to a frame that speaks of carefully honed strength. One arm clutches a duffel bag like it contains his soul.

I plant myself firmly in the doorway. "What do you want?" Years of training keep my voice steady, even as adrenaline floods my system. You don't survive 44 years on this earth by letting strange men into your home at night, no matter how pretty their packaging.

Know your enemy; know your target. This drenched man could be either. Except I have no idea who he is.

He doesn't fit the profile of the island-adventure guests who usually stay at my inn. Even if he did, this is not the time for island adventuring.

"Room for one. This is an inn, isn't it?" His accent carries old money and fresh blood. Up close, I catch the metallic scent that rain can't quite wash away.

That's when I see it—a nasty gash on his temple, still weeping crimson. His white shirt is torn at the shoulder, revealing more than just storm damage.

This man isn't running from the weather…